Memoirs of an Average Man

Tell Me A Story

By Michael J. Walters

ISBN: 979-8-9946977-1-9 (Paperback)

Library of Congress Control Number: 2026907897

This book is a work of historical fiction. Some names and events are drawn from history, while others have been fictionalized for the purposes of storytelling. The opinions expressed are solely those of the author. All material herein is intended for entertainment purposes only and should not be construed as medical, financial, legal, or spiritual advice.

While this collection is based on historical events, some characters, time lines, and dialogue have been fictionalized for dramatic purposes.

Independently published by
Local Media Now LLC
Clinton, MI 49236

Credits:
All photographs and written content herein, except where otherwise noted, were created by the author, who retains full rights. Cover and art designed by the author using ChatGPT Plus. Book design by the author.

Printed by Kindle Direct Publishing
United States of America

First Edition, 2026

Local Media Now
P.O. Box 168
Clinton, MI 49236

www.LocalMediaNow.com

Dedication

To Mona, who always believed in me,

To Nicholas and Debbie, my strength and fortitude,

To Amanda Morris, who always took my side,

To Sue and Chris Salcau, faithful and constant friends,

To Ronald Mysliwiec, a sainted teacher, who instilled a lifelong love of music in me.

This page left intentionally blank.

FOREWORD

I am an average man.

I didn't always think that. I grew up in the sixties and seventies, but eventually I succumbed to the modern, everyone-gets-a-trophy philosophy of individual exceptionalism. While watching television in the early 2000s with my young son, Nicholas, I succumbed to the musical earworm of Barney the purple dinosaur, and soon I, too, believed that I was "special in every way." Years of music reaffirmed this notion:

I'm a "Highway Star." I'm "Simply The Best." "I Am The Champion..." But I know better, Good Reader, because I am an average man.

It was a mantra I adopted when I became a media mogul in 2015. (There I go again -- self-aggrandizement -- as if being average just isn't good enough.) Simply put, I bought a small town newspaper in a quaint village in Michigan for a small price -- about the cost of a mid-sized SUV at the time.

I had been a career teacher and knew nothing about running a business, but I had taken a single journalism course in college; and though I earned a B, I had also won the coveted "Hardest Working Reporter Award" from Professor Phil Pirages.

I bought that small newspaper, The Clinton Local, and almost quadrupled its value through a series of trial and error ventures designed to increase sales and readership. Despite my willingness to take risks as a businessman -- expanding territory, adding staff to improve content, developing ancillary services like photography and printed sports programs -- I hid in fear on the pages of that newspaper for over four years. Each week, I'd produce three to five news articles without my name ever appearing below the masthead. I figured owning the newspaper was enough notoriety. (I even created a Facebook account with Clinton as the first name and Local as the surname, just to avoid using my actual name.)

It took eight days in an intensive care unit in 2019 for my authorial shyness to dissolve. I began writing my own column -- full name attached -- called The Publisher's Pen.

This book is a collection of the best of those stories. I have removed articles that were editorial -- about Covid-19 and the 2000 presidential election -- and retained the fun stuff -- tales of everyday life, which I think are very relatable.

After all, I am an average man.

AUTHOR'S NOTE

I have always loved music. My secret dream as a Motor City teenager was to become a rock and roll star. Of course, that was the dream of half the boys my age in the 1970s. The other half wanted to become the next halfback for Bo Schembechler. Some wanted both.

Entering high school in the mid-70s, homework and scholarship were low on my priority list. The most important thing I learned was the dial numbers of the best rock and roll radio stations in Detroit at that time -- WRIF, W4, and WABX. "Doing homework" was the excuse I used to spend hours shuttered in my bedroom, singing along with the radio and writing down the lyrics of my favorite songs. To this day, a single word in conversation compels me to sing a line or two. This has annoyed many.

For instance, a passerby asks, "What time is it?"

I break into "Does Anybody Really Know What Time It Is?" by Chicago.

My wife asks if I've remembered to take the garbage bin to the curb, and I launch into "Yakety Yak" by the Coasters.

Friends turned up their radios to drown me out as we drove around the Motor City, swigging from brown bagged bottles.

Oh, and that's another annoying habit I have -- I love alliteration, even though I didn't always understand the definition of that word. (There's a story there, on page 135.)

I started writing stories -- personal narratives -- in my Publisher's Pen column for The Clinton Local newspaper in 2019. I couldn't resist making the title alliterative, and, of course, each article included some lyrics to an appropriately related song.

I was more than a little annoyed when I learned in 2025, as I was preparing this collection, that using lyrics of a song requires direct permission from the artist or publisher who controls the rights of the song -- a lot of trouble for a few words. Also, such permission would likely come with a fee to be paid. I wanted neither the extra work nor the additional expense.

Looking further into the law, I learned that the reason using a part of the lyrics without permission was unacceptable was due to proportions; one stanza could represent ten or twenty percent of the work. Seen from that perspective, I was less begrudging as

I snipped the lyrics from the top of each story herein. (After all, I made darned sure I included my very own copyright page in this tome.)

One of my favorite sayings -- my own, I think -- is *"If necessity is the mother of invention, then laziness is the father."* I coined this phrase because I recognize that I am inherently lazy. Rather than decry my slothfulness, I celebrate (some may say justify) the value of this seemingly negative trait by pointing to mankind's most wonderful inventions: modern appliances, modern conveyances, and, of course, a hand-held remote control so that one never needs to get up off the couch.

Necessity -- the desire to save a vestige of the music in each of my stories -- compelled me to further explore copyright law. I learned that one can use the ***titles*** of songs without first acquiring permission, so this is what I have done. Not all story titles are song titles, however. Art, like life, is never that even, never that neat.

This book, Tell Me A Story, includes my favorite tales written when I ran the Clinton Local newspaper. I retained the rights to them when I sold the newspaper in 2022.

Since I am a high school teacher, I was a little self-conscious about sharing this entire collection. (I wasn't a teacher when I shared them in the newspaper, but even if I had been, I'm fairly confident they wouldn't have been discovered by my students -- when was the last time you saw a teen with a newspaper?)

Since I am an average man, some of the stories paint me in a positive light, and some do not. Some show my mean-spirited side, and others show me as vulnerable and sympathetic. In some stories I am a villain, and in some I am a hero. Add them all together, and I am just an average man, and while I'd like to bury my dark past, I share it because it is what makes me... average.

I had a little fun with the story headers just before I finished. The stories that make me feel good, warm, happy, sappy, et cetera, have an angel on my shoulder in the heading image. Stories that I wish I could change to make me look better, or those which feature mostly negative events, or perhaps unkind thoughts from yours truly, have a devilish imp riding my shoulder. Good + Bad = Average.

I hope you enjoy all of them.

Michael J. Walters

March 7, 2026

PLAY LIST: TELL ME A STORY

TELL ME A STORY

"Tell me a story, Poppa."

Stroking the curly hair from her sleepless eyes, he could see that this might take a while. Still, bedtime had become a ritual that highlighted the end of each day. That she always enjoyed his tales, stories from his youth that she couldn't completely comprehend, wasn't lost on him.

'It's the connection,' he mused. 'That's why my little one never tires of my stories...' and the thought unravelled and became a wisp.

"Tell me a story, Poppa, please."

"Tell me a story..."

BREAK ON THROUGH

Before I retired from 31 years of teaching in Detroit Public Schools, I bought the small town newspaper where I lived. The Clinton Local had been owned for 30 years by a larger than life character named Maryann Habrick, a woman both adored and reviled for her weekly personal column she called "Life in the Slow Lane."

Maryann was no Gertrude Stein, but her columns had homespun charm, though quite often, the topics were immodest and even unseemly. (They included an in-depth recounting of her barium enema and the charming tale of two amorous squirrels enjoying each other atop her father's tombstone.) In the days before social media, her weekly column provided enough grist for the mill, as they say, and people in town readily bought her newspaper just to see what she would say next.

In the early 2000s, as social media proved to be more effective at both reporting news in a timely manner and providing juicy topics to scandalize the town, the popularity of her ancient newspaper (established in 1884) began to wane. Her stories began to seem repetitive, and people began to joke that her paper was best used as a teaching tool for children to correct grammar and spelling errors.

I was going to change all that.

I bought the newspaper in 2015, 30 years from the date Maryann first owned it. I quickly learned that, despite the orthographic errors that abounded in her writing, Maryann enjoyed a hardcore following, mostly folks who also grew up in her beloved hometown of Clinton, Michigan.

I realized that I could never replace Maryann, but I found someone who could; Susan G. Salcau began writing a personal column for the very first issue of my Local. She was the literate and witty version of Maryann, and though she hadn't been born in town, her charm shone through, and Susie Q (my nickname for her) hit the spot and mostly squelched encore calls for Maryann.

Yet Susie had her limits, and a newfound respect for Maryann's longevity arose in both of us. Susie started to take a week off here and there, eventually leading to a stretch of months.

I had always wanted to be a writer, but I was leery of "putting myself out there," I guess you could say. I wanted to step in for Susie when she faced writer's block, but I didn't, initially.

My secret purpose for buying the newspaper was to afford myself a platform to write -- and I did. Each week I'd fill the paper with three to six news stories. These were of the objective, matter-of-fact variety. No one would know that I had written them because I left them unattributed. I figured that any story without a byline was by default written by "Local Staff." I was hiding.

Was I embarrassed of my own writing?

The only place I put my name was in a small box on the classified page that identified me as the owner and publisher, but that was it. I even left photos I had taken unattributed.

My friend and assistant, Amanda Morris, encouraged me to identify my work. In fact, she hounded me. Reluctantly, I began

to identify my work with a handlebar mustache icon to represent my own prominent whiskers.

I dropped the coy behavior when I found myself in intensive care for an eight day stretch in the spring of 2019. I wasn't near death, but this reminder of mortality shook something loose.

On the last day of my hospital stay, Deacon Norm from my church visited.

'This must have been serious,' I thought, and my mind turned to those loved ones I had visited in hospital. Memories of Mona, my mother, who died in 2011 after a nine year struggle with cancer, began to play in my mind's eye.

Images... vignettes... stories...

Memories...

~~~

"What do you really want to do with your life, Michael?" Mona, asked me as I stared at a two foot
~~~

stack of uncorrected assignments I had brought home. I was in my second year of teaching middle school social studies in Detroit Public Schools; not my desired subject, not my desired age level, and the kids were challenging, to be polite.

Sighing, I told her I didn't know. She did know, however, so she asked again.

"What do you really want to do, Michael?"

"I'd like to be a writer," I said with rare candor.

"Then be a writer…"

I told her that I couldn't just quit and become a writer, that it didn't work that way, that there was no way Dad would allow me to live under his roof without an income, chasing a pipe dream. Mona refuted every assertion, God bless her, but I had plenty of excuses…

… until that day in the hospital.

'Why not?' I thought as I waited for my friend, Mark Smith, to pick me up. 'I'll tell the story of my eight day hospital stay. It will be my barium enema story!'

And with that ignoble topic in mind, I began writing my first personal narrative, "How I Spent My Spring Break," as my hospitalization occurred during that festive week.

In the three and a half years I had owned The Clinton Local, this was the first piece of fiction I put into the newspaper, though it reads like an autobiographical account. I had just discovered enough nerve to put my name to my own writing. I didn't yet have the gall to be a real investigative journalist, though the opportunity was there, as you shall see…

How I Spent My Spring Break (and What I learned)

Originally published April 11, 2019

As a former teacher, I'll admit that I assigned essays to students returning from vacation breaks as time fillers, in addition to providing writing practice, of course. Usually, the essays were unremarkable and could be interchanged from one student to the next, but, occasionally, one or two were noteworthy due to unusual content.

I assert my Spring Break was unique, and, therefore, possibly of interest to you, Good Reader.

What did Mike do for Spring Break?

Why is there a new Editor?

Why is Mike referring to himself as the Publisher?

Monday, April 1, 2019 3 AM

Spring Break is in the wee hours, but it already seems like much of it will focus around health issues for me. After hours of up and down, bed to bathroom activity, I'm driving myself to Herrick Hospital in Tecumseh, a five minute trip. I have a pain in the gut, and it has been getting worse every hour since the evening before. I believe in doing things local (of course), and Herrick is quiet and accommodating, with only two other patients there at the time.

I get attention immediately. An initial prognosis from James, the physician's assistant, is pancreatitis. I panic initially, thinking 'pancreatic cancer,' until James educates me. No food, no water, rest and painkillers are prescribed. I check in.

I learn that Herrick, while operating on a smaller scale, is a good place to go for general and emergency care.

Tuesday, April 2, 11:15 PM

The plan had been to wait it out at Herrick until my pancreas calmed down. Once the swelling subsided, a clear diagnosis could be made as to the cause of this painful ailment.

I learned that pancreatitis is mainly caused by excessive consumption of alcohol. The second likeliest cause is gallstones.

The doctor prescribed pain medication to be injected every three hours. I got my first shot on Monday at 9 AM. Shots continued every three hours until 9 PM Tuesday, when I was again calling for my medication. A little after 11 PM, I was abruptly awakened by two nurses standing over me, asking me if I could feel how fast my heart was beating. I hadn't noticed, but I was aware that I was sweating. Over one nurse's shoulder I could see that my pulse was 184. (Low 70s is normal.) A couple times my pulse dropped to the 80s, and my heart felt tired.

This sequence happened several times until the EMS arrived to take me to Bixby Hospital in nearby Adrian.

Wednesday, April 3, 12:15 AM

I find myself face-to-face --well, not really -- face-to-screen with a doctor at Bixby who tells me that it looks like I just had several episodes of atrial fibrillation. They now check me into the critical care unit, give me pain medication and medicine to slow down my heart, and I see more doctors and nurses in person in the morning.

I learn that it is not uncommon that hidden ailments can surface when the body experiences trauma.

"A-Fib" is a rapid beating of the heart that can cause coagulation -- blood clots. Blood thinner is added to my growing list of medications. Spring Break is just getting started!

Thursday, April 4, 2019

Both Herrick and Bixby are staffed by many talented, caring medical professionals. At one point, I overheard two debating the painkillers given me -- Dilaudid -- a medication used to help relieve moderate to severe pain by working in the brain to change how your body feels and responds to pain, according to WebMD.com. Dilaudid, also called Hydromorphone, belongs to a class of drugs known as opioid (narcotic) analgesics.

I learn they are often abused, and many times people will enter emergency rooms claiming pancreatitis to get the drug. Apparently, some at Herrick thought that might have been why I came there -- me, a druggie! I worry about the addictiveness, but not so much as to refuse the relief. It really knocks out the pain.

Friday, April 5, 2019

Pain medication is switched. I don't remember the name, but it is much more effective, lasting longer and allowing me to feel normal. The swelling in my gut is going down. (There's a six pack under there somewhere.)

Room switch to a single today, and I started receiving

visitors. I learned that (when the shoe is again on the other foot), I shouldn't shy away from visiting the sick in the hospital, something I always avoided, thinking it would take too much time. It's lonely in the hospital, and even short visits are nice.

Now that I was on the other side of the bed railing, I realized that an extended hospital stay can feel like an eternity to the patient, yet because of pain and fatigue, the patient is relieved to see you go after a 15 minute visit.

Saturday, April 6, 2019

Test results came back on the pancreatitis. My doctor -- one of them, I now apparently have three: a primary, a cardiologist, and a gastrologist -- tested the parathyroid gland to see if it was the culprit for causing the pancreas to overwork. It was not.

Now we wait on another inquiry he made to the Cleveland Clinic, this one based on an even rarer deficiency.

I learn that doctors, while extremely intelligent, don't always know all the answers. What makes them really smart is that they are not afraid to say so.

Sunday, April 7, 2019

I'm still not ready for release until my cardiologist makes a dosage adjustment to the A-fib meds. (Look at me -- a real hospital veteran throwing around abbreviations.)

Getting up that morning to bathe, I walked the 10 step trip to the bathroom by myself. Before I got back to my bed, the nurse rushed in,

"Are you OK?"

My pulse had shot to 140 on that little jaunt, and I was tired! Early in the afternoon, after the adjustment, I begin to feel better than I had in a week. A deacon from my church came to visit me, bringing communion, and I learned that many were praying for me, both from my church and Facebook friends. It was a comfort.

Monday, April 8, 2019

I'm ready to check out, but the wait is long. I learn that my discharge must be approved by two doctors -- the "hospitaler" (a newer concept, I was told, like a supervising case manager) and my new cardiologist. Unfortunately, this delays the discharge until the afternoon, but gives me a chance to try the hospital cheeseburger, which I had been avoiding due to a tender tummy. (Solid foods had only been allowed since Saturday.)

Now I am home and trying to get back into the swing of

things, but it looks like it will be a slow go.

I am fortunate to have family and friends in my life, and I need to enjoy them and God's creation, which is why I am now slipping toward the role of publisher. I will still oversee operations, but Amanda Morris, quickly introduced in last week's issue, will serve as editor. Please continue to submit your information to editor@theclintonlocal.com. I look forward to continuing to serve the community as publisher of the Local.

***

This was my first effort to step out from the role of editor and into that of feature writer. It took a near death experience -- literally -- to bring me out of my shell. (This account of my ailments and hospital stay was milquetoast; it was much more serious than described above.)

While doctors are concerned with malpractice, newspapers are concerned with libel, so, being a natural born coward, I avoided telling the truth when it came to my care at Herrick. The only competent and dedicated worker that I met there was "James," whose name I changed from Patrick, if memory serves me now. He was the only one I met at Herrick who seemed to care about the job, and it manifested in an unexpected way.

> "Are you sure?" Patrick asked me for the third time. It was almost 6 a.m. on April 1, 2019, and my gut still throbbed with pain from the newly diagnosed pancreatitis.
>
> "Yeah, I'll stay here. It's close to home."
>
> I didn't want to think. I just wanted a bed and some pain killers, and then I could start making phone calls. It was the day before put-the-paper-together-Tuesday, after all, health emergency be damned. I gritted my teeth.
>
> "Why do you keep asking if I want to go to another hospital?"
>
> "It's just that most people don't stay *here*; they either go to Adrian or Ann Arbor. I'd go to Ann Arbor, if I could," Patrick advised.
>
> I had been in such pain that it hadn't even regis-

tered with me how strange it was that a physician's assistant would be recommending *other* hospitals in different cities. As far as I was concerned, the care I had received up to that moment was just fine, most of it coming from Patrick. I later realized that he had a pretty good idea of the quality of my future care in that institution.

"There's only one other patient, an old lady, and she's heading off to hospice this morning," he added. His underlying message, which I had missed, was that people *literally* did not want to be caught dead in this place. He tried again. "It's a short ambulance ride to either Ann Arbor or Adrian."

Despite my gut pain, my internal cheap-O-meter was still working fine: ambulance ride = $140 fare.

"No," I said flatly. "Just get me checked in here."

Patrick gave me a knowing, sympathetic look, affirmed my decision, and left. Before walking out, he told me the doctor prescribed a dose of Dilaudid every three hours, to begin when I was settled into my room.

Over an hour later, a nurse came to wheel me to a room. I had been left waiting there in pain, but I was able to make all the necessary phone calls. I called my wife, Debbie, who was now awake to start her day as a childcare provider in our home. I called my business partner, Kurt, who was also a teacher, to ask him to bring my laptop to me. I called another teacher, Amanda, my long-time coworker and helper, and promoted her (officially) to editor of the newspaper, and then gave her a list of tasks to complete before meeting me at the hospital the following day.

I got the first shot for pain at 9 a.m., and it knocked me out immediately. Dilaudid was like a mule kick -- seconds after the plunger was depressed, my eyes would roll back, and my head would drop to my pillow, lights out for almost two hours. The third hour would consist of alternating groggy wakefulness and light slumber, with a gradual return to clarity. As the third hour progressed, so did awareness of my pain, so much so that I began watching the clock's minute hand, mentally willing it to hit the top of the dial faster. When it did, my eyes eagerly trained on the door, looking for my angel in white.

My noon and 3 o'clock came roughly as scheduled, and I luxuriated in the deep peace brought by the narcotic. It was easy to see how one could become addicted.

The minute hand crept past its marker -- 6 o'clock becoming five after, then ten after. Annoyed and with the pain in my side now returning to levels I felt at check in, I thumbed the red call button and glared at the doorway.

I did it again less than a minute later.

And then again.

Here she came, a new nurse, burly, blond and bilious. She marched toward my bed, and I became dimly anxious for my personal safety. She cancelled the call button, seemed to realize the attitude she was projecting, and smoothed her white scrubs with both hands. Now composed, she forced a false fairy tale princess voice.

"What do you need?"

"It's time for my meds," I snapped quickly.

"Oh, you don't need those," she said as she began to head for the door.

"The doctor said every three hours!" Alarmed, I nearly shouted it.

"Oh, he was just snowing you," she said, and was she now smiling or was my pain causing me to take it as a taunt?

"No, he wasn't. Those were the doctors orders. **You have to follow doctor's orders."**

Telling that nurse how to do her job wasn't going to win friends, but it did get my medication, and like a 'good junkie,' that was all I cared about.

The three hour cycle quickly ran its course, and at 9 o'clock I renewed my call. Yes, I realized that the new three hour mark would be 9:15 p.m., but I decided that I'd start early to account for resistance.

While I waited for the top of the hour to hit, I listened to chatter in the hallway just outside my door. As I grew more lucid, I could discern at least eight different voices, and my mind attached bodies to those eidolons -- nurses, janitors, candy stripers, clerks, and EMTs. It sounded like they were having a party.

'Am I dreaming? Is my brain still swimming in narcotic soup?'

Then I remembered what Patrick had told me: the hospital would have been empty if I hadn't decided to stay. A party had been planned, and I was an uninvited guest. While I mostly stayed sedated, I did wake up and demand attention from time to time. I was a buzz killer, in other words.

I decided to listen longer and to wait until 9:15 p.m. so there could be no reason for debate. In the meantime, I listened.

It really was a party.

"Turn up the radio," a male proclaimed.

"The patient will wake up," a female cautioned.

"Give me another rum and coke," said another male voice.

"Me, too," said another.

"We better keep it down," said the same female voice, presumably the on-duty nurse, "He might hear us."

"Then turn up the radio," the first male demanded. Someone complied, and the voices were mostly obscured.

I lay in bed for the next ten minutes listening, and I figured I heard seven or eight distinct voices, though it sounded like there may have been more people out there. Even though this was a Monday night, it seemed like a routine. The hospital had been "closing" for almost a year. That, and its declining reputation, kept it mostly vacant. These workers were used to partying on the ghost shift like kids at college, and my presence was like having a dorm monitor right down the hall.

Eventually, I grew bored of hearing other people enjoying themselves, and I thumbed the call button.

A minute later (faster this time!) a pretty young girl came in. She wasn't dressed like the other nurses. Was she a candy striper? I don't know, but she did have what I hungered for -- the needle. Without ceremony, she lifted my arm, stabbed me with the needle and pushed the plunger down quickly. I felt my eyes roll back in their sockets and my head immediately lolled backward. The last thing I registered before I dropped into oblivion was the alarm on the girl's face.

<Beep> <Beep> <Beep> <Beep> <Beep>

Alarm sounds. Equipment flashing red. Shaken awake. Nurse in my face.

No, two nurses, worried faces.

"Do you feel that?" one nurse asked.

Huh?

"Do you feel that? Do you feel your heart racing?"

I looked over her shoulder and saw 184 BPM on the monitor, and then I noticed that my heart was hammering. It went on like that for a while as the nurse explained that my stay there was over; they were going to transport me by ambulance to the hospital in Adrian. They were going to get rid of their unwelcome guest after all.

When my heart slowed -- down to 80 BPM -- I felt tired, and my heart actually felt sore, like a bicep might feel after several sets of curls in the gym. A few minutes later, it revved up again. The EMTs rushed in, slid me on a gurney, and raced me to their vehicle.

I arrived at Bixby Hospital in Adrian, Michigan, shortly after midnight on April 3, 2019. Bixby had opened in 1957 and would close in 2020 as the new ProMedica Charles and Virginia Hickman Hospital opened in September, 2020.

I hadn't thought of my situation as serious until they sat me up in front of a monitor to discuss my condition with a heart specialist whom they had to wake at his home. Though sleepy looking, he was intelligent and reassuring, telling me what tests and treatment I was to receive that evening, and that he would see me in the morning.

I was wheeled to ICU, poked and prodded as they took blood samples, established an IV in my left arm (no small feat considering my phantom veins), and, most importantly, injected me with the pain killer I was really coming to enjoy.

I slept.

***

With Amanda taking over the primary editing duties, I was free to do more writing. That doesn't mean it happened, of course. My next Publisher's Pen article was about the various public parks in the area, perhaps because I was learning to "stop and smell the roses" after my hospital stay.

Eventually, I began to write about events in my life, both current and past. It was the easiest way to begin.

So now, Good Reader, please allow me to share my favorite stories from those years of writing for the local newspaper. Some have been lightly edited to provide a better read.

The next story here, as you will see, was originally printed in August -- four months after my ICU tale, which had been a shy peak from behind the doorway of my room. Eventually, I came out all the way and even had fun with it.

I hope you enjoy these tales.

With A Little Help From My Friends

Originally published August 8, 2019

I need a vacation, but I know I just don't have time for it!

Oh, I know the Clinton Local will be in good hands with my helpers -- Amanda, Sue and Chris.

No, I just need a vacation from getting ready for vacation.

First, I have an ongoing master bedroom remodelling project that needs to be wrapped up before we go. Fortunately, I got some help from Ted Talvitie, who finished the painting for me.

As part of the project, I decided to install all new light switches and electrical outlets -- ten in all. I'm not a licensed electrician, so when I had my son turn the breakers back on, I stood ready with the fire extinguisher.

All but one worked. Overall, I was pleased.

Of course, I had to get the newest gizmo -- the modern day "Clapper" -- a bluetooth controlled light switch. Now I will be able to turn the light off and on by using my phone, tablet, or even a whole house device like Alexa. (Who needs to get up?)

Surprisingly, that installation worked, though the bathroom switch with automatic moisture sensor did not. (This was to be my answer to forgetting to turn on the fan.)

I am lucky enough to live next door to Jeff Szczesniak, Local sports columnist and electrician, who gave me a lesson in wiring as well as some tools and equipment. With his help, I managed to fix the non-working switch.

The pre-vacation to-do list is long, however, and it seems to keep getting longer. There's moulding to install, as well as a new toilet. After that, everything that's been piled up in our living room the entire summer must go back into the bedroom. (My wife has been so patient that I'm the one annoyed by the clutter.)

As I said, the list seems to keep getting longer and new tasks seem to be added daily. For example, as I left for work early in the week, one of my wife's day care parents pointed out a tree in the backyard.

"Looks like a hornet's nest," she said.

"No, it's probably silkworms," I replied, squinting to see. The object was bigger than a football. I was sure hoping it was just silkworms.

I grabbed one of those trimmers with the extension poles and marched to the back yard, figuring it would just be a couple minutes.

Turns out the object in the tree **was** a hornet's nest, and as a bonus, there was another in the neighboring tree.

Extension pole or not, I knew I needed to get rid of the wasps before I cut the branch. (I've seen the Hunger Games movie and enough Winnie the Pooh episodes to know better.)

Back to the garage I marched to get the spray, which promised a jet of twenty-seven feet. Maybe it works, but not twenty-seven feet straight up into the air, which, by the way, wasn't my brightest moment either. (Bug spray for breakfast -- **not** recommended.)

Despite the drenching, one angry little hornet found me -- ouch! Time for the big guns!

Chain saw in hand, I started chopping, and before I knew it, I had half of one tree down and two-thirds of the other down. I spent the next few hours chopping the limbs into pieces and still didn't finish.

And so, the list gets longer -- move furniture back into the bedroom, chop and remove tree limbs, and, yes, pack for vacation.

Thankfully, I always get a lot of help there, too. My wife, Debbie, should be awarded an honorary engineering degree for her ability to pack the family vehicle for vacation. Luckily, I usually just have to pack my own luggage.

I think I can handle that?

***

Even though this isn't much of a story, it was my real starting point. I had found a formula that worked -- self deprecation. It's probably the last safe form of humor. In most of the tales I tell, I paint myself as a buffoon, even though I clearly am not.

No, really, I'm not. I'm actually quite smooth and cool, filled with élan and swagger, the prince of panache, the fakir of flair and flamboyance, the gaucho of gusto, the...

I hear you, Good Reader: "Thou dost protest too much, methinks."

Day's Dawning

Originally published August 15, 2019

Farm fresh eggs every day!

I'm on vacation, and I've been waking up every morning to the sound of a rooster. Actually, it has been the sound of three cocks crowing, not a single cock crowing three times, as in the Bible. (I'm not sure what that means for this weeks article, but....)

When I moved to Clinton in 1998, I had to make a few adjustments, me being a city boy from Detroit.

For one, it was really dark out here. Growing up in Detroit, we had lights everywhere. Every porch had a light, and people kept them on all night. Many living room lights were also kept on all night. And, of course, there were the much talked about street lights, which seemed to shine every twenty yards or so on our city streets. (In my Clinton subdivision, outside of the Village, we also have streetlights, but they are few and far between.)

The lack of lights in the VOC (Village of Clinton) has its advantage. The further from the big city you are, the better you can see the stars, and that's a good thing. You can't reach for the stars if you can't see them! It's one of the good things about Clinton, and one of the reasons we chose to have a family here.

Another thing I noticed shortly after I moved was the smells. Gone were the sulfurous smells of leaded gasoline that stung my nose as we played our youthful street games in the city. We'd play those games -- football, whiffle ball, Frisbee, curb ball, statues, kick the can, pickle, etc. -- until one of us saw a car approaching, then he'd yell, "Car!" Everyone would dutifully step to the curb. Had I been smart, I'd have held my breath as those old polluting machines from the fifties and sixties chugged by, but I took in my lungful just like everyone else.

Shortly after moving to Clinton, I noticed the smells that, for me, marked the approach to my new home as I returned from my daily commute from downtown Detroit. I grew to love those smells, foreign to my city-born nostrils, the smell of manure -- horse, sheep, pig, and cow. (I don't remember the exact order, or the exact odor, for that matter, as I retired three years ago and no longer make that commute.) Coming home to Clinton meant peace and tranquility, a slower pace and a friendlier vibe, and that was good -- another great reason to raise a family here.

Growing up in the city, you learn not to look people in the eye as you approach them on the sidewalk. Instead, you learn to steel your gaze and look resolutely forward, setting your teeth and perhaps even balling a fist. I'll admit that wasn't a very friendly posture, but it wasn't meant to be -- I grew up in Detroit, not one of its suburbs, and looking tough was a necessity sometimes.

In Clinton, I immediately noticed the warmth and friendliness of the residents. Even when we were driving, as we'd come upon complete strangers, the hand of the oncoming driver would come up in a friendly wave. I learned to wave back, and it felt good. Clinton was and is a friendly place, and that's another reason to raise a family here.

Prior to moving to Clinton, we did our research. We explored the neighborhood we hoped to live in. In our car, we cruised by the front of our prospective new home many times. We even got out and walked through the woods behind our neighbors' houses so we could sneak a peek at our future back yard. (Had we done that in Detroit, I don't know how it would have turned out.)

We went into town and walked the streets of Clinton, stopping at Stormy's Bar (now Captain's) for some refreshment. We met Clint Hoelzer there. (Clint is the owner of Hometown Pizza and a generous benefactor to hundreds of little league teams and other causes over the years. I add this information for those distant readers who may not know him. Of course, everyone in Clinton knows Clint.)

Clint, who we discovered was to be our new neighbor, gave us the story of Clinton. I don't remember the details of that conversation, but I do remember being impressed when he told me he was named after the Village. I took that as the deepest expression of hometown love by his parents. I stretched my memory and could not recall anyone naming a child after any of my former places of residence. As a teacher, I came across a wide variety of unusual names, but I never ran into anyone named "Detroit."

Of course, the top reason we chose Clinton to raise our family over other locales was the school system. Children are always our number one concern, right? We researched the schools back in '98 and learned they were exceptional. I think the Clinton Community Schools may even be better today than they were then, if that's possible.

We chose to live in Clinton, and we're happy we did. Even so, like everyone else, we take a vacation away from our beloved Village, and that's a good thing, too. As they say, absence makes the heart grow fonder.

***

Another ploy utilized early in my creative writing venture is known as pandering; how could anyone object to an article praising the home town and the local school? As an added bonus, I found a way to kiss up to one of the main advertisers, the owner of Hometown Pizza, Clint Hoelzer.

It didn't make for exciting tales, but I was just getting started...

Leavin' On A Jet Plane (or Big Fish)

Originally published August 22, 2019

This is week two of my vacation, and I've now enjoyed two idyllic settings -- Up North, Michigan in the Sleeping Bear Sand Dunes area, and, as of this writing, San Diego, California.

Each place had a signature morning wake-up sound, I noticed. The former was marked by crowing roosters and the latter by airplanes taking off, both much different than my regular Clinton mornings, but both signalling the start of another day in paradise.

Up North, I enjoyed the dunes, the beaches, the tourist town of Glen Arbor, the hospitality of my cousins Anthony and Anne, my Aunt Alberta, and my wife and son.

In San Diego, I enjoyed the perfect year round weather and the comfort of my youngest brother's mansion, which looks like something off the old show called "Lifestyles of the Rich and Famous." I also enjoyed the company of my brothers -- Paul, Mark, Joe, and David. We met many interesting friends there, and it was all on my brother-in-law's dime -- thanks, Jeff.

Two perfect locations in two

My youngest brother, David, has a stunning view of San Diego Bay, making his place a five-star place to visit!

weeks. So why am I feeling so peevish as I sit here typing on the final flight back to Detroit Metro Airport?

Could it be the turbulence? It's Sunday night, and the plane's captain warned us it would be a little bumpy, as a storm had passed through the area earlier. (It's more than a 'little' bumpy to me, but I **am** able to continue typing.)

No, that's not it.

Is it the baby that's been whining non-stop since we boarded? I'm trying to avoid complaining like an old curmudgeon, but then I realize that the crying is not the ultimate reason for my annoyance.

What has really got me more rankled is the lady in front of me. In particular, her jacket.

The seats are awfully close to begin with, and she has her jacket hanging over the back of her chair and into my space. I flapped it back over a bit, and she flipped it back even further, so now it's about nine inches from my nose. I realize now it's either war or I try to find a way to become Zen about it and 'let it go.'

We take off. It's dark. The lights in the airplane cabin are low, and I can barely see the offending jacket. I press the button on my chair and my seat slides backward. Now my face is a full twelve inches from the irritating apparel.

I start to relax and get deeper into this week's column as I begin to put a finger on the source of my annoyance.

Like almost everyone, I enjoy vacation time. Also like everyone else, I imagine, the travel time is what really gets to me. I don't like to travel much because of, well, because of the travelling, if that makes sense. I like being there, but I don't like getting there. (The days of the Star Trek teleporter cannot arrive soon enough for me.)

Travel time aside, vacations have always been about family, and there are many memories.

~~~

When we were kids, our family vacations for many years were to Camp Dearborn, which is actually in Milford, Michigan. Camp Dearborn is a huge area that features camping for RVs and hundreds of wood-framed tents on concrete slabs, complete with outdoor kitchenette areas.

We looked forward to those vacations. For one, Milford was only about an hour from home in Detroit, so travel time was next to nothing.

For another, we typically had many relatives join us. I was
~~~

This is a typical Camp Dearborn Walters family portrait, taken quickly and facing into the sun circa 1975.

raised in a large Italian family on my mother's side. We got to know our cousins well because they, too, had tents at Camp Dearborn. There were years when we had 10 or 12 tents in a row, each with a family of relatives.

At Camp Dearborn there was a beach at a man-made lake. There were paddle boats. There were early morning swimming lessons in an unheated pool, and there was fishing with bamboo poles and little bits of hot dog or cheese on the hook.

You didn't need a fishing license to fish in the lakes there, which were stocked with bluegill, sunfish, perch, and catfish.

One year, when about thirty cousins were there, we decided to have a fishing contest. We were going to catch enough fish to have a fish fry!

We told my mother, and I remember her telling us to ask her brother, my Uncle Ralph. I can still remember the conversation as all of us swarmed him at the tent.

"How many fish would we have to catch for a fish fry?" we asked him with our eager eyes fixed on his face. He looked down at the bucket we had -- that morning's catch of 8 little bluegill and catfish -- and chuckled.

"That small!?" he said. "You'd need a hundred at least."

Looking back on that, I know he meant that as a deterrent and probably felt confident that would be the end of it.

Unflappable, our group of young fishermen headed back to the lake. As we walked, our talk got bolder.

"We can catch a hundred."

"Sure we can."

"Heck, if those are so small, let's catch two hundred!"

"Why stop there? Let's just keep catching fish until Friday afternoon."

(Friday seemed like a natural deadline to us, as it was the last day before the vacation ended, and we were raised Catholic.)

So we caught tiny fish after tiny fish after tiny fish. They all went into the bucket, then into my mom's camp freezer.

"Is this one too small?" one of the kids would ask, holding up a two inch perch on the end of their bamboo rod.

"If it can bite the hook, it's big enough," another of us reasoned.

At some point early Friday afternoon, we arrived with our final buckets of fish, and my mother broke it to Uncle Ralph. The look on his face was priceless.

"You're joking," he said, staring at her, then back to the buckets of freshly caught fish.

My mom smiled. Like Mary at the wedding feast at Canaan, she knew he'd do anything for her.

"Well, OK, this should only take a few minutes," he reluctantly agreed.

Then mom pulled out the rest of the fish from the freezer. He stared at her again, then laughed and dropped to his knees on the cement, fillet knife already starting to work. The kids gathered around him. He was our hero.

What I didn't notice then but can't help reflecting on now is how scarce the rest of the fathers were during the fish cleaning process. Nonetheless, three hours later, as the first fillets were coming out of the pan, everyone was there with plate in hand. It was a feast, and my cousins and I were proud to have fed the entire family that day -- with the help of Uncle Ralph.

I'll be back on the beaches of northern Michigan in no time. Toes in sand, umbrella overhead, and the memories of vacations past coming in like the waves.

***

There are more Camp Dearborn memories herein, and one of them gets a little... sticky. For now, Good Reader, let's stick to the chronological order in which they were written.

The next piece takes us back, way back...

Back to School

Originally published August 29, 2019

It's time to go back to school, and I've got to admit that I don't miss it at all.

One of my earliest memories of school is of the first week of first grade. Because we were raised Catholic, and because we lived in an area where the safety of the Detroit Public Schools was in question, my parents sent us to the nearest parochial school -- St. Christopher, an oasis near one of the nation's largest housing projects. This was in the 1960s, before charter schools and schools of choice, so Catholic schools were a popular alternative for many urban parents.

I still don't really know how my father managed financially, paying tuition for five of us, but it was truly a simpler time, with fewer wants and needs.

My first grade teacher was Sister Tarcisius. (She took the name of a 3rd century Roman martyr.) Sister Tarcisius was a devout and strict nun. She wore the conventional black habit with the white band across the forehead. She was a member of the Sisters of the Holy Family of Nazareth, which was a teaching order.

Most of the teachers at St. Christopher were nuns, especially in the lower grades. They worked without pay and often without much thanks, so I will thank them here, even Sister Tarcisius, before I tell my tale.

~~~

It was the first week of school, maybe the first day, and we had already begun academic work. Gone was the frivolous fun of kindergarten. We were real students now. And though our feet dangled above the floor as we sat in our perfect rows of desks, we were expected to demonstrate maturity.

Sister Tarcisius called ten of us to the front blackboard where she had written ten simple addition problems. I say 'simple' now, but it may as well have been a quadratic equation to me at that time.

My best friend, Ronnie, and I simply stared at each other, then at the board, then back at each other.

"Do you know how to do it?"
~~~

I asked Ronnie, who was my neighbor from across the alley and my buddy, though unfortunately not a whiz at math. He shook his head.

I was no genius in math either, but I knew who was. I looked down the board at the other standing children and saw Margie (a nice girl I think I had a crush on) and Grace, my cousin. They were finishing and walking our way.

Now, I did learn one thing at school that week, and it was the procedure for returning to your seat. Teachers in those days were very big on procedure. My little brain probably couldn't hold the math lesson that came later, but I did know the procedure.

When you were done at the board, you didn't just walk back to your seat. First, you walked along the front of the room toward the door. Then, after snapping a ninety degree right turn, you were to walk the aisle along the wall -- all the way to the back of the room. After snapping another crisp right turn, you could then walk to your row, snap another right, then walk down the row to your seat. All of this was to be done while holding your hands together in front of you as if praying, and to be honest, after that day, that's exactly what I did!

I had mastered the procedure for returning to my seat, but I had apparently missed the math lesson that had preceded it.

"Margie, help us. Help us!" Ronnie and I pleaded as she walked by, the picture of excellent posture and proper hand form as she shook her head in revulsion at our request.

Chastised, Ronnie gave up. I could see it in his face. But I had an ace in the hole -- my cousin Grace! We're family -- on the Italian side -- that had to mean something. Surely she would help.

"Grace, help me do this problem," I said as she approached on her way to her seat. Ronnie was my friend, but you know what they say about desperate times. It was every kid for himself at this point.

"Grace, Grace, Grace...."

She walked by like she didn't know me, but I detected an odd look in her eyes. Was it fear? Was it pity? Probably a bit of both. Ronnie and I were the last kids standing. The clock was ticking louder, and I remember sweating profusely.

Sister Tarcisius got up from her desk. She walked slowly over to us. She stood between us and the class, looming, her voice ominous in our ears.

"Do the math!" she said, pointing with both hands to the two incomplete problems.

We stood there,between her and the math problems, looking at each other, hoping for some inspiration.

"Do the math!" she said again, this time a little louder and much more insistent.

At this point, being a child of mid-sixties discipline methods, I knew what was coming. Prayers to all the Saints, Euclid, Archimedes, and Pythagorus couldn't have helped us. We were like deer staring into headlights, eyes locked on math problems that would never solve themselves.

"Do the math!" she said, and this time she grabbed our ears.

<Bam> <Bam> <Bam> <Bam>
<Bam> <Bam> <Bam>

I think I may have literally seen stars, or perhaps they were tiny cherubs floating around my head. The good thing about having our heads banged against the blackboard was that the disagreeable math problems were almost totally erased, so Ronnie and I were dismissed to our seats.

That evening, Ronnie's mom and my mother talked across the back fence. I remember my mom telling me to move away before they talked. I played contentedly in the dirt of our yard, clueless as to the conversation nearby.

The next day, as we sat properly in our desks, feet dangling, there was a knock at the classroom door. Sister went to answer it, and there was shouting almost immediately -- including some 'grown-up' language, though I don't remember the words, just that I was shocked. It was Ronnie's mom, and when the shouting stopped, she poked her head into the room and called Ronnie out.

I wasn't the smartest kid in the class (obviously), but I knew that was my best friend's last day in that school.

We settled back into our lesson, and there came another knock.

I stiffened. As I feared, it was my mom's voice. Strangely, I worried that my mother would repeat the performance Ronnie's mom gave, and I didn't want to leave that class, despite the physical math lesson a day earlier.

But Mom wasn't yelling. Her voice sounded pleasant and soothing.

"Yes, sister. Okay, sister," I heard her say, and began to realize I was going to stay after all.

Years later, I realized this set up my entire grade school career, but that's another story. I will leave you, Good Reader, with the thought that I am grateful (in the long run) for the nun's discipline, even if it turned me against math for most of my youth. I'll also share that years later, when my little brother David had Sister T, she had changed her name to Sister Maria and became, in his words, "just the sweetest old lady imaginable."

Go figure.

***

Some readers in this sensitive age were appalled when they read this in the newspaper and expressed their concern for me as if I were still that little boy. I was amused. In the years that followed first grade, I became the go-to kid whenever the overstuffed classroom needed a reminder of who was in charge.

When Mona, my mother, stopped by that day following Ronnie's mom, I imagine her full conversation went something like this...

"Yes, sister, I understand," Mona said placidly. "You do **whatever** you need to do to 'educate' my son."

"Anything?" said Sister T, a leering smile breaking across her countenance.

"You have my blessing, sister. I know what hard-heads my boys can be."

The Sisters of the Holy Family occupied a convent on campus. They lived together, ate together, prayed together, and, presumably, discussed work together. The value of having one of the five Walters Boys in class was like drafting a blue chip athlete.

"I just don't know how to get my students to listen," a young acolyte might say over the evening meatloaf at the nunnery.

"Do you have a Walters boy in your room?" asked the elder Sister T. "Then it's simple...."

By middle school, I was aware of this educational technique, enough so that I began to read the nun in front of the room like a seismologist reads a volcano.

I had Sister Blandine in the eighth grade. She was an elderly nun, too. (For their sacrifice, God apparently granted the sisters longevity; they almost all looked ancient, especially to my youthful eyes. The only exception was dear Sister Vincent, my second grade teacher -- a sweet woman, though an ineffective teacher -- she never struck me. I mostly played hockey on the floor in the back of the room using pencils and erasers while she created new bulletin boards tracking the number of "pagan babies" we had saved by collecting our pennies in cardboard rice bowls.)

By the eighth grade, I had grown strong and wild. (My six foot athletic frame allowed me to make the cut on all the sports teams, even though my skills were limited.) Sister Blandine, however, knew my fatal flaw -- Mona, my obliging mother.

One morning, the class was very talkative. It may have been Pączki Day, a full day of celebration in that Polish parish, which meant it was a day in hell for all teachers -- raffles announced every fifteen minutes on the PA system, hot dogs (yes, real hot food!) for lunch, a trip to the gymnasium to buy penny candy (for all-day nibbling), and, of course, sugary pączkis for breakfast.

We were wired.

Sister B walked slowly to the front of the room in her black, flowing cassock, determined to teach despite the odds. She was a heavy and elderly woman, so she moved slowly. She stood patiently at the front of the room, hands folded prayer-fashion as she called for our attention.

"Class... Class... Class..." I was reminded of the Cheech and Chong skit with Sister Mary Elephant, and started to giggle. Sister Blandine did not look happy. In fact, she was starting to simmer, turning red as she stood there looking around the room. My eyes followed hers.

Margie -- Goody-Two-Shoes Margie -- was talking away, ignoring Sister Blandine. My cousin Grace, a perennial teacher's pet, was totally unmindful of Sister B's mounting rage. My eyes glanced furtively between my oblivious classmates and Sister B.

'What's black and white and red all over?' I thought with a final, ill-timed snigger. 'Sister Blandine!'

I could have gotten away with the untimely smirk had I not locked eyes with her at that moment. Her face reddened even deeper, and then she relaxed, apparently remembering her dinner table training in the convent.

Now calm, Sister B walked deliberately down the aisle toward my desk, which had been in the center of the room. Around me, students continued to chatter, ignoring my approaching doom.

I could see the look in her steely eyes and could think of no way out. Running was not an option, so I did the next best thing. I folded my hands on my desk top, straightened my back, and looked straight forward, hoping to avoid the coming maelstrom. Ironically, despite my perfect Catholic school boy demeanor, at that moment I stuck out like a sore thumb in a room full of teens hopped up on jelly donuts. Sister Blandine was undeterred.

She stopped at the side of my desk, a dark cloud of gloom hovering to my right. I tried not to look at her, but the force was strong with this one, very strong.

I looked up, locking eyes. Her eyes softened, making her look almost grateful to me. Then she removed my glasses, folded them calmly, set them on my desk beside my hands, and executed a remarkable imitation of Jake Lamotta backing Marcel Cerdan into a corner in the ninth round. Of course, Sister B used open palms. Fists would have been unladylike.

Somewhere between the fourth and fifth slap, my classmates stopped their chatter and turned as one to admire Sister's ambidexterity.

Tiring, Sister B eventually stopped, took my glasses from the desk, and gently set them askew on my face before calmly returning to the front of the room.

"Now that I have your complete attention..."

~~~

I joke about these events because I was never really injured and because it was a different era. (And because I was more than a little devilish in middle school.) I often attributed my 20 year span as a middle school teacher as penance for my youthful mayhem, possibly the result of earnest prayers by the good sisters.

"...And Lord, as we sit down to enjoy this blessing of meatloaf, mash potatoes and boiled peas, please give us some recompense by making young Michael become a middle school teacher himself one day."

"Amen!"
~~~

The Things We Do For Love

Originally published September 19, 2019

Last Wednesday, I stopped in at the Clinton United Methodist Church, which is just a short walk from my house. They were hosting the bi-monthly Clinton Blood Drive. That news reminded me of going to my first blood drive.

~~~

It was at my high school, and most of us seniors (high school seniors, not senior citizens) were eager to participate in something that represented adulthood. Like voting, or even drinking (remember, the drinking age went down to 18 for a year or two in the late 70s), giving blood was a grown up thing to do. Because of that, many were eager to sign up.

I had my own motivation, however.

I signed up so I could impress a girl.

Her name was Ann, and she was my crush throughout most of high school. I say 'crush' because I can't really call her my 'girlfriend', though we dated a few times. You see, despite what those who know me now might think -- that I'm a suave, smooth-talking Casanova -- I was pretty awkward around the ladies back then. (My wife might say that I'm still awkward, but... never mind.)

I dated Ann a few times throughout high school. One uncomfortable time was on a double date with my friend and his girl. I was quiet, which motivated Ann to move next to my friend's date. They spent the entire time chatting together. My buddy wasn't happy, but we were at a University of Michigan football game, and it gave us a good reason to focus on that. Go Blue!

A couple other times I took her to the movies, and that allowed me to carry out my strong, silent type persona -- fortuitous, since I tended to freeze up when I tried romantic patter.

So, when I saw Ann sign up to give blood, I signed up right behind her. There would be plenty to talk about, and I felt pleased with myself at this "impromptu date" during school hours. Ann laughed when I did
~~~

it. She laughed a lot. (Was it with me or at me? I've never been certain.)

The next afternoon was the big day. Our class was called, and I made sure I strolled (quickly) to walk apace with Ann as we went downstairs to the old cafeteria where the Red Cross had set up. As luck would have it, my normally uncooperative brain and tongue did not desert me this time as I made small talk about donating.

"Is this your first time?"

"You know it is, Mike!" She said with a trill.

"Are you afraid it will hurt?"

"No, my sister said it doesn't hurt." She said, and then, with an air of accusation, "Are you afraid?"

I was horrified that she might even consider that I was afraid of a little needle. I was, after all, a captain on the football team. If that didn't pass for tough-guy credentials, I don't know what did!

Luckily, before I could voice my protest, I was called to the table. The phlebotomist, a person professionally trained to draw blood, had the needle in before I knew it. Ann was watching with a smile on her face. I returned her smile with my tough-guy smile. Like a stone, no one could see pain there. No one.

It was working. I could see she was impressed by my toughness, until...

"Mike, is that your name?" said the professional phlebotomist.

Yes."

"I can't find your vein. Do you mind if I search around a bit with the needle?"

"Go ahead."

"Great. Now hold still. This might hurt a little ..." And she proceeded to dig around in the crook of my right arm with the needle, desperately searching for the elusive vein. Cognizant that Ann was still in line watching me, I put on my toughest face, like Rocky Balboa in the first movie, after Apollo Creed pummels him. Even so, I must admit that it hurt more than "a little".

But now I could see Ann being called from the line and walking over to the nurse's area. I must confess that I looked forward to commiserating with her afterwards.

"Mike, would you mind if I tried the other arm?" my highly trained professional phlebotomist asked.

I assented. Why not? I could compare my battle scars with Ann afterward. The bruise on my right arm was already forming, and it was about the size of a small apple. Surely my wounds would draw some sympathy, perhaps even triggering the Florence Nightingale effect. At least it would lead to conversation that would take the rest of the class period.

I looked up again and saw Ann stepping off the doctor's scale near the nurse's station. She was heading for the exit.

"Bye, Mike. See you tomorrow in class!" She said as she headed out.

"Aren't you going to give blood?" I called across the room. "Ouch!"

The nurse decided to stick my other arm while I was distracted. She commenced to root around under my skin with the needle almost immediately. Off guard, my face contorted in pain.

"I can't," said Ann with a laugh. "I'm underweight."

She left, and the nurse continued her efforts, eventually striking pay dirt. By the time I got out of there, class was over, and the school bell rang for dismissal. That 'date' turned out to be typical as far as things went with Ann.

Even though I left with two good bruises, one on each arm, I gave blood again after that first time. It is a noble thing to do.

Someone needs blood every two seconds, according to www.givingblood.org. One pint of blood can save up to three lives. So, consider giving blood.

It really doesn't hurt (much), and it may just save a life.

***

While my love for Ann was unrequited, I found true love with my first and only **canine companion -- Floozy**.

An old friend, Bob Leach, called me one day, saying his wife had picked up a stray near work. I drove to his house right away.

"She loves men," Bob mentioned. The small mongrel, a mixture of spaniel and whatever else, had greeted me enthusiastically.

I had been listening to the radio on the way there, of course, and the last song I heard as I killed the engine had been Aerosmith's "Somebody." It was still in my mind as I stroked the dog's long fur. Bob asked me what I was going to call her.

The lyrics in my mind stopped mid-song, and the name came forth: "Floozy!"

"What kind of name is that!"

"You said she really likes men, didn't you?!"

Ghost Riders in the Sky

Originally published October 31, 2019

Last Saturday, the Clinton Historical Society, in conjunction with the Clinton Inn, hosted a "Spirit Walk," a guided tour of five Clinton locales that some have claimed to be haunted.

Talk heard from empty rooms. A woman seen on the stairs. Those were the type of phenomena mentioned in the Clinton Inn and at each stop along the way.

The weather was cold and rainy, but the intrepid spirit walkers had come prepared with umbrellas and a lighthearted mood of adventure. I stayed near the back most of the evening because I've had enough experience with haunted houses to last me a lifetime...

***

Before I moved to Clinton, I owned a small home in Redford, Michigan. I bought it because it was cheap, made of brick, located in a good school district, and close to my workplace. It was also close enough to my parent's house, but not too close.

When I was living with my parents in my early twenties, I spent most evenings out with friends, more often than not wasting my time and money at one or another watering hole. Those were some good times, to be sure, but I wish I could recapture some of those hours (and all of those dollars) to be put to better use in the present!

When I bought the house in Redford, I became like the guy in that insurance commercial on TV nowadays. In other words, I became my father. I no longer wanted to go out every evening. Instead, I'd invite my friends over.

"Hey, Mike, let's go out this Friday night," one of my buddies would suggest.

"Why don't we just hang out here?" I'd answer.

"What are we going to do here?"

"We could buy some beer, cook burgers on the grill... It would be fun," I said.

"Sounds boring," said another of my soon-to-be-distant friends.

"Boring!" I sputtered, flab-

The Spirit Walk participants line the staircase of the old Clinton Inn.

bergasted.

"Yeah, B-O-R-I-N-G!" said a third traitorous ex-friend. "We want to go to bars to meet women!"

"We can invite them here," I said before I realized what would come next. I had just invited their cold, silent stares of disbelief. I steeled myself for their derision.

"Oh, sure! Mike's going to invite the women to come here!"

"Why didn't I think of that?"

"How many are there?"

"Funny, I don't remember seeing ANY women here before!"

The festival of sarcasm went on for several minutes, until I finally relented.

"Okay, we'll go to the bar -- again!" I said.

So you see, my house in Redford was a lonely little house. Naturally, I needed companionship, and I found it with "Floozy," a stray mutt I adopted. Floozy went with me wherever I went. She was a great companion, and she's a big part of my "haunting" story.

One evening, after I had gone to bed, I heard the front door slam -- loudly. Floozy perked up and looked in that direction. Scared, but young, strong and maybe not so bright, I walked to the front door just like the people in horror movies do. The little voice in my head told me not to, but another voice said I had to do it -- if my home was being invaded, then I needed to be the "Man of the House." This was in the days before cell phones, so I couldn't just quiver in bed and dial 911. The only phone in the house was attached to a wall in the kitchen, which may as well have been miles away for all the good it did in the moment.

Slowly, I opened my bedroom door and walked down the hall toward the front door.

Nothing. There was absolutely nothing there.

Floozy came up alongside of me and started growling at the door. More accurately, she was growling at the open air just inside the front door. Her teeth flashed and her hackles were up, but I could see nothing.

I looked at the door, still closed tight and locked, just as I had left it.

Trying to be rational, I decided I needed to check every room in the small house. I went downstairs and Floozy followed, seeming relieved to have an opportunity to get away from whatever she sensed. There was no one downstairs, but I heard walking on the hardwood flooring above. I ran upstairs with my faithful mutt trailing me. I checked all the rooms this time -- closets, windows, doors -- nothing.

I decided to go back downstairs to finish the investigation. Again, I heard the footsteps above. This time I was locked in place for a while. Back and forth he/she/it paced. I tried to compose myself, tried to explain the sounds rationally, but failed. Floozy and I both stared at the ceiling. Floozy whimpered and my skin crawled. After a few minutes, the walking sounds stopped.

It was late, but not so late that I couldn't give my mother a call. I wasn't going to scare her with my story, but I knew that talking to her would help settle my nerves.

I walked upstairs to use the wall-mounted phone in the kitchen. As I went to reach for the handle (but before I actually touched it), the pencil, which I had kept perched atop the phone, shot like a bullet across the room. Determined (or perhaps a little dazed by that manifestation), I picked up the phone and put it to my ear.

No dial tone or busy signal, just white noise, the kind I have never heard on any phone before or since.

Totally spooked, I checked all the doors again, went back to my room, prayed, and eventually went to sleep.

Over the eight years I lived there, the sounds of footsteps and door slams were a common occurrence. The phone event never repeated itself, and I never saw anything like a ghostly apparition. These phenomena were also experienced by a friend who house-sat five days for me and by cleaning people, all who swore they would never return to my "haunted house."

Somehow, however, I must have made peace with my "ghost." On several occasions, when I came home from work and walked through the front door, I was greeted with a cloud of perfume -- not visible, but very strong and certainly there for the nose to smell. Again, as my friends had so dramatically pointed out, I almost never had female visitors, so there was no logical explanation for it.

Though my house was apparently haunted, I did hold onto a bizarre satisfaction that the ghost who was living with me was happy enough to greet me at the door, and evidently she wasn't so bored there that she needed to leave.

After I moved away, my niece, Tina, who knew the folks who bought the house from me, reported that they experienced much of the same.

Now I live in Clinton, in a house too new for ghosts, so I'll just have to enjoy those spirits that will roam the streets in Downtown Clinton tonight.

Happy Halloween!

***

Floozy was a great dog, but I wasn't a great master. I was always too busy to stop back at home after work to take care of her, so I left her outside most of the day.

Eventually, my neighbor, Mike, took her in, feeding her roast beef dinners from his table, or so he said. I couldn't compete with that, so I relented when he suggested I give my dog to his sister, a recent widow. A week after I did so, he caught me as I came home.

"Your dog is there when my sister comes home. She's there when she goes to bed. She's there all the time -- just jumping into my sister's lap every time she sits down," Mike said.

'Uh, oh,' I thought. 'She wants to give the dog back...'

"My sister loves that dog!" Mike concluded, and I breathed a sigh of relief.

Three weeks later, he told me Floozy had died quietly in her sleep.

Dashing Through the Snow (Old Blue, Part One)

Originally published November 14, 2019

The first big snow of the year, like the one we had Monday when Clinton got almost eight inches of the fluffy stuff, floods my mind with as many memories as there are snowflakes: hot cocoa and cartoons after hours spent outdoors; sledding and tobogganing; Christmas caroling with my church choir along Detroit streets; and, of course, shovelling.

Now, let me be clear; shovelling snow is not a memory I relish, nor is it one I recall with any amount of detail. Usually the recollection is about not shovelling as much as it is about shovelling, and often it is associated with driving.

My first vehicle was a 1972 Ford Maverick. I bought it in 1982 for $250. Being my first vehicle, she was my first love, as any boy from Detroit might tell you. I called her Old Blue, and she was a solid little car, perfectly functional until I loaned her to one of my brothers, who will not be named since he is a subscriber and, more importantly, since he usually invites us over for Christmas.

After this brother borrowed Old Blue, the reverse no longer worked. She still drove wonderfully in forward, though, so I never dreamed of replacing her. (Parallel parking along Anthony Wayne Drive near Wayne State University was quite a spectacle, I imagine, as passersby would see me "driving" in reverse a la Fred Flintstone -- door open and left leg pushing off against the pavement. Luckily, I was strong-like-bull then, and the Maverick was light.)

The lack of reverse gear in the vehicle is an important part of this story, which I will begin now.

It was 1983, and the Detroit area had seen its share of snow. It came early and often, and it also came late. On March 23 of that year, six inches of snow were added to the ground cover that stubbornly stayed. It was still on the ground in April, even as we looked for the first signs of spring -- red-breasted robins on the lawn, tiny buds on the branches of trees and bushes, and Dairy Queen coupons in the mail.

It was those coupons that brought Joe "The Nez" Naglik to my door on April 1.

"Hey, did you see that the DQ is opening?" The Nez asked.

"Better than that," I said. "I have the coupon right here. Two for one on Peanut Buster Parfaits!"

They always say great minds think alike, so I wasn't surprised to see The Nez had the same idea as me. Our excitement began to wane, though, as we both realized how late it was. The DQ was open but had early hours until full summer. We had to be there by 9 p.m., but it was already 8:47 p.m.

"We'll have to fly," said The Nez.

"Let's go," I said. "I'll drive."

Great minds might think alike, but they don't necessarily drive alike. And while I have never been a big lead foot, I had driven with The Nez, and he could make a church bus look like a Formula One car.

We hopped into the Maverick. I put her in drive and took off, taking a right at the first intersection -- a T-section that ran along what we called Ford Field at that time.

"No, we should have gone left," The Nez cried.

I could hear the strain in his voice as he obviously thought we would miss out on that first-of-the-season treat. I knew I couldn't let my friend down, so I did what had to be done.

"I'll turn around," I said.

"You don't have reverse," he reminded.

"Who needs reverse?" I said heroically. "I'll pull a U-ee."

Pulling a U-turn in the snow would be easy (and fun), and my blind faith in the little Maverick was not unfounded. All winter I had driven her through snow banks piled two and three feet high. Given the right velocity and a limited path, she made it through everything that winter.

In fact, one time, as I was traveling in the snowy and icy ruts of my street, with cars almost everywhere on either side, a Ford Bronco approached. The Bronco didn't seem to want to stop or pull over, so I revved up and barreled into the piled snow to my right, schussing through it as the Bronco passed on my left, keeping just enough momentum to drop back down into the tracks behind the bigger vehicle.

It was that level of confidence which informed my decision to make that U-turn, even though the back end of it would take us through snow-covered Ford Field. The Nez did not object.

So I gunned it, flipped the wheel to the right, then a full, hard left. We spun around through the snow, entered the field's edge at about 30 mph, got halfway through it and

<CRASH>

We hit something. Old Blue came to a sudden and complete stop. We got out to look around and saw nothing but snow.

"Maybe we hit a rock," I said. "I'll try to get us off it as you push."

Motivated by the fleeting image of soft serve topped with salty peanuts and thick chocolate fudge, The Nez pushed as I rocked the car back and forth by shifting the automatic transmission.

"We're never going to make it," he said.

"Yes, we will," I insisted, but five minutes later I resigned myself to no ice cream that evening. Worse, I realized I would have to deal with my vehicle problem. Because it was dark (and cold and wet), I decided to deal with the car in the morning. I also put it off because, while The Nez was a good friend to hang with when it came to sports, he knew even less about cars than I did. For that problem, I needed Pete and Partlo -- true Detroit motorheads.

The next morning, accompanied by Pete and Partlo and armed with a snow shovel, I went back to the scene. I dug the snow out from under the car. No rock.

Partlo slipped to the ground to examine underneath my car.

"Not a rock," he said, brushing away snow with his hand, "bed springs."

"Bed springs?" Pete and I said in unison.

"Yep, looks like you wrapped it around your trannie and drive shaft pretty tight," Partlo said, chuckling in a way that said 'What an idiot! I can't believe you did that.'

It ended up making a bit of sense, really. People dumped all kinds of things in that field, which was on the Dearborn side of Paul Road, a one mile stretch that, at that time, had no lights and no stop signs. It would have made a perfect drag strip, except for the million-and-one potholes. Legend had it that neither Detroit nor Dearborn could ever agree on repairing the road properly, so for decades the only attention it got was some infrequent hot patch to fill in the biggest holes.

Ironically, if it hadn't been for the snow filling in those potholes, I never would have driven on that road that night. Everyone who lived there avoided its moon-like surface.

That was not the end of that 1972 Maverick, but it was the last time it moved under its own power. I had thought of cutting out the floorboards to make it a full Flintstone mobile, but once in a while common sense peeks through the clouds, and eventually that was it for Old Blue.

So I'll leave you, good reader, with a wish that you drive safely this winter as you dash merrily through the snow!

***

It took three months for me to complete the story about Ol' Blue. In the winter of 2020, I was pleasantly surprised by the positive responses to my personal prose as I bumped into people during my normal, weekly news beat.

Something I did not learn right away was that newspapers, especially weekly newspapers in small towns, are often not read right away. They linger on coffee tables for days and weeks after an issue is released. Sometimes, they never get read. Sometimes, they are gathered and stacked for "later." Other times, they are read when the mood strikes or to relieve boredom. Feedback on my writing came in slowly, which might account for the three month interim between part one and part two of this story. I wasn't sure the story was appreciated, so I put off writing again.

Though I always think of you, Good Reader, as I write my tales, I eventually learned that the tale must be told regardless of outside interest. That is, if an author has a story to tell, he ought to tell it, sales and readership be damned. I think that's what Mona was trying to tell me decades ago -- just do it, just write.

I'm In Love With My Car (The Continuing -- And Final -- Saga of Old Blue)

Originally published February 20, 2020

A few people told me they liked the story I told some time back (after that big November snow storm?) about "Old Blue," my 1972 Ford Maverick that met its demise when I ran it over some abandoned bed springs. When I told that tale, I suggested that I wasn't quite done with her just yet. A couple people asked me to tell "the rest of the story," as Paul Harvey would have said.

~~~

After Pete, Partlo and I cut the bed springs from around the transmission, drive shaft, and axle, we tried putting the car in neutral to push it back to my house. That didn't work, so we removed the drive shaft. We pushed her into my parents side yard, and I let her sit there as long as I could. (Which meant until my Dad got tired of seeing what he called "junk" sitting in his yard.)

I wanted to repair Old Blue since she was my first love, so to speak. (This story's song title by Queen resonates with more than a few men of my age, I'm sure.)

I had heard that a mutual friend, Chuckie, had a 1970 Maverick that he wanted to sell. I learned that the parts were about the same, so I hatched a plan to swap Chuckie's transmission into Old Blue. I walked over to his house and, one hundred and fifty dollars later, I was the proud owner of a second Ford Maverick.

Chuckie thought of himself as a real lady's man, so he had decorated the interior of his Mav' with a leopard skin print on the inside roof, some kind of fluffy fur cover on his back seats, Cheech and Chong style dingle balls rimming the roof line, and the crown jewel of fashion on this chic machine? -- a two foot by four foot mirror mounted over the back seat.

Still, it ran, and as long as you didn't take your hands off the wheel, it was reliable. (If you did take your hands off the wheel, the car would take an immediate hard left.) I used it for a couple months as a substi-
~~~

tute for Ol' Blue as I waited for the weather to get good enough for outdoor repairs. My plan was to take the transmission from the Chuck-wagon and put it into Blue.

I didn't know how to do it, but I knew who could....

Pete and Partlo, strangely, made themselves unavailable. While I was looking for another mechanic, I learned from a mutual friend -- Sabbatino, AKA Sam -- that Chuckie had a harrowing experience prior to selling me his rolling chick magnet. Apparently, according to Sam, Chuck's brakes had failed as he was heading into a busy intersection, so Chuckie threw the car in park. I was no mechanic, but I guessed that event might make his transmission less than desirable.

One day my mother asked me what I was going to do, now that I owned two old cars. (Her tone suggested that I should get rid of one -- soon.) I told her about the curious absence of my backyard mechanic friends, and she saved the day by suggesting my older cousin, Anthony.

Anthony was my hero as a kid. He was super cool. He played piano, built and flew remote control planes, and some other stuff I won't mention here. He was also super smart, and I was not disappointed when I asked him on the phone later that day.

"Anthony, I've got these two Mavericks, and I'd like to put the transmission from one into the other. Would you be able to help me do that?"

"I don't see why not," he said. "What shape is the other transmission in?"

I told him about Chuckie's mishap, and he told me I should buy another transmission. He told me they had car parts in the classified section of the newspaper all the time. I looked, called a number, and the person on the other end told me they had what I needed.

"Where are you at?" I asked, ready to pick up my car part.

"Oh, I'll deliver it to you -- same price -- forty bucks," he said.

"Okay, that sounds like a good deal," I said.

He showed up with his trunk flopping open, and he promptly asked for my money. I should have been suspicious when his next question was where he could buy marijuana. (Forty dollars was the price of an ounce of the stuff at the time... or so I'm told.)

He helped me take the transmission out of his car and

place it into my yard. It looked a little rusty, and I asked him about it. He assured me that he guaranteed all parts, asked me again if I knew where he could score, then left.

I still remember the look on my cousin Anthony's face when he came over to help me fix Old Blue.

"This is the transmission you bought?" He asked, barely containing his laughter.

"Well, it is a little rusty, but..."

"The rust isn't even the problem," he said, now unable to hold back his laughter. "Look at the teeth!"

Again, I was born in the Motor City, but I had none of the car common sense that most of my friends had. At the time of the transaction, I hadn't even noticed that the "new" transmission I had bought was missing half the teeth on the flywheel. In other words, my backyard tally was now two cars and three transmissions, and only one of them functional, and poorly at that.

Within the week I was calling the scrap yard. They towed Blue with the rusty trans in her trunk and I drove behind in the Chuck-wagon. Pete did step up and help as my ride home.

I'd be lying if I said it was a bitter moment for me. Sure, Old Blue was my first love, but my next love was even sweeter -- a 1965 Chevy Bel Air that I picked up for another $150. But that's another story....

***

... And that story is included in this book, Good Reader, in three parts. My luck with cars, or lack thereof, was legendary. This book contains most, but not all, of those tales. Amanda, my editor, protested in Billy Idol fashion -- "more, more, more" -- but I won't budge.

"Next time..."

...but wait, if you email me at ***LocalMediaNowLLC@gmail.com***, I'll send you the story of my 1980 Volkswagon Rabbit diesel engine, and you'll be placed on an email list to get updates on future books.

May You Live In Dull Times

Originally published January 16, 2020

Sometimes the writing muse doesn't come to me right away. I had that problem this week, exacerbated by the fact that my editor, Amanda, is on vacation in sunny Florida, leaving me to pull together the newspaper on my own for the first time in almost a year.

Since it had been so long, I decided to print out a hard copy of the paper at my office after I got about three quarters done. There were lots of gaps, but page by page I filled them in with a feature here, a submitted article or photo there, and occasionally my own writing.

The Publisher's Pen came last, like most weeks.

Why?

Well, it's what I call a personal narrative, and sometimes it is hard to share personal thoughts with countless others. (No safety net of Facebook, either. Once an error or dumb statement is out there, it's out there. No editing save running a correction the following week. That's the impetus behind state laws requiring local governments to publish their meeting minutes in the local newspaper -- the immutability protects the public.)

Don't worry, my muse today isn't Jimmy Stewart's Mr. Smith. I'm not going to continue to talk about it.

My inspiration actually came from those printouts. As I looked at the gap left from deleting last week's article, I kept reading and rereading the title, lyrics from a song U2's Bono sang in 1983 about the silence one hears on New Year's Day.

For a while, the song stayed on my mind, but then it tumbled around in my head for two days, got shortened, and morphed into "All's Quiet on the Western Front," the title of a World War I novel by Erich Maria Remarque, which I had read in high school. I guess that thought arrived courtesy of the trailer for the newer movie, 1917, which I had seen at the Clinton Theatre. Maybe my subconscious has been worrying about the recent tension between the United States and Iran?

It's odd how the mind works,

shunting thoughts of war and the very real death that is the end result for too many people. But now I remember a few of those thoughts.

I remember the real look of fear in my son's eyes as he learned he needed to register for the draft when he registered to vote. It was neatly disguised as academic incredulity by him, and equally camouflaged by me with a statement I hoped would be predictive.

"Don't worry, the chance of war, much less a draft, is low in this modern era," I said.

That was a couple years ago, and I was able to push it out of my mind then. But not now...

~~~

I remember "playing war" in the back yard with Ronny, my childhood friend from across the alley. Visions of John Wayne and other movie war heroes flashed in our minds as we went to battle, using Ronny's brother Eddie's '67 Impala as a tank or a fortress, depending on the scenario of our game. Eddie went to Vietnam, and his car waited there on cinder blocks. When he came home, we stopped playing in Ronny's yard. I stopped going over there, in fact. Eddie was scary. I couldn't explain it.

I remember the neighbor four doors down from us, the brother-in-law of the homeowner, Cloyd Swope. I don't remember his name, though I remember hearing he was a veteran. He had survived the Battle of the Bulge, the last major German offensive of World War II, which yielded the highest number of American casualties in the war. Every afternoon he would return from one of the corner bars which dotted every other street corner in those days. He would stagger home, talking to himself or to ghosts. I didn't understand it, but I didn't laugh at him like some of the other kids. I thought it was scary.

I remember how proud, how strong and fearless, my cousin Joe Stumpo looked when he returned from 'Nam, sitting on his Harley Davidson motorcycle, long black hair, long black beard, and the biggest black handlebar moustache I had ever seen. He seemed invincible, but years later the memories of death and battle and atrocity ate away at him, too. He died -- too young -- a shell of that man who was a living hero in my youth.

I got lucky. The sacrifice of others, those I have named and those unnamed and unknown by me, kept me from harm during my youth. I no longer have a fear of conscription -- for my-
~~~

self.

Now, I pray that our world will remain peaceful, for my son and for your children, too.

There is an old saying which is commonly called 'The Chinese Curse.' -- "May you live in interesting times."

I hope we will be able to greet each other with the inverse:

"May you live in dull times."

***

Some stories are emotional for me, and this one gets me every time I read it and envision my cousin Joe. The glory of his post Vietnam youth is described here, but the first image that comes to my mind is the sallow, grey-skinned, chain-smoking bitter man he became as he hit middle age. Thankfully, he mellowed and seemed to enjoy what he had in life -- children and grandchildren -- before he eventually died, too young, of course.

The other image in this piece that grabs my heart is that of my son looking frightened about the draft. That same fear I saw on his face welled in my heart and threatened to spill out. But it's a father's duty to stand strong, like The Duke, right?

Writing this book of memories is mostly for you, Good Reader, but this piece is for my son. It is my way of letting him know, before he has his own family, that fear for one's child is as natural as love.

***

The next piece is a bit ironic. As I sit here, I am in the first week of a medically supervised liquid diet designed to eventually help me shed over 100 pounds. I hope to become thinner, as my brother Paul did years ago, and eventually drop a few of the weight-related maladies in the process.

When I wrote "Count Me Out," the next story, I had actually begun an exercise regimen that I continue today; it evolved to five days a week within a year.

The difference now is that I no longer deny that I have been taking in extra calories. I had regularly professed to be clueless as to why I couldn't lose weight consistently. Tracking calories works only if you are honest with yourself, and I had been a big, fat liar!

By the time this is published, I hope to be half way to my goal. I hope to become half the man I used to be.

Count Me Out -- of the 15% Category, That Is!

Originally published January 30, 2020

For those of you who know me, or at least have seen me, you know that I am overweight. In fact, I am classified as 'morbidly obese' on the medical charts. The title is both distasteful and scary.

It is scary because of the plethora of health issues brought on by or exacerbated by excess weight: hypertension, diabetes, heart conditions, sleep apnea -- almost every ailment known to doctors.

It is distasteful to me because I used to be relatively thin and athletic -- a long, long time ago -- and I had sworn then that I'd never let myself get fat.

When I was a kid, growing up with my four younger brothers, I was thinner but not nicer. In fact, I was a relentless bully, especially toward my brother Paul, who was always heavy.

I made fun of him at every turn, creating chants and jeers like some loathsome bard.

"Super-fat, we know that, Paul is that. Oh, yeah!"

"Hey, fatster shu-batster!"

"Chubby-wubby flubby dubby..."

And other such nonsense, though I spewed it proudly, like I was Lewis Carroll reading Jabberwocky.

Some may call it Karma, my life as an overweight adult a fitting retribution for the cruelty of my youth.

Since then, I have apologized to Paul. (But if I haven't, Paul, let me apologize here and now!) Being obese is no picnic. (Egad! I can't even avoid food metaphors!)

Though I'm a little late for a New Year's Resolution, I have pledged to diet and add exercise to my regimen starting last week. I signed up for the Weight Loss Challenge at Simple Nutrition in Clinton, and I started to actually use my gym membership, going three times in the past five days!

I have already begun to annoy my wife and friends with unrequested exercise and diet reports.

"Guess what? I did 30 minutes on the treadmill today!"

"Did you know the steak and cheese wrap at Hometown is really filling?"

"I figured out a way to do sit ups, even with my big belly!"

And so, I have probably started to annoy you, too, Good Reader. I wouldn't risk that, however, unless I felt the message to be an important one.

According to results of a Center for Disease Control and Prevention (CDC) survey released this month, an average of 15% of all adults are inactive, defined as engaging in no leisure-time physical activity during the past month. Michigan had 25.1% of adults reporting inactive, according to a CDC report.

So my message this week is a two-part request.

First, if you happen to see me, ask me about my regimen of diet and exercise, or tell me about your own. I think such regular conversation will help me stick to it. After all, if I quit my efforts to diet and exercise regularly, I will have to make an equally public announcement on these pages, with an embarrassing title like...

"Enough, Already! I'm Fat, So Leave Me Alone!"

Or perhaps...

Publisher Proud to be BBOM (Big Beautiful Old Man)

My second request is that you join me in improving your diet and exercise regimen in 2020. Proper diet and regular exercise can help prevent or manage many health problems and concerns, including: stroke, metabolic syndrome, high blood pressure, type two diabetes, depression, anxiety, many types of cancer, arthritis, and falls, according to the Mayo Clinic. Regular exercise can also improve mood, boost energy, and promote better sleep.

I'm looking forward to a happy and healthy decade, for you and for me. Join me in getting a good start in 2020!

***

One friend of mine, John "The Incredible" Hauck, took me up on the offer and remained my workout partner for years, until I went back to teaching and adopted a 5 a.m. exercise regimen. (I just can't discipline myself to hit the gym after a day of work.)

And now, back to the car stories...

My Goal Line Girl (part 1 of 3)

Originally published February 27, 2020

After Old Blue had gone to that great junk yard in the sky, I was without wheels for a while. Mona had been gracious enough to drop me off at work for a couple weeks, but seeing that I started at 5 a.m., her hospitality wore thin in a hurry. At that time, I was a short order cook -- first shift -- at a restaurant called Lee's Family Diner on the busy corner of Ford and Telegraph Roads in Dearborn Heights.

Old Blue was purchased from one of the regulars at Lee's, and now I had another offer from a patron. He was a gruff, older man who always sat at the end of the counter. He told me he had an old car -- "a classic" -- that he was selling. He said the cook on the afternoon shift wanted to buy it, but he liked me better and wanted me to have her. He said he thought she was perfect for me. I hadn't read Stephen King's Christine yet, or I may have been turned off by that line. Instead, I was honored, and bought her sight unseen, right there at the counter.

Later, I met the old girl -- a 1965 Chevy Bel Aire. She sagged from a broken rear coil spring on the passenger side, her golden paint had long been oxidized, leaving bare patches of metal on her hood and roof, and the seats were threadbare. (You could see the springs in places!) The tires were bald. But she was a '65 Chevy -- a classic, so she was perfect in my eyes. I was already in love.

"She burns a little oil," he had said, "but she doesn't leak a drop."

I was 21 at that time, and that was the biggest understatement I had ever heard up to that point -- and for years afterward -- but I was happy with her. So happy, in fact, that I could envision my ugly duckling transformed into a swan. Mentally, even though I possessed no skill in mechanics or body work, I could see myself transforming her into a real show car.

First things first, a fancy car had to have a name. I rolled some ideas around in my head and came up with a name from a song that had been playing on

The 1965 Chevrolet Bel Aire

the radio at that time -- Southern Cross by CSN. I would call my new love "Goal Line Girl."

Funny thing is, like so many other lyrical misinterpretations, the song never said that name -- it didn't say "Goal Line Girl," it said "woman girl." Yet I was proudly certain, and I would sing that song (with my lyrical error) every time I filled up her engine with oil.

Hubris is the folly of man, and pride goes before the fall. In my youth, I would posture as THE EXPERT in lyrics. For instance, I would correct Chuckie (my backup Maverick connection from down the block) when he sang, "he's got such a so caress" instead of the real lyrics in Pinball Wizard.

I knew everything, of course, so when my friends tried to talk me out of restoring her, I didn't listen, except when they told me she'd need a lot of money.

I decided to get a second job -- delivering pizza. Despite her many frailties, Goal Line Girl was reliable in that she started every time, though I found myself travelling with a 5 quart jug of K-Mart motor oil in the back seat. About every second or third delivery run, I'd have to stop and add oil. Once, I got adventurous and drove her out to Kalamazoo to see my buddy Ralph at college there, playing AM radio the whole way and grooving on "65 Love Affair" by Paul Davis -- a hit at that time -- in between stops for more oil.

Despite this hindrance, after a few weeks I had accumulated enough money to start considering repairs, so I talked with my longtime mechanically inclined friends to attempt to enlist their help. Partlo was apparently too canny to be lured in, as was Pete. Sometimes, however, you find friends in need, and that is how the restoration process started.

I mentioned that I worked as a cook during the day in Dearborn Heights, though I lived in Detroit. What I neglected to mention earlier, when I listed the deficiencies of Goal Line Girl, was that she also had a missing exhaust pipe and several lights out -- headlights, brake lights, and turn lights. Detroit Police had a reputation for being somewhat laissez-faire when it came to vehicles, at least compared to suburban officers, so I devised a route home from the restaurant that took a series of side roads and less travelled byways. I kept to the same path each afternoon, which may have been a mistake because one diligent officer in Dearborn (home of the toughest cops in the area at that time) seemed to be waiting for me one day as I roared by.

He gave me so many citations that I felt like I was holding a deck of playing cards -- tickets for speeding, excessive noise, no brake lights, etcetera.

"If I fix all of these things, will these tickets get dismissed?" I asked the officer as he nursed the cramp in his writing hand. He gave me a look that spoke to my sanity.

"You really want to fix **this**?"

I resolutely told him I did, and he told me I had to have it done by the date on the back of the tickets, bring all my receipts and the vehicle to the courthouse, and if, after inspection, it appeared they all were satisfied, the tickets would be dismissed.

"Or you could just drive this to a junk yard and bring that receipt to the judge," he said. "It'd be a lot cheaper."

I tossed the tickets into the back seat of the vehicle with the hundreds of paper receipts from several weeks worth of pizza deliveries. Then I went to share my dilemma with my mechanically inclined friends. I had already lost Blue; I wasn't going to lose my Girl.

To my surprise and delight, Pete enthusiastically volunteered to help me make the necessary repairs. We made a date for that Saturday, and there I was, for the first time in my life, under a car on a beautiful summer day instead of out playing ball somewhere. I felt accomplished as we fixed her up, step by step, and pride of ownership soon made my chest swell.

My buoyant mood was to be short lived, unfortunately, but that will have to wait until next time....

Goal Line Girl (part 2)
We Didn't Start the Fire

Originally published April 30, 2020

About two months ago I left you with the first half of the story about my all-time favorite car, which I called Goal Line Girl. It was a 1965 Chevy Bel Air that had no exhaust system, a broken rear coil spring, bad shocks, bald tires, burnt out lights, and an engine that burned more oil than gasoline, but it was my baby, and I intended to fix her up eventually.

That timetable was moved forward when I received about a dozen tickets for the listed defects (as well as speeding). I tossed the tickets into the back seat of the car, where they rested on the seat with hundreds of old receipts from my pizza deliveries from the previous weeks.

It was time to call my friend, Pete. You might remember that he, along with Partlo, were what I called "motorheads" because they spent all their time under the hood of one car or another. Lucky for me, Pete agreed to help, and we came up with a plan for all those repairs.

We started with the exhaust and walked into a store that had a complete system in stock for about $100, which was about what I took home in a week for 40 hours of work delivering pizza, including tips. We also bought rear shocks, light bulbs for the tail and headlights, and then hit the junk yard for two used coil springs. We planned to begin repairs that Saturday at 8 a.m.

Pete showed up on time, and the two of us got to work. It took a while with just the car's jack -- no blocks or hoist to lift the car. I remember finishing in the late afternoon. Pete and I decided to clean up and then take the newly repaired vehicle on a maiden voyage to Partlo's new apartment in Ypsilanti.

We got in my car and hit I-94, heading west from Detroit. I can still see my hands on her big steel steering wheel as we cruised around a curve at 70 mph. I remember saying, "Wow, she really rides nice with the new shocks and springs. Imagine how smooth she'll be with new tires!"

And that's when I really began visualizing what she might look like. Would I paint her cherry red or keep the golden color? How would I get the threadbare seats repaired? Should I rebuild the engine or get a bigger one? Stock or street modifications? Automatic or manual transmission? Fuzzy dice or dashboard Jesus? So many decisions to make now, and Pete and I discussed them during that ride to Ypsi.

Pete reminded me that my next step had to be to take the repaired vehicle to the courthouse with the tickets to get them dismissed.

"You still have the tickets, right?" Pete asked.

"Sure."

"And the receipts for the parts?"

"In the back," I said, hooking a thumb over my shoulder and pointing to the assorted slips of paper that littered the back seat like leaves on an autumn lawn -- tickets from the Dearborn Police, receipts from auto parts stores, and hundreds of pizza delivery stubs. (In those days, they wrote the address on the receipt so the delivery person would have not only the address but also the price to charge at the door -- GPS was unavailable then.)

We got to Ypsilanti and found the apartment, which was a lower flat in a duplex home near the Eastern Michigan University campus. Like most older towns, there wasn't much available parking, so we drove around the block a couple times. Frustrated, I declared that we would be taking a spot in the alley behind someone's garage. It was marked 'no parking.'

"Are you sure that's wise?" Pete asked.

"It's not a real sign. We can't get a ticket," I said. It had apparently been placed there by a frustrated homeowner, but I didn't have the slightest clue as to how truly frustrated she was until later.

"Should we roll up the windows and lock the car?" Pete asked.

"Why bother?" I said. "It's a nice night. Let the car air out."

And it was a gorgeous August evening, warm without the usual high humidity. We arrived around twilight, and it was just beginning to cool off. Pete shrugged his shoulders and tossed his prized WABX radio baseball cap into the front seat. We headed toward Partlo's.

Now, in my youth, Good Reader, I did a few things I am not proud to recount today. One of those was my propensity for unbridled gusto when it came to partying. I was, for a few years there anyway, a 'party animal.' As soon as we arrived, the party began. Pete, normally the most reserved, even participated with more zeal than usual. He cited the long day of car repair as his reason.

"Hey, that's right, Partlo! You've got to see my new car," I said, and I started to list all of the future improvements that would make my Goal Line Girl a real show girl, er, show car.

"I've been looking at that car all day," Pete said. "He can see it when we leave."

We all agreed to that, then Pete went to the bathroom.

We had some loud rock and roll playing the entire time, though I can't remember the tunes. It was so loud that we never heard the sirens.

"Hey, where are those flashing red lights coming from?" I asked, noting the blinking pattern on the walls of Partlo's kitchen.

"There's no blue in them, must be a fire truck," Partlo said, then added with a laugh, "maybe Pete set your car on fire."

Before the lights appeared, Partlo and I had been calling out jokes to Pete about how long he remained in the bathroom. If he responded, we didn't hear it over the music. Partlo and I cracked jokes and shot the breeze for about 15 minutes in his living room. At the end of that time, I began to take Partlo's joke a bit more seriously, not the part about Pete, but the part about fire and my car. I mentioned it to Partlo, who thought it was unlikely, but I got him to get up, and we both knocked on the bathroom door until Pete answered, then we headed outside.

Both Partlo and Pete were well over six feet tall, but Pete walked with a pronounced limp due to a pellet gun accident as a teen. One of his eyes didn't work well either, so as we walked out to the alley where my car was parked, Pete split from us and headed toward the car from a different angle.

As Partlo and I turned the corner, I saw my car, my beautiful dream car, smoldering as firefighters continued to spray water on it. The fire had been so hot that the glass melted before shattering, and the roof warped into a contorted mess. Just a series of intertwined wires and springs, the seats inside were now totally threadbare! I stood there gaping, then my eyes shifted to a short woman with a dog on a leash. She was being questioned by someone who must have been the fire chief.

"Did you see anyone strange around, Ma'am?"

"Well, there was this man," she said, looking past the chief and in the direction of Pete. "He was tall, blond, and walked with a limp."

I stepped forward. The chief turned to me. I confirmed that I owned the vehicle, then he asked me if I thought Pete might have set it on fire.

"No way! He worked on that car with me all day," I answered, but then a flicker of doubt entered my mind. After all, he had been in the bathroom for a long time. 'Could he have snuck through the window?'

"Okay, do you want us to haul it to the junk yard for you?"

Horrified, I said, "No, I'm going to fix her up!" I proceeded to rattle off my plans as I had on the ride earlier, and the fire chief just looked at me with a mixture of disbelief, pity and mirth.

"Okay, but this is an arson case, so do you mind if we hold the car for a couple days in our impound until we figure out who did this?"

Not sure where I would begin with the repairs, anyway, I agreed. His plan also appealed to my sense of righteous indignation. How dare anyone treat my Girl like this?

Partlo ended up driving us home that night. And to my surprise, Good Reader, the story does not end here. Stay tuned for part three...

Claus Peter Buseman
April 13, 1958 — August 28, 2024

Goal Line Girl (part 3)

Gone, Gone, Gone

Originally published May 7, 2020

Partlo drove us home, and on the way we mentioned to Pete that his name was brought up as a suspect. Partlo thoroughly enjoyed giving Pete a hard time about it. As for me, though I told the detective that I was sure Pete wouldn't have done it, I was starting to visualize how he might have snuck through the bathroom window and ignited the car. Was his envy of my (soon-to-be) beautiful classic car strong enough to drive him to such extremes?

"You forget that I spent all day working on that car with you," Pete said in his defense.

Still, I was running the scenario through my head, trying to calculate just how long Pete had been in the bathroom. Could he have made it out the window? What did he use to start the fire? How did he get back in through the window? I was almost ready to ask Partlo to turn the car around so I could examine the scene as any proper detective might. (I had, after all, been an avid reader of Sherlock Holmes stories.)

I was starting to simmer, ready to launch an accusation like it was a game of Clue: "Peter with the lighter in the alley." Partlo continued to throw fuel on the situation with more jokes. Fortunately, Pete spoke up with his best and most irrefutable defense.

"You guys seem to forget that I lost my (W)ABX hat in that fire, too!" Pete said with a finality that left us silent.

We all knew how much he cherished that cap, though the audacity of equating his loss with mine was rather galling. However, if Pete had torched the car, he would have rescued his cap -- case closed.

So I again brooded in silence as we cruised east on the freeway, wondering how my car had come to be a mid-summer bonfire. Fortunately, as a youth, my spirit was resilient. (Or you could say that I was a slow learner.) My mind started to turn to ways I could still repair her. In fact, since the roof melted down, I figured I could make her a convertible. How cool would that be?

Unflappable, I began to share my revised plans with Pete and Partlo. They politely listened, then Pete asked, "What are you going to do about those tickets?"

"I'll just have to show the court the fire marshal's report," I said.

"Good luck with that," they both said.

On the following Monday, I called the Ypsilanti Fire Department. The chief said he had nothing solid to report, asked me again if I thought my friend had done it, then asked if he could hold the car until Wednesday because he had a lead to follow. I said okay.

Since I had no wheels, I had to ask my brother Paul for a ride on that Wednesday.

My brothers and I love each other, but you might remember me mentioning in another story that I picked on Paul mercilessly when we were younger. I mention this, Good Reader, to be fair, so you have all the data when you hear what happened next, lest you begin to have too much unwarranted sympathy for me.

"You need to pay me for gas," said Paul.

"Okay, I'll pay for the gas." I said. "Here's ten bucks. It won't take more than that."

"And my time..." Paul said, hand still extended.

I tried to look incredulous, to run the "but we're family" line on him, but it really wasn't unexpected. He had me where he wanted me.

"Twenty bucks," he said. "Extra." And then he added, "Each way."

I was outraged, but deep down couldn't blame him. Besides, it was for my Girl, my Goal Line Girl, my one true love. I acquiesced, but added a trip to the bank to his chauffeur's route. We stopped at the bank and I withdrew $50, which, after the repair parts purchased the previous Saturday, left my bank account dry.

One step at a time. That was my mantra, though in hindsight I wish I had more of a chess player's view on the world -- the ability to see many moves in advance.

We drove back to Ypsi that Wednesday in the morning and met with the fire marshall.

"Someone threw a road flair into your car," he said. "That's what started the fire."

'A road flair,' I thought. That definitely rules out Pete. Then I asked, "Did you find out who did it?"

Having been an avid fan of detective stories and shows, like Columbo, McCloud, Hart to Hart, and the like, I expected that he would have already apprehended the culprit. After all, he'd had three days.

"No, but we think it was someone who had escaped from a group home."

"A group home?"

"For the mentally disturbed," he said. "We had a report of an escape around the same time the fire occurred, and the two events were in the same area."

I asked if the suspect was arrested, and was told there was no evidence. I was feeling a little indignant about justice not being served. That feeling, however, was greatly amplified by the next exchange.

"So, the investigation is over? Can I get my car?" I asked.

"Sure, just take this slip to the impound lot. Pay the man there for three days, and then you can take your car."

I'm sure my jaw dropped as I stared at him.

"Pay? You never said anything about paying," I said, outraged. "I let you hold the car for your investigation!"

"And I thank you for that, but you still have to pay if you want to get it out of impound," he said. "It's $60 a day and $40 for the tow."

Now I really did feel like a victim as I totalled the cost -- $220!

"That's insane," I said. "That's over two hundred dollars! I don't have that kind of money."

Next to me, very quietly (and did I hear a chuckle in his voice? I think so) Paul spoke up for the first time.

"I do."

On the way to the 'impound lot,' Paul negotiated his usurious price for the loan. Twenty percent for three months? No, he wouldn't hear of it. Double his money in the same time period?

"Not good enough," Paul said simply. I was desperate to get my Girl back, so I made my best offer.

"How about my stereo system?" I offered. It was a component system with top quality speakers and tuner, and a mid quality turntable and cassette deck. Combined, it had cost me over $1,200, and I had owned it for little over a year. Certainly, it was a steal for $220.

Never one to let a golden opportunity pass, Paul countered, "and your record collection!"

Outraged, but drawing close to the impound yard without the money in hand to ransom my Girl, I made a compromise.

"One hundred albums, but I get to set aside my top 50 first."

The attendant there was a good ol' boy with a straw hat and bib overalls, and he came out to me to get the scoop on why I was there. I told him my dreams for the car, and he looked at me like I had fallen off the turnip truck. In a deep southern drawl, he managed to talk some sense into me.

"Boy, you crazy t'think this is fixable," he said. "Leave 'er wit' me. You can buy another t' fix up, an' I'll give you sixty bucks fer scrap."

Maybe it was the way she looked in the harsh daylight. Maybe it was thinking of my Dad's reaction to having this in his driveway. Maybe it was the thought of negotiating another sum of money from Paul to pay for the towing from Ypsi to Detroit. Or maybe it was because this was the first time in a week that I had an offer of positive cash flow -- whichever way, I took his offer and said my sad goodbye to my Goal Line Girl.

***

My Goal Line Girl wasn't the last vehicle I anthropomorphized, but it was the last one I truly loved...

...sigh...

Giving her up to the junk yard at least had the benefit of allowing me to keep my stereo system and albums, at least temporarily. Just about a year later, Paul was able to claim the prize when I had yet another car dilemma. Stories about my next vehicle (yes, several tales of woe) would have come next, but they were preempted by Covid...

The End of the World (or Glory Days)

Originally published March 19, 2020

I had really planned to keep it light this week and avoid talking about THE topic -- CO-VID-19, AKA The Coronavirus. After all, what could I add to the conversation?

I've received reassuring emails from my banks, insurance companies, mortgage companies, health care providers, my fourth grade teacher, the company I bought my business cards from, Rotary International, Costco, and even Shoe Carnival.

I, too, wish to assure you that your Local newspaper will endure this crisis, bringing you the best local news we can get under the circumstances.

With the state mandated school closings issued last Friday, the Local lost one of its most consistent news feeds -- athletics, arts, and sciences in the local schools. Consequently, we have trimmed this issue by four pages.

I had thought to create a section in the absence of high school sports called "Glory Days," in homage to the Bruce Springsteen song by that name. For those unfamiliar with the tune, the feature would be about athletic tales of old, as told by individual guest writers. My editor thought that would be an eventual train wreck, so we canned the idea. Still, I find myself stuck on the idea and feel compelled to see it through. Blame it on my OCD, baby.

~~~

When I was in middle school, I always made the school basketball team. Even though I was clumsy and got nervous and agitated when I happened to get the ball, I had three redeeming qualities that kept me on the team, albeit on the bench:

1. I was almost 6' tall, even then.
2. I was able to play defense against anyone.
3. I shot over 95% from the free throw line.*

That last detail has an asterisk because that was my practice statistic. I was a perfect 100% from the charity stripe in games.
~~~

I played for the Saint Christopher Crusaders of Detroit. We were pretty good, and we usually won the league or lost to our arch rival, the Saint Alphonsus Arrows of Dearborn. It was kind of like Bo Schembechler's Wolverines versus Woody Hayes' Buckeyes of the 1970s. We were the two big teams in the league.

Near the end of the season, we faced the Arrows in their house, and we needed the victory to keep our title hopes alive. I sat on the bench for most of the game, as usual. After all, my real value on the team was in practice -- I played hard and was a good defender to challenge our ball handlers. I really didn't expect to get in the game, and to be honest, I didn't really want to.

As I mentioned, I usually became so nervous when I got the ball that I would be called for traveling or get the ball stolen away. Then I'd face the derision of my teammates and my coach. Truly, it was much better to sit on the bench and cheer.

But with little over a minute left, one of our guards fouled out.

"Walters, get in there!" my coach yelled, clearly unhappy to be calling for me.

He wasn't the only one.

"Just play defense," he added.

Before I got into the game, we had gone down three points, a practically insurmountable deficit in the days before the three point shot. Time was ticking down, and with less than 10 seconds left on the clock, the Arrows had the ball. Their guards were cagey and fast, but I managed to tip the ball away from the dribbler in front of me. My teammate, Dean Frankiewicz, seized the opportunity and dribbled the ball toward our basket. Dean was fast and surehanded, so I relaxed as I ran down the court after him. He would certainly score for us.

But he didn't.

The ball hit the backboard, the rim, then bounced back to me as I was running full speed. Practically under the basket, I tossed the ball up without looking...

... And it went in!

Our fans exploded with excitement, and their cheers went on and on. I couldn't understand why. Then I realized I had been fouled, and the rules at the time called for me to shoot "one and one." If I made the first shot, I'd get a second shot. Incredibly, I had a chance to win the game.

The Arrows coach called back to back time outs. I later

understood that it was an effort to "ice the shooter," but to me, the break was welcome. I settled my mind and body even as my coach's intensity was increasing.

The thing I did best was free throw shooting, and I had an odd yet helpful ability to block out everything but the front of the rim. With the same rhythmic pattern I used in practice, I prepared for my first shot: dribble, dribble, dribble, place tip of finger on inflator valve, bend knees, body and arms coil slightly and then release...

SWISH

And then the cheers.

And then again...

SWISH

And just like that, we had won the game.

My joy was to be short lived, however. In the locker room, where I thought I would be celebrated by my teammates (if movies are to be believed), I was met with icy coldness. The coach had immediately launched into a 15 minute rant about how bad the team played -- "except Walters" -- which left the others with nothing but disdain for me.

I walked out of that locker room feeling robbed, though the look on my father's face and his enthusiastic hug as I met him to go home made all the difference.

If the end of the world is coming, and we can't go to theaters, to restaurants, or to other events, we still have our memories and our stories from the "Glory Days" to share.

***

After scoring the winning baskets in that game, Mona felt I had earned a spot in the starting rotation. I knew better, realizing my two point lay up had been sheer luck. Nonetheless, she grilled me after each practice.

"Did you tell the coach you should be a starter?"

"No, Mom, I'm not a starter..."

"You need to tell him. You're better than those other boys..."

Bless her heart, she went on like that all the way home. My father steered clear of this campaign. He knew the unwritten manly code: he let the coaches do the coaching. After a few days of Mona's post practice questioning, she decided to go into the gym to give the coach "what-for." After that, I quit the team, with her blessing. She was indignant. I was embarrassed. But God, I love her for it.

Any Major Dude Will Tell You

Originally published April 2, 2020

Last week, it all started to get to me, and I must apologize to you, Good Reader, for losing my cool. I felt like (and sounded like) Chicken Little running in circles and proclaiming that the "sky is falling."

For those who don't remember, I went on and on about the price of the Local and the need for an increase. My panic was unnecessary for several reasons: faith, loyalty, and ingenuity.

As for faith, I have always liked the phrase, "Let go and let God." Recently, I was speaking to a worker in a local grocery store, and she said the atmosphere was "&#@* crazy!" We were talking about the mad rush to snatch up toilet paper. I shared the following quote from the Gospel of Luke 12:24:

"Consider the ravens, for they neither sow nor reap; they have no storeroom nor barn, and yet God feeds them; how much more valuable you are than the birds!"

And yet, less than a week later, there I was, panicked -- "Oh, ye of little faith!"

Determined to begin practicing what I had been preaching, I decided to take last Thursday off. I started the day by doing some much needed early yard work, which I had been neglecting for years. I trimmed some long-overgrown bushes and then started on the fallen trees in the back of my yard. I listened to the birds sing, the woodpeckers tap time, and I sang "Bungle in the Jungle" by Jethro Tull as I chopped away.

Even with the occasional burst from my chain saw, it was peaceful -- serene, even. I looked at a sparrow bringing a twig to one of the birdhouses I had mounted with my son years ago, amazed they were still deemed useful by our avian friends. I recalled the article shared last week by Reverend Jon Turner of the Clinton Baptist Church, and I remembered that God provides, maybe not all that we want, but certainly all that we need.

Later that afternoon I spent a few hours sitting (six feet apart) with my friend and Local subscriber, John Hauck. We fished for catfish from his pond and talked about family and times past. We watched the unbridled energy of his dog, Ringo, as he ran around the pond at full speed. We listened to the spring peepers in a bog near the edge of his property and the sound of someone target shooting (I hoped!) behind his acreage. As we talked and he asked me questions, I was reminded of the fierce loyalty that is part of every Local subscriber I've had the pleasure of talking to in person or in writing. There is loyalty to the Village of Clinton and to its newspaper.

The next day, last Friday, I went to the office (lonely now due to the virus) and struck upon an idea. I had said the Local needed to either double its fees or double its subscribers. Seizing on the latter, I created an old school promotional campaign -- go door to door in Clinton and leave flyers -- trying to double readership in the Village. I created my flyer to go on top and began to rubber band them to leftover papers from the week. (Quite a few since school was out and several of our business stands were closed.)

That evening, I began the door to door process, but tuckered out after only an hour and a half. I did get a chance to

When Life Gives You Lemons

Worried about shortages of critical suplies?
We've got the answer to your problems!
Call 555-1212 to order your supply now.

This was a fun project, though I never actually ran it in the paper.

admire the variety of architecture in one of the village's older neighborhoods, and I did get some much-needed exercise. Even so, I decided to subcontract the rest of the job to the Smith Twins -- Samantha and Stella -- under the guidance of their father, Mark.

During my short-lived paper route, I recalled my first job.

~~~

When I was about 12 years old, my brother, Paul, and I pestered our mother to let us have a paper route. She checked into it and got us what's called
~~~

a "shopper" -- those advertising papers that are delivered to every house in a neighborhood.

We were excited the first week, but after doing the route for a couple weeks, we quickly grew tired of it. The hours were long and the money was insignificant, especially when compared to the earnings our friends boasted about from their "real" paper routes with the Detroit News and Detroit Free Press.

When the papers came next week, I had a plan to avoid that work. (People talk about Millennials today, but kids of every era could exhibit slothfulness when left unchecked.) We still had to roll and rubber band the papers, of course, because that was done at home with Mom watching. Then Paul and I set out to do our route.

"Are you sure this will work," Paul asked. I always accused him of being our mother's pet, and I'm sure he didn't want to disappoint her as much as anything else.

"Sure, we'll deliver a block or two. When we get far enough from the house, we'll dump the rest in the field," I said. The field was owned by Ford Motor Company and sublet to a farmer, who tilled most of it. Further down from our house, however, was a copse of small trees, saplings really, where someone had posted a hand-lettered sign that read 'Passion Pit.' At the time, I had no idea what that meant, but the grass was tall there, and our treachery would go unnoticed -- of that I was certain.

Craftily, we meandered up and down a few blocks on the way back home, just to kill some time. When it felt like we had exhausted the right amount, we headed home. Mom was waiting for us at the screen door.

"How did your paper route go? she asked.

We muttered "fine" and "okay," but we could tell "the jig was up," as they used to say in the old movies.

"Where are the papers?" she asked.

"We delivered them," I gamely asserted, but my gaze wavered. Paul was looking at his shoes.

"No, you didn't," she said, and her confidence in the next statement puzzled me. "Go back to those trees where you dumped them and finish your route."

Flabbergasted.

In those days, even in the big city, everyone knew whose kid you were and how to get in touch with your parents. And they weren't afraid to do so.

Paul and I fulfilled our duty that day, then we quit the route.

Older and wiser, but perhaps still a bit lazy, I've struck upon an easier method once again. During the crisis, we will be sending sample copies to Clinton residents who currently do not subscribe. It is our hope that they will avail themselves of the offer below and join our community of subscribers to the "Best Little Newspaper in Clinton."

My own crude sketch (above) sought to generated sales during the Covid pandemic, though looking back, I should have asked for more.

***

For a three year commitment of $60 total, new or renewing subscribers got the newspaper and a decent tee shirt. The campaign was successful in one way -- about 60 people took advantage of the offer.

I say took advantage because that's what I let happen! Craftier business people at the time offered much less and got much more, some flat-out asking for "support" via GoFundMe and other methods.

I did have fun sketching the above promotion and subsequently designing the tee shirt, using professionally drawn graphics for that!

Almost Cut My Hair

Originally published June 11, 2020

I've been singing that old song by CSN, "Almost Cut My Hair," a lot recently, mostly every time I look into a mirror. Sometimes it pops into my mind when I recall that I do own a home barber kit, purchased shortly after retirement as a hedge against runaway expenses. (I retired the kit after a couple catastrophic attempts at self-grooming.)

I also thought about the tune as I drove into Ohio last week to pick up my camera, which had been sent in for cleaning before the pandemic struck.

Covid restrictions are different from state to state. Ohio barbers have been open for a while; even so, it somehow felt disloyal to our local barbers, so I brushed the hair out of my eyes and headed straight home.

Saturday evening the song came to mind again in Downtown Clinton as about 130 people participated in a peaceful protest as a part of the Black Lives Matter movement.

The song, you see, was really not about haircuts at all, but about protest and revolution, and it hearkens from an era that produced some of my favorite music of all time -- the late 60s and early 70s.

Long hair is something that has been associated with protest, in my mind, since I was quite young.

~~~

I was too young to be involved with the Flower Power movement -- "make love, not war" -- but I was not too young to be fascinated by their style. I wanted to look like them, or at least like Micky Dolenz of the Monkees.

For my thirteenth birthday I asked for and received a two-inch-thick, green suede-leather wrist watch band. (I already had the watch.) The band was hot and sweaty, but I wore it with pride all that summer of 1974. That I had managed to cajole my mother into buying it was a triumph of my blossoming independence, in my mind. I still wasn't able to get my father to allow me to grow my hair like a Monkey, however.
~~~

My father, Ralph, took great enjoyment in cutting our hair, and he was never more in his element than when he had an audience.

Summer shearing was the worst. He'd call us in from our perpetual bike riding around the neighborhood.

"Mike, Paul, Mark, Joe, David!"

No, Good Reader, this was not done over a cell phone. It was an old fashioned cattle call, and when Dad called (especially when Dad called) you knew you'd better get there fast. Our friends knew the routine. Mom usually called us in for mundane things like meals and bedtime. When Dad called, they knew it was about to be show time.

My heart sank as I saw Dad standing with the clippers by the picnic table in our back yard.

"You first, Mike," Dad said. "Oldest first."

I tried my best to protest, but gave in to the eventuality that I was never going to grow my hair long. Sighing, I held onto my hippie watchband for comfort as my father ran the clippers back and forth across my scalp. I looked like Sinead O'Connor, or, keeping with the era, Telly Savalas.

Our friends, of course, had a good old time watching the spectacle of the five of us getting scalped. It was better than any western on the tube.

I had come to resent my father's hair cuts, and, unfortunately, as I grew into my teen years, I had also come to resent him.

Ultimately, I got my revenge -- twice.

The first time came that very school year. At the first parent conference, the music teacher, Ron Mysliwiec, approached my mother and told her he hoped I would play the part of Nanki Poo in the spring operetta. In seventh grade, I had played Doctor Quackenboots, a role my teacher added to the original H.M.S. Pinafore. Apparently, the music director wanted to cast me as the male lead in The Mikado!

But that wasn't the best part.

The best part was that he asked my mother to let my hair grow for the rest of the school year. Dad wasn't happy about it, but Mona got her way when she wanted to, so it happened. By spring, I was blissfully looking through my hair like a sheep dog.

After that, my brother Paul and I went to the Detroit Barber College for hair cuts. In 1977 Saturday Night Fever came out, and we had to have our hair "feathered," like John Travolta. I stuck with this style through the summer of 1978, and got my senior photos right before I had to cut my locks for football. (Our coach, Ted Mac, had a high and tight crew cut for as long as I knew him, and he wouldn't let you play if your hair showed when you wore your helmet. No debate. No compromise.)

My father voiced his objection to my long hair for my senior photos, of course.

"You look like a girl," he said. "Do you really want to be remembered that way?"

And I did, especially when I recalled his delight at shearing us like so many sheep all those years ago -- in front of our friends. I was a senior in high school -- a grown man, as far as I was concerned. As a grown man, I was going to make my own decisions, and if long hair was what my father did not want, then I was keeping it. It was my ultimate revenge.

Of course, as you might already have guessed, Good Reader, I did not have the last laugh. Just a few years later, men's hair styles grew shorter and shorter. Over time, I became more embarrassed of that senior portrait, sliding it behind other photos on the mantel at Mom's house. Did they retouch those photos back then? I think they did, and as I grew older it looked like I was wearing rouge and lipstick. I was never prettier. Egads!

Haircuts continued to be an issue for me in college. When I came home for Christmas break during my first year, I decided I needed a trim. My youngest brother, David -- AKA Dewey -- volunteered to cut it. He made mistake after mistake, and we laughed and laughed as he tried to repair the damage.

"Here. A little more off this side," Dewey said in between snips. "Oh, wait..."

"What do you mean, 'Oh, wait?'"

"Oh, nothing," he said, snorting laughter through gritted teeth. "Nothing, really."

I went back to college in January, 1981, as a punk rocker, spiking my hair up to hide the defects. I was quite avant garde, being the only one on campus with that style at the time.

As I look at my long hair now, I wish for two things. One, of course, is the reopening of our local salons and barber shops. The other is a wish for peaceful protest and expression of ideas.

Yes, I really feel like we owe it to someone.

Ring My Bell

Originally published June 18, 2020

Graduation Day, 1979 -- I can remember it like it was yesterday. Well, at least a few bits and pieces.

~~~

I remember that we had rental gowns back then, and they were quite heavy and hot. I think they may have been velvet. (The gowns used now are thin to the point of being sheer, and students can buy them at a cost that is usually less than what our rental fee was over 40 years ago.)

I grabbed my rental gown and hopped into the family's lemon yellow Plymouth Duster. It was the first time I had been allowed to drive it since the accident. (Yes, my automotive misfortunes abound -- there is another story there!)

I drove the six miles to the graduation ceremony, playing the radio and smoking Parliament cigarettes the entire way. I thought I was the coolest. I remember Anita Ward's "Ring My Bell" playing on the radio as I pulled into the parking lot, so I stood there with the door ajar, car running, smoking and listening to that old disco tune. (I had been a staunch "Disco Sucks" rock and roller in public, though I confess to you now, Good Reader, that I was a closet disco fan. Some of it was pretty good.)

I waited by my car until it was time to assemble with my fellow graduates and don our caps and gowns. During those last days of school, our schedule had changed dramatically. We didn't have as many classes together in the last few weeks. Finals came and seniors were in the building at random times depending on their schedules. It hadn't occurred to me what would happen after the graduation ceremony until I was walking up to our gathered class on the steps of St. Scholastica Church in Detroit, where the ceremony was to be held. I just assumed there would be a graduation party somewhere.

My parents had offered to take me out to celebrate after the ceremony. Our family was half Italian (Mom's side), so celebrations meant feasts. Many of my best memories come from
~~~

such celebrations -- Christmas dinner at Mom's, Easter at Grandma's, Thanksgiving at Aunt Lily's, Fourth of July at Uncle Tony's, and countless family weddings. What I wouldn't give to have family celebrations like those again...

A week before the ceremony, Mona had proposed a grand feast, including all my younger brothers, grandparents, and possibly my cousins. I don't know the details because I rejected that idea immediately.

"I'm going to celebrate with my friends," I told her. Even though I hadn't heard of any parties yet, I was sure they were in the offing.

I was wrong.

As I strolled up the steps to join my class, I asked a few friends for the scoop on the after parties. The answers varied.

"Not sure."

"I haven't heard."

"I'm just heading home."

Our senior class sponsor called us to order, we got in line, marched, sat through well-intentioned speeches that none of us remembered even five minutes later, grabbed our diplomas, then marched out. It was a blur, and it was hot. We were glad to return our rented robes and caps immediately after the ceremony.

Again, I persisted in asking about after parties. I don't know where or how I got the idea that a party with friends after graduation was mandatory, but I would not let it go. I finally managed to get my high school crush, Ann, to agree to go out afterward, but only if she wasn't the only one. 'Two is a date and three is a party' was her standard for that evening, and she was not about to go on a last minute date. I think she felt it was beneath her, or, as I eventually figured out, she just wasn't that into me.

I recruited my friend, Greg, whom I called Scotty, after the Star Trek character -- I was Captain Kirk, of course. The three of us drove around town for the evening.

Ann had us stop at a party store to buy beer, which surprised me. I had always thought she was so innocent, but apparently one advantage of not being the oldest child in the family was being able to use your older sibling's ID as your own. Yes, they checked identification then as now, but the penalties weren't as strict, and most store owners seemed to think it just wasn't cool to deny minor children their smokes and booze.

This was going to work out perfectly, I thought. As Ann

was in the store buying beer, I worked on Scotty, whom I had, until that moment, considered to be the perfect wing man since he didn't drink.

"Switch seats with me, Scotty."

"Wouldn't you feel silly sitting in the back and having me up front with Ann?"

"No, I'll get her to sit in back with me, and you can drive."

For some reason, he balked at the idea of being chauffeur. The conversation was cut short as Ann came back with her brown bagged six-pack -- Miller, specifically "Light Beer from Miller," a repackaging of the Meisterbrau recipe, as I learned while writing this piece.

We started driving again, and Ann cracked a can. She asked Greg if he wanted one, and he declined. I waited patiently for several minutes, then asked for one.

"Oh, no, you're driving. That wouldn't be safe."

And I couldn't really argue with that. I hadn't really had that much experience with drinking at the time, and my driving record was already bad when sober. I gave no thought to possible serious consequences, being young, dumb and immortal, of course.

"Do you want to pull over, maybe go to a park?" I asked.

"No, this is fun," she said. "Let's just drive around."

And so we did just that -- for hours. Eventually, Greg decided to have a "brew-ski," as he called it, and then another. As a newbie, it hit him hard. Soon, both he and Ann were giggling and laughing, shouting "turn here" and "go there" to me as I drove around the northwest side of Detroit.

'Ah, well, at least she didn't jump in the back seat with him,' I thought.

Hours later, I dropped them off at their respective houses and headed home, sober and regretting that I turned down Mom and her offer for a family dinner party.

What I wouldn't give today to have just one more gathering like that!

And that is why I will dare to say that the Class of 2020 is actually blessed. This weekend, they will line up outside with their classmates. They will process down the steps at Wegner Football Stadium while remaining six feet apart, and then they will stand with their own two family members, spaced 10 feet apart on the track near the scoreboard end zone. After each grad receives their diploma, they will leave with their parents. Due to the COVID-19 restrictions, they will be compelled, at least publicly, to remain with their families.

I hope they spend the rest of that special day with their families, savoring the time they have together and celebrating as only families can celebrate. There will always be time for friends, but family celebrations, well... the memories can last a lifetime.

Congratulations, Class of 2020!

***

The lemon yellow Duster was an iconic car in our family. I had borrowed it to drive to and from summer football practice my senior year, and I got side-swiped while driving a teammate home. (There is a longer, more interesting story there, but I'll share the nutshell for now.)

Dad was upset, even though the accident wasn't my fault. He didn't want to make an insurance claim, so I came up with a home repair for the shattered passenger door window -- Plexiglas with two hook-and-eye door latches to hold it in place. It worked, though it was unsightly.

I went off to college after graduation, hoping to take the Duster, now an extra car in the household, with me. I was rebuffed.

The next year, my brother Paul came to the same college, not by train, but behind the wheel of the Duster! I tried to pull rank as eldest brother, but he was to big and too smart for that by that time. The entire next year I cringed at my friends' comments...

"Hey, Mike, drive us to that party at Western (Michigan University)... Oh, that's right... your brother won't let you borrow the car!"

You remember when I told you that I was the mean one, Good Reader? Well, I knew my brother would one day rue his decision.

On Halloween, the small campus at K-College was unusually wild, with multiple "trash can" parties. (Bibulous events where everyone brought what alcohol they could and dumped it into a trash can. We lined the can with a trash bag first, of course -- we weren't barbarians!) Everyone, especially the football team, had indulged heavily.

Into the evening, someone came to tell me that my brother was in a fight with the senior running back. He clearly expected me to jump to the rescue. I shrugged and dipped my cup into the trash can. "That'll teach him..."

A Day at the Races

Originally published June 25, 2020

Last week, I wrote about my graduation "after-party" experience, which wasn't much of a thrill. My purpose for writing was as much to remind myself to cherish time with family as it was to encourage graduating seniors to do the same.

In that tale, there was some underage drinking, and while I think I made it seem like a stupid, moronic thing to do, I did not directly say so, and that has worried me since. For the record, I do not advocate underage drinking or drinking and driving. I don't want to preach, so I'll leave it at that.

I overheard one senior talking about heading to Mackinac Island as a celebration destination, and I recalled my senior trip way back in 1979.

~~~

Our class went to Cedar Point for its senior trip, I think. I didn't go because, like most athletes, we were still in season as our track team went to its fourth straight state championship meet. (We were Class C State Champions three of four years, though it had little to do with the athleticism of yours truly, to be honest.)

Feeling a little cheated, some of us decided on a June trip to the island. We piled into the car -- Spencer, Pierre, Jim, Webster, and me -- and headed north for the day. We caught one of the ferries and made it to the island around noon -- the whole day ahead of us.

First we decided to rent some bikes and tour the island. We were all young, strong, and foolhardy, so we planned to take the bikes not only around the island but also up to the top of the island, to Fort Michilimackinac and, of course, the Grand Hotel.

This trip was to replace our senior trip, which, as I said, was preempted by the track finals. Spencer was a state champion pole vaulter. I was a discus thrower. Jim and Pierre were not competitive athletes, but they could hold their own in a game of pick-up.

There was only one problem -- Webster. While he was everyone's friend and had a
~~~

great sense of humor and was possibly the smartest person in the class, he was also a person with dwarfism -- average head and torso with shortened limbs. When we got to the bike rental booth, the complications of that fact became apparent.

"Oh, heck no!" Webster said as he looked at the bikes available for his size. The only ones he would have been able to ride himself were child-sized, and the only one of those available at the time (mid-day in June) was a pretty pink one with streamers coming from the handle grips. I couldn't blame him for not wanting to ride that one.

"I can take the training wheels off," the vendor said hopefully. That didn't seem to improve Webster's mood.

"Forget it. You guys can go without me," he said as he started walking off.

Like I said before, Good Reader, we were friends, and I've always felt friends should stick together. So I spoke up.

"Wait! We can ride a tandem -- a bicycle built for two!"

The words weren't out of my mouth before I realized the problem with that -- his legs wouldn't be able to reach the pedals. Now, you might think that's not such a big deal because he was "diminutive." You would be wrong. Webster checked in at a solid 140 pounds, something that made him a hard-to-tackle ball carrier in pick-up football.

We started riding, and then, of course, Spencer led the group up the hill to the Grand Hotel. Webster was a dead weight behind me, but I was young and in the best shape of my life. (I doubt I could ride a bike with my own weight up such a hill today.)

Eventually, we traded our bikes in for horses, and that's where the real excitement began.

Approaching the stable, Pierre took over, saying he knew about horses from being on his uncle's farm in the summer. We were all city boys, born and raised in Detroit, so that classified him as the expert in our eyes. (Besides, Pierre always wore cowboy boots, so of course he was the expert! Duh!)

"Who has the most riding experience here?" the stable owner asked. We all looked at Pierre, and he was assigned a horse named Diablo. (I felt like I dodged a bullet there! That name alone spoke volumes!)

"Who else has experience?"

We all looked at each other. After an uncomfortable silence,

I remembered that I had ridden a horse before. Well, actually, it was a pony, and it threw me from the saddle the one time I tried riding it. (I came up under the electric wire fence and thought someone had clubbed me with a two-by-four. Ouch!) Despite the glaring fact that this experience should have kept me from volunteering, I stepped forward and was rewarded with Frederic.

'Great," I thought, 'how bad could a horse named Frederic be, especially compared to one named Diablo?'

"Frederic is named after that hurricane last year, the one that killed five people," the owner said, and then he actually smiled. "But you shouldn't have any problem with him, *as long as he stays with Diablo.*"

He went on to explain that all of the *other* horses, which had soft, friendly names like Buttercup, Boopsie, and Ralph, would follow Diablo no matter what.

The horses plodded here and plodded there. We could barely get them to move, and when we reached a grassy meadow at the top of the island, they stopped and grazed. This was not working out as we had planned. The horses seemed to have a mind of their own. Apparently, they were unionized, this stop for grazing being one of their mandatory breaks. Even Pierre, who turned out to be only marginally more experienced than me in equestrian skills, couldn't get his horse to budge.

Finally, as the day waned, we realized we needed to head back in order to catch the last ferry to the mainland. Pierre dismounted and started to walk his steed out of the meadow, and it seemed to be working, our horses followed all the way to the dirt path which led to the brick road that headed down the hill. All the horses followed, except Buttercup, upon which sat Webster. He kicked and cajoled his pony, but she was really enjoying the long grass and would not even look up. Pierre decided to help, and he walked the twenty yards back into the meadow, bringing Diablo with him.

Frederic looked back at Diablo, looked over his shoulder at me, and then whinnied. (Or did he knicker? I'm not sure, but it certainly sounded like a laugh.) Then Frederic looked at that steep downward slope and bolted.

Apparently, I had the luck of riding Frederic on the day he decided to usurp the crown of "Leader" from Diablo! He galloped downhill on the brick pavers. Terrified, I held on and hoped he wouldn't break both of our necks. Thankfully, he managed to avoid the carriages, bicycles, and pedestrians that shared the road. Behind me I heard Pierre and the others, shouting at me as if I had purposely decided to throw caution to the wind and run my quarter horse downhill at almost 50 mph.

Near the bottom of the hill, about 50 yards away and out of sight from the stable, Frederic slowed and the others joined us. It was almost as if he didn't want his owner to see the way we had come down the hill at break-neck speed. And I wasn't going to tattle on Frederic, either, and thus reduce my esteem as a 'real horseman' in the eyes of the stable owner. Such was my vanity, even after what felt like a near death experience.

This summer, I hope to enjoy a beautiful, if less exhilarating, vacation, and I hope you, my Good Readers, do the same!

***

I can still recall every detail of that harrowing downhill trip, and I marvel that I'm still alive to tell tales!

***

Next up are more vacation memories, with quite a few at Camp Dearborn, in Milford, Michigan. It was an affordable place for family vacations, and we went there for maybe 15 years straight.

Reading through all of my stories in this collection, I notice how many have to do with vacations. I never thought about it at the time, but running even a small town newspaper was a lot of work; it must have been -- for me to be so preoccupied with vacations!

Above left: a tent at Camp Dearborn; above right: the Canteen

Buddy Holly

Originally published July 9, 2020

When we were young, we went to camp Dearborn in Milford, Michigan every year for two weeks of summer vacation. We looked forward to it, mostly because we were there with our cousins. In fact, our extended family reserved between eight and ten tents every year.

What they called tents in Camp Dearborn were really wooden frames set on concrete slabs, enclosed with hard steel screens and draped in a very heavy, olive-drab canvas. Each "tent" had a canvas awning over a picnic area that held two picnic tables -- big enough for almost any family back in the 1970s. There was a kitchenette area that had an electric stove and a refrigerator enclosed in a wooden cabinet. All this was set on the same large concrete slab. The slabs sat in rows, about 10 feet apart, and there were many, many rows back in that time. Together, it was called "Tent Village."

For us kids, this was the perfect vacation. There was a vast playground area, a sandy, man-made beach, a large swimming pool, a fishing lake, a paddle boat lake, arts and crafts every morning and organized sports every afternoon. The pièce de résistance, however, was the canteen.

The canteen was near the beach, and it was a fair but not impossible walk from all of the tents in Tent Village. The canteen served burgers, hot dogs, fries, and other short order food. Most people, however, stopped there for one of two things: hand-dipped ice cream and frozen Coke. I had my first frozen Coke at the canteen; this was years before 7-11 stores began springing up with their variety of "Slurpees." It was the only place to get a frozen Coke, so naturally, it was one of those must-haves every vacation.

I have many memories of Camp Dearborn vacations. Some are brief, like the memorable family portraits. (A sample is on page 31.) One of the things they did every year at Camp Dearborn was come around and offer to take a family photo. Mom would corral us before we ran off to one destination or another and make us wait for the photographer. Trying to keep five boys around the camp when the playground, ball diamond and lakes were calling could not have been easy, so I don't think she can be blamed for failing to anticipate my younger brother Mark's clothing malfunction. Like Janet Jackson's infamous 2004 Super Bowl halftime show, Mark's clothing failed to cover everything when he sat down. Those were the days of fringed denim shorts, usually homemade back then, and Mark's shorts were more fringe than shorts. I don't think anyone noticed at the time, but when we noticed later, we didn't let him live it down.

The author, 1974

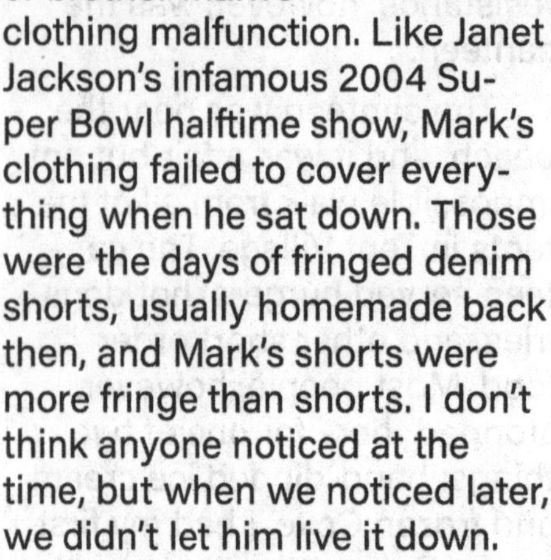

Most of the photos were funny for one reason or another -- each a slice in time preserved for later. In another memorable one, almost all of us were scowling, especially Mona, probably from a fight just before the photographer arrived. These were taken back in the days of flash and film photography, and you didn't dare ask for a retake unless it was the photographer's fault.

Another family photo was amusing because of our elephant bells (bell bottom pants -- the pant legs so wide at the bottom they covered your shoes), tie-dye shirts, headbands and wristbands right out of Woodstock.

One of the photos that sticks in my mind is probably when I was about 12 or 13 years old. In that photo, I was gangly, pimply, and wore Buddy Holly glasses. Now, don't get me wrong -- Buddy Holly glasses were cool in the 50s and 60s, and they may even be cool now, but in the 70s, if you had to wear glasses, they had to be wire rimmed, like John Lennon, John Denver, or even Elton John. If you really think about it, Buddy Holly is similar to Albert Einstein -- you want to *be* like him but not necessarily *look* like him.

As I mentioned at the beginning, many cousins joined us there in Tent Village, among them were Grace, Ann, and Anthony. I didn't get to hang out with Anthony until I was a bit older, as he was several years my senior. Ann was just a year older than me. Grace was my age, and we shared every class all the way through school. She was the social butterfly. Together, Grace and Ann introduced me to the other attraction of the canteen -- the nightly teen dances.

The dances began around 7 p.m. and lasted until 10 p.m., concluding each night with "Stairway to Heaven" by Led Zeppelin. That song ended the night for many years, through 1975 at least, though it was released in 1971. In fact, the entire three hours of music was virtually the same each night. There was a DJ who would encourage people to dance and count down the last few songs of the night, but he probably was using a pre-recorded reel to reel.

I loved listening to the music and slurping frozen Coke, and on occasion, I might suggest to my friends that I was thinking about asking a girl to dance. I was terminally shy, and it was apparently my cousin Grace's mission to help me get over it. After a futile night or two of exhorting me to get off the sideline (actually yellow parking bumpers, as the dance took place in a roped off parking lot), Grace set a trap.

~~~

It was Friday -- the big night before everyone left camp and went home. Grace, who made friends easily, mentioned that we were stopping to pick up a friend of hers as we were making the nightly trek to the canteen. We stopped at a tent several rows over, and Grace came out with a beautiful blonde girl about our age. Grace introduced her friend to all of us -- Ann, my brother Paul, and me. Then she turned to her friend.

"Well, what do you think?"

Blondie (I don't remember her name) made a non-committal, guttural, somewhat unladylike sound. Grace took that as a cue to resume our walk toward the canteen. Grace and Blondie led the way, but they weren't so far ahead that we couldn't hear their conversation.

"He's cute, isn't he?" Grace said, trying to sell Blondie on the idea of dancing with me -- her terminally shy cousin -- when we got to the dance.

"Hmm, maybe, I guess if he got rid of the glasses," Blondie said.

"Mike, take off your glasses," Grace said.

I looked at her like she was crazy, mostly because I knew I wouldn't be able to see a thing, but also because my glasses were a big part of me by then. Nonetheless, I complied. Grace asked for Blondie's evaluation again, and this time she was slow in responding.

Meanwhile, I was doing my best not to get tripped up by objects in my path; the lack of 20/20 sight didn't do anything to improve upon the awkwardness of my young teenage body.

"No, I don't think so," Blondie
~~~

said dismissively. Grace was not to be deterred, however.

"Mike, push your hair to the side...."

I put my glasses back on and took another look at the sourpuss face of Blondie, now not nearly as pretty as I had first thought.

"Forget it, Grace," I said. And we continued to the canteen in silence for a while, letting Grace and Blondie pull ahead.

I didn't ask a girl to dance that night either, but thanks to Grace, I didn't spend the night worrying about it. It was the first dance that summer that I truly enjoyed -- talking with the guys, listening to that old time rock and roll, and sipping frozen Cokes in the warm summer night.

***

I may sound like a sympathetic character, Good Reader, based on that last tale. Remember, however, that I am an average man, with both virtues and flaws. This next story about our times at Camp Dearborn balances that scale.

I shared this next tale, "Rocket Man," in response to the community vilifying a high school student for an inappropriate post on Facebook. The post was racist, and I did not condone it. Appropriate discipline was called for and carried out by the school. The backlash on social media, however, was extreme -- calls for the student to be expelled from school and stripped of his wrestling medals, for starters. The young man deserved to be castigated, not castrated.

I share my embarrassing tale that follows to say, "Hey, we all get stupid sometimes..."

Rocket Man

Originally published July 16, 2020

When I first moved to Clinton and discovered the Local over 20 years ago, I used to flip to Maryann Habrick's "Life in the Slow Lane" column, which she wrote pretty much every week. Oftentimes she wrote about people she grew up with here in Clinton, and though I didn't know them, I found the tales interesting. The most memorable columns, however, were the occasional ones that had, shall we say, irregular topics. For instance, the two I remember most involved a detailed description of a medical procedure and the antics of two amorous squirrels in Riverside Cemetery. (No, not all together -- those were two separate stories!)

I read "The Slow Lane" just about every week. To be honest, I looked forward to it. (Recently, Carl Habrick mentioned his desire to anthologize the column, and I look forward to that, too.)

While I am unable to retell stories of Clinton from my youth, many people have told me they enjoy my tales anyway. I am grateful for that, as they are the only tales I can tell. Like Maryann, my personal confessions here can sometimes be embarrassing, and, on occasion, outlandish. This tale is one of those, but before I go further, I'd like to express a few thoughts.

I am glad I was born in a simpler age. (I know I sound like a geezer when I say that, but it's the truth!) I thought about this recently, with all the craziness and stupidity going on out there. I'm glad there were no cell phones with voice and video recording features when I was young; I can't imagine all the stupid, careless, and thoughtless words and actions of my youth being recorded and shared with everyone, available forever somewhere in the cloud. The thought is mortifying, which is probably why I limit my digital exposure even today.

That said, I am about to share an embarrassing story of my youth -- one of *those* moments.

Last week I told a tale about being at Camp Dearborn with the cousins on my mother's side of the family. This week, I recall one from my father's side.

~~~

Uncle Roy and Aunt Beverly had seven children, six of them boys. Kevin, the eldest, was a couple years older than me. Kenny, who was smaller than the rest of us, was about my age. One night, our parents charged us with the care of all the brothers who could walk -- about ten of us in all. I think I remember Karen (who usually got saddled with baby-sitting) heading to the Canteen with our other cousins, Grace and Anne, the three of them eager for a girls' night out. Since Karen was otherwise busy, Kevin and I were the new baby-sitters, probably because we were so mature and responsible. (Yeah, right!)

Our story takes place around 1974. I was about 13 years old.

We left our parents at the tent and headed to the playground. Even though it was dusk and the playground was unlit, nobody really policed it until much later at night. Kevin and I did what "mature" teenage boys would do -- we got the little ones on the merry-go-round and spun it as fast as we could, trying to get them to fly off. We pushed them high on the swings until they cried. We basically terrorized the little ones and thought it was grand fun.

This rocket has been modified -- the slide lowered to the second level. The original, before the days of rampant liability lawsuits, was attached to the third stage, at least two stories high!

Then we came to the rocket.

Camp Dearborn had a rocket ship climber in the middle of the park. It was very visible, and today it would make liability lawyers drool. It was about three stories tall and had a slide (with no protective railings) at least 20 feet off the hard
~~~

ground. (There was no mulch or rubber pellet base to cushion your fall, either.)

Naturally, we all had to climb it, so we made it a contest to the top. Kevin and I, being the oldest and strongest, made it to the top first, declared ourselves winners, sang a few lines from "Rocket Man" by Elton John, and started climbing back down.

We stopped our descent at the slide and decided to take the easy way down.

Once down, we grew bored as we waited for "the little kids."

"I'm heading to the outhouse," I said.

"I've gotta go, too," Kevin said.

We wrangled with the issue for a minute, both of us expressing the urgency of the moment. Being responsible and mature, of course, we recognized that we couldn't leave the little ones unsupervised.

I'm not sure who got the idea first, but one of us started to go right there by the slide.

Realizing no one could see us, the other joined in. I don't know who took the next step, but soon both of us were relieving ourselves on the slide itself, creating a disgusting and smelly slip-n-slide.

But it gets worse, Good Reader, because we then exhorted our siblings to slide down -- into the smelly pool that we had created at the bottom. Kenny came first, and his dawning recognition of what he had just experienced came slow enough so that all of the others also made the trip.

"You guys are going to pay for this," he yelled. Kevin and I just laughed. In fact, I'm ashamed to admit even now, we hadn't stopped laughing since we began our foul creation.

Kenny was furious. The more we laughed, the more his ire grew, until he finally played the big trump card, reserved only for little kids or desperate times.

"I'm telling -- both our parents," he said, and the conviction he put into those words stopped our hysterical convulsions immediately.

"You wouldn't," Kevin and I both countered, but we realized, finally, that we had crossed a whole bunch of lines at that slide. Kenny was serious, and he meant it. Naturally, we did the only thing we could think of -- we began to beg.

Kenny stood with his arms crossed for what seemed like an hour as we begged and pleaded with him not to tell on us. As we imagined our parents hearing what we had done (and the subsequent punishment for it), our supplication became more earnest.

Kenny stood there like a rock -- arms crossed, head high, and face grim -- but then a smile broke on his face, and we thought we saw a glimmer of hope. Was there forgiveness in that look?

No, not at all. It was the smile of sweet revenge. Kenny told us what it would take for him not to tell on us, and Kevin and I grimly complied.

We climbed the rocket and heard Kenny's next command. "Wait until I say we're ready, and then slide down."

From that height we couldn't see anything in the darkness below, but we heard the sound of splashing, or more accurately, the sound of several "splashings." On command, Kevin and I slid down to our fate.

Now all of us were soaked and smelly, with nothing to do but return to camp for fresh clothing. One of us made the argument that our parents would surely smell us and know, and that we couldn't go back camp. Someone else suggested we go to the beach and jump into the water, clothing and all. Yet most of us were so disgusted with ourselves by that time that we didn't care. We couldn't stand how we felt and how we smelled, and we just wanted to get out of those clothes. Fortunately, our parents weren't at the tents, so we changed and went on like nothing happened.

At the time, we were sure we had pulled it off without our parents' knowledge, but I find it difficult, in retrospect, to believe that Mom (who did the laundry) didn't notice a thing.

~~~

As kids, we sometimes do and say stupid things. Sometimes our actions and words are offensive, even abhorrent, and yet, we find forgiveness due to our youth and the belief that we can all learn from our mistakes and grow to become better individuals.

During these trying and testy times, when even our friends, neighbors, and relatives might express opinions that differ from our own and subsequently upset us, I hope we can remember that we've all made mistakes.

Hey, maybe even us "older kids" can become better people, too...

***

My summertime teenage depravity continues with this next tale from Camp Dearborn...
~~~

Good Vibrations (You Had Me At Hello!)

Originally published August 8, 2020

Previously, I shared two memories of vacationing at Camp Dearborn in Milford, Michigan. Both of those memories involved evening activities, though of course, most of the activity really happened during the day.

When I was younger, I was content with the arts and crafts every morning (especially on the day we made tie-dye tee shirts), playing basketball, volleyball, or softball in the afternoons, and, of course, fishing in the man-made lakes. As I grew older, encountering "the fairer sex" became a high priority.

As I've mentioned before, my early high school life (and consequently my early love life) was plagued with a profound shyness. I would turn beet red, sweat like a marathon runner, grow a second left foot and become uncomfortably dumb-witted in a matter of seconds when confronted with an opportunity to talk to a girl. My cousin Grace was always willing to be a matchmaker for me, but I knew it would do no good if I didn't have "game." I decided to fix that, so I caught up with my cousin Anthony, who was at least four years older than me.

One summer, it may have been 1976, Anthony decided to spend a few days at Camp Dearborn with his family. (He was working full time and going to college by then.) Anthony always had beautiful girlfriends, and he seemed to be confident about everything. One bright summer afternoon, as we walked to the canteen barefooted and bare chested, I asked him to give me some lessons on talking to girls.

"Okay, watch this," he said as two beautiful girls in bikinis came our way.

"Hi there!" he said with the biggest, cheesiest smile on his face. I thought it looked too big, almost like the Joker from the Batman comic series, but then I heard the girls giggle. They were practically purring when they returned the greeting. They continued to coo as we moved past them. I was impressed, and I told him so.

"Did you get a good look at them?" he asked me.

"Yeah, they were foxes!" I answered, trying to impress him with my use of cool 70's slang.

"No, I mean, did you get a good look at them, a really good look at them?"

I confessed my ignorance. I didn't have a clue what he was talking about.

"Watch them closely this time," he instructed. "Don't look at me."

We continued to walk, now heading toward the beach. Despite going shoe less most of the summer, my feet started to sizzle on the sidewalk, and I started to do that little hot-foot dance.

"Straighten up. Look tough," Anthony said, coaching me in machismo. "Here comes another pair."

I looked forward and, sure enough, we were on an intercept course with another pair of bikini clad beauties, probably headed to the canteen for frozen Cokes. I watched them closely, which normally would have been difficult for me, especially if either had made eye contact with me. I was safe, however, as Anthony must have already had a lock on them, and their eyes were obviously transfixed to his. When they were about ten yards away, he whispered to me.

"Okay, now watch closely," then he loudly added for them, "Hi there!"

I could hear the cheesy grin again in those words, and these girls responded the same as the others had -- with giggles, coos, and a purring echo of "hello." What was different, now that I was watching them, was their body language. They were blushing, and one of them flipped back her hair, a sign, Anthony assured me, that signalled her willingness for more direct contact.

"Did you see them?" he asked me again as they passed out of earshot.

"Yeah, that was great," I said, enthusiastically. I was ready to learn more from my older cousin, who apparently held a master's degree in women. "They were totally into you!"

"But did you see *them*?" he asked again with the patience of Master Po, the blind mentor who trained Kwai Chang Caine, AKA "grasshopper," at the Shaolin monastery on the 70's TV show "Kung Fu."

"Yeah, I saw them. They were giggling and whispering to each other," I answered, then added, "and one of them was blushing."

"No," he said, still patient. "Did you see ***them***?"

Anthony then went on to explain to me the desired response he was seeking when he smiled and said hello to those bathing beauties we had encountered. According to him, the response, a physiological one usually associated with a sudden drop in temperature, could best be observed if I focused my attention toward the bikini tops of the intended targets. He insisted that he was able to elicit such a response -- on demand.

"No way," I said once the meaning of his assertion broke the veil of my naivete.

To prove himself, he proceeded to demonstrate on several pairs of passers-by. He even managed it with a trio. I was flabbergasted. I had already held him in high esteem, but that day he ascended to god-like stature in my pubescent mind.

"Now you try it," he said, as any good teacher would -- model, then practice -- but I couldn't do it. After all, it would mean direct eye contact. Besides, I had many more shortfalls than just my lack of confidence. Anthony was muscular, darkly tanned, had a full mustache and an impressive amount of chest hair (still popular back then). By contrast, I was pale, hairless, pimply, and had thick black glasses, not hip wire rims.

I didn't overcome my preternatural bashfulness that summer, but gradually, I began to conquer it that fall, not on the beach, but in the hallways of my school. (It was a lot easier with the girls fully dressed, anyway.)

Eventually, I learned that confidence is the key to success in all walks of life -- in the halls, on the beach, or on the streets.

***

I began to develop confidence that next school year, my junior year, and it led to my first and only successful election, highlighted in the next story.

I declined to run the following year when my "friends" encouraged me to run for Student Council President so that an African American student wouldn't get the role. I liked my would-be opponent. (His name was Terrance.) So I declined to run, and he won by default. I lost my taste in politics until years later, when I lost several times attempting to get a seat on the local school board. Current politics have helped me completely lose the desire to serve.

I Wanna Be Elected

Originally published July 30, 2020

Sometimes my inspiration for this column comes from a song, and sometimes I have to scratch and scrabble for an appropriate tune to match the week's theme. It's a "chicken or the egg" conundrum.

This week, my inspiration comes from all of the political talk with the coming presidential election. I've tried several times to get elected or appointed to political-type positions, with no success, at least in my later years. My very first attempt to win an election, however, was met with rousing (and surprising) success.

Most of you who have been reading this column know that I may be characterized as a bit of a rascal in my youth, though that wasn't always the case. Near the end of the eighth grade, a transformation occurred, and I can remember the day well.

We were in our seventh grade homeroom class at St. Christopher School in Detroit. (Home of the Crusaders, by the way.) Sister Blandine called us all to stand in the front of the room (no social distancing then!), and we crowded together along the blackboard and along the side of the classroom. She announced that she was going to call off test results from a standardized test that measured our grade level ability in reading. I don't remember the test because I had always been careless when it came to academics, at least up until that time. I had, in fact, trained my parents not to expect too much from me, so report cards were never an issue. They were happy that my final report card every spring reflected that I would move on.

Seated at her desk, Sister Blandine called names one by one, announcing the reading scores by rank, from lowest to highest.

"Robert, reading grade level 5.5 -- you should be ashamed of yourself. Sit down," she said.

Each student was called by name with their score and a comment out loud for the entire class to hear. Such public humiliation wouldn't be tolerated today, but this was 1975, long before we became a "kinder, gentler nation." I wasn't worried about it anyway. I expected to be called soon, and I would laugh it off just like I did regular class assignments and tests.

Sister went on and on, and, to my surprise, I remained standing -- and the reading levels kept going up, 9th grade, 10th grade, etc. She explained that the decimals stood for months.

I continued to stand there with a 'What am I still doing here?' look on my face. It was the same look I got from many of the other kids, the smart ones who were shocked and disappointed to be told to sit when she called grade 11, and then grade 12.

Eventually, I was standing in front of the room with Kelly Alfastan, a tall girl I didn't know very well despite being in the same school building with her for almost eight years.

"We have a tie," said Sister Blandine. "You both have a reading score of 12.7. Congratulations!"

Shocked, I returned to my seat. Maybe I wasn't as dumb as I thought I was....

That event motivated me to study when I became a freshman in high school, to prove that I could really do it. The strangest thing happened though, the more I used my brain, the less I was able to employ social skills. I became terminally shy.

When I started sophomore year, I was determined to become more socially adept, so I began talking to everyone. By the end of the year, I decided to test my newfound skills and run for student council office for the following year. Juniors served as student council vice president, and I only had one opponent -- Julie Wiszniewski. Julie was very popular, being a majorette, a volleyball player, and an honors student.

On the morning of elections, the entire student body of 750, plus faculty, gathered in the gymnasium. Each candidate was allowed two minutes, and Julie and I were near the end of the long list of speeches, as they had next year's sophomore, junior and senior class officer candidates speak before the student council candidates.

Julie and I approached the microphone stand together. It was placed in the middle of the gym floor, with no chairs and no tables. It felt like walking out on a cliff.

Julie spoke before me, and though many eyes had glazed over by then, I saw quite a few members in the audience perk up when she grabbed the microphone, most notably the guys in the front row. (Julie was a pretty blond.) Her speech was received warmly, and she smiled confidently at me as she handed me the microphone.

I began my speech, rambling aimlessly, and I could see the boredom in their faces. For some reason, I focused on the face of Marty Doyle, an athlete in the upper class. His face was at least neutral, and I took solace in that.

My speech was not going well -- when would these interminable two minutes end? I was sweating profusely. I was repeating myself. Finally, the moderator signalled for me to finish, and so I concluded.

"If I'm elected to the student council next year, I promise a successful year for everyone!"

I was staring at Marty Doyle, and he was staring at me. The slack look left his face and his mouth opened to form an "O" of surprise. In that second, I realized what I had actually said:

"If I'm elected to the student council, I promise everyone a suc-**sex**-ful school year!"

In that moment of realization, my mouth opened in dawning horror, and I covered it quickly with my free hand. What had I just said -- *out loud* -- in front of everyone -- in my *Catholic* high school?

Suddenly, everyone realized what I had said, and cheers went up that rivalled those at championship basketball games. Guys pumped their fists in the air and shouted my name. It was crazy, being my first glimpse at the real nature of politics.

At the end of the day, the election moderator, a teacher I was sure had been pulling for Julie, told us the results.

"It was close, but Mike won," she said, with no small amount of disappointment evident, at least to me. Julie's jaw dropped so low it looked like a cartoon. She left the room in tears, but returned to congratulate me a day or two after the event.

It was my first, and last, successful campaign, and also like most politicians, my campaign promise was never fulfilled.

***

Sex sells, right? Even the empty promise of sex sells!

Let's veer toward more wholesome tales now, Good Reader, ones that come from my more recent, mature days...

Petosky Annie spies Morel mushrooms as easily as Petosky stones!

Petosky Annie and the Lazy River

Originally published August 27, 2020

I just got back from a two week vacation. Well, almost two weeks -- it was broken up by trips back here to take care of the newspaper on Wednesdays. (That's when we label and deliver the paper each week.)

Even though the vacation was truncated, I feel rejuvenated and will (hopefully) retain some of the peace evoked by the sound of Lake Michigan waves crashing against the sandy shores.

One way or another, my vacations have always involved water, and as I soaked in the sun on the beach, I was reminded of a water related incident involving my wife, Debbie, my son, Nick, and my cousin, Anne.

I sometimes call my cousin "Petoskey Annie" due to her uncanny ability to find Petoskey stones, even while just casually walking on the beach. The Petoskey stone, composed of a fossilized rugose coral, is Michigan's state stone. It is unique to the Great Lakes and can be found along the shores of Michigan's lower peninsula, *according to www.michigan.org*

Anne's husband, Gerald, has lived in northern Michigan his entire life, and he is the embodiment of outdoorsmanship. Not a day goes by that doesn't find him outdoors -- hiking, swimming, or bird watching. The two of them could have their own TV special -- a modern day Mr. and Mrs. Grizzly Adams!

At least that was how I always thought of them, especially as Anne led us to this secret trail or to that hidden beach. I began to insist that she should become a tour guide in her retirement. I even had her logo and slogan figured out: "Explore Every Nook and Cranny when You Book Your Tour with Petoskey Annie!"

That always made her laugh, and I realize now that she didn't know how highly I *honestly* regarded her outdoorsmanship.

About eight or nine years ago, we were vacationing in the Sleeping Bear Sand Dunes area, which is near Petoskey Annie's home. It has now become an annual vacation location, but at that time it had been maybe just our second year there. Annie had been a wonderful hostess and tour guide that first year, showing us all the neat places to go, so we looked forward to seeing some new places that we missed the first time around.

We enjoyed kayaking the sandy and shallow Crystal River the first year, but now we were going to switch to the Platte River. We also decided to switch to using tubes instead of kayaks. Buying tubes was cheaper than renting, and Gerald agreed to drop us off at a likely starting point along the river. The three adults had tubes, and Nick, about 12 years old then, had an inflatable kayak, which turned out to be our salvation.

Annie is about my age and is also a retired teacher, so we have a lot in common. Often, while on vacation, we have to self-consciously curtail the urge that every teacher seems to have -- to talk non-stop about school and students. It can be annoying to others who might want to get in a word edgewise. Nonetheless, Anne and I found ourselves pairing up more often than not along the river.

Eventually, the river spilled into a lake. There was a nice sand bar at the mouth of the river as we entered the lake. Noting how others had "parked" there, we circled up and rested. The exit to the lake -- the continuation of the river -- was about 90 degrees to our right and about 100 yards away. Parked on the sand bar, we chatted for a while as Debbie passed out cold beverages from a cooler strapped to the back of Nick's Kayak. Eventually, Annie and I engaged in "teacher-talk," and Nick, a restless pre-teen, paddled toward the exit. Debbie followed him.

One of us, either Anne or I, realized we were still sitting there while the other two had already made it to the exit point of the lake. We pushed off the sand bar and headed toward them...

...Well, at least that was the plan.

Debbie, Anne and I each had tubes, as I mentioned earlier. For most of the trip down the winding river, we floated with ease. On a few occasions, we had to use our hands to paddle away from tree branches that extended into the river. Debbie, being light and long-limbed, rested easily on top of her tube, which allowed her to use her cupped hands as paddles. She easily kept up with Nick.

Anne and I sunk into our tubes, content to let the wind and current do the work, and that worked out just fine -- until we pushed off from that mid-lake rest stop.

"Do you think we should paddle, Mike?" Petoskey Annie asked me as we drifted southwest, away from our river exit in the northwest corner of the lake.

"Why bother?" I replied. "The current is definitely going to take us out."

Annie looked at me with some doubt in her eyes as she said, "Okay."

In moments we were being pushed into the reedy beds on the southern shore of the lake. The wind (which I had not taken into account) had driven us away from our exit and was continuing to push us away.

"I think we're going to need to paddle," I said.

"Oh, really?" said Annie, who had already begun to feverishly paddle from within her tube.

We both flailed at the water for several minutes, sitting with our butts sunk into the tube's hole, lying back and doing what could best be described as a twisted butterfly stroke.

"Is that the same tree?" Annie asked. "Right there on our left?"

"Can't be," I said in between puffs of air and exhausting strokes of my arms. "We've been paddling for five minutes!"

But after another few minutes I looked, and though I didn't want to admit it, the tree was the same that was to our left when we had started. If anything, we had lost ground. I said as much to Annie.

"Do you want me to jump out and pull us?" she asked.

Now, Good Reader, I'd like to blame my reply on my state of combined exhaustion and frustration, but that would be too simple. There are moments in your life when you are clearly thinking only of yourself, and later you realize your self-centeredness. This was one of those moments. In my mind I checked off the following:

1. We are stuck, and no amount of paddling is going to get us out.
2. Help is out of sight. Deb-

bie and Nick are down the river, and everyone else wisely stuck to the northern shore.

3. We are wearing wet shoes, so swimming out of here will be difficult.

4. Luckily, I'm with Petoskey Annie, Outdoorswoman Extraordinaire; If she thinks she can pull us out, she can do it! So I said,

"Yeah, that would be great, Annie!"

So she flipped out of her tube...

...and sunk to the bottom of the lake.

At first I thought it might be a trick, like something from an Aquaman movie, and I expected to see her begin to walk along the murky bottom while pulling the tow ropes on both our tubes. After a few seconds, as she thrashed her way to the surface, I realized that was not part of the plan.

"Annie, are you struggling?" I asked, confused by the disparity between the mythos of Petoskey Annie and the reality that I saw there in the water that sunny afternoon.

"I'm not a very strong swimmer," she gasped.

With some work, Annie managed to loop her arms into the tube, and I used my big mouth to shout for Nick to return with the Kayak. We formed a daisy chain and, with an incredible amount of effort, managed to get out of there alive. I think that was the last time we ever tubed that river.

We joke about that day now, and we've (almost) forgotten the moments of panic we experienced then.

Life is good, but life is short. The best times are spent with family and friends, pursuing an adventure or sharing the simplicity of our daily lives. I thank God for that.

***

This is one of my favorite memories, and I'm glad I can share it with you, Good Reader. I'm also extremely glad that it didn't turn out worse; in my attempt to humorize events, I sometimes skim over the very real fear of the moment. When Anne went under, I was stuck in the tube so tight, my bottom sunk so low, that my feet pointed skyward; I was in no position to get out of my tube if she actually needed some help. I thank God that she managed to get her arms back into her tube.

The next tale involves some embellished fear, which I prefer over the occasions when life and limb are actually threatened.

Highway Star
(Dirt Track Terror)

Originally published September 10, 2020

Usually, over the Labor Day Weekend, I labor. I will typically spend the entire weekend working around the house; that's been my tradition for many, many years. This year, however, I departed from tradition and spent most of the weekend doing enjoyable activities.

On Saturday, my son, Nick, and I went up to Houghton Lake to see my brother, Mark, and sister-in-law, Larisa's new house -- smack dab on the waterfront. (And he's not even my rich brother!) The house has a wonderful view and is very big. I'll admit I was a little jealous.

We spent the day in the company of family, enjoying the surroundings and getting a rare opportunity to visit with my niece Amanda and her daughters, Raelynn and Kylie.

Toward the evening, Mark took us out to the back roads near his home in his Polaris Ranger, which looks like (at least to me) a cross between a golf cart and a Jeep. My wife used to call this activity -- driving along back-country dirt roads -- "two-tracking," but my brother called it going "side-by-side," which he later explained to me had to do with the seating arrangement within the vehicle.

If I don't have the terminology correct, I'll ask to be excused, as my brain may still be a little joggled from the ride.

You see, Good Reader, this was one of those activities that separates people into two categories -- the "men from the boys," so to speak. My brother, and apparently my son, both considered the experience exhilarating.

"Terrifying" was the word that first popped into my mind.

The event consisted of going through muddy terrain -- on purpose -- and travelling at high speed along bumpy dirt roads. The vibrations alone were enough to shake loose fillings.

"This really does a number on the L5, doesn't it?" Mark joked over the roar of the engine as we rattled and bounced through a particularly rough

One man's delight is another man's terror.
From left to right: the author, Nick Walters, and Mark Walters

section.

Now, I'm no chiropractor (and neither is Mark), but I knew where L5 was located based on what I was feeling as we flew across the washboard road.

Suffering roads like that would normally lead me to place a complaint with the county road commissioner's office, but, apparently, my brother and a good number of other enthusiasts seek out roads like this.

In fact, he seemed to avoid the smoother, drier parts of the road in favor of muddy trenches and troughs of pooled water.

Perhaps the most harrowing experience, though, was crossing the main road in this lightweight, off-road vehicle.

"Put your door up," Mark said as he looked both ways at the four lanes of traffic traveling almost 50 mph on the paved road that stood between us and the comfort of home.

I looked to my side and saw a net with a plastic clip. I held the clip and just looked at Mark in disbelief.

"Put your door up before we cross the road," he repeated. "It's the law."

I continued to stare at him. We certainly had broken a few laws back there on the trails, but before I could get his attention, he got that maniacal look in his eyes as he revved the

Despite the large number of yard signs supporting President Donald Trump at Houghton Lake, nearly every driver on the dirt track displayed solidarity with Black Lives Matter by throwing up a fist as they passed.

engine. Apparently, he had seen his window.... I snapped the "door" on and we darted across the road.

As we returned to his peaceful home on the placid waterfront, I began to relax.

I took note of the preponderance of "Vote for Trump" signs on the lawns of the homes in his new neighborhood; they were everywhere, and I was surprised.

"Wow, Mark, there are a lot of Trump supporters in your neighborhood," I said.

"So."

"So, it just seems to contradict all the people we crossed paths with on the trails," I said.

During our outing, we must have crossed three dozen others on "side-by-sides," dirt bikes, and four-wheelers. More than half of those riders threw up the "Black Lives Matter" fist as they passed.

I found the incongruity interesting, and I told him so.

It was his turn to stare at me, and then he started laughing. He nearly flipped us, so he slowed the vehicle and pulled over.

"Oh, so you think the other drivers were throwing up the 'Black Lives Matter' symbol while they were out riding their side-bys?" He started chuckling as he continued. "Boy, people around here must really take their politics seriously! They take every opportunity to express their politics, even out on the trails in the backwoods!"

He carried on a little longer, continuing the sarcasm in between guffaws and snorts of laughter. He was truly enjoying himself.

It didn't take too long (honestly, not too long...) before I began to realize that the fist pump by those drivers must have meant something else. Mark explained the meaning.

The dirt roads serpentined through the woods, limiting vision around corners.

Trains of drivers would raise fingers to indicate the number of followers behind each of them, with the last one raising his or her fist, not in solidarity with a political movement, but merely to indicate that no one was behind them.

Mark enjoyed telling his family about my misunderstanding that night around the campfire, and I'm sure he'll enjoy re-telling it again at a later date. (That's just what we do in my family.)

Nick and I left the next morning after a hearty breakfast. (All of my brothers can cook, but Mark may be the best of the bunch.) We headed downstate and stopped at a golf course -- North Star, near Lansing. In between my wild swings at the tiny golf ball, we rode the gentle slopes of the course in a slow-rolling, standard golf cart, which was more than alright with me.

***

I've referred to my mother in previous tales as "Mona." That nickname is explained in this next piece.

I had the comfort of my mother in my life until I was 50 years old. Mona died in 2011. Despite having her in my life for a relatively long time -- five decades -- I still feel like I've been orphaned.

I'll give this advice to you, Good Readers, especially those younger men following along:

No one will ever love you like your mother.

Period.

No one.

Mona Lisa's Best Friend

Originally published October 1, 2020

Saturday was my mother's birthday. She would have been 84 this year, but she succumbed to cancer in 2011 after a nine year battle.

The death of one's mother leaves a scar, even when you are older and the death is expected.

My mother's name was Joan -- Joanina to her Italian parents, Joanie to her friends, and Mona to me.

I came up with the nickname of Mona from the 1971 Right Guard television commercial. It was the one where the guy opens his medicine cabinet only to find the neighbor from the next apartment staring back at him. The neighbor says, "Hi, guy!" and then launches into a song and dance about the deodorant. Our protagonist then calls for his wife in dismay,

Joan "Mona" Walters on a balcony at the Grand Hotel on Mackinaw Island

"**Mona**!"

I used to imitate him whenever I was looking for something around the house.

"Mona, where are my socks?" But it's usage soon expanded.

"Mona, what's for dinner?"

"Mona, can I go to my friend's house?"

"Mona, Mona, Mona..."

Now, some of you may consider my behavior -- calling my mother out of her name -- disrespectful. She even brought it up once (perhaps out of embarrassment) when we had family over, but my Aunt Alberta came to my defense, telling her it seemed like a term of endearment. I heartily agreed, even though at age 10 I didn't know what that meant. (I did know -- too well, however -- the consequences of disrespect!)

So, "Mona" it was, and I not only used it to replace the title of "mom" or "mother," I also used it in song.

I developed at that time and still have the habit of bursting into song at the slightest provocation. Growing up in my parents' household, every now and then I'd burst into a Mona song.

There was, of course, "Mona Lisa" by Nat King Cole, "My Shumona," a derivative of The Knack's "My Sharona," and (credit to my father) the "Mona in the Morning" song, which went as follows:

"Mona in the morning
Mona in the evening
Mona at supper time
Won't you be my Mona
Moanin' all the time?"

Dad and I would often sing that one as a duet.

It all sounds pretty silly, I know. And what prompted this juvenile flashback? Last week, one of my mother's dearest friends -- one of those who would call her 'Joanie,' also died.

MONA LISA'S BEST FRIEND

Over the years my mother had many friends, but outside of her true best friend -- her own mother -- she had only a few close friends. There was Caroline 'Mum' Stawacz and 'Patsy' Frankiewicz, but perhaps her closest friend was Pat, who died just last week. Patricia Fagan Waynick, a proud Irish woman, died at the age of 78.

Patricia Fagan Waynick

As kids, we spent many summer days with Pat and her children. Pat had four children. The eldest, Randy, was my age. With my four brothers, the nine of us made quite a gang. We hung out a lot in the summertime, especially at their house because they had a pool. (I can still hear Pat telling us to remember to use the bathroom before swimming, or the 'special purple dye' she'd put in the pool would give us away!)

My most vivid memory involving Pat was the time the whole squadron of us went up to Ford Park in Dearborn, just a half mile from our house in Detroit. Mona and Pat drove the little kids there, while the older ones rode our bikes there.

The park had a walking track that encircled it, similar to the one we enjoy at Tate Park. Naturally, being young boys and seeing that track made us want to race. Randy and I challenged each other. Around the third lap, still exchanging leads back and forth, we saw our designated finish line in sight. Bearing down for all it was worth, I stood up on my pedals and 'floored it.' Randy did the same.

I felt like a NASCAR racer, like Mario Andretti anticipating the checker flag. Randy was making a move, coming up on the inside. I was giving it my all, but he was still gaining. His front wheel was now equal with my rear wheel, and still he was gaining ground. The finish line was now a mere fifty yards away. We were traveling at top speed, the wind whistling past our ears and throwing back our shaggy summertime manes. The glory of youth -- the combination of speed, strength and endurance, was a heady experience.

Randy was going to pass me, and I couldn't let that happen. Still thinking of Mario Andretti, I decided a little bump might send him onto the grassy infield, slowing him enough in that crucial final stretch to guarantee my victory. With a slight jerk on my handlebars, I veered into him. It worked. My body hit his handlebars, causing him to veer, but before he left the track, my pedal caught in the spokes of his front tire.

The calamity that befell us was and is to this day just a painful blur. Both bikes and both riders did three or four painful somersaults along the asphalt track. On the first tumble I remember trying to break my fall. Instead, I broke my left arm. It was the only time in my life I had actually 'seen stars,' just like in the comic books. We laid there on the pavement, a tangled mess of broken bike parts and bruised and bloody body parts. After the initial seconds of being dazed and confused, Randy started laughing.

"Looks like I won," he said, pointing out that he had tumbled further across the finish line than I had. That made me laugh, too, until I remembered the pain I had briefly (but very clearly) experienced in my left arm.

"I think I broke my arm," I said, and then we carried our bikes and ourselves to the picnic area where Mona and Pat sat talking.

"What happened to you?" Mona asked.

"I think I broke my arm," I repeated.

"You'd be in a lot of pain if you broke your arm," she said with a look of disbelief.

"No, really. I think I broke my arm," I said, now sounding like a broken record. I then described the end of the race in detail.

Mona was still disbelieving until Pat interjected.

"Joanie, I think it's possible," she said. "Maybe you'd better take him to emergency?"

I don't remember much after that point, but I do remember having a cast on my arm for the rest of that summer. I remember Pat testifying on my behalf all those years ago. I remember the massive bouquet of flowers she sent for Mona's funeral, and I remember her deep and abiding friendship with my mother.

Patricia Fagan Waynick -- may she rest in peace.

***

The next item on our list is a rare attempt at creative writing. I think my inspiration came from the 2006 movie starring Jim Carrey -- "Click." Unlike the movie, this story is not especially good, but I include it to demonstrate, perhaps to my current students, that to grow as a writer one should start first with their own stories and then move outward.

One day, perhaps, I will have the courage (and the talent) to move outward...

Ticking

Originally published September 24, 2020

In a world where time is measured digitally, Old Man Time himself still holds on to the old ways. If you care to listen closely, you might just hear the gears of time turning...

<Click>

Roger Chesterton had a really important decision to make today. It was Labor Day, and though most of the country was off work, Roger wisely scheduled his time to meet with the representative from Abraxas Media.

"Honey, there's bacon and eggs on the stove for you, " said Roger's wife, Pam, knowing it was futile to try to stop her husband when he was on a mission, but feeling duty bound to try. When he declined, she shifted gears.

"Stay and have some cereal with PJ," she suggested.

On a typical holiday or weekend, the family would laze around their updated farmhouse in their idyllic small town in rural America. Not today, however. Today, Roger had a really important decision to make.

"Oh, Pammy, my little love muffin," he replied, lightly pinching both of her cheeks as he drew close to kiss her. "It's a big day!"

<Click>

PJ, who had recently graduated from the terrible twos, either wasn't listening or just didn't get it. She looked up at her father, milk dribbling down her chin to the wet bib below, and said, "We play horses, Daddy?"

"Oh, pumpkin, if Daddy plays it right today, you'll be playing with real horses," Roger said, playfully tweaking his daughter's nose.

Pam gave a look that said, 'Don't make any promises,' but then switched on the smile that had captured Roger back when the two were still in school.

<Click>

Roger went out the side door of their old farmhouse and crossed the big yard to his vehicle. Bounder, the chocolate-colored Labrador he and Pam bought as a pup right after they got the house, came running to greet his master with the usual canine enthusiasm.

"Down boy, down," Roger commanded, lifting his knee into the dog's chest. Normally, Roger would have accepted the customary greeting -- paws on shoulders and sloppy kisses -- but not today. He had a really important decision to make.

Pushing Bounder away, Roger made a beeline to the car.

He walked past the gazebo he had built during their first summer in the home. Pam planted rose bushes around it. The two of them would have their morning cups here before PJ came along, sipping coffee (for Roger) and tea (for Pam) and reading their small-town newspaper, digital for Roger and newsprint for Pam.

She was a quirky one, his Pammy, but it was why he loved her. Pushing those thoughts aside, Roger turned his mind to his meeting today as he got in his car.

<Click>

He drove through the heart of his village's downtown business district. A dozen people walked here and there in small groups, looking in store windows and carrying their bags and bundles.

'Like something out of a Norman Rockwell painting,' he thought, and then, 'Small potatoes.'

<Click>

Roger drove slowly through the village, reminding himself that one of these days he should go to a meeting and get the speed limit raised. His mind slipped back to the decision he was to make today, but then his reverie was interrupted by the sound of the emergency siren, a blaring noise that could even be heard all the way out at their farmhouse.

'Pammy always worries when that thing blasts, says prayers, like that will help!' he thought, shaking his head and smiling for his Pammy, 'poor, quirky, adorable Pammy...'

"Ridiculous," he said out loud as he waited at the intersection for the fire truck to pass. Grown men and women, dressing up as firefighters and riding their shiny red truck.

When the firefighters passed, Roger slipped his car back into gear and continued on to his office in the much bigger and more modern city just east of there.

<Click>

Roger pulled into the lot, got out of his car and walked to the door of his office building. The entire facade was glass and chrome, and the morning sun was fiery and blinding in the reflection. As he neared the door, he noticed a dark rectangle about head high. It was an envelope taped to the glassy surface. Roger opened it.

"Roger,

I'll have to take a rain check on that meeting. I'm taking the family out to the lake.

Bill"

It had been written on the fancy Abraxas stationary Roger always admired.

<Click>

Roger's mood deflated, but only momentarily. There was still plenty of day to salvage. He would just go home and let this Labor Day play out like any other holiday -- relaxing with family...

He started humming to himself as he turned the corner to drive the final mile to his home, barely aware of the smoke and sirens as he approached....

***

Family is important. It may be the most important thing in the world, the best, yet simplest, gift God has given us on this earth, and it's one we often take for granted. It's why I keep the schmaltzy story you just read, Good Reader. It's also why there are more than a few tales in this tome that focus on family.

The next one focuses on my father, with whom I had a changing relationship. As a youth, I was in awe, yet fearful. As a teen, I was defiant and resentful. As a young adult, I was dismissive and disdainful. As I entered my 30s, however, I became aware and grateful. I began to admire my father.

How did he do it? Can I ever be the man he was?

I am thankful I made it to that age; some men get caught up in one of the earlier stages.

Donald Barthelme, an American satirist from the 60s and 70s, opined that a young man needs to "kill the father." I guess, in a non-literal way, that's true. Or perhaps we just need to rewrite the father, to take the prototype and reconfigure it anew with each generation?

In any case, fathers are important. If you are reading this and you intend to become a father, know that you will make a world of difference in the lives of your children, especially your sons.

Hang in there, fella!

My Number One Fan

Originally published October 15, 2020

While working on a feature story this week about football, I couldn't help recalling the moment I first decided to play the game.

I was a sophomore in high school and had dutifully gone out for the baseball and basketball school teams since sixth grade, always at the **urging** of my father. I bold the word "urging" because it was not subtle or gentle.

My father, Ralph, was really into sports. The thing that kept him from getting us into football and hockey leagues when we were younger was the fact that little league participation required equipment fees. We were a family of seven with one income. Dad worked for the US Army as a civilian auditor. He made a fair living, almost bulletproof against lay-offs and job loss, but not exactly lucrative.

I remember him talking with another parent about the little league hockey team, the conversation coming to an abrupt end when the other dad shared the cost of equipment.

At my father's behest, I grudgingly played basketball and baseball every year, which is ironic because on any given spring, summer, or fall day you would find me in the neighborhood playing pickup games of basketball, strike-out, curb ball, four square, street football -- you name it. I was a sports junkie, but I wanted it to be on my terms, I guess.

When high school arrived, I honored our long-standing and unspoken agreement by trying out for the basketball and baseball teams. To my surprise, I got cut from the freshman basketball team, and I got cut from the junior varsity baseball team. It stung, but I got over it and gradually came to enjoy this new level of freedom. No organized sports -- yeah! I made the honor roll all four quarters that year, but looking at an all-A report card was a hollow substitute for watching his son on the court or on the field. I knew it without even looking at my father.

One hot August evening found us sitting at the dinner

table in our small bungalow in Detroit, windows open and fan blowing. (We had been a very traditional family until Mom entered the workforce in the late seventies.) Looking at us sitting there, you might have thought of us as a sweaty version of the Brady Bunch -- without all the pretty girls.

"Anything new happen today, Joan?" Dad asked.

Just like the old television shows, where the working father expected a full report on the family, my Dad came home, read the evening newspaper, and expected dinner to be piping hot, delicious, and laid out on the table for him at the appointed time. Mom only had two small victories in those days; she insisted my father come to the table fully dressed and that he leave the newspaper in the living room and the television off.

I would have preferred the television remain on, as that would have kept Dad from asking me questions. Heck, it would have kept him from speaking at all. My father, like me, had boob tube myopia, a common affliction that males are prone to develop when left in a room with an operating television. In severe cases, it may cause drooling and even loss of bladder control.

The television was off during dinner time at our house, however, so the conversation flowed.

"Paul got a postcard in the mail today," Mona said in response to Dad's question. "It's from the football coach."

This was a surprise to me, and not a good one. I looked at my father from the corner of my eye and could see his interest pique at the mention of football. I tried to sink back into my chair, to become invisible, but at age 15, I knew that was impossible. I decided to remain quiet and immobile.

"Football! Does the coach want you to play?" Dad asked my brother, who was an incoming freshman at the same high school. I had never seen my father take an interest in Paul, not like that. Paul always tried out for sports in middle school, but always (to the best of my knowledge) got cut. The next oldest brother, Mark, who was probably the best athlete in the family, had been distracting Dad nicely with his success in middle school sports.

The possibility of having a son play football -- the pinnacle of all sports -- inevitably led Dad to imagine an even better dream fulfilled (and I could see it welling up out of the corner of my eye) -- *two* sons playing football!

Even as my brother was explaining that he was thinking about trying out for the football team, I felt my father's gaze turn toward me.

"How about you, Mike?" he said, and I know that sounds innocent enough, but you have to understand the level of my father's fanaticism to truly appreciate my discomfort.

During my middle school career in basketball I had exactly two moments where I scored points, one of them being a game winner, and my father "went fruity," according to Paul Mungia, a teammate at the time. In baseball, I almost never got into the game except as a pinch runner. (I was fast, believe it or not.) Yet my father went to every game -- *every game* -- and most practices when he could make it. He was my number one fan, and I love him for that now, though at the time I sometimes prayed for the indifference other parents apparently had for their children's activities.

I looked down at my plate -- mashed potatoes and peas in a gravy from some kind of meat I had already finished. I didn't dare look up as I quietly answered, "I don't know."

"What do you mean, 'you don't know,?' Your brother's going to play, and you're going to play," Dad said with a finality that quashed any disagreement or discussion.

"I guess," was my only response, though I knew better and kept it a silent response.

In that moment I felt I knew what it was like to be Jesus carrying the cross to Calvary, sacrificing my time and physical well-being for the sake of family accord. When Mona read the postcard aloud, announcing the date and time of try-outs, I felt the scourge. Then she read one final line and looked at me.

"It says here that hair should be cut above the collar of a dress shirt," Mona said, and I felt like the crown of thorns was being pressed against my temple. In eighth grade I was allowed to grow my hair long for the school play, and I had managed to keep Dad's clippers away from it since then. Dad looked delighted, and announced "fresh haircuts for everyone after dinner."

The next week, Paul and I went to the try-outs. I was disappointed to learn that they didn't cut anyone. After a month of waterless, two-a-day practices on a dusty, hard-packed field, something happened and I think I finally found my sport.

Thanks, Dad!

Basketball Jones

Originally published October 22, 2020

Sunday in church our pastor read the gospel story of Jesus being confronted by the Pharisees, who had hoped to trap him into making treasonous statements against the Roman government.

His response? "Render unto Caesar the things that are Caesar's, and unto God the things that are God's" (Matthew 22:21)

It's one of my favorite passages, both divine and practical, as much of the Bible proves to be.

What does it mean? Most Christians realize that our souls belong to God and are ultimately fulfilled by spending an eternity reunited with Him.

My pastor's focus, however, was on the temporal meaning -- the giving unto Caesar part. His point was that we not only can, but should, participate in earthly government, and that it is our obligation to vote.

It seems like many people, Christian or not, are heeding the call to vote this election, with record numbers filling in absentee ballots.

As you know, Good Reader, I attempt to walk a neutral line when it comes to politics and this newspaper. I'm not neutral, of course, but I make the effort to present both sides as evenly as possible -- within reason. That's not always easy, nor is it always possible. It's about as difficult, in fact, as trying to be a good Christian in this day and age, especially with the political banter flying around.

One way to remain neutral is to remain grounded in faith. When I hear of the shenanigans of our political leaders -- on both sides of the aisle -- I try to remember to pray for them. They must be under tremendous pressure, especially in this political campaign season, to say and do some of the crazy things we read and hear in the news. So, I try to remember to pray for our leaders.

It's not easy. And, of course, I'm tempted to pray a little harder for one over the other.

Last Saturday afternoon, I was aided in my effort to be a

better person and Christian. I attended a prayer service in Tecumseh on the lawn of Saint Elizabeth Church, of which Saint Dominic Chapel of Clinton is a part. The prayer service was modeled on the Prayer March in Washington, DC on September 26, 2020. The service had seven prayer focuses.

The first focus called for us to turn from our wicked ways, and how revealing it was when the question was asked, "Did you think of someone else when you heard the word 'wicked'?" The answer, honestly, was yes. I thought of the other side of the political aisle. (Prayer was the correct answer -- prayer for healing to come to our divided country.)

It's a forest-for-the-trees conundrum, the ability to see the splinter in your neighbor's eye but remain oblivious to the log in your own, and I should know better. I had my first lesson back in high school.

~~~

During my senior year in high school, I decided to volunteer to coach a little league basketball team at my church in Detroit. The kids were in fifth and sixth grade, and I felt like a big shot. As those of you who have read this column know, I was not so great at basketball, but hey, those kids didn't know any better.

As it turned out, teams were selected days earlier by experienced fathers who had coached for years. They left me the table scraps as far as talent -- with one exception -- Donald "Disco Misco" Miskovich, who had not been selected due to a reputation as a hard-to-manage troublemaker. Disco and I got along great, however, and our playbook was simple -- Disco right, Disco left, Disco up the middle. The other players were told to keep out of the way and, if through some odd quirk they got their hands on the basketball, they were to find the quickest way to get it back to Disco Misco.

While it's true that I didn't have an extensive playbook, I had studied coaching enough to know how a coach was expected to behave.

Unfortunately, it was the legendary Bobby Knight I emulated.

I screamed; I shouted, and I berated the referees without mercy. (It was expected, no?)

The league manager, Ron Sappington, spoke to me on a couple occasions, reminding me that the refs were volunteers, but that made little difference to me. Near the end of the season, he found another way to im-
~~~

press the message upon me.

I arrived early for my game -- more than an hour early -- and spoke to him in his office to kill the time.

"Hey, Mike, I'm glad you're here. You can be a big help," he said as I entered his office.

I waited, then asked how I could help.

"I need a ref for the next game. The little kids -- third and fourth graders. It starts in 10 minutes, and I've got nobody," he said.

"Oh, I couldn't help you there, Ron," I said. "I don't know anything about being a ref."

"Sure, you do," he said, concealing what I'm sure must have been a smile below a stony facade. "I've heard you from the sidelines during games. You know how to call 'em. You know what to look for!"

"Well, I'm not..."

"Sure, you are! Here's a whistle." He jumped up and hung a lanyard over my neck, adding, "Don't worry. I'll be out there with you."

Ron and I took the court, both wearing the traditional black and white stripes of a referee. Ron left me at mid court and went to give the other coaches pregame instructions, or at least that's what he told me. I realized later that those instructions were far from typical.

Play moved up and down the court -- much faster than when I enjoyed a sideline seat. I saw foul after foul being committed, but by the time I had decided that I should blow my whistle, play had moved on to the other end of the court. Both coaches were starting to express their anger at my lackluster performance.

"Hey, didn't you see that foul? What are you -- blind?" said Coach #1.

"Come on, ref. Those guys are mugging my players," Coach #2 screamed.

"What's wrong, ref? Did you swallow your whistle?" Coach #1 asked.

If I had swallowed my whistle, people might have at least heard a peep from me. The longer the game went on, the more frozen I became, until the only thing I could do was run up and down the court.

As any sports fan knows, play will get rougher if referees don't call fouls. Not a single foul had been called in the first half. Game play resembled a tank of piranha targeting a single goldfish. It was becoming a bloodbath.

At halftime, Ron, who also had not used his whistle

(though the two coaches seemed to be fine with his lack of involvement) gave me some more advice.

"Just blow your whistle," he said. "You can decide what foul to call after you stop play."

So that's what I did. I blew my whistle on the very first play of the second half.

"What are you doing?" screamed Coach #1 after I blew my whistle. I pointed to his guard, who had been dribbling the ball.

"Foul," I said meekly.

"What foul?" he shouted, turning red. I turned to Ron, who quickly looked away.

"Travelling?" I answered, so low that I had to repeat it three times until the offended coach shouted it back at me. He added a few extra disparaging opinions on my first call ever as a referee.

Later, I called a foul on the other team just to balance it out, and I ended up being praised by Coach #1 for finally getting it right.

At the end of the game, the players took their little bruised bodies from the court, casualties of my lesson in sportsmanship. I left with only a bruised ego.

Upon reflection, it reminds me a little of politics and the media. The real problem is that nobody notices the bruised children.

Let us remember to pray for our political leaders and get out there and vote!

***

Today, I barely keep track of politics. I don't read news on my phone, computer, or in print. I don't watch it on TV or listen on the radio. Despite this embargo, I usually get wind of the major calamities and absurdities of the political world.

Perhaps I should engage?

My high school civics teacher, Mr. Bosley, extolled the need for an involved citizenry. Yet, for the last couple decades, it seems we just don't want to listen to anyone not espousing our own views. For all I know, Good Reader, you've stopped listening to me already.

Good Reader?

... Good Reader?

Wash His Mouth Out with Soap

Originally published November 5, 2020

It's 2:30 in the morning as I write this, and we still don't know who has won the election for President of the United States. A quick glance on Yahoo shows Biden leading Trump with 225 electoral college votes to Trump's 213. Yet Biden has only 3 undecided states leaning his way, if the colorful map on my screen is to be believed, and those states hold a mere 21 electoral college votes. It appears that Biden won't have enough to get the needed 270 votes, unless at least two of the six states shown to be leaning toward Trump (with their total of 80 electoral votes) do a dramatic flip. It appears that President Trump will get a second term, yet I hesitate to put that on the front page this week, fearful I'll be the creator of another "Dewey Wins" headline.

It's much safer to announce the winner of the Clinton Township supervisor race, Basil Greenleaf. The ballot counting here in Clinton is done -- and it was done on election day, though maybe not at 8 p.m., as I had hoped. I was able to walk out of the Township Hall at 10 p.m., thanks to the hard work of Clerk Joann Steffens and Deputy Clerk Barb Merritt.

I'm grateful, but I'm also tired... and not just from lack of sleep.

I'm tired of the vulgarity and meanness of the campaigning done this season. I'm not going to name names -- there's been plenty of it to go around on all sides.

One Local reader sent me a question earlier this week. (For reference, when I say "Local Reader," I mean Clinton, Manchester, Tecumseh, Tipton, Saline -- everywhere within a ten mile arc. I like to think big.)

Her question concerned the placement of a sign in one of the above mentioned locales, a sign that said "No More Bullsnot." Of course, it didn't say snot, it said SH*T, and she felt it was crude.

I have to agree that it is crude, and our acceptance of it and other base language during this political season, both from candidates and with each other on social media, has diminished us, reducing our society to a primitive version of itself. We're better than that.

Though I can't say that ***I*** always was, as I recall needing to be taught a lesson in that department more than once.

~~~

When I was very young, perhaps four or five years old, I got my mouth washed out with soap for saying sh*t.

My brother Paul and I were at the table having lunch -- Spaghetti Os, I believe, when one of us said it. (It was one of my mother's favorite curse words, so I think I know where we got it.) Mona scolded us for saying it, then one of us laughed, and it was off to the races.

"Sh*t, sh*t, sh*t!"

We took turns repeating it and laughing, doing a little seat dance/wiggle, unyielding to our mother's insistence that we stop.

"Joanie, wash their mouths out with soap," said our beloved Grandma Grace. She had been quietly sweeping the kitchen floor, giving Mona room to be the parent. Clearly at this point, however, she had enough. Paul and I stopped our filthy chant and earnestly began apologizing.

"No, please, please, please, no, no, no, sorry sorry, sorry...," we stammered, as if the frequency and speed of our apologies would somehow alter the decision.

Mona was firm, apparently eager to impress her own mother with her discipline. She hustled us to the bathroom, grabbed the bar of soap and, since I was the eldest, shoved it into my mouth first.

"Make sure you get it on their teeth, Joanie," Grandma said from the hallway. Mona was thorough, if nothing else, and she managed to get soap in between most of my front teeth -- top and bottom -- as well as into the crevices of the molars, again, top and bottom.

I never forgot my first mouth washing, and many years later I brought it up to them, but they both disavowed any knowledge of the event. They had become kinder, gentler parents.

When I was about 25 years old, I found myself as an assistant coach for a Catholic high school varsity football team. As a young assistant, I got to stand on the press box roof and spot for the head coach, who kept his feet safely planted on the sidelines. I was an avid football fan, just having finished my own brief career in college, and I sometimes became agitated
~~~

and vocal when the officiating didn't go our way.

Now, I know, Good Reader, you're thinking that I must have learned my lesson about yelling at referees when I was younger. After all, my experience as a hapless basketball ref was humbling indeed.

But no, I was a hard-head, and I yelled at the officials on the football field almost every play.

Being on the roof of the press box had its advantages -- a great line of sight and a wonderful platform for broadcasting one's voice. It was tantamount to being a yodeler in the Swiss Alps.

I got so caught up in the game that I paid little attention to anyone but the players and the refs, yelling at one or the other nonstop. I never really noticed the row of nuns, dressed in their traditional attire, seated at the fifty yard line directly below the press box.

Another bad call went against us, and I let the referee have it.

"That's bullsnot, ref. BULLSNOT!"

Like a group of synchronized swimmers, five nuns turned my way, looking up at me with disgust and shock.

"Oh, sorry, er... sorry about that," I said sheepishly, stepping back on the roof to get out of their line of sight. I actually considered stepping off the roof and ending it all right there, such was my embarrassment.

Since then I have become keenly aware of my environment, for the most part. There are certain times and places that crude language may even be considered quaint, or homespun. But it is always better to err on the side of caution.

My wife, Debbie, shared an encounter she had at a "local" establishment last weekend. The more I think about it, the more disturbing I find it. At the establishment she asked a young male worker a question about the number of guests allowed in the building at one time. Both of us have become very concerned with the reported increase in COVID-19 cases, and, in order to avoid closing her business, Debbie does her best to avoid crowds.

"F-Covid," said the young worker to my wife. Except he didn't abbreviate it. And this wasn't like the "F-Cancer" bumper stickers you might see here and there, which are expressions of grief and frustration. He then went on to express disdain for the safety precautions that have become expected during this pandemic.

I respect everyone's right to an opinion, and for those who don't want to wear a mask or limit numbers indoors, I say fine. I can choose to avoid you.

I do, however, take umbrage with a twenty-something worker dropping the F-Bomb, as we used to call it, in conversation with my wife. (I am, of course, assuming my wife didn't open the conversation with, "Hey, what's the F-ing limit on crowds in here?")

Both my wife and I have decided to limit our exposure to this establishment, which is a shame because we have grown to enjoy going there.

Personally, I feel sorry for the owner. I can't imagine running a business where its reputation is so reliant on employees, some who are immature and under educated. What can an employer do? The boss can't follow that worker around all day.

Maybe he should wash his mouth out with soap?

Grandma Grace, a staunch advocate of oral cleanliness, and Mona, wielder of the soap bar, flank Uncle Ralph Aiello (center), the sainted man who took his filet knife to hundreds of tiny pan fish so that his nieces and nephews wouldn't be disappointed.

Calf's Heart Stew

Originally published November 12, 2020

Birthdays in my house were special as I grew up. No, it's not that we got big, fancy gifts. In fact, gifts were often necessities like socks and underwear, though on occasion we received a more personal gift. For instance, I can remember receiving a super cool green leather watch band once. I called it "super cool," but it was also really hot. I never knew I could perspire so much from the wrist!

Speaking of wrists, another vivid birthday memory I have involves my right wrist and the two scars that are still visible today.

I may have been about 8 years old, which would put the year at 1969. It was summertime, as I am a July baby, and we had a picnic birthday party planned in our backyard.

Perhaps the best birthday gift my brothers and I looked forward to was the opportunity to name the family's meal for that day, which usually defaulted to the nearest Sunday because it called for a more than average effort in the kitchen from Mona.

My go-to meal every birthday was Calf's Heart Stew. I think I selected it for two reasons. For one, it couldn't just be whipped up at a moment's notice; it required Mona to place a special order at the butcher store -- Podgorski's, Michalak Meats, or one of the other three that ran along the two-mile strip of West Warren Avenue north of our house in Detroit. (That strip had an equal number of bakeries, and at least twice as many bars. It was the good old days!)

The second reason I always selected that meal was because one or more of my brothers didn't like it. As I've confessed before, Mom called me her 'mean one.'

But I could also be helpful, and so that Sunday evening, as our nearby relatives joined us for my birthday meal and later for cake and ice cream in the backyard, I insisted on helping to carry the food out to the picnic table. Mona was in the kitchen gathering forks and spoons and bowls, laying them out for me to carry outside. She had also made a secondary entree, probably mostaccioli, for those unwilling to sample the culinary pleasure of my favorite stew. Every large family gathering also included Mona's signature Italian Potato Salad. As usual, she had prepared a big bowl of it.

"Are you sure you can carry that?" Mona asked as I grabbed the large glass bowl of potato salad and headed toward the side door which led to our yard. "It's heavy!"

"I can handle it," I said, eager to prove myself. And I could! It was heavy, but I was a sturdy lad, so I bounded down the steps and pushed the door lever on the screen door.

I use the term "screen door" loosely here because we almost never had the screens in place. The screens were torn beyond repair years earlier, probably from us kids bouncing balls or throwing frisbees against them. In any case, they sat unused in a corner of our basement. Instead, even though it was mid-summer, our screen door had a storm window in it. This was well before widespread use of safety glass or even Plexiglas. Our screen door had good old-fashioned glass glass.

So, I bound down the three steps to the door with my heavy bowl of potato salad and pushed the door latch. The door swung into the yard, then swung back quickly to close with me still inside. (We always kept the spring set high so the door would close even when there was a strong breeze.) With my left hand I balanced the bowl against my chest and pushed the lever again, with the same result -- the door snapped back to the closed position, automatically latching before I could get out.

Undeterred, I smacked the handle again, forcing the door to swing even wider than before. I repositioned the bowl in my left arm and stepped forward quickly, but I was still too slow. The door was already on its way back toward me, this time with even greater speed. My right hand shot out to push the door back before the latch could reset, but this time I missed the handle and punched my hand through the glass pane. Shards from the 3' by 4' storm window sliced my wrist as glass rained down on the driveway below. I think I managed to save the bowl of potato salad and return it to the kitchen, though Mona wisely discarded it before we ate.

Back in those days, folks believed in home remedies, so Mona got a towel and wrapped my wrist in it until the bleeding stopped. Later, she wrapped bandages on it. I never saw a doctor for that one, so my scars look like ones made in an attempt to flee this world voluntarily.

Despite the pre-dinner drama, I think we ended up continuing with the festivities. I was well enough to blow out the candles on my cake, though I think I may have taken a rain check on the blood red Calf's Heart Stew that evening.

Next week, my son, Nicholas, is celebrating a birthday. It's a special one for him and for his parents, as he'll turn 21 years old. I don't have to tell parents how that feels, both the nostalgia of reflecting on the growth over time and the pride of looking at your child with new eyes -- as a young adult. (It's been an ongoing process since he moved out of the house, but age 21, for me, seems to be a milestone.)

We'll probably take him out to eat for his birthday, but if he asks, he might get his mom to make his favorite homemade chili, or perhaps stuffed peppers made by yours truly. Either way, I hope to help make his birthday a special and memorable one -- without any drama.

Happy birthday, Nicholas.

***

Nicholas ended up celebrating his twenty-first birthday as his mother and father both did when we were that age -- by drinking alcohol with his friends. Debbie and I were aghast when he described being carried back to his dormitory by friends after consuming an indeterminate amount of vodka. Though we both had our moments when we were his age, it felt different imagining him -- our baby -- hanging one foot over the side of the bed to reduce the "spins," or even worse, "riding the porcelain bus."

Thankfully, it's over. He survived. And he's smart enough to know better next time. Smarter than his old man by a country mile, at least...

Calculus for ~~Dummies~~ Me

Originally published January 7, 2021

I received many nice gifts for Christmas, and one of them was **not** the "Calculus for Dummies" book I received from my son, Nicholas. I say that jokingly and with affection because he seems to have gained his sense of humor from me.

You see, I asked for it.

Nick is now 21 years old and matriculating into his senior year in college. Academically, his pace and level of success outstrip his 'old man' by a wide margin, but there was once a time when I was of help to him when it came to the books. The extent of my usefulness, however, expired some time around the sixth grade. Since then, I have jokingly (my wife says annoyingly) continued to offer my help with homework.

"Nick, do you want me to help you with your physics homework?"

"Really, what do you know about physics, Dad?

"I know if you drop a Fig Newton from a tree it always hits the ground," I said, and added sagely, "and that proves the theory of gravity."

Nick just rolled his eyes.

"I'm good for now, Dad, but maybe later?"

Strangely enough, mathematics is Nick's forte. It's strange because it is most assuredly my Achilles heel, and Nick knows it. Thus, it is what I offer to help with most often.

"Nick, do you want some help with that calculus homework?" I have asked many evenings while standing in the doorway to his room.

Over the years, he has become wily in his response, until the most recent exchange caused me to finally stop asking....

"Sure, Dad, can you use the chain rule to compute the derivative of the composition of two or more functions?"

My slack-jawed stare was telling, but being *my* son, he couldn't resist pursuing the line of questioning.

"Could you help me solve a differential equation?" He asked, seeming to enjoy himself.

I stopped him before he got out another question, fearful my head might explode if I actually tried to formulate an answer.

"Excuse me? What's that?" I said, hand cupped to ear. "I think I hear your mother calling! Oh, that's right, I told her I would help her with ... something. Gee, I am sorry, Nick, maybe later?"

I left the vicinity so fast that you might have expected to see a cartoonish swirl of dust in my wake.

Over the years I have enjoyed the jesting repartee we have when it comes to calculus, and I must confess that I've become lazy; I'm now grateful he no longer needs my help with schooling, freeing up time for my own academically appropriate pursuits, like watching Family Feud reruns.

Once upon a time, however, I had not resigned myself to failure in the world of mathematics.

I've already shared the story with you, Good Reader, about my first experience with math in the first grade, and that set the tone until grade 9, where, to my surprise, I had a bit of success. In fact, Mrs. Henson, my algebra teacher, recommended me for the honors class at the end of freshman year, and that ended up changing everything.

In a small school, when you end up in one honors class, your schedule becomes so constricted that you end up with the same students in just about all your classes. I saw the same thing at Clinton High School when my son went there, though the "honors" classes are now called "AP" (Advanced Placement).

While I had been successful in freshman algebra, sophomore year brought a combination of geometry and trigonometry in the honors class, and my grades started to drop. Junior year brought more trigonometry and something called analysis. Calculus came senior year, and I didn't need math to calculate that the slope of my GPA was going to continue downward.

The first quarter of calculus brought a "C," which was really a gift. A "D" followed in the second quarter; it was a real Christmas present because by then I was completely clueless. I spoke to the teacher after class before the second semester began, drop slip in my extended hand.

"Why would you want to drop calculus, Mike?" asked Sister Mary Kay, my math teacher for the previous two and a half decreasingly successful years. I looked at her with amazement, then with amusement, and finally, with anxiety. It was clear she needed to keep her numbers up to justify keeping the class open. It was a Catholic school, and she was a nun, but she couldn't seriously believe I would be able to reverse the trend -- that *would* be a miracle!

It took some convincing, but I persevered and finally insisted that she sign my drop slip. Walking away, I felt some relief knowing that I wouldn't have to sit in her room for 55 minutes every day, feeling like the class dunce for 53 of those minutes. (The two minute roll call attendance was okay.)

I also felt disappointed in myself. My father had taught me not to quit -- mostly in reference to sports, but that's one of the good reasons to involve all children in some form of athletics -- the transference of principles.

I had ,in fact, quit, and it stuck with me. Nevertheless, I moved on to college, entering a pre-medical program. (How hard could it be?) Little did I know that to become a dentist I would need to take FOUR terms of calculus.

There I was, less than a year later, sitting in a college calculus classroom of about 25 students with Professor Fink at the front of the room. Five or six students in the front row could barely contain their zeal; every question posed by Fink caused their hands to rocket upward and their throats to produce guttural moans like Arnold Horshack, one of the sweathogs from TV's "Welcome Back, Kotter."

I sat in the back with a large comic book question mark over my head, but only for a few weeks. This was college, after all, and they didn't take attendance. Sleeping in was a better use of my time, I judged. Unfortunately, I didn't think about dropping the class, and I took my first "F" ever, or at least the first I can remember.

After my second year there, I decided to become an English teacher. I was tired of being broke, so I took Mona up on the offer of free room and board until I finished my bachelor's degree. I moved back home to Detroit in 1981, got a job, transferred to Wayne State University, and was ready to start over.

But first, I needed to settle my score with calculus.

I enrolled in a summer calculus course at the University of Michigan Dearborn. I was one of 30 students in the classroom, and, looking for every angle, I was hoping that the instructor would grade on a curve and that I could just be better than half of the class.

It was during that summer

course that I learned how many students manipulated the system to broker a higher GPA.

In week one, we had our first quiz, and I had studied hard for it. My parents had a small fifth wheel in the backyard, and I stationed myself there every day for four hours, reviewing the class notes, completing homework, even going back to rework the problems from the day before in an effort to master the skill. I had never worked so hard on anything, and, though it was a cooler than average summer, the little camper was like an oven, with no AC and tiny windows that only partially opened.

I looked forward to learning the results of that first quiz and went to class that second Monday with confidence. There were fewer students there -- only about 25 -- and another student opined that they must have thought the quiz was too hard and just "dropped." It was a new concept to me, so I asked about it. I learned that students could drop the class at any time up to the final exam. The only penalty was financial. You could expect a partial refund all the way through week eight of a ten week course.

I got my quiz grade -- a "B" -- and forgot about the rules of "dropping" until the next class. Eight more students had disappeared, apparently dissatisfied with their first quiz grade.

Now I was beginning to feel outraged.

'Suck it up, buttercup,' I thought, wishing I could say it to the anonymous faces of those who had dropped the class.

I was becoming worried that the 'class curve' was disappearing, and that I would again, as usual, settle like sediment at the bottom of the math pool.

I went back to the hot-box trailer and redoubled my efforts, realizing that I could only control my own behavior.

Four more students dropped the next week.

Six followed them in week four.

The final week available for dropping (without a negative mark on transcripts) saw seven more join the exodus from the class, leaving eight of us to find the Promised Land on our own.

In the last week or so of the term, the guest instructor had each student schedule an appointment. He asked about my interest in math. I was honest.

"Look, I just want to pass the class, hopefully with a 'B.'"

After repeatedly confirming that I would not attempt to go

further in the world of mathematics, he complied. Weeks later, my report card came with the desired "B."

I consider it one of my greatest accomplishments in life. In fact, I might even want it incorporated on my tombstone with the following epitaph:

"Here lies Mike...

He passed calculus -- with a "B!"

***

Apparently, I really needed to fill some space this week: this piece ran much longer than the usual. In the newspaper, I even filled the rest of the page with "Dad Jokes" -- something of which I am truly fond, yet cannot claim original authorship of a single one. Even years later, I knew those "bad-dad-jokes" had been "borrowed," so snip, snip, snip.

Bad jokes aside, that "B" in calculus remains my most highly valued academic achievement. Crazy, but true. Although a "B" in linguistics rates a close second.

I honestly never worried about getting B's instead of A's, except for my freshman and sophomore years in high school. This cavalier attitude toward grades came around to bite me when I entered my master's program at Wayne State University, getting my only "B" in the first semester -- and shrugging it off. That's an interesting story, but I'll save it for another time...

Breathless

(A Poet Who Didn't Know It)

Originally published March 25, 2021

I was speaking to a friend and Local subscriber last week, and I asked him about his choice for the new mascot name; Clinton Community Schools will soon be selecting a new mascot to replace the "Redskins" name.

As a refresher, in case you didn't see the choices, they are (in alphabetical order): Cardinals, Cobras, Coyotes, Red Hawks, Red Wolves, and River Hawks. An online survey, open until Sunday night, gave community members and alumni an opportunity to vote.

My friend said he liked the alliteration afforded by the first three options, and I confessed that I have always been a big fan of alliteration, even though I didn't always know what it meant...

~~~

After eight weeks of purgatory studying calculus in the back yard hot box that was my parents' camper, I went back to college in the fall of 1980. Passing calculus the second time around gave me some satisfaction, but I was through with math. I did some soul searching and figured I would go with what I felt was my strength -- I was going to become an English major.

My first course in my new major was poetry with Professor Hilliard, an interesting, good natured, red-headed fellow who seemed to enjoy his chosen field. The course drew an interesting variety of students, too -- much different than those in the science and math classes I concentrated on the previous year.

Three students in particular stick out in my memory: Gushing Glenna, All-Natural Ned, and Artsy Alvin.

The poetry class met three times a week, and on Fridays we were expected to bring two poems to share with the class, distributing print copies to all and then standing at our places to recite them. Presentation was key, Professor Hilliard explained, and he told us to "bring your words to life."
~~~

No one was better at this than Gushing Glenna.

Gushing Glenna, or GiGi, usually volunteered to go first. She bounced around the large, round table as she gave each of us her poems for that week, breathlessly sharing with us the backstory of each piece as she came full circle to stand in her place, continuing without skipping a beat or taking a breath.

"Okay, now I really like this first one, it reminds me of what I really am, I mean when I'm deep within myself, like when I'm meditating, and I'm thinking about what I really want to be, or who I really am, you know, the real me, and I go deeper and deeper into myself and then I ..."

After the first session, Professor Hilliard knew that GiGi needed a little help getting started. Like an old crank-start automobile, he would have to gently nudge her forward or we would never get through her two poems.

"I can't wait to hear your poems," Hilliard would interrupt smoothly and with perfectly genuine enthusiasm. "Why don't you just start right in?"

"Oh, okay," GiGi would say, then she'd begin.

"Flowers for Me,

I hope you don't forget to bring

Some flowers home for me!!!

Any kind will make me happy,

Merry, joyful and carefree!!!"

There was more to the poem, of course, but this portion is enough to demonstrate how Gushing Glenna earned her nickname. She was liberal in her use of exclamation marks in writing, and she is perhaps the only person I've ever known who also *spoke* with three at the end of every sentence -- you could really hear them! Every poem had the same high level of enthusiastic vocal inflection regardless of the topic -- flowers, books, office furniture, dead cat -- you name it.

All-Natural Ned was the opposite of GiGi -- think Pig Pen of Charles Schultz's Peanuts meets Schleprock from the Flintstones. All doom and gloom and dirt, he read his poems in a deep monotone.

Don't get me wrong; I'm sure I can't claim to have been the model of personal hygiene in my college days, but Ned pushed the envelope, and he celebrated his back-to-nature philosophy in his poetry.

"The Real Me, by Ned.

Wake up in the morning -- the natural me

But Society says I must conceal, Cover up!

Aluminum chloride, aluminum chlorohydrate complexes, and aluminum zirconium complexes to cover my smell

Triethanolamine, glycerine, emollients, emulsifiers, and foaming agents to shave my beard

Fluoride in my mouth and chlorofluorocarbons in the air around my head...

...Now I'm ready to face the world.

Doesn't that feel better?"

Hilliard was delighted by Ned's poem decrying modern hygiene products, but I'm sure I wasn't the only one to think that it explained why others gave him a wide berth at the table.

I remember Artsy Alvin most, probably because I learned something from him.

Alvin was a few years older than most of the students. One of a few "lifers" on campus who seemed content to squander daddy's money on learning for the sake of learning -- a ridiculous concept to me at the time. He was skinny, with long hair and a pencil thin moustache. Alvin looked like a cross between 80s hair band rockers and Zorro, and the girls in class cooed over his poems every week. I don't remember his poems, except that they were typically short, and that he avoided capital letters like e.e. cummings.

I also remember Alvin because he was the most critical of the work of his classmates, including mine. Most of us had developed an unspoken truce. For instance, I would praise the enthusiasm of Gigi's work, and she would later give me kudos -- mutual back-scratching. I didn't care if it was honest.

Alvin, however, was always brutally honest. And after weeks of his candor, I began to brace myself for his appraisal after I recited my poems for the week.

"There's a lot of alliteration in your poems," Alvin said around mid-term after I had just finished presenting my weekly poems. "In fact, all of your poems are loaded with alliteration."

I sat across from Alvin, and my face burned. I was getting angry.

'This was the last straw,' I thought. 'Every week he's got some kind of criticism -- like he's perfect!'

I couldn't control myself, and I blurted in anger,

"You know, you think you're so perfect. I may make a mistake or two, but I know how to read and write as well as you!"

I crossed my arms and glowered at Alvin, who looked at me, blinked, and calmly (and compassionately) said, "I didn't call you illiterate. I said you used a lot of alliteration -- two or more words strung together with the same beginning sound."

I don't remember what my response was at the time, but really, what could it have been? "Oh." Or perhaps a defensive, "Yeah, I already knew that!"

Despite my embarrassment, by the end of the term I had collected over 50 poems, and I began to regard myself as a poet. Professor Hilliard actually liked about a dozen of them, marking them in my final poetry portfolio. I was even beginning to think of poetry as a career path.

The next year, I enrolled as an English major at Wayne State University in Detroit, where I could live at home and work while going to school. I signed up for a creative writing course that Fall, and it ended up being half poetry. I proudly shared a freshly typed copy of my portfolio with the new poetry professor. He hated the poems Hilliard liked, but liked many of the others.

Though prize winning British author Julian Barnes once said, "Poetry is a subject as precise as geometry," it's noteworthy that his writing career is based on novels, essays, and short stories. Eventually, I turned from poetry to the more practical career of teaching.

***

I will admit that poetry is truly fun. I enjoy it on the rare occasions I try it now, usually when doing mini lessons with students. (Most of them despise that week or two each year, preferring more concrete work like grammar, vocabulary, and reading comprehension questions. Education, especially for the young, is grade oriented, and students like to be able to predict their own grade with the certainty that comes only from assignments with answer keys.)

I eventually felt that to make a living as an English major, I had better do something practical, so I became a teacher. Today, I think it is a fine profession, and I have done alright following this path, though I am unsure if I'd repeat my steps if I ever got a "do-over," as you will learn from the next story...

Mammas, Don't Let Your Babies Grow Up to Be Teachers

Originally published April 1, 2021

Once a teacher starts talking about teaching, it's hard to get him to shut up about it. For that, I'll apologize to you in advance, Good Reader.

Teaching was my field for 32 years, and all in all, it was good to me. That said, I don't recommend it to those younger than me. In fact, I discourage it.

Case in point, about 10 years ago my wife and I were talking with our son, Nicholas, as he sat on his bed relaxing and playing a hand-held electronic game. (He was 11 at the time.) My wife, Debbie, interrupted his reverie with a question.

"Nick, what do you think you want to be when you grow up?"

Nick lowered his game to his lap, looked up at us, and with a solemn expression said, "I think I'd like to be a teacher like you and Dad."

"Noooooo!" Deb and I shouted simultaneously, causing Nick to start and toss his device into the air. Nick's eyes filled with alarm and locked on his parents, disregarding the game as it clattered to the floor. I don't think we had ever both yelled at him like that before. Deb and I looked at each other, silently conceding that we may have overreacted, then worked to smooth it out.

"It's not that there's anything wrong with being a teacher..." Deb said.

"It's just that you could do so much better than your parents..." I added.

"Maybe you'd like to become a doctor or a lawyer?" Deb offered.

"Or a butcher, a baker, a candlestick maker?" I added, until Deb's glare suggested I stop. "Or anything, anything other than a teacher."

After that, Nick didn't dare to tell us what he wanted to be until he was about to graduate from Clinton High School in 2018.

"I'm going to go to the University of Michigan, and I'm going to become a computer engineer," he told us matter-of-factly that spring.

Panicked that our lesson all those years ago made too deep an impression, Deb and I began to counsel our son to lower his sights.

"Maybe you should have a backup plan, Nick?" Debbie asked.

"What if U of M doesn't accept you?" I asked. "You need to at least *apply* to another college."

We went one for two, getting Nick to apply to one additional college. Fortunately, his resolve paid off, and he is now one term away from his chosen degree from his chosen university.

Over the past few years, I occasionally worried that we may have traumatized our son when we scared him away from the teaching profession. My guilt was mostly erased this spring, however, when he told me about his student internship with Amazon. He will be able to work from home while earning more than I ever earned at the pinnacle of my career. On top of that, he also received a large signing bonus.

When I think about my "internship" as a teacher, the last vestige of guilt slips away entirely.

I began my teaching internship, also called student teaching, at Wayne State University in my junior year -- about 1983. Wayne State had a three semester program for student teaching, which they touted as superior to others. And it really should have been, as the 18 total credit hours meant that it cost almost $11,000 in today's dollars, and that was on top of all the other required courses.

For that money, student teachers committed themselves to increasing levels of servitude under a string of school teachers at the closest public school -- Murray Wright High School, which was just down the block from Wayne State.

My first term of indentured servitude was with a young, bitter woman named Miss Shine, who explained to me during our very first session that she was never going to let me teach her class (one of my requirements to pass that term), and that she was never going to give me anything greater than a "B," since that is what she earned when she was in my position.

Delightful.

So I dutifully went there three times a week, sat in a chair by Miss Shine's desk like a trained Pomeranian, and watched her in action, or should I say inaction? Miss Shine had the lesson on the blackboard before any students arrived, so most days she would just sit in her chair, scowl at the students and tell them to read the board.

The next term I got Miss Lynn, who was also the teacher liaison with Wayne State. That meant she had the afternoon free of regular classes so she could meet with the future teachers in our own on-site classes. It also freed up her afternoons for much, much more!

It was the fourth week of the fall semester for Detroit Public Schools, but it was our first week in the teacher's program. I knew Miss Lynn, so I was comfortable reporting to her room, which was the theater -- down a long hall and near the back parking lot. Miss Lynn told me I wasn't her first choice as a student teacher, but since a female student teacher had been sexually assaulted last term in her classroom, she wanted a male this time. She seemed a little happier when I agreed to arrive half an hour early each morning to make the coffee.

The terms of my servitude in this second term were every day, 8 a.m. to 11:45 a.m., including every Wednesday afternoon to meet with the college liaisons and the other student teachers.

On my first morning I gamely made the coffee. I had told her I knew how to make it, but really I had just watched the waitresses make it at the restaurants where I'd worked. I took my best shot at it, and when Miss Lynn and her fellow teachers arrived that first morning, my coffee making skills were up for evaluation.

"How many scoops did you use?" said one teacher. "I've got whiplash from my eyelids slamming into my head!"

Bright-eyed and ready to go, I entered the classroom with Miss Lynn, prepared to watch a real teacher in action, not just sitting behind a desk.

I got action, alright. Miss Lynn was out the door in a matter of minutes.

"Take attendance from this sheet," Miss Lynn said as she began slipping on her coat. "Send the absences down to the office. Have the students read the chapter, and write the answers in their notebooks. Collect the notebooks. Take them home. Grade them and I'll see you tomorrow."

She was halfway to the door before I realized her intent.

"You're just going to leave me here with the class?" I asked. She just looked at me and smiled.

"You'll be fine," she said, flinging her scarf over her shoulder and turning again to the door.

"Wh-what chapter are they on?"

"Ask Shanelle, or maybe it's Raquelle -- the girl in the front row with the braided hair..."

I made it through that period with the help of that girl, whose name was really Danielle, and by some miracle I made it through the rest of the morning. I learned a lot. I learned that even though it was the fourth week of school for these students, Miss Lynn still hadn't made up her grade book, nor had she graded a *single* assignment. She had considerately left all that for me, so that I might benefit from the experience.

Miss Lynn did return that afternoon to check in on me, but I never saw her in the classroom again. She came in every morning, had coffee, left, and came back to freshen her makeup in the afternoon before slinking out the back door with the principal, a married man...

Miss Lynn had gotten so comfortable with the arrangement that she called dibs on me for the next and final semester, which would be a full day of student teaching. I knew I didn't want to do even more of that, so I came up with a rational excuse; I told her that because Miss Shine's class focused on speech and her class focused on theater, I really needed to work with a teacher who focused on writing skills. Never mind that I had learned precious little about either discipline from the two of them; we both knew it wasn't really about that.

Still, she had to acquiesce, and I was placed with Miss Minor, who was tall, bespectacled, and hilarious. I learned a lot from her, including that you had to be yourself as a teacher. (My early efforts at being Miss Minor Part Two were dramatic failures.)

For some reason, probably stubbornness, I stayed in teaching, but I don't think I got to be any good at it until somewhere after year six. That may have been due to the sketchy start described above, but I'd also attribute it to the level of difficulty, which only teachers can truly appreciate.

Teaching is probably one of the most difficult professions to do well, but it remains one of the lowest paid professions considering the amount of education, the ongoing training, and the level of complexity involved. In our society, a paycheck is not only survival, it is also respect.

I'd like to think my son would have eventually become a great teacher, but I just couldn't let him grow up to become one.

The Great White Hunter

Originally published November 26, 2020

Last Saturday, I was talking to Antonio Cerroni, the owner of Poplar Glen Farms. I had stopped at his place just east of the Village to get some farm fresh eggs and locally grown, pasture raised steaks to celebrate my son's birthday, and we started talking about deer hunting. He told me of his exploits, both in the past and from that morning. I shied away from sharing the tale of my first (and only) deer hunt with Tony, but since I've always been open with you, Good Reader, I've decided to tell all, no matter how embarrassing.

~~~

I was in my late twenties and had just purchased a house in the Detroit area. A friend of mine needed a loan, and I accepted a compound bow as collateral. I hadn't been in the market for a bow, but he eventually talked me into accepting it in lieu of repayment. Since I was single and had more money than sense, I accepted the deal and began to buy the accoutrements and trappings needed to become a successful archer and bow hunter. My friend gave me a few lessons, and I quickly realized that I was pretty good at shooting bow and arrow.

My brother, Paul, became an avid hunter after marrying Kathy, a Yooper (person from the upper peninsula of Michigan) who could hunt and fish with the best of them. (To this day, she usually gets a buck before my brother.) I told him I had gotten a bow, and he invited me to join him for some target practice. I impressed him with my accuracy, and he offered me the chance to go hunting with him on a piece of property he had bought for just that purpose.

Paul had been baiting the property. (It was legal then.) He gave me the tree stand right above the bait pile. (I was relatively slim and agile back then, for those of you trying to imagine my current physique climbing up a tree without assistance from a crane.)

We got there about 6 a.m., and I walked past the pile of turnips and carrots and began the assent to my tree stand with
~~~

my bow inside its case, slung over my shoulder. I asked Paul where his tree stand was, and he just laughed and pointed to a camo-colored tent-like structure on the ground about 60 yards away.

"I'm not climbing up a tree," he said. "Are you crazy?"

And apparently I was, because it was November, and all I wore was a pair of blue jeans and a fairly light jacket. I didn't even think about gloves. That is, until I had been in the tree stand for about half an hour.

Paul's tree stand was exactly that -- a tree STAND. Since then, I've seen them at Cabela's, often with comfortable looking chairs and cup holders. Paul's "tree stand" was a few two-by-fours nailed together that barely spanned the length of my foot. So, naturally, I stood in my tree stand, leaning against the tree and trying to remain silent so the deer would come in to feed, unaware that I was ready to make it their last supper.

Almost two hours had passed, and there was no sign of life out there. In fact, signs of life in the tree stand were also beginning to diminish, as hypothermia was beginning to set in.

Shortly after getting in position, I had wrapped the soft bow case around my legs for extra warmth. I hesitated to put my gloveless hands in my pockets at first, but after thirty minutes, I figured it was imperative if I intended to use those hands later. I looped my arm through the bow and tried to keep my teeth from chattering...

And then it happened -- I saw a deer trotting toward the feed pile below me. I pulled my hands from my pocket, nocked an arrow, and took aim, but the voices in my head, perhaps brought on by some sort of cold-induced phantasm, wouldn't let me fire. I was frozen, not by the cold this time, but by my conscience, which decided that twenty feet up a tree in freezing temperatures was a felicitous time for debate. It was like the old cartoons, where the protagonist has a devil on one shoulder and an angel on the other.

The deer that presented was a fawn, and she couldn't have been even a year old.

"You can take any size deer during bow season," my primitive, devilish side reminded. "Shoot."

"Yes, but this is Bambi!" The angelic side firmly scolded.

The two contradicted each other like that, back and forth, as I nocked and unnocked the arrow, drawing the bow and then letting it down again.

"You won't get meat any more tender than that," said the horned figure's voice, now seeming to come from my belly. It was effective, as most appeals to the stomach have been with me over the years.

I drew back on the bow-string and took aim, visualizing the arc of my arrow as it descended toward the lungs of the young deer, which was really no bigger than a medium-sized dog. Then another thought entered my mind before I could release the arrow.

"How can I bring that to someone to be cleaned. They'll laugh me out of the butcher shop!" And I relaxed the bow again. My mind went back and forth like that for several more minutes as the young deer nibbled on the veggies below -- yes/no, bow raised/bow lowered -- until I heard a snort nearby.

After a few minutes, I realized it wasn't one snort, but two. They sounded like cows, but that couldn't be possible, out here in the woods. I looked left. I looked right. I looked straight ahead, but for the life of me, I couldn't see a thing but trees and bushes. Eventually, I figured it must be mother deer coming after her babe, which had scampered off when the snorting started.

I stood there ready to shoot; there would be no embarrassment in bringing in a big doe. Of course, I had to see her first.

After about half an hour of deer snorting and me posing like an archer, my brother came bounding over.

"What are you doing, Paul?" I said, indignant that his noisy entrance caused the snorting to stop. He clearly scared off my quarry.

"Hey, if you're not going to shoot, we might as well leave," he said.

"What do you mean?"

"You were just staring at them, and they were staring back at you," he said. "Did you plan on killing them with your eyes?"

He went on to explain that he had watched them approach my stand, and that he was amazed I hadn't even seen them. So much for me becoming the Great White Hunter!

Perhaps I'll ask Tony to part with some venison when he gets a deer this season.

I SAW AUNTIE KISSING SANTA CLAUS

Originally published December 24, 2020

Now, you probably won't believe this tale, but I actually caught Santa kissing my mother once, long ago. I also caught him kissing my aunt. Apparently, Santa was quite a rascal back then...

I can still recall the first time I met Santa in person. I can play it like a movie reel in my mind. There we were, my brother Paul and I, tucked in our single beds upstairs in the dormer of our small bungalow on Woodmont Avenue in Detroit. I can still see the Brenda Starr, Star Reporter bed sheets on the bed. (I wonder if that had anything to do with me ending up as a reporter all these years later? Who knows?) The sheets displayed a worried red-headed Brenda wondering how "Tiny Tembo," the elephant, was going to make it on his own in the jungle. I can't tell you how that drama played out, Good Reader, because we never got the part two bed sheets, if they even existed.

So Paul and I were tucked-in that Christmas Eve; being very young, we had bought the old line of getting to bed early so Santa would have time to come -- a crazy notion now, as everyone knows Santa can warp time, causing it to stop as needed during his annual trip around the globe.

Not knowing any better then, however, we dutifully went to bed early.

"Do you think Santa's going to come tonight?" Paul whispered to me in the darkness.

"Sure, he always comes," I said with sufficient certainty, being the older and wiser brother.

"Mom says she might wake us up when he comes," Paul said.

I immediately dismissed the notion; it defied all the rules. Kids had to be asleep for Santa to come -- that was just how it was and is. Period. I told Paul so, but he seemed stuck on the notion, which, I'll admit, irritated me because he apparently was privy to intel that Mona had kept from me.

"Stop talking and go to sleep, or Santa will never come,"

I said, and flipped to face away from him.

Though I intended to go to sleep immediately, it didn't happen that way. I thought of all the television shows and cartoons I'd seen featuring Santa, and remembered that there were occasionally ones where the kid would get lucky, wake up, and find Santa there in the house, drinking the milk or eating the cookies that had been left. Or did that only happen in the Grinch?

As my mind replayed old footage of Santa, I eventually relaxed and fell off into a deep sleep. I don't recall the dreams (I've never been able to do that), but they were pleasant enough, I'm sure. Visions of sugar plums and toy soldiers and trucks and...

<LIGHTS ON>

...The sweet dreams were interrupted by the glare of the overhead lights. Mona had turned them on from the bottom of the stairs, and she was calling up to us.

"Michael? Paul? Are you awake?" she said from below.

I heard the sound of someone coming up the steps, and vaguely wondered why she would be coming up after tucking us in. I could tell by looking out the window that it wasn't morning, and it wasn't a school night, either.

The footsteps kept coming. Paul and I rubbed the sleep from our eyes.

"Santa!" We both shouted as we saw the Big Man in Red crest the banister of the staircase. Mona followed Santa toward our beds, where he sat on the corner and asked us what we wanted for Christmas -- after he confirmed that we had been good boys that year, of course.

And we must have been really good that year in comparison to other years because it was the only year Santa made a personal stop at our house. After that, we had to catch the Old Elf in the stores or in parades like everyone else.

Of course, our family -- the extended Italian side of our family -- was big enough to warrant a special trip from Santa every year. One of my great aunts, Aunt Cam (short for Camilla), apparently had some inside connection with Santa, and she was always able to get him to appear at our family Christmas party. They were always held on the first Sunday in December, early enough in the month to avoid Santa's busiest time.

My big Italian family probably looked similar to so many depicted on television, except we didn't have any members in the mafia (I think). We were "il cougino" -- cousins -- and if I had one cousin, I had a hundred cousins. After a while, you stopped keeping track of second and third and fourth. Some of the older cousins we addressed as aunts and uncles, which became confusing as we grew older ourselves.

The Vorase family, the foundation of this group, was itself a large family, and it was dominated by the seven sisters, who were my great aunts -- Rose, Stella, Cam, Marion, Mary, Grace (my grandmother), and Lily. They took turns running the family Christmas party over the many decades it lasted.

For most of those years, we held it at the Dearborn Civic Center. The Civic Center was a magical place. There was a game room in the basement, and several rooms had televisions, each with different shows playing. We mixed with other kids whose families were hosting parties in different rooms there, and it was all friendly fun -- until Santa came.

Our parties ran from noon to about 4 p.m., not that we kept track of the time back then. Santa would usually show up around 3 p.m. He entered through the large hall, and all the kids there would shout his name and run up to him. I confess I was a bit territorial when it came to "our" Santa's arrival.

"He's coming to see us, not you," I'd tell the strangers who, moments ago, had been my playmates, then I'd run ahead to our party room.

Someone, usually Aunt Lily, would lead us in a song like "Here Comes Santa Claus," and we'd all clear a path for him to the special chair at the end of the room. Santa had a large sack when he entered, and somehow several more large sacks, filled with gift wrapped presents, appeared. Aunt Cam always helped Santa by reading out the names on the labels, and young and old came forward to sit on Santa's lap as their names were called. Excited and armed with our gifts, we'd return to our seats to open our new treasures.

One year, remembering my manners and recalling that Santa and I were old time buds (He did come to my house, after all!), I decided to catch up with him as he was leaving -- to say thank you. I stepped into the hall and almost dropped my candy cane.

Santa was kissing my Aunt Cam!

Worse than that, my very own mother appeared to be in

The Vorase Women (six of seven): Stella, Lily, Cam, Grace, Marion, Rose.

line to do the same!

And she did... Mona!

Outraged, I ran in to tell my dad, who just laughed. It was not the reaction I had expected, but I knew Uncle Deno, Aunt Cam's husband, wouldn't take it so lightly. I looked around for him, but he was nowhere to be seen. Did he see it, too, and depart in anger?

When Uncle Deno finally came back into the room he looked flushed and sweaty, and I figured he must have caught up with Santa and let him have it. I never did hear anything more about it, but every year after that time I noticed that Uncle Deno would leave before Santa's arrival, clearly trying to avoid any conflict with the Old Elf.

I felt bad for Uncle Deno, one of my favorite uncles, until a few years later when Santa sent a peace offering...

Santa came and went again, another party over, and everyone was gathering their toys, casserole dishes and coats to leave. Uncle Deno had prudently ducked out to avoid Santa again this year, but now he came in to help clean up. Aunt Cam was gathering Santa's discarded bags and stopped in the center of the room.

"What's this? What's this?" she declaimed, holding one of the bags up. When everyone in the room stopped to look, she reached in and pulled out a small gift box, apparently forgotten by Santa.

"It says, 'To Deno, From Santa,'" Aunt Cam said.

Uncle Deno took the gift in his hand, wrapped his arm around Aunt Cam's waist, and gave her a big kiss -- in front of everybody!

"Santa knows how to put everyone in the Christmas mood," I said out loud, and my Dad ruffled my hair.

Merry Christmas, everyone!

Slow Ride

Originally published January 14, 2021

I drove to Madison Heights last Saturday evening to photograph the Clinton Football Regional Championship game. It was thrilling, and I'm not talking about just the game (which was thrilling in its own right).

I'm talking about the hour and fifteen minute ride there.

When we were much younger, my brother Paul, nicknamed "Death Racer" (by me), was the very definition of an aggressive driver. He would insist on driving anywhere we went, and I would sit, white-knuckled, in the passenger seat, singing his theme song to the tune of Speed Racer, the cheesy anime classic from the late 60s.

"Go, Death Racer

Go, Death Racer

Go, Death Racer, Go!"

Neither my singing nor occasional heartfelt pleas could make Paul slow down; he'd continue his daredevil course, loudly complaining about "old men with hats."

While he railed at elderly drivers in general, calling them "Q-Tips," Paul had a theory that the slowest and most dangerous drivers on the road were old men, and those who donned chapeaus were the worst. Paul would whip past any such car, giving them a wide berth, regardless of their apparent driving acumen. It was like he couldn't bear being near them.

I thought of Paul as I drove the metropolitan freeways of Detroit on my way to the game last weekend...

It has been five years since I raced along with morning traffic during my 60 mile commute to teach in Detroit. I know that I 'kept up with the flow of traffic' then, but I can hardly believe it now.

Cars were on my rear bumper almost the entire way. I'd look down, and yes, I was going the speed limit.

Merging onto the expressway was another hostile experience, as I turned on my blinker, brought my car gradually up to speed to merge seamlessly with the cars currently in the right lane -- only to have the car behind me roar into that lane, pull next to me and glare. Blocked, I had to renegotiate my merge, hoping that the next car behind me wouldn't do the same.

That happened more than once, and combined with the occasional car doing 20 over the limit and weaving in and out of four lanes of traffic like an arcade game, my nerves were nearly cooked.

The final straw came from my Google Maps program, upon which I relied for directions. It decided my best route was I-96 to the Davison Freeway to I-75.

Vehicularly speaking, the Davison was a walk in the park, with lower speed limits and multiple lanes -- think Washtenaw Avenue in Ann Arbor. The drivers were just as aggressive as those on the expressway, but the speeds were much slower.

My distress from driving the Davison came from memories of one of my places of employment called Detroit City High School. It was a violent place, and someday I might just share those stories.

I reached the field of play safely, despite the harrowing journey. I would have kissed the ground if it weren't asphalt.

After the game, I looked forward to a shorter drive to my brother Mark's house. It was dark, but hopefully that meant less traffic. I took a few deep breaths as I entered the car. I said some prayers as I turned the ignition. I steeled myself for the 25 minute ride to sanctuary. Then I looked around the interior.

"Blast! Where is it?" I thought as I continued to search.

I got out, went around the back of the car, popped the deck lid, rifled through compartments, searched the back seat -- for naught.

I was searching for that one talisman that might protect me from danger on the road.

'A hat, a hat, my kingdom for a hat!' I thought, then slipped my hoodie over my head. 'It will have to do.'

***

From being an admitted old man to the days of my youth ... up next ...

Let Me Roll It

Originally published February 4, 2021

Recently, I've been grooving on the latest Paul McCartney album -- McCartney III, which was released in December, 2020. McCartney turns 79 this June, and his music is as good as ever, with new songs that take the listener back to his younger days as a Beatle and as a soloist. "Lavatory Lil," for instance, is reminiscent of "Magneto and Titanium Man" from the 70s, or perhaps the Lennon penned "Polythene Pam" and "Mean Mister Mustard" from the later Beatles albums.

I could write an entire review of the album, but I won't make you suffer. I'm a 'fanboy' when it comes to Sir Paul -- ever since I was about 13 years old.

~~~

It was early in the summer of 1974, and I was riding my Schwinn stingray on my usual course up and down our block, Woodmont Avenue in Detroit, a quarter mile stretch between Paul Road and Whitlock Street. (I looked up the house we lived in at the time -- all five brothers, mom, dad, and dog -- and was surprised to see that the square footage listed for the house is 768.)

Spending so much time riding my bike, I would often stand on the pedals to stretch my legs. Sometimes this was done while also pedalling (in order to go super-fast), and other times I would just coast that way, taking in the scenery.

Back then, we shared things as a community, sometimes for good and sometimes for bad. One neighbor was 'sharing' her music, blasting WRIF radio from her backyard. If I had to guess, she was sun tanning, probably doused with baby oil, a common tanning aid used back then. (Skin cancer hadn't yet been discovered, apparently.) While I am sure the loud music must have been an annoyance to some of the neighbors, I was transfixed. I'll never forget that moment when music found me, and I found it.

It is one of those simple memories, a little mental video clip that can be replayed in the mind's eye with fidelity, transporting the viewer to the past.
~~~

There I was, standing on the pedals of my powder-blue Stingray (with banana seat) and coasting toward Whitlock, when the first guitar notes of "Band on the Run" floated across the street to me. I turned my bike around and circled the street in front of that house until the song ended, then I pedaled home as fast as I could, ran into the den, opened the lid on my mother's stereo console and turned it on. Over the next few weeks, I spent hours each day seeking out rock and roll stations -- WABX, W4, WRIF, and WDRQ.

I soon commandeered that room as my bedroom, claiming the privilege of being the eldest and enlisting my grandmother's support, all to the chagrin of my brothers, especially Paul. After moving my bed into the chamber, I proceeded to hang music posters on the walls, many from McCartney albums, and then I'd intersperse clippings and photos from Cream Magazine. I had become a full-fledged fanboy.

I felt grown up, becoming a teenager that summer, discovering music and getting my own bedroom. It was a heady feeling, and the excitement crescendoed that summer when I held hands with the new girl across the street, Kathy L. Soul.

Being teens, Mona would let us hang out even after the streetlights came on. We would stand on the street corner in groups, talking and joking around after a game of tag, kick the can, or statues. It was a new experience that summer, mixing with the girls so much. Up to that time, the boys would spend all day and evening playing sports -- no girls allowed! Now, it seemed the other guys were eager for the evening to come so we could involve the girls. I didn't understand the shift, until that evening when Kathy grabbed my hand.

We were standing around under the streetlight, talking about music, sports, and bikes -- the important stuff. Sam, who lived down the block, and Patty, one of the Soul sisters, were holding hands, impervious to the jokes made by the rest of us. Sam announced that they were "going together," though to this day I'm not really sure what that meant. Then Sam really got things going.

"Why don't you go with Kathy?" Sam asked, looking in my direction.

"What?" I said, dumbstruck.

He repeated himself, then added, "Everybody knows you like her. You stand next to her every night."

I was unable to deny it, and

as the truth of this revelation dawned on me, my face turned red, then redder, as I felt Kathy slip her hand in mine. All I really remember of it was that it was a sweaty experience, standing there holding hands and feeling guilty every time I had to pull my hand away for a few seconds to dry it off on my shorts.

As I said, I had no idea what "going together" meant, but to Kathy, it apparently meant that I had to grant her access to my growing record collection, among other acts of fealty. Reluctantly, even though I wouldn't even let my brothers touch them, I loaned her a few albums. She offered to reciprocate, but I declined. Her collection seemed to focus on Teen Beat icons like David Cassidy and the Jackson Five.

One evening, I learned that this new sense of shared ownership extended to bicycles. Specifically, she wanted to ride my bike, which was another thing of mine that I never let anyone else touch. Already I was beginning to doubt the value of this couples thing. A few pleasant tingles evoked by sweaty hand-holding seemed to pale when compared to this new conjugal sharing of all my favorite things. 'Hmmm, I might have to rethink this....'

Nonetheless, she insisted, and I relented. She took off on my bike, and as she pedaled away, I thought of something.

"Hey, I need my bike back. I have to go home and get something," I shouted, but she was quick, and with a broad smile on her face she headed off, presumably to demonstrate to the others the newly elevated status of our relationship. (I could practically hear them -- 'Wow, Mike must really like her if he let her ride his bike.')

Still pedalling away from me, she shouted over her shoulder, "You can use my bike."

I didn't want to use her bike, but I did want to follow her to make sure she didn't **ruin** my bike, so I walked over to her big, black, scratched-up Huffy cruiser. It had hand brakes, and the front tire rubbed the fork a little, but I soon got it up to speed.

Determined to catch up with her and my treasured bike, I stood on the pedals and pumped for all I was worth. By mid-block, I was up to maximum speed, which wasn't horrible, considering it was a girl's bike. Still standing on the pedals, wind blowing back my hair, I started to coast.

On the sidewalk, Mona was walking up the street toward me. She said something I couldn't make out, then beckoned me to stop.

So I squeezed the two hand brakes... and that was when I learned that only the front brakes worked.

My perspective of the world shifted -- repeatedly and for the next three seconds -- as I tumbled across the asphalt in the center of the street, just me and Kathy's bike, head over heels and heels over wheels.

I came to a stop about thirty yards past where Mona stood on the sidewalk, calling my name and asking if I was alright. Lifting myself off the pavement, I realized that I wasn't alright -- abrasions covered my body from head to toe, though remarkably I had no broken bones. I pulled Kathy's bike to the side of the road and left it there, going home with Mona to get bandaged up. My Aunt Alberta came over with some kind of ointment and some tweezers to pull the pieces of gravel from my skin.

The next day, I went over to Kathy's house to get my bike and my records back. I had had enough of the whole "going together" thing, having fallen out of love, I think, somewhere between the first and fifth tumble in the street the night before.

The pain and heartbreak of young love wasn't done with me yet, though. As she handed me back my albums, I noticed she had colored in Bob Seger's name on the Beautiful Loser album jacket. Silently outraged, I grabbed my bike and concluded our breakup without looking back.

But the sting of love wasn't done with me. When I got home I inspected my cherished albums and noticed they were all scratched. I later learned that she used one of those automatic devices that allowed you to stack vinyl records -- something an audiophile like me would never have done. I think those scratches hurt more than the ones all over my body.

Perhaps my musical selection for this piece should have been "Love Hurts" by Nazareth, but that song was released in 1975, placing it a year or so after the events just described. Then again, it is now featured in commercials for Aspercreme, which may make it the most appropriate song after all.

***

The original title for this piece had been, "Falling Head Over Heels Out of Love."

You Can't Always Get What You Want

Originally published February 18, 2021

Tuesday was a snow day for most in our area, as the predicted six to ten inches of powdery snowflakes did, indeed, come down overnight.

I remember looking forward to snow days, which meant time off from school, both as a student and then again as a teacher. Nowadays, it just means shovelling.

~~~

As a child, one snow day I remember vividly involved me, a sled, and our icy driveway. I was probably 9 or 10 years old, and our father was at work, which meant the driveway was empty, as Dad took our only car, the family station wagon. This would have been around 1970, and though women were entering and reentering the workforce, Mona remained at home to care for the five of us.

My brothers and I took turns sliding down our icy driveway on the old sled -- the kind with the wooden platform and metal runners. Down we went, into the street -- unworried about cars since we lived near the intersection of Paul Road, a thoroughfare most drivers avoided. We sledded for hours, built igloos (real ones with snow roofs), and even fashioned our own spiral slide, which wrapped around our neighbor's elm tree.

After hours of sledding, Paul and Mark, who were younger than me, went inside. I wanted to do a few more runs down the ice covered driveway, so I continued. Mona told me I had 15 more minutes, then I had to come in for a while. (Those were different times; if we could be outside, we were outside.)

Sledding is a youngster's sport, which most of us discover as we age and realize how much energy is expended getting back up the hill. It's probably why ski resorts, with their chair lifts, are popular with adults. (My wife and I took Nick, our son, to the Wegner Field hill in Clinton when he was young. It was great fun, and we have some fond memories, but I'll have to admit that I don't miss the walk back up those stairs.)

In an effort to get in as many more trips down the driveway
~~~

as possible that day, I started to shorten my return path, eventually just walking up the icy drive. I also found it was quicker to carry the sled on my head than to pull it behind me.

You don't have to be a fortune teller to know what happened next.

I slipped and fell as I neared the top of the hill. Since I was holding the sled over my head, my hands were unavailable to help stop the fall, and I struck the ground face first. (Some might say that explains a lot!)

Ouch!

It hurt, for sure, and I was crying, but real horror dawned when I realized I had broken my glasses. Like Ralphie in Jean Shepherd's "A Christmas Story," I was terrified of the imagined reaction by my parents. Most of us who have been bespectacled since our youth know the feeling, planted in our minds the day we got our first pair.

"Don't you ever break those, or you'll be walking around like a blind man," parents would threaten, or something like that. I don't recall the words, but I know the dread of breaking my glasses was tangible.

Still crying, I picked up my broken frames and the lens which had popped out, and I went inside. I made a beeline to my bedroom, still crying, and threw myself down on the bed. A solution presented itself to me; pray for a miracle.

I placed the pieces of my broken glasses under my pillow and began praying fervently.

"Dear God, please fix my glasses...."

I went on in that vein for minutes that seemed to stretch into infinity, occasionally peeking under the pillow to see if my request had been answered. My specs remained in pieces. I was disappointed.

As an adult, I look back on that and realize that our prayers *are* answered, but like the 1969 Rolling Stones song, "You Can't Always Get What You Want," God instead gives you what you need.

Mona came to my bed and sat on the side, rubbing my back.

"What's the matter?" she asked.

Miserable due to the lack of a miracle and fear of my parents' ire, I blurted out my problem.

"They're just glasses," Mona said, still soothing me. "We can fix them."

I told Mona about my prayers going unanswered, and she told me one of her favorite quotes: "God helps those who help themselves." (Which is attributed to many different sources, including -- erroneously -- the Bible.)

She took me downstairs, got out a roll of tape, and repaired my glasses the old fashioned way. I wasn't the only kid in school with tape on his glasses, and her repair job was just what I needed.

Paul, Joseph, David, Mark, and the author, some time before he reached third grade and got his first pair of spectacles.

Manic Monday
(Or The Little Truck That Could)

Originally published January 28, 2021

Commuting to Detroit from Clinton for eighteen years left me with more than one tale to tell about snowy and icy roads, but the one I call "The Little Truck That Could" stands out.

My family had been in Clinton for a few years, and I had become used to the 60 mile (each way) commute to teach in Detroit. It was probably 2001, and by then I felt I was clever in 'discovering' the back roads to US-23. They weren't necessarily faster than the more direct route along US-12, but it was more consistent -- usually.

One of the unpleasant realities of a long commute was that travel time easily doubled during inclement weather. When we had a big snow, such as we had last week, I usually tried to leave by 5:30 a.m. to make the 8 a.m. first hour bell at school. Arriving on time was almost an impossibility, and more than once I found myself singing "Manic Monday" by the Bangles.

Another unpleasant reality was the delay in decision making from a school district not exactly known for its efficiency. In other words, on many snowy days I found myself pulling into the parking lot at work -- after an arduous three hour trek -- only to find my school building closed.

"It was on Fox Detroit," my assistant principal would say the next day.

"I only get Toledo stations," was my reply.

"You could go online to check," came the helpful response.

"Yes, but they didn't announce the closing until 7 a.m.," I'd answer. "If I'm not already half way here, I'm going to be late."

"Oh," and then they'd usually turn away.

The best solution I came up with was to stay at my parents home in Dearborn Heights the night before if a big storm was predicted. That worked out well, but I still got caught by surprise on occasion.

~~~
~~~

One morning, I woke up to learn that we had an overnight ice storm. The roads were slick, but it was February, which meant all the plows and salt trucks knew the drill -- they got out early and helped make the roads drivable.

I was driving a Chevy S-10 pickup truck at the time. I usually threw bags of sand or potting soil in the back; they added weight and helped the light back end on the rear wheel drive truck hold the road.

Making it out of my subdivision was the first challenge, as it usually gets plowed later in the day by the county.

I took my back road route into work that day out of habit, and it was fine until I turned north on Platt Road, off Stony Creek Road. I had never noticed before, but just before you get to Willis Road, Platt starts a long, gradual incline. I also had never really thought about the fact that once you passed Judd Road, you were committed to continue until you reached Willis.

Two inches of solid ice made me take notice.

I was queued behind six or seven other cars on a segment of road that somehow escaped the salt trucks that morning. None of the drivers in front of me dared to attempt a U-turn, and so they proceeded up the hill -- very, very slowly.

"I'm going to be late. Come on!" I shouted through my windshield. I knew it was icy, but they were being far too cautious...

Fifteen minutes and six cars later, it was my turn, and as soon as I hit the gas I realized I owed my predecessors an apology. My truck fishtailed, so I eased off the gas and got her pointing north again. The S-10 was a four cylinder with a manual transmission -- no traction control, no anti-lock brakes, no four wheel or all wheel drive. Heck, it didn't even have positraction, just standard two wheel drive.

I depressed the accelerator ever so slightly and tried to slowly nudge her across the ice without spinning out. I was moving along at a brisk three feet every 10 seconds or so, and then I noticed that I was approaching a hill.

In all the mornings I had travelled that route, I had never noticed that the road ran uphill the last 200 yards or so before you reached Willis. Still carefully keeping my foot steady on the accelerator, I hit the beginning of the incline and slowed to a standstill. My drive wheel was still spinning, but I was going nowhere.

Since I was no longer moving forward, I decided to stop accelerating, to hit the brake and take a moment to figure out what I was going to do. At that moment, my truck started sliding backward on the ice. I turned to look over my shoulder, thinking I might just slide onto the shoulder and wait it out, or perhaps call a tow truck. The driver behind me changed my mind.

Evidently, she had more faith in my driving skills than I did, as she had steadfastly followed right behind me up the hill. In a second, I was going to crunch into her front end.

I hit the gas and the truck fishtailed, but I managed to correct in time. I had arrested my descent into her grill, but now I was at a stand still again. I had no other choice; I put the pedal to the metal, as they say, and my truck started to actually move forward -- inch by syrupy slow inch.

The progress was agonizing, and my mind raced right along with my engine.

"Will I blow the engine running it full out in first gear like this?"

"What if I hit a patch of dry pavement or salt?"

"What happens if the hill gets too steep up ahead?"

With my window rolled down, I leaned out to look ahead for dry patches. It took nearly 15 minutes to traverse the 100 yards to the crest of the hill, and I was white knuckling it all the way.

Sometimes, Good Reader, you find yourself in situations where you can't appreciate words offered by someone else due to the circumstances, like when you hit your thumb with a hammer and someone asks with compassion, "Are you okay?" You can appreciate their concern later, but not at that moment. It was like that as I was nearing the top of the hill and a big Chevy Silverado was coming the other way. I saw the driver roll down his window and lean out toward me, grinning. He and his passenger both started chanting.

"I think I can."

"I think I can."

"I think I can."

Grimacing at the time, I now appreciate the humor. I think I may have even laughed back then, though not until I started the downward slope and headed to a pay phone to call work. (School in Detroit was open that day, but not for me.) I headed home, grateful for flat roads and the warm cab of my little truck that did.

Cold November Rain
(Sometimes It's Okay to Quit)

Originally published March 4, 2021

Last week, I went to the Clinton Middle School girls basketball game to take some action photos. While our newspaper sports section often focuses on high school sports, I try to include the middle school at least once a season. I'm glad I did because I learned something.

In the middle school girls league, teams play three (3) five minute periods in the first half, and the winning team for each period gets one point, regardless of the actual score. No pressing is allowed during these periods, either. The goal is to let younger players develop skills in a game situation.

You might think that would also naturally be the goal of every coach, but you would be wrong. You may remember me telling you about my first coaching experience with young basketball players. My goal then was win, win, win; It is a fever that most coaches catch, and most coaches, at least at the lower age levels, should try to keep it from consuming them.

This is not to suggest that I don't believe in competition or that I feel that every child deserves a trophy for participating. I just think we need to keep it all in perspective, like CMS coaches Steve Degood and Sue Cornish. They strike a good balance between winning and teaching. Coaches have a responsibility to guide young people in so many more ways than mere technique and the X's and O's of the game.

And sometimes, if the coach is unable or unwilling to be a teacher, then the job falls to the parent. This story is about one of those times.

~~~

My son, Nick, grew up with Clinton Youth Soccer, but around 2011, as he headed into middle school, offerings for boys at that age dropped off, with most boys transitioning to football or even fall travel baseball. To continue his soccer experience, we enrolled him in a soccer league in a nearby city.

The coach of this new team, which I'll call The Devils in this
~~~

story, was an experienced and educated man. I later learned he was a member of my church, too (though I can't say I'd ever actually seen him there).

Like my father, I had always been one of those dads who went to and stayed for every practice. There were usually three of us at each Devils practice. We'd sit in our lawn chairs and discuss politics, jobs, and sports in between second-guessing the coach (as parents often do).

At the end of the first week of practice, the coach held an intersquad scrimmage, and Nick scored the first goal on a brilliant maneuver around two defenders. I was ecstatic, but the coach was even more enthused.

"Good job, Nick. Way to go!" he shouted.

Oddly, a good deal of anger began radiating my way, and it was coming from my sideline buddies, the mood changing from collegial to adversarial. I was surprised, but I honestly didn't really mind. I'm ashamed to admit that I adopted a rather unchristian mind-set.

'The conversation isn't really that great,' I thought, 'and if their boys aren't as good as mine, maybe I shouldn't associate with them...'

I moved my lawn chair a few yards away, though still close enough to hear if they made any more negative comments.

Later, on the drive home with my son, I brought up the goal, hoping to revel in his enthusiasm, but he wasn't very loquacious on the subject. In fact, his demeanor was subdued, so I chalked it up to preteen malaise and quietly replayed the goal in my mind as I drove home, smiling and imagining Nick leading the Devils down the field for goal after goal once competition began.

Little did I know that was to be his last goal of the season. In fact, after that practice, his performance showed a dramatic drop. He seemed to be avoiding the soccer ball, sometimes even appearing to run away from it. The other sideline dads made sure to comment, offering the opinion that Clinton players were not welcome.

I asked Nick about his declining performance after practice on several occasions, though I never got a response until one cold day in November as we drove into the city for an end-of-the-year tournament.

It was raining steadily. About halfway there, Nick spoke up from the back seat. "Do we have to go to this tournament?"

"Of course we do," I snapped back automatically.

"Why?"

"Because we never quit," I said, finishing before I realized how much I was sounding like my father.

Nick was silent, surrendering to what appeared inevitable.

I drove through the rain, windshield wipers thumping back and forth, my only son sitting in misery in the back seat.

<thump> <thump> <thump>

The rain was cold and relentless. I pulled into the parking lot. I looked into the rearview mirror at my wonderful, normally happy son, and then I looked at my reflection and repeated his question silently.

"Why?"

Wipers still thumping, sitting in our warm car, I asked him aloud, "Why don't you want to join your team for the tournament?"

I expected a complaint about the weather, but what I got was a story of bullying. According to my young son, shortly after his impressive goal in practice, the city-living Devils made it clear that he was not to touch the ball again, but if he did, he was to pass it to them ASAP. Nick wasn't the only one, and his compassion for a teammate in similar standing outweighed his concern for himself. What I found unbelievable was his assertion that the coach was aware of it but had purposely ignored it all season.

"You're not going to play soccer today, Nick," I said as I unbuckled. "Stay here."

"Can't we just go home?"

"No, I've got to talk to your coach," I said, and marched through the biting rain to the field.

The head Devil himself (AKA coach) was standing in the center of the field; I approached to inform him that my son was not going to play and that I was pulling him off the team. I also told him of the bullying, and I mentioned a few of the little Devils by name. Silent, he just stared at me, but I could read the look in his eyes.

'This has absolutely nothing to do with soccer.' And...

'I'm trying to win a tournament here.' And...

'Big deal—it's not like your son contributed much anyway.'

I shook my head and walked away, remorseful for what I made my son endure for so long, but thankful that I had both taught and learned a valuable lesson — sometimes it's okay to quit.

That Smell

(or The Green, Green Grass of Home)

Originally published April 21, 2021

Yesterday, when I got to my office, which is now in Downtown Clinton, I noticed a smell I haven't noticed since last spring at the very least, maybe longer. It was a smell that once was completely unfamiliar to my city-nose.

I am a city boy, as most of you know -- born and raised in Detroit. I moved to Clinton when I got married, to a subdivision south of town, and I guess that's about as close to farm living as I'm ever going to get. I never would have thought that I'd get used to that smell, much less enjoy it, but I have a confession...

I love the smell of fresh manure. And no, not in an "I love the smell of Napalm in the morning," Apocalypse Now kind of way. I've genuinely come to enjoy it.

From 1998 to 2016, I commuted from Clinton to Detroit and back again every workday during the normal school year, and often for summer school, too. I admit that I really don't miss the driving, which took about an hour and a half each way. It was the commute home, however, that I began to embrace, and it was that smell of spring agriculture that I was surprised my city-nose grew to love.

On the winding road from Saline to Clinton, I would pass horses grazing in the fields near the road, sheep in their corrals, pigs in their sties, and each had its own special aroma. After smelling truck exhaust fumes along most of the commute, the farm smell was in stark contrast. It was natural.

But it was the emotion it evoked that made it a good smell. It signaled the return to hearth and home, to kith and kin, and the relaxation and love of family, of spending time with my wife and son. I think that's why I grew to love that smell.

Of course, the smell of manure has not always had a pleasant connotation for me.

There were many occasions when this city boy would get stuck behind a semi-truck hauling hogs to the market. Not only did I find the smell unpleasant, but I'll confess to being a little squeamish at seeing my favorite breakfast food so early in the food chain. I can honestly do without that. On a platter with two over-medium eggs and some hash browns -- that's how I've always preferred to view my pork!

Of course, there are other memories evoked by the smell of manure -- changing diapers, for example. I have heard some mothers say they don't mind the smell of their own baby's diaper, but I must be honest. I love my son, and I willingly changed his diapers (when I couldn't get out of it, of course), but I won't say that I enjoyed THAT smell.

THAT smell -- the smell of human waste -- usually evokes bad memories, like spending time in a nursing home to visit a dying loved one.

THAT smell summons one particularly bad memory for me, though I find it comical in retrospect.

~~~

I was in fifth grade, about 10 years old, and I decided to follow the crowd and join the Altar Boys at my grammar school -- St. Christopher Catholic School in Detroit. The Altar Boys (and it *was* a boys-only group back then) was popular; all the boys wanted to be a part of it, not due to our devotion to the Lord, but due to the promised end-of-the-year trip to Boblo Island. Nearly the entire class of boys went to the first practice session immediately after school that fall of 1971.

It was just after Labor Day. Practice was long and hot, as air conditioning was still a luxury rather than a necessity. My classmates and I spent most of the practice on our knees at the altar, listening to one of the two adult leaders lecture us on the structure of the Mass and our roles in it. I'm not sure why we had to spend so much time kneeling, but we were told it was crucial for us to remain motionless -- like statues -- until we were called to duty. I watched our leaders, two brothers in their mid-thirties who seemed to have eyes in the backs of their heads, looking for an opportunity to shift my weight, to temporarily ease the burden on my protesting knees, but they were shifty and lightning-quick, pacing the altar with pointers wielded like machetes, waiting to snap us back to attention.

I'll call them the Special K Brothers because they were truly special. They resembled the Doctor Seuss characters -- Thing One and Thing Two -- in that they were tall, gangly, had
~~~

Brillo-pad hair, and ultimately wreaked havoc on the lives of children, though I won't go into detail about that here.

The Special K Brothers went on and on for over an hour, demonstrating various tasks which we were to perform when we finally had our opportunity to serve, then they announced a short break, to be followed by a second practice for our investiture ceremony. I hadn't known about that.

During the entire first round of kneeling practice, I had not only been concentrating on the pain in my knees, but also on the increasing agitation in my gut, which was gurgling and rumbling loudly, probably from eating one of Mona's famous room temperature tuna sandwiches at lunch. (They were cold when she packed them, but they didn't stand up well in the heat -- definitely a winter sandwich.) I knew I was going to need a bathroom, so I took my five minutes to search for one. I headed toward the main entrance where I knew one to exist -- locked!

The rumble moved lower in my gut, and panic began to bloom. I headed to the altar, where an older student told me there were bathrooms in the back. I went back there, moving as fast as I dared.

'There's a bathroom,' I thought. I reached for the knob and twisted -- locked! One more chance in the next room.

Special K One was coming out of the bathroom there -- I could see the commode -- and the door was closing behind him. I made to rush past him and get inside, but he grabbed my arm.

"Where are you going?" he said.

I thought it was obvious, but I responded anyway.

"To the bathroom."

"No, you're not. Break's over. Get back out there," he said as he gave me a little push.

"But I really have to go!"

"You can go when you get home," he said, and he glared at me with beady, dead-black eyes. He released me and headed back out to the altar, and, as if reading my mind, added, "It's locked anyway."

And it was.

Now I really had to go, but cutting out of practice didn't even occur to me, so I went back to the side of the altar and knelt in place for another hour.

The good news was that my knees didn't even bother me, what with my focus being elsewhere.

Once released, I wanted to

run home, but I didn't dare. My Glutei Maximus (That's the plural form, I learned) was clamped like a vice. It was the only thing that got me through the second practice.

So I started to walk home, looking like a bizarre, young Pee Wee Herman with my light beige, tight, high-water, khaki floods.

'I'm never going to make it home,' I thought with certainty. In my mind, I reviewed the houses along my half-mile path. 'Do I know anyone along the way?'

The answer was yes, of course, but the second question was key.

'Is there a bathroom along the way I could use?'

The answer to that, upon consideration, was "No." This was not going to be a delicate little pitstop.

So I ambled down the street with my odd, clenching gait, sweating as much from the sheer mental anguish as from the physical effort. I got a little more than half way, just south of Warren Avenue, a major road, when the horrible reality could no longer be denied --I had to go now -- RIGHT NOW.

I was just three doors away from Greg Gurka's house. He was a classmate who later became a friend, but at that time, I barely knew him. I just knew he was the tallest kid in the class and that he lived alone with his mother, who was divorced, a relatively rare thing in 1971.

Nonetheless, I had to **Go Right Now,** so I picked up my speed, unclenching slightly to move faster...

...and I did move faster, or rather, a part of me moved faster -- an internal part...

I stood there on the sidewalk, both ashamed and relieved. Horrified by the squishy feeling and the ripe smell, I was also grateful I hadn't gone up to their porch. Apparently, no one knew I was there, so I made the uncomfortable walk the rest of the way home without further incident. (Of course, what else could go wrong after that?)

Mona never commented on the mess, nor did she comment on me showering in the middle of the day, something parents know never happens with preteen boys. That experience foreshadowed my career in general as an Altar Boy, as it turns out; I was kicked out of the group two years later.

Like most life experiences, it turned for the best. And who knows, the experience may prove invaluable as I age; I guess it all Depends. :)

Pennies From Heaven

Originally published April 28, 2021

For a couple years now, I've fancied the notion of literally paying a penny for the thoughts of some people. For instance, I'd be really interested in the thoughts of some of the people who buy the Local off the newsstands, particularly the honor stands.

Honor stands are those that have a payment container, usually a small cylinder with a hole for coins, into which customers may drop payment for that week's newspaper. It's called an "honor" stand because customers are on their honor to pay the listed amount for the paper, which currently is $1.

I remember Maryann Habrick, my predecessor and publisher of the Local for 30 years, occasionally writing about the lack of honor or honesty that was apparent with some of her customers. You see, it's a simple fact of counting the number of papers taken and then counting the money -- when the ratio is not one-to-one, it's fairly obvious someone took papers for less than the listed price. (To be fair, occasionally there is a five or ten dollar bill in the container, so it seems that some people catch up, too.)

Over the years, I've learned to accept that some don't pay, and I try not to think of it as disrespectful. Instead, I try to adopt the mind-set of one of my former high school teachers, Mister Poslako. He was a laid-back dude with a bushy mustache and a tweed jacket, complete with professorial patches at the elbows. He once told me he didn't mind when students kept books they "borrowed" from his classroom bookshelf because he hoped that they benefited from reading it.

I'm truly no longer bothered by underpayment at my honor stands. I'm just glad they're reading it. It does cause me to chuckle, though, especially when I go to one rack in particular.

About two years ago at this particular rack, I noticed a single penny as well as many folded bills. Each week there would be an additional single penny representing one of the newspapers sold. The match was perfect, week-to-week. In the second year, I noticed two pennies each week in addition to the bills. Again, the two pennies were a perfect match for two additional newspapers taken.

Recently, there have been three pennies each week.

The fact that this happens in a restaurant is not lost on me, and this week I had intended to tell the story of The Late Night Term Paper, Mona, and Me. (It follows this story.)

But as I researched the meaning of pennies and finding them, my mind went further afield...

Finding a single penny has positive meanings, more than I initially thought, and I realize that I, too, think of a single penny as a positive thing.

For instance, I always stop to pick up a penny when I see one on the ground. I consider it lucky. I adopted that habit from my former football coach and mentor, Ted Mac. I remember seeing him get so excited when he would find a penny on the ground in the field house. In fact, players got in the habit of dropping pennies on the ground just so the coach could find them.

I found an article about an American practice that I had never heard of -- placing a penny on the gravestone of a military veteran. According to the article, leaving a penny on the headstone of a veteran or military member that you don't know is a sign of respect and gratitude for their service.

Another bit of penny lore I'd never heard came from the internet. It is the story of a man picking up a penny, looking at "In God We Trust," and affirming that he should put his trust in God, the penny being a reminder from God to do so.

Coins have been an important part of my life, not just collectibles, but all coins. I usually avoid spending coins. Instead, I hoard them -- filling jars and cups and canisters. I've only relinquished them on rare occasions.

Once, when my son was in Karen Tice's kindergarten class, they collected coins for the Miles of Pennies collection, started many years ago by long time Local reader Dorrie Blom. The winning class at the elementary school would get a pizza party, and that was all the motivation two helicopter parents (my wife, Debbie, and I) needed. We cracked into my penny collection and sent our young son into school every day with 1,000 pennies. It's heavier than you might imagine, but Nick carried his burden for two straight weeks. Our goal was $100 worth of pennies. His class won the pizza party.

Debbie thought it was newsworthy, and I always took the opportunity to chat with Maryann back when she operated out of the old brown, two-story at 108 Tecumseh Road. I stopped by with a photo of Nick and gave her the information. Being a good reporter, she pulled a little more info out of me than I had intended to share.

"Where did he get all those pennies from?" she asked.

I told her about my stash of pennies, and so the story went from "Nick Gathers and Donates $100 in Pennies" to "Little Kid Dips into Dad's Treasure Trove to Win Pizza."

When we got that week's Local, Debbie was surprised by the slant. I swore up and down that I didn't tell Maryann they were my pennies, that she must have gleaned it, or maybe I just didn't remember telling. (I was just trying to escape my wife's wrath, like most husbands.) Eventually, Debbie and I got a laugh out of that.

Money -- coins in particular -- have been at the center of humorous stories on other occasions.

The first time I took my wife to Las Vegas was in 1996. When she asked about bringing gambling money, my mind went to my coin stash. (I really was in love!) I pulled out the coins and dumped them out, and the two of us spent hours sorting and counting. We pulled out over $300 in quarters and put them in a canvas sack. It bulged like it held Fred Flintstone's bowling ball, but it must have weighed three times as much.

Being nearly half a decade before 9-11, airport security was relatively relaxed, but that didn't stop the security officer at the conveyor belt from opening our luggage.

"What's this?" he said, lifting our canvas sack of quarters a few inches out of the suitcase.

"Quarters," Deb and I said in unison.

"Quarters?" He said, and the look on his face was priceless.

"For the slot machines," Deb answered.

He closed our suitcase and zipped it shut, probably convinced that two people this simple could only be a threat to themselves. As he shook his head and chuckled, I noticed the ATM at the airport, and it dawned on me that there would likely be one when we reached Vegas. In fact, I realized, there were probably many ways the kind people at the casinos could help you get at your money to gamble.

Debbie and I laughed about it on the plane, and flattered ourselves with the thought that we would have a jump on everyone else in that we would be ready to gamble right away.

We came home from Vegas much lighter, if not poorer. (Deb is a lucky girl, but she wisely let them convert her winnings to foldable money instead of refilling our sack.)

One final piece of internet lore on pennies captured my mind -- the belief that the dead -- deceased loved ones, in particular -- use pennies to talk to us. Based on my love of collecting pennies, I think I could believe that.

The three departed loved ones I think of most often are my mom, dad, and Grandma Grace. I'd like to think those pennies represent them.

So now, when I collect from that honor stand, I caress those pennies from heaven that represent my deceased loved ones, and I smile.

They're still with me.

***

Did I really take such a noble stance about being cheated out of 99 cents times three? Heck no! What made me even angrier about that stand, which was at the local Big Boy restaurant, was that someone regularly opened the cheap lock on the box (a recommissioned ballot box) and took most of the folding money, too. For a while, I thought it might have been one of my son's friends who worked there, but it could have been anyone. The total amount taken, I learned after I changed to a thick Master lock, was between $8 and $11, week after week.

So, if you ask me again, Good Reader, if I really had adopted the Zen-like acceptance that my old English teacher had toward theft?

No, it ain't me, babe! No, no, no...

The Late Night Term Paper, Mona, and Me

Originally published May 6, 2021

Growing up, my mother, Mona, and I used to watch old movies together. She had a love of musicals, and I came to share that love. She also loved gangster movies. (Really, just about anything in black and white.)

I remember asking her to watch my all-time favorite black and white movie with me -- Young Frankenstein by Mel Brooks. She liked the character of Igor, in particular.

"He has a face only a mother could love," Mona said of the great comedic actor Marty Feldman, who was known for his peculiar appearance -- big nose, bulging eyes and thick eyebrows. As Igor, with his migratory hump, Feldman was one of the highlights of the movie.

"A face only a mother could love" -- doesn't that summarize mothers perfectly? They are the people who love us, all of us, despite the pimples, scars, and many flaws -- both internal and external.

I have found myself shaking my head at the mothers of convicted criminals, who cry and insist that their baby is a 'good boy' -- all the way to the electric chair. But that would be my mother, too, if I were in the same position. I think it would be the same for all mothers.

No matter how bad, how dark, how selfish, or how embarrassing we are, mothers still love us unconditionally.

Most often, in the recollections I share with you, Good Reader, I might seem to be a wonderful guy. Sure, some of the stories are filled with pathos from a universe aligned against me, but that generally makes me a sympathetic (and hopefully humorous) character. Rarely do I share stories which shine a light on my less attractive nature.

In honor of Mother's Day, however, and inspired by last week's piece, I am going to tell the tale of "The Late Night Term Paper, Mona, and Me."

~~~

After five and a half long years, I was finally nearing the end of my bachelor's degree
~~~

work at Wayne State University in Detroit. (Indecision as well as a few failures added the extra year and a half to the normal duration.) During my time at Wayne State, I worked full-time -- at least 40 hours per week -- and kept 'full time' credits, a minimum of 12.

Not wanting my undergraduate work to take an even 6 years, I took 19 credits in my final semester in the summer of 1984. I also added another full time job to pay for car repairs (times two) to my 1980 Volkswagon Rabbit Diesel. (That's another story, or maybe two!)

I was chronically fatigued that summer, and I took it out on those around me.

Once, coming home from work, I asked my youngest brother, David, AKA Dewey, who was about 13 at the time, to toss the car keys to me from the porch. He did.

Apparently, lack of sleep had a significant impact on my reflexes, because the keys went right past my outstretched hand and clunked me in the face. It really was *my* fault on at least two levels, but I took it out on him. I sprinted to the porch and gave him an uppercut to the solar plexus.

"Oooof."

He didn't say anything else, and neither did I. At the time I felt he deserved it, but that sound and the image of him doubled over and looking up at me in pain is still clear as anything in my mind. I think I have since apologized to him, hopefully more than once, but if not, let me do so again. I'm sorry for that, Dewey. Please forgive me.

That same mean spirit was not limited to family.

Mona worked for the Detroit Public Schools Board of Education at the School Center Building on Woodward Avenue. She was a secretary in the special education department, and she was a great typist. Her other skills included being able to decipher my scrawling penmanship. Naturally, I took advantage of her good nature and her lunch hour and made my way across the Wayne State campus to her office on the fourteenth floor whenever I needed a paper typed.

One day, I had worked most of the night on a particularly long paper that included footnotes. Back in those days, some professors allowed you to identify your sources using notes at the end of your paper, which made typing easier. Others, however, insisted that footnotes belonged at the foot of each page, which made typing a real challenge in the days before computers and word processors. I knew Mona could handle that with ease, so I headed to her office with 15 pages of nearly illegible notes in hand.

"Hey, Mom, do you have time to type a paper during your lunch today?" I asked, confident that she wouldn't think of declining -- and I was right.

"Sure, just let me check with my boss," she said. "How much do you have?"

I held up the wad of papers.

"That's nothing," she said. "Do you want to go for lunch afterward?"

I knew she meant that she would treat me to lunch, as she always did, but I felt I had to show some gratitude, so I insisted it would be my treat.

Mona typed the paper faster than I would have imagined, and I sat in the chair next to her desk, half dozing as I waited for her to finish. When she finished, we headed downstairs and decided to try a new restaurant in the same building.

We were early for lunch, and the place looked like it had just opened. Wait staff was running hither and yon, taking chairs off table tops and wiping everything down.

We requested coffee as we were seated. It was really the only thing on my mind at that time. I wasn't much fun in the way of conversation to start our lunch date, and I got even worse as time passed. Mona tried pleasant small talk, but, after pulling an all-nighter, I was focused on one thing -- coffee.

There were only a few other patrons there, so I figured this wouldn't take very long. I was mentally planning the rest of my day as Mona and I sat there:

1. Drink coffee,
2. Turn in paper,
3. Drive home,
4. Sleep for 10 or more hours.

I watched as the wait staff ran back and forth, but nobody came our way -- with or without coffee. In fact, nobody even brought us a menu or water. We sat there and watched servers buzzing by to tables near us, bringing drinks to customers who entered after us. Still no one came to our table.

Being a participant in the food service industry for most of my youth, I wondered how long it would take for a waiter or waitress to get to our table. I calculated the deduction in tip as the minutes went by. Like a student in a classroom, I raised my hand; I even waved my hand, but servers seemed to be wearing blinders as they walked past, on their way to serve yet another customer before us. I grew angry, and I started to complain loudly.

"I can't believe it!" I said in a loud voice. "What kind of place is this? How long do we have to wait for a cup of coffee?"

The staff seemed to be wearing earplugs, as well, because my tantrum didn't even elicit a single flinch. It was like we were in another dimension, invisible and inaudible since the moment we took our seats.

"Don't worry, Mike. I'm not in any hurry. I can get back to work late," Mona said. Of course, at that time, my selfishness kept me from even considering the impact on her.

"No it's not about being in a hurry, Mom. It's about service."

"Relax. It'll be okay," she said, trying to sooth her twenty-something toddler. "We'll just sit here and have a nice conversation until a waiter comes by..."

"Relax? How can I relax? I need a cup of coffee!"

At that point, I knew we weren't in the Twilight Zone because patrons from the tables closest to us began to stare at me. Perhaps my Aura of Anger radiated out from our table, repelling wait staff like some invisible force field. Today, I can imagine their conversation as they glided past each other and past our table.

"Are you taking that table over there?"

"Are you kidding? That's not my section."

"Marge is supposed to cover that area. Where is she?"

"Don't know -- I haven't seen her since steam started coming out that dude's ears."

Mona and I sat there for nearly 30 minutes as people around us began to get first their drinks and then their food. Finally, I said I'd had enough and pulled two pennies from my pocket. I placed one where my lunch should have been placed and the other at Mona's place setting.

I made sure to stop to complain to the manager on the way out. Later, I realized that it was a new restaurant with a new wait staff, and there was obviously some confusion about who covered which table. I also realized how embarrassing I must have been to my mother as I sat there complaining loudly from my seat, then complaining to the manager and placing those two pennies -- the ultimate sign of displeasure in the restaurant business.

Despite all that, Mona accompanied me to another nearby restaurant where we grabbed a carry-out meal and took it back to her office to eat. She never complained about my behavior or said I embarrassed her that day. I don't think I saw anything but love in her eyes.

At that time, with my angry temperament and ugly face, she loved me as only a mother could.

Thank you, Mona, and Happy Mother's Day to all mothers; your unconditional love is a true gift.

***

Stories like this one are difficult to include; we like to edit our past; don't we, Good Reader? Cut out the ugly parts and embellish the mediocre -- it's what we do when recounting our lives.

My initial thought, on reading this again five years after it was originally written, is how the food service industry has changed due to Covid 19. Servers sneer at tips below 20% -- even 25%.

My wife, who loves Facebook, told me someone recently reported enjoying a fine dining experience that yielded a bill of about $120, for which they left a twenty dollar bill as the tip. The post went on to say that, as they left, their server caught up with them by the door and said, "If you can't afford to drop a fifty (as a tip), you shouldn't go out to eat."

Being the marvelous mathematician that I've described heretofore, I recognize that the original tip was below 20%, which has always been a traditional mark for good service. A $50 tip on the same bill, on the other hand, would have been a 40% gratuity.

Excessive, in my book, but my brother, Dewey, and his friend, Vance, espoused the same steep expectation when they worked as waiters at a fancy Italian restaurant in Detroit around the time of my story. Their philosophy had been that if you were wealthy enough to afford an expensive meal, you were also rich enough to over-tip.

In the name of self-preservation (and with the hope of ever being served a good meal in public again), I'd better stop right here. Moreover, if I do venture into a restaurant again in hopes of good service and an unadulterated plate, I'd better wear my pandemic outfit, shown on page 186, minus the printed identifier.

As a "media worker," I was considered an essential worker during the pandemic, and the outfit shown was my favored garb.

The Art of Short Order Cooking

Originally published May 21, 2020

I enjoy cooking at home. I always have. Now that we are required to eat all of our meals at home (during Covid) -- even those we pick up from a restaurant -- cooking them at home has lost its sparkle. There is a growing desire to once again sit in a restaurant and dine OUT! I'm sure I'm not the only one to feel that way.

Thus thinking of food, as I do far too often, I recalled my first experiences in the culinary arts.

~~~

I turned 14 in 1975, and the allure of having my own spending money --- real cash, not the crumbs I had been getting from infrequent lawn mowing jobs or unsuccessful paper routes -- made my ears perk up when my friend and neighbor, "Alpo," mentioned that the corner restaurant was hiring.

Alpo lived across the street and was the younger brother of my best friend at the time, Geo. Alpo, named Alfred by his mother, was a cook at the Clock Restaurant on West Warren Avenue in Detroit. He told me they needed a dishwasher, and since the place was only half a mile from home, I eagerly walked there to apply.

I was hired to work the weekend breakfast shift, which apparently was unpopular with other workers, but I was glad to be able to take those hours since I could continue even after school resumed in the fall.

We were paid every other week, and my first check grossed $51.20 for the 32 hours I worked. (Minimum wage then was $1.60 per hour.) After taxes, I took home almost $40 a week -- a lot of moolah, in my young mind.

I held that job for two years, and in the spring of 1977, when I was 16, they started to put pressure on me to learn how to cook.

I had washed dishes for the legendary Mike Nice (pronounced like the city in France). Mike was a thin fellow about four years older than me. I learned a lot about short order cooking from him, and when he got busy, he'd call me in to assist -- making toast, side dishes,
~~~

and soups. On Sunday mornings during 'church rush,' the sixty-five seat restaurant would fill up all at once, making it difficult for even Mike to handle by himself.

As the summer of '77 approached, he got the directive from the manager to train me to cook, so I spent as much time in the kitchen as possible, running back to the dishwasher to keep up in between stints as his assistant.

It was short order cooking; flipping burgers and pancakes and frying breakfast meat on a grill doesn't seem to be that tough. However, Good Reader, let me assure you that there is some skill involved.

For one, flipping eggs to make them "over easy" requires a touch that only comes with practice. For another, cooking a steak to satisfactory specifications -- rare, medium, medium rare -- was another skill that required experience. And, of course, cooking multiple orders at the same time required practice, practice, and more practice.

Mike trained me for a couple weeks. He let me try some of the above, but, being proud of his reputation for fast, quality service, he'd quickly step in and take over when it appeared I wasn't getting it. After two weeks, he recommended I train on the afternoon shift as it was typically slower than days. That's when I met Vasco.

Vasco was a short, skinny man with an accent that I placed as somewhere other than rural or urban U.S.A. (Well, I was no linguist, after all!) He loved talking with the waitresses, or rather at them.

Whereas Mike was obviously well liked by the waitresses (They fairly purred when they spoke to him.), Vasco was coarser and, consequently, barely tolerated by the waitresses. I can't repeat his rambling patter here, but the common theme focused on how he -- and he alone -- knew exactly how to make any woman happy. He would occasionally pantomime his vile thoughts. As I have noted in other stories, I was a naive young man, and "training" under Vasco was as uncomfortable as it was uninstructive. I learned nothing about cooking from him; all I learned was "The World According to Vasco," which I was sure would never prove useful to me. After two weeks of that, he pronounced me ready to handle my own shift.

I still didn't really want to become a cook, and I told the manager so. That's when she called in her son, who also cooked. He was in his 30s -- ancient to me then, and he used the age gap to impress upon me his sagacious world view.

"If you learn to cook, you'll always have a job," he said. "Look at me; I'll always have a job because people always have to eat."

Now you might think that was it, Good Reader, but you would be wrong. He managed to go on with the theme for what seemed like hours to me, as I stood there by the dishwasher looking up at him. There was an urgency in his voice, and he apparently was not going to relent. Worn down, I agreed to be promoted to cook.

Due to my youthful naivety, which I have mentioned in other stories, I hadn't taken their eagerness to "promote" me as anything other than good intentions. Moments after it was announced that I would become a cook, however, one of the main waitresses walked around proudly telling everyone that now both her daughters could work with her, the youngest taking my slot as weekend dishwasher.

I was beginning to realize that the declarations of Mike, Vasco, and the older and wiser cook meant nothing. I wasn't ready to cook by myself, and I knew it.

"Don't worry," the manager said, "We'll start you off on a midnight shift during the week. It should be slow."

It sounded right to me on the surface. How busy could it get on a Thursday night from 10 p.m. to 6 a.m.? Hey, maybe I could handle it.

When the big night came, I showed up to work and Sandy, the sole waitress for that midnight shift, met me with a less than warm and fuzzy greeting. That's probably because she wasn't a warm and fuzzy person. I knew Sandy from Saturday and Sunday mornings, when she would be signing out as I was signing in. She was a big, tough, brusque and hard-edged woman, and I choose those descriptors as a kindness when compared to the alternatives.

"What are you doing here?"

"I'm the cook," I answered proudly as I tied on my apron.

"Oh, #@*% NO!" she said, picking up the telephone to call the manager. When her demands that "a real cook" be sent immediately seemed to be ignored, she hung up and tried the owner. She even tried calling Mike, who must have certified that I was "ready." The Mike Nice stamp of approval seemed to calm her.

"You'd better be able to handle it," she said, still glaring, though the smoke had stopped pouring from her ears.

At that moment I felt anger toward her, indignant over her doubt and lack of faith in me. A couple hours later, I was starting to relate to her doubt in me, and by the middle of bar rush, I was actually feeling sorry for *her*.

It was supposed to be a slow shift, but nobody apparently told the bar go-ers across the street. Maybe someone was celebrating a birthday, or some drunkard loudly offered to treat everybody to a late/early breakfast. Either way, the sixty-five seat restaurant filled up all at once around 2:30 a.m., and Sandy began posting meal tickets to the cook's wheel with lightning speed.

I made a lot of dishes that night, most of them much slower than an experienced cook, but many may have been okay. The real problems surfaced as I tried to hide the fact that I had yet to learn how to flip an egg without breaking it. I tried to hide it with the toast, but some of the patrons weren't drunk enough to settle for that. Sandy brought breakfast order after breakfast order back to my window. I'd dump dozens of eggs before I got one unbroken pair of over-easies, but then the order was sent back because everything else was cold. And, of course, I had several steak orders from the big spenders. Sending food back that evening seemed to be a running joke throughout the dining room, and I think even Sandy was getting some enjoyment about making me cook so many dishes over. It was as if she was saying, "See, I told them you aren't a cook."

The shift couldn't end soon enough, but I didn't quit. My Dad taught us never to quit anything, and that, for the most part, has been good advice for life.

I didn't have to quit, but I wasn't fired. I simply was never scheduled to work again. I remember asking the manager for my dishwasher's job back, and that was when I realized their plan.

"That position is filled," said the manager. "We'll call you when something opens up."

As I said, I was pretty naive then, but at least I knew better than to wait by the phone.

Sylvia, Sausage Gravy, and the Mechanical Cook

Originally published June 4, 2020

Last week, Good Reader, I told you about how inept I was as a short order cook. Nonetheless, when I returned to my parents home in Detroit in the middle of my almost six year undergraduate stint, I decided that I would apply for jobs as a short order cook. Like the Little Engine That Could, I found myself repeating the mantra, "I think I can. I think I can."

I knew I couldn't go back to the Clock Restaurant. (Someone might remember me!) Since my parents had moved west to Dearborn Heights while I was in college (And, yes, they did leave me a forwarding address!), I decided to look in that area. I put in applications up and down Telegraph Road (US-24) in Dearborn and Dearborn Heights.

By the time I hit my 20s, my confidence was so high that I thought I could do anything. So when I walk into the Ram's Horn restaurant, the owner gave me an interview on the spot.

You may have come to think of me as a steadfastly honest person, Good Reader, and I do try! However, I must warn you ahead of time that the following discourse is riddled with fabrications and truths stretched like taffy in a Mackinac Island fudge shop. Since my experience at the Clock, I hadn't touched a frying pan outside of my own house. (Mom was a good cook, but my brothers and I always made our own breakfast.)

"Short order cook, huh?" the Ram's Horn owner asked.

I blinked. Maybe twice. I hadn't expected to be interviewed, but I slipped into con-artist mode with alarming fluidity.

"Yes, at the Clock in Detroit," I said, and that was true -- technically.

"How long?"

"Oh, about two years," I said, rolling my years as a dishwasher into it. I had, after all, helped the head cook for most of that time.

"You know John Kanakas, the owner (of the Clock)?" he asked, and this time he locked eyes with me. I imagined him making a phone call to check my story. These restaurant owners must all know each other! My slick veneer cracked, exposing a look of panic, just for a second. I started to stammer, but he interrupted me.

"There's a guy who's opening a new restaurant down the street," he said. "He needs some experienced cooks to help him open it."

At the time, I thought he had fallen for my deception. Later, I realized he was sending me to his future competition. If he thought I had the right pedigree, he'd have kept me for his own restaurant.

I went down to the corner of Ford and Telegraph Roads in Dearborn Heights, the future home of Lynn's Family Restaurant. Leon Lynn met me there, interviewed me, and asked me to demonstrate my skill by making breakfast for him. Just my luck, he wanted his eggs over easy. I flipped and flipped, breaking yolks each time. He was patient and understanding when I explained that I was rusty after years away from the profession. Or perhaps he was just desperate for a cook. Either way, I made it past the egg test.

"You'll get better with time," he said. "Do you know how to make country gravy?"

Lee was a southerner. It was obvious in his dialect. I was a sheltered Detroiter, and I had never heard of country anything. The way Lee's eyes lit up, I knew it was something special to him, so I happily followed instructions and made a batch of country gravy, frying the sausage and saving the grease to make a roux. He had me try it, and I'll admit that I not only enjoyed it, but I ate it with gusto. I think my display of appreciation for his favorite food was what got me on Team Leon, so to speak.

Eventually, I got pretty good at short order cooking. Lynn's seated about 50, including 10 stools along the counter, which faced the grill. I remember really being in rhythm one busy morning and hearing a child behind me tell his mother, "Look, Mom. He's moving like a robot!"

At first it was uncomfortable cooking with my back to the audience, especially when the customers wanted to converse, but I gradually grew used to it. What was more uncomfortable was working with Sylvia.

I was originally paired with a waitress named Audrey, a beautiful (but spoken for) brunette. Sylvia filled in when one of the full time waitresses was absent. When Audrey quit, she became my full time partner.

Sylvia was an older lady who kept her silver hair in a tight bun and always wore a smile. She was pleasant to work with, except when she needed to walk to the other side of the counter. As I cooked, with my back to the customers at the counter, Sylvia would try to squeeze by me to get to a customer on the other side, which was where the regulars sat. If I was preoccupied or not fast enough, she would already be upon me, leaving me with no choice except to push up against the grill as tight as I could in order to allow her room to get through. I neglected to mention, Good Reader, that Sylvia was a large woman -- one of the largest I have ever seen.

Pushing against the grill was uncomfortable, to say the least. It was hot, and it was belt high -- almost. Actually, it was about four inches lower; like I said -- uncomfortable.

I began to challenge myself when I noticed she was coming my way. I'd sprint to the opposite end of the counter and wait for her to pass, hoping to return to the food I had been cooking before it burned. Then, when she had taken the order or refilled the coffee, I'd do it again.

Such gymnastics had its own benefit. I was never thinner than when I cooked there.

It was mostly good to work with Sylvia, though there was one day that was not so great.

One day, when I was training under Mike Nice at the Clock (while still washing dishes), he got into it with one of the waitresses. As I had said last time, the waitresses uniformly adored him, and he was generally charming to them, except for the time one of them "jammed him up."

The waitress may or may not have realized it, but she filled the wheel with order after order for the Great Mike Nice. He grinned and called me in to work toast and side dishes, and then he went into overdrive. Moving with aplomb and precision, he loaded one grill with hash browns, another with bacon and sausage, and got eight egg pans prepared. He stopped me when I started putting down toast.

"We're going to put these all up at the same time," he declared, then he explained he was teaching the waitress a lesson for "jamming" him. When he had filled the warming counter with dishes and had the overflow sitting on the boards in front of and behind him, he began calling the offending waitress's name and ringing the bell repeatedly.

"Order up! Order up! Order

up!" he said in staccato, interspersed with the ringing of the bell.

He had made his point.

This event flashed through my mind one Sunday morning as the church rush flowed into Leon's. I watched Sylvia make her way to table after table, taking order after order. Incredulous, I even watched as she walked past me with her nearly full pad to take counter orders, too. After she took everyone's order in the restaurant, she started putting the orders up for me. Running out of space, she began to neatly line them up along the salad bar all the way to the coffee machine -- about eight feet of tickets with two, three and four orders apiece. I didn't move a muscle until she was done. I stood there waiting for her to respond to my glare, but she didn't. She simply picked up the coffee urn in one hand, the decaf in the other, and made her rounds.

I admit to having a mean streak, Good Reader. Even my own mother once called me her "mean one." So I can't deny I'm a bit ashamed to say that I "pulled a Mike Nice" on Sylvia and piled up the orders for her. Unlike Mike, however, I had no bell to ring, but got satisfaction for a minute or two by calling, "Order up, Sylvia! Order up!"

Guilt set in quickly, however, or perhaps it was the pride I had developed in my cooking. I certainly didn't want these culinary masterpieces to go cold before they got to table, and if I let my retribution play out, I might end up recooking some of the orders, and then the joke would be on me. Plus, I had begun to feel sorry for Sylvia. Maybe it had been a momentary lapse of judgement on her part.

I picked up platters of food and began to deliver them. Later, I apologized to Sylvia, and we came to an understanding about spreading out orders.

I left Lynn's restaurant after about two years of working there, and about a month after I left, arson investigators were knocking on my door. Someone had torched Lynn's Family Restaurant. I was a former employee. Did I have a bone to pick with Leon? I told them that, in fact, I liked the guy. They seemed satisfied and left.

Up to this moment, I never realized that summer should be dubbed "The Summer of Arson," as it was also the time when my car was torched.

As I said last week, I look forward to enjoying a meal while seated in one of our fine local establishments, but until then, Good Reader, "Bon Appétit!"

Field of ~~Dreams~~ Tomatoes

Originally published May 20, 2021

I finally made it to a home baseball game last week on Saturday. The weather was beautiful, and it was the first day of no Covid-19 masking, at least outdoors.

I still wore my dark, wrap-around sunglasses, though. They are the kind that prompt complete strangers to walk up to me and ask, "Have you just had eye surgery?"

(I'm not kidding. That's happened twice in the past few months.)

Those shades were useful in the bright sun, though they proved to be a disadvantage, too.

I strolled into the ballpark, watching the action on the field and daydreaming about one of those great baseball movies.

I should have been watching

My pandemic gear.

where I was going...

Down I went -- on both knees and one hand. The other hand held my camera aloft. I racked up my left knee a bit, but the camera was safe -- bonus number one. Bonus number two was that I went down behind the bleachers. No one saw me, or perhaps, since it was on the visitors side, no one cared.

I wasn't hurt much, though I could see by the darkening circle in the dust on my jeans that I had somehow skinned my knee through my pants.

What really hurt was my pride. I had tripped over a dried up rut in the dirt that had been left by a truck passing through during the rainy season, which led to several game cancellations earlier in the year.

I tripped on a rut?

Worse, as I was gathering

myself there on the ground, a toddler trundled by, easily navigating the odious rut. He was smarter than I had been; his eyes were fixed on the path ahead.

Inspired by his success and eager to avoid further embarrassment, I finally got up, brushed off the dust and continued forward.

A young mother came to gather the toddler as he raced past me, and I recognized Kristi Shadley, who was probably there to watch her son, Nik, play varsity ball. She asked if I was alright. (Apparently, I had not gone unnoticed.) Her concern was a balm of comfort -- better than a bandage.

I felt like a toddler myself, and I started to think about growing old and how we tend to retrace the steps of our youth -- in reverse, both physically and mentally.

I didn't stay in that mental rut for too long, thankfully. The task of taking photos demanded my full attention, particularly when I reminded myself how much more a fastball to that knee would hurt, as I planned to take photos from inside the protective fencing.

Between innings, my mind wandered, and I started to think of great baseball movies again. One of them was "Field of Dreams" starring Kevin Costner. In my mind I could see the endless fields of corn, and my mind wandered again, crossing over to another recent conversation about gardening.

~~~

And then it was the early 1990s, and I was in my little backyard of my 960 square foot brick home in Redford, Michigan. Most of my yard was concrete, but I left very little lawn in the back, preferring to till most of it for gardening.

I planted a peach tree, a pear tree, grape vines, strawberries and the usual garden veggies. Being single, though, some years I would get too busy to plant, and my seedlings would wither in the sun before I got them in the ground. Other years I would be too busy to harvest.

One spring, I got out with my roto-tiller in early April and cultivated the whole garden area, turning all the old mulch, branches, and tomato bushes from the previous year back into the soil.

Then I got really busy, and I didn't get out to the backyard again for anything but a casual glance until almost 2 months later, after Memorial weekend. That's when I noticed my Field
~~~

of Dreams, which was actually a field of tomatoes.

Apparently, when I cultivated in the fall and then again in early April, I tilled hundreds of tomatoes that I had left to rot. All of those seeds germinated and grew, and now I had a field of tomatoes!

I almost couldn't bear to destroy *any* of the plants, but I knew that they all couldn't produce fruit, crowded as they were, so I started thinning the field. I weeded them out until I had a mere 72 tomato plants standing. I spent a pretty penny on tomato cages that year, but I looked over my field of dreams with great pride for the next month or so.

Eventually, I realized that there really *could* be too much of a good thing. What I was going to do with all those tomatoes?

I began to distribute them to coworkers, neighbors, and family, until they began to balk at my generosity.

I mentioned my bountiful harvest to my grandmother, Grace Aiello. She offered to give me her 14 quart canner.

"You'd give me your canner, Grandma?" I asked, touched by her generosity.

Granny was always generous, especially when it came to food. She'd empty her "ice box" anytime one of us grandchildren visited. Even as accustomed as I was to her generous nature, I had to reject the offer.

"Oh, I really couldn't take that, Granny. Didn't Grandpa give that to you?"

"Non si preoccupi. Pasta fagioli. Ho un sacco di polpettone," she said, though it was probably something else that sounded like that. I added the Italian to give this tale some authenticity, even though the above reads, "Don't worry about it. Pasta with beans. I have plenty of meatloaf."

I had always heard that Grandpa had given Granny the pressure cooker, aka canner, as an anniversary gift, and that was true. What I failed to realize, being relatively young and unmarried, is that Granny loathed the item, never used it, and probably brought it up whenever she needed to put Grandpa back in line.

So I took Granny's canner and even got about 100 mason jars from her neighbor across the street. I took everything home and told my brother, Mark, who was living with me at the time. He came up with the brilliant idea to make and can homemade salsa.

Mark and I canned all Saturday afternoon one day in August, filling over a hundred jars with his homemade salsa. It was only after we finished that I considered that I didn't really even like salsa that much and wouldn't possibly ever eat that much, so now I found myself giving away jars of homemade salsa instead of fresh tomatoes.

Despite the nightmare of overabundance, that garden really was my field of dreams. I've never had such a prolific garden since. I intend to plant a garden again this year, but on a smaller scale. If I am lucky enough to have extra veggies, I'll bring them to the Clinton Farm Market, which should be starting soon.

If that doesn't happen, I'll just put them on your porch, ring your doorbell and run!

***

As I prepared the above recollection, I grew nostalgic. I'm unsure if I prepared much of anything that year. It feels like ages since I've gardened!

I wouldn't mind trying my hand at it again sometime -- as long as it wouldn't require me to dig in the dirt, sweat in the hot sun, or do any physical labor whatsoever, for that matter.

Do you have a garden, Good Reader?

Maybe I could come over some time? I'll bring my folding chair, umbrella, and a cooler of refreshment for two...

Deal?

***

As I reflect on the next story, I am a full week into a rather extreme, medically supervised diet through the University of Michigan. I needed it, as you may have been able to discern by previous stories.

Success when dieting is all about attitude, and I need to change my attitude (and consequent behavior) toward food. Here are two deleterious precepts I've lived by in the past, demonstrated in the next tale:

1. Never waste food.
2. In order to truly celebrate, you need to be eating!

I'll just blame my Italian heritage...

Fool for the City... Chicken

Originally published June 10, 2021

Last weekend, my wife, Debbie, and I went to Grand Rapids to celebrate the wedding of our nephew, Joseph Earl Conklin, to his lovely bride, Emily. One of the highlights of any wedding, after the exchange of vows, of course, is the wedding feast.

The food at this reception was delicious, and, as you can see by my picture on this page, I am far too often preoccupied by food, but there you have it.

They started with hors d'oeuvres immediately after the wedding ceremony, and finished with a delicious meal. My wife had the chicken, and I had the beef. Both were delicious. (I sampled hers, too.)

Thinking about wedding cuisine caused me to recall my own wedding and our subsequent banquet. We held it at a Knights of Columbus Hall in

Debbie and I pose for a picture at her nephew's wedding reception in 2021.

Detroit and made use of one of the wonderful Polish cooks that populated the area. We had the usual mostaccioli, but we also had Golumpki (otherwise known as stuffed cabbage) and City Chicken.

City Chicken is a dish, believe it or not, that doesn't typically involve chicken at all. It consists of battered, breaded, and skewered chunks of pork and veal, roasted in an oven. To my surprise (and secret delight), we had at least a whole pan of the stuff left after our reception, probably 60 kabobs, or so. Never having been one to let food go to waste, I insisted we take it home and have it for the gathering of close friends and family the next day at our house.

That next day, we parceled out City Chicken to whoever would take some, but still ended up with two large freezer bags full. We put those in the refrigerator.

Two days later, we were to begin our honeymoon -- a romantic trip to destinations between Las Vegas and San Diego. We had saved (and spent) all our money on the wedding and reception, so this first honeymoon was mostly on a budget, part of it to be spent in a free Las Vegas condo given to us as a gift and part of it to be spent on a good friend's living room floor in San Diego. Despite the parsimonious nature of this trip, we decided to splurge on the first night, which we were considering our "real honeymoon night."

We arrived at Paradise Point Hotel in San Diego in the early afternoon, and though our check-in time was 3 p.m., we were invited to enjoy the pool.

"We can check your bags at the desk until your rooms are ready," said the helpful concierge, "then we'll deliver them to your room."

"Sounds great," Debbie and I said in unison.

We turned to go, eyes on the sparkling pool with its waterfall and swim-up bar, when I remembered something that was sure to make the afternoon perfect...

"Hold on. I want to get something from my luggage," I said, and pulled out the remains of the last bag of City Chicken, which I had securely tucked between my underwear and my socks.

Debbie and I staked out prime spots near the pool, right in the California sun so we could get a tan. (That's what we did in those days!) It was late June in southern California, so the weather was, in a word, perfect -- 80-some degrees with low humidity and a sweet, salty breeze coming off the bay. I set the bag of City Chicken on the hot cement next to our pool recliners while we enjoyed the pool and the swim-up bar. After a couple hours of drinking and swimming, we returned to our recliners.

"I'm hungry," I said, and immediately reached for the Bag-O-City-Chicken.

"Think it's still good?" Debbie asked.

"Of course it is," I said, feeling the bag. "In fact, it's nice and warm, almost like it just came out of the oven!"

Now, most of you out there know where this is heading, even though I didn't see it coming at the time. I really should have seen it, however, in the eyes of the lady in the pool side recliner next to Deb, when she politely -- but *very* firmly -- declined my proffered bag of pork on a stick.

"It's delicious," I said around another mouthful, "Are you sure you won't try just one?"

Debbie, my faithful new wife, however, was not shy about it, probably knowing that this was going to be the only dinner offered by her frugal new husband.

We sat there for a few more hours, watching the sun slide westward in the sky, nibbling on our sun-warmed pork and continuing to drink the fruity adult beverages that were part of our honeymoon suite package. Other patrons had been steadily leaving pool side, leaving us in relative solitude, and our conversation turned intimate.

Tonight was going to be the big night of romance, especially since the rest of our vacation was planned for my buddy's floor.

Debbie made a flirtatious remark.

I followed with what I thought were romantic and irresistible lines. (Don't ask me what they are now. I've been married for over 20 years!)

Deb said something in a sultry voice, and that was enough provocation for me.

"Come on, baby, let's go to our room," I said confidently. This was going to be a honeymoon night to remember! Visions of the ultimate sensual encounter filled my mind, so much so that I could barely see the walkway in front of me, or was that due to something else?

When we entered the honeymoon suite, Debbie excused herself to take a shower. I looked out the window at the romantic sunset that was waiting for us, radiant light flashing on the gentle ripples in the bay, sailboats silhouetted in the distance, kites soaring from a nearby dock, and all I felt was...

...sick. I was sweaty, and my stomach started to flip, turning itself into a tight knot. I fell to the bed, not daring to move, as the pain spread to my lower intestines. Debbie came out of the shower -- sans towel -- and I let out a moan -- which she realized was one of pain. Eventually, she joined me in bed, and we moaned for hours, but not in the way that honeymoon suite was accustomed to, I'm sure.

We both passed out sometime early in the evening, but in the morning, we were fine.

There were a few skewers of

City Chicken left, and I'll admit that it was with some hesitancy that I threw them away -- waste not, want not.

We left those fine digs for eight days of enforced celibacy on a living room floor, but we had a marvelous time in San Diego nonetheless. So much so that I suggested to Debbie that we uproot and live there.

***

Now, I am aware that half of the "Good Readers" out there are of the feminine persuasion, so I'll add here that Debbie did get a much better honeymoon the following summer when we took a two week Caribbean cruise aboard a three-masted tall ship named Mandalay.

It was a small ship, with fewer than 50 passengers, and we helped hoist the sails, took rugged inland tours, climbed small mountains, and drank cool drinks while reclining on the sandy shore of a deserted island. We even learned a new language -- "Dos cerveza, por favor!"

It was glorious -- an experience we always said we would do again, perhaps when our son became a teen. That never happened, though just this year we finally booked a second cruise, this one to Alaska, aboard one of those huge floating cities. Debbie and I feel blessed that our 26 year old son is still willing to go along with us.

Time spent together is a real gift, as I'm sure you know, Good Reader, and it is the main theme in the next short, short piece.

Pay It Forward

Originally published June 17, 2021

The funniest thing happened to me Saturday morning as I was heading to man the registration booth at the Summerfest Antique Tractor Show.

I decided to start my morning with breakfast. Not so unusual in itself, as I usually do have breakfast, though this morning I thought I'd be good. As I placed my order for hot tea in the drive thru at Biggby, I averted my eyes from the placard advertising the bagel sandwich, complete with sausage, egg, and cheese – yum! Instead, I decided to commit to my effort at dieting and ordered the blueberry yogurt parfait. (It was delicious and completely satisfying, as I learned later.)

As I pulled to the window to pay for my order, the young lady there told me that the gentleman in the black pickup truck ahead of me had paid for my order. I don't know who it was, as I didn't really pay much attention, but as I headed toward Tate Park I thought of the "Pay It Forward" philosophy that was popularized over two decades ago with the movie starring Kevin Spacey, Helen Hunt, and Haley Joel Osment. The concept, simply put, is to show your gratitude for kindness or gifts you've received by giving gifts or kindness to others -- even complete strangers -- often anonymously and without the expectation of reciprocation.

In my mind, I started to wonder whether I had done anything to "pay it forward" recently?

I took up my station at the park and enjoyed meeting many different people, including a few multi-generation families. Summerfest always draws families together.

I saw one father with his young son (grandson?) sitting in his lap as he drove his tractor to its parking spot for the show, and I thought of Father's Day, which is this weekend. I thought of how fathers regularly, day-in and day-out, "pay it forward" for their children, with no thought of repayment. I thought of my father.

Ralph William Walters was not a perfect man, nor was he a

perfect father, but he did "pay it forward".

Dad taught us through sports, often by coaching us and our friends in one activity or another. He started coaching me in bowling, baseball and basketball at age 8. As I grew older, he remained in the lower levels to coach my four younger brothers, but he didn't neglect me.

Some fathers raced to the bar after work each day -- not mine. Every day, my Dad came to the end of every practice -- football, basketball, track, and baseball -- all the way through high school.

Of course, he never missed a game, even when I rode the bench during my freshman year in college football. He would drive more than two hours from Detroit to Kalamazoo, watch the K College Hornets get drubbed (We were abysmal that year), have a quick lunch with me, then make the trek back home.

His attention to his children in sports didn't just lead to better play on the field or the court; it led to us becoming better men. Many of the good qualities my brothers and I share can be attributed to our father -- loyalty, persistence, commitment. Dad sacrificed his own pleasures to "pay it forward" with his sons. Thank you, Dad.

So, until I figure a way to "pay it forward" myself, I'd like to offer warm wishes for a Happy Father's Day to all fathers out there -- especially those who have coached their children in sports, trades, music, or other skills.

A free breakfast is nice, but time spent is a gift to be cherished forever.

***

A few weeks after this was published, I learned my mystery breakfast provider in the black pickup had been George Ames, a nice man and a great father, who also spends an inordinate amount of time coaching his sons in sports. He's one of the good dads.

***

The next story is another of my car stories. This one is related to my father, in a way. Though I have not included stories about my 1980 Volkswagon Diesel Rabbit that I purchased from my father in 1984, I will tell you about the last car I bought from him over 20 years later...

Cast but a Glance at Riches

Originally published July 1, 2021

This weekend's rain and subsequent flooding made me think of another of my many vehicles, this one a short-lived car, though probably the nicest vehicle I have ever owned.

The vehicle was a 2004 Ford Taurus, purchased from my father, who had decided it was to be the last vehicle he ever owned. (Like many, he leased cars from that point on, preferring to avoid the maintenance that comes with older vehicles.)

I had a habit of purchasing old vehicles from my father, and none of them ever worked out -- not a single one.

This Taurus was a beauty. Richly appointed, it was a full-size four-door sedan with air conditioning and power everything -- heated seats and steering wheel on top of all that. I had never before nor ever since enjoyed such luxury in a vehicle.

Unfortunately, I only got to enjoy it for a few short months.

I picked it up in the fall of that school year (2007) and drove it into Detroit on my morning commute everyday. Winter that year was warmer than usual, and we had a lot of rain. One day, or maybe it was several days, in February, 2008, we had rain that just didn't seem to quit --the kind of rain that causes complete strangers to remark to each other...

"Enough rain for ya'?"

"Any more and we'll need to build an ark!"

"Too bad it doesn't come when we need it!"

The year 2008 was not a very good year for many people, for many reasons, and it really wasn't a good year for me, either.

At that time, I decided I would avoid taking US-12 for my morning commute. It was usually backed up, so I found alternatives, eventually reaching the on-ramp for US-23. From that point, it was a jaunt to I-94, then I would cruise past Metro Airport and into Detroit.

On that morning in February, after days of non-stop rain, I took my short-cut, turning on to Clinton Macon Road. The rain was coming down so hard that high speed wipers could barely keep the windshield water free.

I wasn't going too fast, probably not over the speed limit, but I know I wasn't going too slow, either, despite what conditions demanded. I was, after all, commuting to work, and it was all about getting to work on time.

The day seemed darker than normal. It was about 6:15 in the morning -- almost an hour before sunrise -- and the sky must have also been overcast. It was pitch black, the darkness seeming to swallow the porch lights on the intermittent houses as I pushed past Billmyer Highway.

It was dark and hard to see, headlights glaring in the rain, and I came up over a familiar hill that I passed every morning, houses sitting on either side of the hill just before the road sank into a valley. As I crested the hill, my headlights reflected on the road ahead of me. It was different than usual somehow.

'Why is my light reflecting off the road like that?' I thought.

'For that matter, why is the road so wide?'

I'll confess to being a little slow thinking that morning, so I was still going at 45 or 50 mph when my tires came upon the answer to my questions.

It wasn't a road anymore, after all.

It was a pond.

The rain came down so hard and for so long that the road had flooded. I hit the brakes, but that just slowed me down a bit, not enough to prevent me from hitting the water. My car began skiing, and I actually floated right out into the pond, slightly off to the side of the road for good measure. I was truly stuck.

My car stalled, and it was never going to start again.

The other problem was that the water, which was almost up to the outside door handles, was rising inside my fancy car, first covering the floor, and then covering the bucket seats (made of fine Corinthian leather).

Luckily, I still had electric power, at least for the moment, and I opened up the moon roof. (I told you it was a fancy car!) I started to climb out the top of the car, but realized the extent of the newly formed lake. I was easily ten yards from dry land. I squatted with my feet on the center console and my torso extruding through the roof of my car.

It was still pouring rain, and I was getting soaked.

I called my wife to tell her what happened, and then I

called the county sheriff's department.

As I was waiting, two Clinton school buses passed. I was sure I knew the drivers, but I may have been wrong. In any case, they wouldn't have recognized me in my new car, and frankly, I wasn't sure I really wanted to be recognized. It was pretty embarrassing. I could see the tense looks on their faces as they drove through the pond, their high tires easily keeping the cab of their vehicles above the water line.

The wake from their passing caused my car to rock in the water like a buoy, sending me even further out into the pond and off the road.

Ten minutes later, the cavalry arrived, and I was relieved. I still had to face the inevitable, however.

The sheriff pulled up safely at the roadside edge of the pond. He got out, and we exchanged pleasantries in the cold rain, then he stood there looking at me.

I looked at him.

He looked at me.

Then he spoke.

"Would you prefer to wait there until the tow truck comes, or do you want to get out of the rain?"

'Get out of the rain' sounded good, though it wasn't that simple. I had to finish climbing through the roof and down the side of the vehicle, followed by a jump into the waist-deep, frigid February water and then an invigorating wade to the shore line.

Reluctantly, I took the plunge, arriving at the shoreline moments before the tow truck driver pulled up. I was towelling dry and warming up inside the sheriff's cruiser when he tapped on the window.

"Where you want me to tow 'er?" he said, pointing to my beautiful but soggy luxury car.

I told him to take it to the Ford dealer in Clinton. (The building now houses the Solid Rock Church.)

"Too bad you got all dried off," he said. "I coulda had you hook up this tow line fer me."

He smiled, and I did my best to return one, though I was still a little sickened by the brevity of my good fortune. I'll never be rich, and I may not get to enjoy 'the finer things in life,' but life is good all the same.

"Cast but a glance at riches, and they are gone, for they will surely sprout wings and fly off to the sky like an eagle" Proverbs 23:5

Oh, You Beautiful Doll

Originally published July 8, 2021

This holiday weekend I travelled up north to Empire, Michigan with my son, Nicholas. It was a good time -- one for the old memory banks. We golfed 3 days in a row, hit the beach twice and had campfires both nights we were there.

The highlight of the weekend, however, was the family Fourth of July party held at my Aunt Alberta's house in Traverse City. It was enjoyable to see all of my relatives there, and a special treat to see my cousin Grace, her husband, Jim, and their daughter, Ann, who came in from Minnesota. Grace and I were very close as kids, especially in middle school, and there are lots of stories to tell, Good Reader. (You might remember the story about my first experience with mathematics at the chalkboard.)

We had a picnic style dinner, sang patriotic songs, celebrated the birthday of little Lily, who is my second cousin twice removed and not really my third or fourth cousin, as I had thought. (I can't keep track of it, anyway. When we were kids, we just called everybody cousins.)

One of the fun things we did there was have a doll counting contest. Aunt Alberta has a vast doll collection. To say that she enjoys collecting dolls is to understate it to the power of ten. She hosts a monthly doll club at her house, and, except for last year's COVID cancellations, never misses the annual statewide convention. She has over 300 dolls of various shapes, sizes, textures, and eras. I tried to guess the exact number of dolls, like everyone else, and came in second place behind young Oliver, who was adept at gauging his grandmother's collection.

My Aunt Alberta is also my Godmother, and thinking of her reminded me of one of my earliest memories. (No, not of her holding me next to the baptismal basin. My memory goes back, but not that far back!)

I was reminded of the time when she came to my rescue.

It was back in the late 1960s, and I was a young student in my elementary school

Nick, Aunt Alberta, and I pose in front of her doll collection of hundreds.

years at St. Christopher School in Detroit. It was a fairly big school that ranged from first grade through eighth grade and was run by the Sisters of the Holy Family of Nazareth.

As a class, we attended church once a week, where we were reminded to sit and kneel straight and to respond and sing loudly. Religious education was one of the most important areas of study to the Sisters, and May Crowning was the most important religious event of the year, at least of those that involved their students.

May Crowning was a religious ceremony dedicated to celebrating Mary, the mother of Jesus, and her role in our Savior's life. (Some believe that Catholics worship Mary, but that is untrue. Catholics *revere* Mary and hold her in high esteem as the mother of Jesus -- a *distinct* difference.)

The Sisters were not the only ones who looked forward to May Crowning. Girls in the eighth grade held their breath through the month of April in anticipation of the naming of the May Queen -- the eighth grader chosen to place the crown of roses on the statue of Mary during the evening ceremony. Margie Szuba was May Queen in our eighth grade year. (I'm pretty sure the race was between Margie and my cousin Grace, with Margie, who lived just two blocks from the convent, perhaps gaining sympathy from the untimely death of her father, though it could have been the result of a well-timed delivery of freshly baked chocolate chip cookies to the nunnery. Who knows?)

The year of my memory, however, goes well before my eighth grade year. I think I was probably 6 years old, which would place it around 1967. We were dropped off at school prior to the evening service, and I reported to my classroom with my cousin, Grace. We lined up in our rows, practicing our posture for the processional.

Sister Tarcisius moved like lightning, checking our hair, smoothing our attire, and correcting our posture. With fifteen minutes to go, we poured out of our classrooms and lined the hallways, hundreds of students filling the darkened corridor. Our music teacher, Ron Mysliwiec, stood in front of us and led a rehearsal of the processional songs.

We started the procession. (It would be irreverent to call it a parade, but for my readers with less religious experience, that's what it was) Hundreds of students flowed out the school doors in two lines, hands folded as in prayer, singing in unison. The sound was either beatific or hideous, all those voices together as we marched toward the main door of the church; I don't know which it was, as all I focused on was remembering the words of the songs we had practiced in music class for the previous month.

Being in the first grade then, I was near the front, and as I entered the church I couldn't even see the May Queen, who would have been in the back. I did notice, however, that there was some lag in the singing from the front to the back, almost like a roundelay, like when we sang "Row, Row, Row Your Boat" in music class, with the three parts overlapping.

We walked down the center aisle and took our seats by class, boys separated from girls, of course, and participated in a ceremony that lasted close to two hours. Our parents sat in the rows behind us, wherever they could fit. It was one of the few nights when that large church was completely full, the other night being Christmas Eve.

By the time the service was done, maybe 9 p.m., it was dark. I was short, being six years old, so when everybody stood up and filled the aisles, I couldn't see anybody I knew. I couldn't see my parents, and I couldn't even see my cousin, Grace. I was lost in the crowd. Being young, I soon became overwhelmed and started to cry.

I don't know if you can

remember what that feeling was like, Good Reader, but I know how I felt then, and I was on the other end of it once with my son, Nicholas.

It was when he was about four years old, and I was playing with him one weekday after getting home from Detroit. I laid on the couch with my arm extended, manipulating toys on the floor with him. I dozed off, and for some reason he wandered off and then lost track of me, went outside and got himself locked out of the house. It was pouring rain and dark, and his cries finally pierced my slumber. Hearing the terror in his voice -- "Daddy, Daddy, Daddy" -- I raced to the front door, the back door, and finally the side door. When I finally got to him he was soaking wet, and his little body was heaving with sobs.

My experience in church in 1967 was similar. Sobbing and crying, I walked around completely lost. The church was starting to empty, and still I couldn't see my parents; I couldn't find my cousin; I couldn't find anyone.

Finally, there she was, my Godmother, standing like an angel in the side doorway of the church. She rushed to me and scooped me up, holding me for several minutes and assuring me.

"You'll be okay. You're okay, Michael. You're okay. You'll be okay. Hold my hand. Squeeze my hand. You're okay..."

Her words soothed me, and I began to settle down as she walked me to the car, holding my hand and reassuring me all the way home.

Her 90th birthday is coming up soon, and I hope she has a wonderful time. I hope that her daughters and sons are there to hold and squeeze her hand, and share their love with her on her special day.

***

And my cousin Anne was there a few years later, holding the hand of her mother, my Godmother, when she passed on. It was a heart-wrenching experience for Anne, but it was also a blessing as she was able to hold her mother's hand one final time.

How many men does it take to replace railroad ties? Five!

Working on the Railroad

Originally published August 5, 2021

I'm on my third day of vacation as I write this piece, and one of the things that makes a vacation both good and bad is the change of scenery. The most dramatic and fundamental change, as I grow older, is the place where I sleep.

Most vacations since I was a kid have been camping trips, and sleeping arrangements are always an important part of the plan. I had never been a 'particular' sleeper -- I could sleep anywhere when I was younger. I'd sleep in the car on the way to the campgrounds, then doze in a lounge chair at the beach, and have no problem sleeping at night -- lights out almost as soon as my head hit the pillow.

As when I was young, I still have no problem falling into slumber in the evening. It's staying asleep that's the problem now.

Our campground this vacation is in Traverse City, Michigan and is located less than a mile from the Cherry Capital Airport, with one of its two runways directing planes straight over our tents, or so it seems, with flights heading in and out well past my bedtime. Nonetheless, I easily fall asleep. In fact, I missed a bit of drama in the wee hours on our first night.

"Did you hear the police helicopter flying over our site last night?" my wife, Debbie, asked me that first morning.

"How did you know it was a police 'copter?"

She told me it had been flashing a searchlight, but it could have been an air raid siren, for all it mattered; when I'm out, I'm out.

Waking up is a different matter altogether.

Usually, I wake up at 3:30 every morning. It's an accustomed ritual at home -- roll out of bed, shuffle into the bathroom, then return to bed and venture again to the Land of Nod. I usually wake again around 5:30 a.m.

Our first night of camping mimicked that routine, though my return to slumber was hindered by a flattened air mattress. As a rule, campers can talk, sing, strum guitars, and make noise until about 10 p.m. every night, 11 p.m. on weekends, but after that you can barely hear the crickets. Despite my discomfort, I was resolute not to be THAT guy, to run the air pump in the wee hours, especially since it would likely only afford a few minutes of comfort before it lost its air again.

I rolled around on the hard ground for the next few hours, intermittently catching a few Z's until my bones stiffened, and I was compelled to shift positions again. Finally, I got up and went for a long walk, getting in twice my usual 'steps' for the day, and then had some caffeine to cast off the last remnants of drowsiness.

That evening, we violated one of our usual rules of camping and went to one of the big chain stores to get another air mattress. They sold only one kind -- the type with the built-in pump, and it was expensive. I bought it and another extension cord and walked out of there almost $100 lighter. (I would have willingly paid even more; I'm usually cheap, but a good night's sleep is a precious commodity.)

Resolved to get some good sleep after that miserable first night, I decided to use the nifty car-tent I had brought along. It attaches to the hatch of the vehicle, allowing you to place an air mattress over the folded down seats. As a bonus, it meant not sleeping on the ground.

Getting up from ground level nowadays, with my age and weight working against me, is something like a turtle trying to flip over from its shell -- arms and legs flailing and body rocking until enough momentum is generated for the big flip. Then there's the grunt-and-hoist , the effort of getting from the prone position to the knees and finally standing fully erect. It really should be an Olympic event!

It was getting dark, and I was eager to get my sleeping quarters set. I put the new deluxe mattress in the back of the car and pressed the "inflate" button.

'Neat,' I thought, 'this takes all the work out of pumping it up by hand. I guess it was a good investment.'

About a minute later, it was still inflating.

'Ooh, this is going to be really comfortable,' I thought as I noticed the thickness of the mattress as it rose in the back of my car.

Another minute later, my brow furled with concern.

'How in the world am I going to be able to get in there?'

The mattress was definitely plush -- too plush, if that's a thing. It filled the compartment almost to the ceiling. Had I been able to wedge myself in there, I'd never be able to get out. I certainly wouldn't be able to roll or shift positions during the night. There was so little room between the roof and the mattress top that I wasn't entirely sure I'd get my head in there, much less my belly.

'It would be like sleeping in a coffin,' I thought to myself, then shuddered.

Exhausted from the night before, I considered deflating the mattress, laying on top of it, pressing the inflate button, and then falling asleep. Absurd as that option was, I considered it until I thought of my usual 3:30 a.m. trip to the loo. Eventually, I swapped mattresses with my son, Nick. Though thinner, it was still comfortable and remained full of air all night long.

The next morning, I woke at 5:30 a.m. to the pitter-patter of acorns drumming on the roof of my car. I had slept well, but, determined to make up for lost sleep the night before, I rolled over and drifted off again, even as the city stirred.

I hadn't realized how long I'd been out of the city, and it took a small effort to block the sounds of the city waking up.

- Increased traffic noise from the road nearby?
  - ***Blocked.***
- Joggers and bikers along the trail behind our campsite?
  - ***Not an issue.***
- Early flights taking off overhead? (Mentally, I slip back to a time when those sounds -- the everyday drone of city life -- were the normal sounds of my life -- for almost 40 years.)
  - ***No problem.***

I rolled over in my comfortable sleeping bag and snuggled my pillow. Ahhhh!

Still revelling in slumber at 9 a.m., an obscenely late hour for me in recent years, my ears were greeted with a sound that my mind couldn't categorize and dismiss. A mere 15 yards behind our campsite, a crew of workers began replacing railroad ties at 9:01 a.m. Like most heavy machinery, the railroad-tie-replacement-thingie was equipped with a flashing light and a piercing, oscillating, high-pitched horn. My repose ended, I had to get up and face another day of vacation.

Poor me! ;)

Every Kind of People

Originally published August 12, 2021

Why go camping?

Of all the possible vacation destinations and choices, my family goes camping 'Up North' in Michigan every year. It has been a tradition since I was young, but aside from being "tradition," I sometimes wonder why we do it.

The first item that causes me to question the choice of camping is the accommodations. Like most people, I've worked hard for many years to acquire and maintain a comfortable home. Most of my income, in fact, goes into paying for, heating, cooling and furnishing it. Many hours go into maintaining it and keeping it clean. Yet, when summer rolls around, I abandon my castle and head to the woods, living among the squirrels and mosquitos, cooking on an open fire, and bathing only when the communal showers aren't too busy, which means about every third day. Phew!

"Isn't it great how even the people up north are into the Clinton Local!" I told Nick as we walked in downtown Traverse City. He just smiled...

Instead of looking at my flat screen color TV in the evening, I stare into a fire, trying to ignore my wife and son as they roast marshmallows and place them between two graham crackers with a piece of fresh fudge -- their own version of S'Mores. (I'm dieting, and I'm being strict about it, mostly, though that doesn't mean I'm not envious.)

So I find other things to occupy my mind by the fire -- I look at our neighbors in their nearby tents and Winnebagos.

Another difference between camping and staying at home

is the proximity of neighbors. Most people like to have a little separation, a little privacy, when it comes to neighbors. I'm one of them. In fact, many people erect tall privacy fences (as tall as local ordinances allow) and build houses on larger parcels of land to avoid being too close to neighbors. I know it doesn't sound too neighborly, but it's the truth -- and for good reason. Robert Frost had it right when he said 'Good fences make good neighbors.' As a species, we can only tolerate so much closeness -- and only from those we have either chosen to have near or those who are near due to birth.

That is perhaps the most puzzling thing about the decision to go camping. We leave our home, with its comfort and its fences and its property lines, and we choose to live (two weeks in our case) right on top of complete strangers.

On the positive side, because they are strangers, they can be observed and characterized like figures in a bizarre sitcom. At the campfire the other night, I chose to focus on a few of them when dessert time rolled around.

It really does take every kind of person to make the world turn. Sitting by the fire, I contemplated three that I had met at the campground: Doggie Dougie, Blow Dry Bob, and The AxeMan.

I happened across Doggie Dougie early one morning as he walked his miniature hybrid dog. Dougie had the little pup on a leash, but he allowed it to do its business on the grass near someone's tent. It was the baggable type of business, but Dougie wasn't carrying a bag. Instead, in an effort to pull off a Houdini-like sleight, Dougie whistled nonchalantly and looked up into the air as I passed, and he actually pointed to a tree across the road.

"I wonder what type of bird that is?" he said, trying to steer my eyes upward.

'Not sure -- but I know it's not a doo doo bird, I mean Dodo bird, because those stay on the ground, like your dog's turds...,' I thought, but just smiled as I walked past.

I met Blow Dry Bob in the men's room later that day. This was my introduction to campground passive aggression, something you'd think would be nonexistent when everyone's supposed to be relaxing on vacation.

I was talking on the phone using my earpiece, which annoys some people, I know. I can understand this, especially when it confuses someone in a live conversation. If I intend to talk to someone in person, like a cashier at a store, I'll interrupt or discontinue the conversation with the person on the phone.

I hadn't planned to start a conversation in the men's room with Bob, however. (For my female readers, most men do not consider it proper to start conversations with complete strangers in the lavatory.)

Bob finished washing his hands, and I was talking with my editor, Amanda, who was polishing up last week's paper for me as I was on vacation. Bob started to blow dry his hands. It was loud, so I paused my conversation. Bob stopped.

I resumed the sentence. Bob started. I stopped. Bob stopped again. I started again. Bob started... I stopped...

This went on so long that I wondered if Bob was also drying his hair. I looked over at him to check, and saw him peeking at me out of the corner of his eye. Was that a malicious grin? I think it was!

I was amused by this brief display of passive aggression, writing it off as one odd case, until around day three with our new, next door camping neighbor, The AxeMan.

I knew The AxeMan was mildly quirky from the start when I overheard this snippet of a much longer diatribe directed toward a woman I presume was his wife.

"This is the best axe in the world, I'm tellin' ya. You can't beat an old axe. I've had this axe since I was a kid, and it's the best -- wouldn't trade it for the world..."

Now, Good Reader, I have heard men wax poetic about old cars, former girlfriends, and even great baseball teams, but I've never heard such an outpouring for an axe. (It went on like that for several minutes.) I thought it was eccentric, until The AxeMan decided the best time to use his axe was when his neighbors went to bed.

So every night, for three nights in a row, The AxeMan came out of his camper, picked up his axe, and began splitting wood. From 10 p.m. to midnight, he split wood, even the night before he left. I never looked closely at his fires the next day, but he couldn't have had much more than kindling left.

Why didn't I stop The AxeMan, who was certainly imposing on those around him who were trying to sleep?

The answer is simple and self-evident when rephrased properly: Why didn't I stop the axe-swinging nut-job in the woods at night?

Sounds like the beginnings of a bad horror story, to me -- no, thank you!

All in all, camping has been wonderful fun over the years, but eventually, I think we'll tire of the outdoors with all the closeness of nearby campers. Maybe we'll get on one of those spacious cruise ships?

***

By this time I had been regularly using a CPAP machine every night while sleeping. Even with that, Debbie often told me that my snoring came through loud and clear.

When we were first married, I stayed overnight at a hospital to participate in a sleep study. The technician at the time wrote, "No apnea, but ***very, very loud snoring!"*** (Yes, she wrote it like that -- in three inch letters and underlined!)

Considering my snoring, perhaps I can now make sense of The AxeMan's behavior. He probably decided that he could chop wood all night if I was going to saw logs...

Nick and I got our camping kicks during the summer after his high school graduation, when we rented this cabin at Interlochen State Park in Michigan.

Learning to Swim

Originally published August 19, 2021

Last week, after heavy rain and wind buffeted the area, causing many to lose power -- some for an entire week -- I considered writing about my camping experience in similar weather up north.

I decided against it. After all, some might argue that camping in inclement weather is a self-inflicted problem -- I could always tuck my tail and head for home...

Instead, I focused on the final two days of my vacation, spent mostly at Good Harbor Beach in Leelanau County. It is the sandiest and prettiest beach in the area, and I really had an opportunity to unwind, sitting under an umbrella and sipping cool beverages. Aah!

My son, Nick, and I walked out into the water periodically to cool off, and I remarked how the sand bar would rise and fall as you walked away from the shore. I told him of a time when I was younger, probably just 6 or 7 years old, and I was walking out into Lake Michigan just like this...

~~~

It was probably 1967 or '68, and my Dad took us to the beach near Mackinaw City, where our grandparents had a cabin. Joining us was Jerry Baxter and his two sons, Glen and Kenny. Dad brought his two eldest -- my brother, Paul, and me. The mothers kept the little ones at home, apparently, or maybe they went shopping. I don't remember which, but I do remember it being a perfect day -- bright sun, warm air and cool water.

Both Glen and Kenny were older than us by a few years, but they were accommodating, and they showed us a lot about nature while we were up there, like how to find leeches under the rocks near the cabin's shoreline and other cool stuff, so when they told us we could walk out to the horizon in Lake Michigan, we followed.

The water level rose as we headed out toward the setting sun, but then the water receded as we crested a sandbar, and we rose out of the water almost to our ankles. We continued,
~~~

following Glen and Kenny, then we'd sink again as we passed the sandbar, only to rise again a few feet later on the next one.

We walked away from shore like that for what felt like a mile, our fathers becoming small dots on the sandy shore behind us.

Dad was waving, so we waved back.

He continued to wave, this time with both arms, so we waved back with renewed exuberance.

Now he was shouting and waving...

Eventually, Glen said that it looked like our dad wanted us to come back. Reluctant to end the adventure, we returned to shore, realizing during that long trek just how far we had roamed.

Apparently, at some point during our trek, Jerry had asked my dad whether we could swim, and when the answer was no, he strongly encouraged our return to shore. Fun time was over, as I was schooled in the art of swimming for the next hour by the helpful gentleman. (How my brother got out of it, I don't know. Perhaps they figured I would be able to rescue my drowning brother if I knew how to swim, or maybe they figured I would teach him?)

The impromptu swimming lesson that day didn't destroy the memory of a great day at the beach, though it did almost suck the enjoyment completely out of our annual two-week vacation later that summer.

I've written before, Good Reader, of our family summer vacations at Camp Dearborn in Milford, Michigan, where we'd spend two weeks roaming in a carefree manner from breakfast to the playground to the kid's activity table to the beach to the fishing lake to the canteen to the campfire and, finally, to bed. Day after glorious day of unscheduled fun, in other words.

Jerry Baxter brought an end to that.

Determined to be a responsible father, my dad enrolled us for swim classes at the pool. We were among the older nonswimmers there, apparently, and for that honor we got to be first in the pool every morning at 6 a.m.

Grumbling and groaning each morning as we were called out of our warm sleeping bags, we were roused by my father's wake-up call:

"Reveille, reveille rise and shine,

You've had your sleep

And I've had mine..." Dad would begin in a loud, clear voice. It was worse than any alarm, though what came next was more annoying -- a string of platitudes that hit our sleepy ears like salt poured into a wound.

Paul and I soon learned to bite back our sarcastic retorts, but only after we had erred in our sleep-deprived state of grogginess.

"It will build character," Dad said.

'Daffy Duck is a character, but I'm not tryin' to be him!'

"What doesn't kill you makes you stronger," Dad said.

'Yes, I do believe you ARE trying to kill us!'

"Hard work always pays off," Dad said.

<Snort>

"This will hurt me more than it hurts you," Dad said.

'We've heard that one before, and we don't believe it for one second!'

"We'll all be laughing about this soon...," Dad said.

'Hardly.'

But here I am, over fifty years later, and I almost find it amusing to envision our scrawny little bodies dripping at pool side, purple-lipped and shivering like lunatic woodpeckers dancing a quick two-step in a vain effort to warm up.

'It could be worse.'

The next story speaks to my brief moment of stardom on the stage. I am the tall one on the right -- Nanki Poo in Gilbert and Sullivan's Mikado. My brother, Paul, and cousin, Grace, were also in the operetta.

Is There a Doctor in the House?

Originally published September 2, 2021

By now you may be tired of me telling you stories of my vacations, Good Reader. This time, however, the story doesn't focus on noisy campgrounds or quirky campers. This time my focus is on the lifestyles of the rich and famous.

On the very first day of our vacation, over a month ago now, Nick and I decided to stop in Traverse City for a bite to eat and a cool drink after the long ride from Clinton. Nick searched his phone as I drove, and we settled on a restaurant called Rad*ish, which shared an open-air courtyard with other stores and a couple food trucks. We felt almost Californian as we sat under the colorful umbrellas and sipped our drinks while nibbling on trendy snacks served on paper plates.

We were truly relaxed and enjoying ourselves, and I started to people-watch -- one of my favorite activities. Moments later, I went to my cell phone to confirm a sighting.

'Was it?'

'Could it be?'

The gentleman sitting at the table behind my son, Nick, sure looked like one of my favorite characters on an Amazon Prime series called "The Expanse." I searched for his name -- Cas Anvar. I was just about ready to go over and get a napkin autograph when a pair of young ladies from the table behind him crowded around him for a selfie. Not wanting to mob the poor guy, I sat back down and sent the photo I had taken (printed on next page) to Nate Adams, the Local's movie and stage reviewer.

"Is that Kal Penn?" Nate responded by text.

"Kal Penn? Who is he?" I shot back.

"He was a doctor on 'House,'" Nate replied.

That made it even better because House was my favorite television show for a long time. It was one of the shows I used to watch with my mother when I'd visit. I really wanted an autograph now, but as the girls

Nick Walters patiently waits for his paparazzo Poppa to zoom in on the bearded gentleman over his left shoulder -- Kal Penn.

lingered with him, my fan-boy fanaticism waned. What would I do with it after I'd gotten it?

Seeing the actor and thinking about that profession caused me to recall my days as a thespian during my late elementary and middle school years under the direction of the best teacher I ever had, Ron Mysliwiec. We pronounced it "missile-wick"--the actual pronunciation of the Polish surname was beyond the ability of most of our tongues. For this piece, I'll refer to him as Mister M.

~~~

I was in the school stage productions all through the early 1970s, and by 1975, as an 8th grader, I was chosen as the lead in our big spring play, 'The Mikado' by Gilbert and Sullivan. It was an operetta, meaning it was part speaking and part singing, and we devoted many hours to practicing both.

I played Nanki-poo, the son of the emperor, who disguises himself as a wandering minstrel to woo a girl named Yum-Yum, who is engaged to the Lord High Executioner.

I was fine with the singing. I was fine with memorizing all the lines of a male lead. I was even fine with the makeup, which was applied heavily.

I was *absolutely* fine with growing my hair out for the entire school year so that I
~~~

could "look the part," as Mister M said. (In fact, I was ecstatic about that. Long hair was cool then, and Dad would never have allowed me to grow it out had it not been for Mona's support of the arts!)

The only thing that bothered me, as we got to the midpoint of the production, was that I was expected to kiss Yum-Yum.

Those who know me today might doubt that I was ever shy, but it was true back then. I had never kissed a girl (moms, grandmas and aunts notwithstanding), and now I had to kiss one in public, on stage, show after show after show.

Looking back, I don't know what I was thinking. Yum-Yum was played by Margie Szuba, a smart girl who was also really cute. Mister M tried his best to help me overcome my awkward apprehension as the kissing scene came up in practice.

"Just lean in and give her a kiss, Mike," he'd say, and I would freeze about six inches from her cheek.

"Close your eyes if that helps..."

But I couldn't, worried that she might lurch forward and plant one on me.

"Would it help if I switch your cousin Grace into the role of Yum-Yum?" he solicited.

I just stared. 'We're cousins, but not kissing cousins!'

"Pretend she's your mother..."

'That doesn't really help, Mister M,' I thought

I looked back at Margie, who puckered up for the big one, but my face flushed a fiery red and sweat dripped down my nose. Now it was Margie's turn to recoil.

"Okay, cut! Let's practice the next song!"

Relieved, I got up and sang my heart out. Certainly Mister M could figure how to write out that kissing scene. After all, he regularly cut and changed lines as needed in other parts of the play.

But Mister M was a man of many things, and determination was one of his strongest attributes. He devised a plan that he never would have been able to execute in modern day schools, but he somehow got away with it. He had clout at that little school. This was, after all, the man who walked out to the playground after school and told my baseball coach that operetta practice had to come before sports -- and he *won* that argument!

What was his plan?

He walked the two of us, Margie and me, to the old library in the back hallway of the school. It was a dark, second story room that was used for storage and seldom visited.

"Now, you two practice your scene," he said with a big, knowing smile, "and don't come down until it is convincing."

And then he walked away, leaving two pubescent teens alone in the darkest, most remote room in the school! I didn't understand which part he wanted us to practice, but Margie did. She held my hand and looked into my eyes...

"W-w-what!?" I stammered. "P-p-p-practice? What are we supposed to do...? Oh, you mean...?"

The room, which was naturally warm and stuffy, suddenly felt like an oven. Sweat poured down my face. Heat rose in my cheeks, and my face turned a color that could have easily stopped traffic. I easily pulled my now slippery hand from hers, but her voice stopped me.

"Mike, why is it so difficult to kiss me?" she asked sweetly, and I stammered something, told her I thought she was nice, and promised I would be able to do it when the time came. Apparently realizing that was the best she could get from me, we went back to the stage in the gymnasium and continued practicing with the group. Mister M seemed focused on the choreography with the sixth graders, and that practice -- our final dress rehearsal -- flew by. Our opening performance was the next morning before the lower elementary classes, and it went smoothly, right up to the, er, you know, the big moment.

Before we stepped on stage for that scene, Margie approached me with an idea.

"You can lean in front of me and if we just touch cheeks, it will look to the audience like we're kissing," she advised.

I nodded, and then thought with an air of nobility, 'I could at least bear a light cheek-to-cheek touch as a sacrifice to my art.'

We stepped on stage, and soon the moment came. I leaned in, confident of the deception. The audience would never know!

But little Margie, sweet little Margie, had her own bit of deception planned.

Margie puckered her lips, as the scene demanded, and I did the same before turning my face away from the audience to lean in for the quick grazing-of-the-cheeks, as planned.

The audience was eating it up. The first graders in the front row were giggling and serenading us with a chorus of oohs and ahhs. Distracted and vulnerable, I detected a flicker of devilish delight in Margie's eyes as her lips formed a quick smile, then quickly re-puckered.

'Look out!' my inner self yelled, but it was too late.

Margie planted one directly on my lips, and I froze there, which made the kiss seem even more intense and romantic. The elementary audience cheered, as did my fellow actors on stage. I was flabbergasted. Fortunately, the kiss was followed by a rousing chorus and very few lines from me for the rest of the play.

The kiss was no easier for the later show, especially since it was in front of the upper grades -- my peers -- but it went off without remark, as did the show that evening for the parents.

We even did a show the following Monday for the students from the public school across the street, and I got my first fan, a younger blonde girl who came to my house every day for about a week straight after seeing the show, hoping to get me to come out and replay the big scene with her, right there on our front lawn.

"Come on out, Nanki-Poo. Your Yum-Yum is waiting," she'd say in a sing-song voice. My neighborhood buddies were there, of course, as they always were when a spectacle arose, and they encouraged her.

I shut myself in the house like a hermit, waiting for the notoriety to fade.

I thought of that as Nick and I walked toward Kal Penn, who was enjoying conversation with his friends at the picnic table. We made eye contact, and I knew he was expecting me to stop at his table. I also knew he was preparing himself to set aside his friends and conversation to politely deal with yet another fan.

I didn't want to be "that guy," so I tucked the napkin in my pocket as we passed his table, and left the area to continue the day with the people who really matter most. Nick and I met up with Deb, my wife, and continued the drama that families weave daily, complete with comedy, tragedy, singing, dancing, and even a little kissing, too.

Oh, Deer! (Part 1)
The First Cut is the Deepest
Originally published October 28, 2021

On August 25, 2021, at nearly one in the morning, a Clinton Police patrol car was struck by a deer while driving on US-12 near Matthews Highway.

Yes, you read that right -- the deer struck the car.

While that's not exactly a 'man-bites-dog' story (the Holy Grail of journalism), it is of interest and worthy of note, especially to a born-and-bred city boy like me.

I have to admit, I certainly was shocked when I hit my first deer, or rather, when it hit me.

~~~

It was around October, 2000, and it was rainy and dark by 6 p.m. -- just like it is now. We were conscientious recyclers even back then, and since there was no curb side pickup at that time, and no bin in Clinton or Tecumseh, I regularly drove our cardboard, glass and plastic refuse north to the recycling center in Manchester, near the market there.

After doing my civic duty, I drove back to Clinton in the dark. I have never liked night driving, and the rain always seems to make it worse. As I was driving south, the bright lights of an oncoming minivan filled my windshield. I winced, and then gasped as I saw a deer on my front driver's side fender. It had crossed right in front of me -- lightning fast, but not fast enough, unfortunately.

My little golden Chevy S-10 pickup was still able to roll down the road, but that deer wasn't going anywhere anymore. The impact propelled it to the opposite side of the road. I sat there in my damaged truck, windshield wipers slappin' time as I stared at the carcass on the side of the road.

The minivan with the bright lights passed me going north, and if I could have seen into the cab of that vehicle, I know I would have seen one relieved driver. I sat there on the road for a few more moments, just staring at the doe on the shoulder of the road.

'So that's how they get there,' I dumbly thought.
~~~

Then I put the truck in gear. It drove okay, so I hobbled home with it and told my wife. Then I called my friend, Vance, another city boy.

"I got my first deer," I told him.

"Oh, you went hunting? Congratulations!" he said. "Doe or buck?"

"Big Doe," I said, now starting to feel weirdly proud, until I remembered how it had happened. "Except I didn't shoot it. I hit it."

"Hit it?"

"With my truck."

"How in the @*%$! do you hit a deer?" he shouted into the phone, laughing.

I echoed his laughter. It was an absurdity that our city-slick brains could not really have anticipated.

"I know. That's what I've always said, but..."

"You must have been going too fast," he said.

"No, I was under the speed limit."

"You weren't watching the road?"

"Of course I was, well, mostly I was watching the oncoming headlights..."

"You should have hit the brakes!," he said.

"I did, just too late. You can't believe how fast they are!"

After I hung up with him, I realized I had to make some calls. First, I called around to see if anyone wanted to pick up some fresh road kill. (After all, I did believe in recycling!) Next, I called my school administrator to let them know I'd be taking off from work the next day to arrange for car repair. After that, there was one more thing I just had to do -- revisit the scene of the crime. The next morning, I went out there and saw the carnage in the cold light of day. I noticed that the deer must have leapt over a berm on the side of the road just before it ran in front of my car. I used that knowledge, and the oncoming headlights, to excuse myself in the death of Bambi.

Later, after I hit deer #2, then #3, and then #4, I came to realize that the best way to avoid hitting a deer is to avoid driving altogether.

Striking so many deer with my cars over the years has cost thousands of dollars and countless hours. You'd think I'd be angry with the species, but I can honestly say I have no beef with them.

Oh, Deer! (Part 2)
Roadhouse Blues

Originally published November 4, 2021

Hitting that first deer with my little pickup truck wasn't to be a solitary experience. About a year later, as I made my way to the expressway along the scenic route, I hit another one, this time a big eight-point buck.

It was the Fall of 2001, and I had discovered a new route into Detroit.

I have always liked driving along 'the road less travelled,' so to speak. When I lived in Redford in the late 90s, I had a seven minute commute to work, almost entirely along Outer Drive, a twisty, scenic stretch of road that wraps around most of Detroit. Comparing it to Clinton, think Michigan Avenue from here to Saline, but slower, much slower.

I was tickled to find a comparatively slower and less travelled route, which led me out of Clinton heading east along Macon Road, then North on Ridge Highway, and then on to...

Well, most of you know the rest, and if you don't, you probably don't need to know about it. The point is that, even though I took that route to travel slower and enjoy the scenery, I often pushed the speed limit. You see, Good Reader, I have a habit of running late. (I think it is a form of rebellion from my youth, but that's another story.)

I don't remember everything very well any more, but there are these few moments of old film stuck in my head, and I can replay them with great clarity.

~~~

I was running late one morning in November, 2001, and I was driving as fast as those back roads would allow. The wooden heart with my two-year-old son's picture shellacked to one side hung from my rear view mirror on a length of twine. It clacked against the windshield as a breeze from the open vent window behind my head sent currents of warm autumn air in a circle around the cab of my Chevy S-10. On the seat next to me was a ten-inch stack of corrected papers, laying criss-cross in organization by class and assignment. It must have been a Monday
~~~

morning because that was a weekend's worth of work -- essays, worksheets, notes from group projects, funny drawings of their teacher inadvertently turned in, etc...

I drove that little pickup truck aggressively, shifting up and down like Mario Andretti, as I came fast upon the hairpin curve on Ridge near Hack Road. Well, okay, it's not exactly a hairpin, but as anyone who's driven it knows, you have to decelerate to about 35 mph, and it comes up on you quickly if you are distracted.

I was barreling toward that point in the dark of early morning, and my mind was wandering. By the time I was on top of the curve, I had to decelerate quickly as I turned. I managed to keep the car on the road without incident, but the stack of papers was another matter entirely.

"God D*$% It!" I shouted as the papers spilled into a pool on the floor.

I bent down to pick up as many of the papers as possible -- while still driving. (I'm a slow learner: on another occasion, when I did the same maneuver, I found myself watching my neighbor's mailbox snap across my hood and then my windshield as I sat back up in my driver's seat.)

I got away with my idiotic driving antics this time, however, though I would soon pay for my earlier blasphemy.

I settled back -- upright -- in the driver's seat and tried to calm myself as I hit the gas to get back up to speed. Seconds later, out of the inky darkness and crossing right to left across my path was a big buck. I managed to hit the brakes, again sending the stacks of papers to the floor, but, nonetheless, my truck struck the buck squarely with the front bumper.

This time I left the papers there, said a prayer of apology and of thanks, and shifted the car back into gear. I drove it up the road a bit, and, realizing it would not make it much further, pulled to the shoulder.

I sat there for a moment, considering what I needed to do, and soon drivers heading the opposite way stopped to help... well, sort of...

"What did you hit?" said one driver in a full sized truck. "Buck or doe?"

"Where'd you hit it?" said another driver through the window of his big pickup. "Are you going to keep the meat?"

Finally, another driver (also in a full sized pickup) stopped and asked how I was and if I needed to use his cell phone.

(As hard as it is to believe, 2001 was still in the infancy of cell phones, and I did not yet own one.) I called my workplace, and I called my wife, thanked him and handed his phone back.

"Could you ask this trooper to tag that Buck for me?" he asked as he tucked his phone into his pocket and pointed at the Michigan State Trooper who had parked in front of my vehicle and was getting out.

I headed over to him and gave him the details. He kindly offered to give me a ride home and waited there until the tow truck arrived. As we waited, the York Township Volunteer Fire Department arrived, and two young, bib-overall-clad volunteers jumped off the truck and headed directly toward my road kill. An older gentleman sauntered slowly toward me and the trooper.

"You hurt?" he asked, still walking toward me, holding a clipboard in one hand, a pen in the other.

I said I was uninjured, but my car was a mess, ha-ha. (I had broken the windshield with my forehead, but I've always been hardheaded, so no damage there.)

"Well, we'd better look you over just to be sure," he persisted. "You never know..."

"I'm sure I'm okay," I said, prideful and trying not to incur a charge for their service; after all, I hadn't called them.

"Well..." he said, and spit tobacco juice into the grass along the shoulder, "Maybe you wouldn't mind just signing this form I've gotta submit to prove that we came out here today?"

As he spoke the two younger volunteers came back, and one of them handed me part of an antler, telling me how I could use it for hunting. The other spoke excitedly and graphically about the damage the buck had sustained. They both asked for the meat, and I figured it was the least I could give them for their trouble. (The helpful truck driver across the road had since pulled away.) The trooper filled out a tag and handed it to them, and off they went, like two kids on Christmas morning.

Not to be left out, the older man thrust the clipboard my way and repeated his request.

"Mind just signing this report so I can get outta here?" he said, grinning.

So I signed his 'report.'

A few weeks later, all the tribulation that comes with such accidents began to settle, until I got the bill in the mail. York Township sent me a bill of $140 for "emergency medical treatment." I called the office immediately and was greeted by a woman's voice. I brought up what I insisted was an erroneous bill.

"Sir, you received treatment on Ridge Road by our EMTs on that date," she calmly insisted.

"But I never *received* treatment. I *declined* treatment," I countered, "and I never called them."

"Sir, you signed the treatment form at the scene," she said dismissively. "Please send payment promptly or you will be sent to collections."

And then she hung up. To spite her (and the nose on my own face) I let it go into collections after my letters refuting the debt were ignored. I endured several dunning letters from the collection agency, but I had a knack for avoiding the repetitive phone calls. I finally paid it after a year in collection.

Today, my wife sent me a photo of deer in our backyard. I'm convinced they come around to taunt me -- a reminder of my many roadside encounters with their kin.

It's mating season (and hunting season), so I'm going to do my best to keep my eyes on the road, my hands upon the wheel, and my bumper away from deer.

***

I realize that these stories may not be very humorous to those who really love animals. Animal lovers might still enjoy these stories, however, if they realize that I always end up on the losing side of the ledger.

In all cases, I did my best to see that the venison did not go to waste, though I learned that on at least one occasion, my bumper had "over tenderized" the meat, rendering it unusable.

One quick story: I took my Prius to Ashley's Body Shop in Clinton, and after he assessed the damage and wrote the insurance claim, Bill, the owner, and I continued to chat.

"You get a lot of business this time of year, I'll bet," I said, talking about hunting season.

"Sure do," Bill replied, "and it's cheap advertising for me!"

"Cheap advertising?"

"Yep," he said, winking, "couple bags of corn sprinkled on the roads here and there... works every time!"

Oh, Deer! (Part 3)

Rocky Raccoon

Originally published November 18, 2021

By now, Good Reader, you know that I have never had great luck with any of my automobiles, despite my attachment to them. (I tend to anthropomorphize them, like a Disney cartoon.)

My current vehicle, a 2008 Toyota Prius, is one of my all-time favorites. No, she's not a beauty, but I've found myself defending her like a man with a buck-toothed girlfriend at prom.

For example, one year, when she was still young and shiny, my wife, son and I got out in a restaurant parking lot to join the larger family for a holiday meal. (For clarification, I'm talking about when the car was young and shiny, not my wife. She *always* shines in my eyes.)

As we headed toward the door, a grizzled old man waited, eyeing me as I approached.

"If you'd have bought American, I wouldn't be out of a job," he said.

'Happy Easter to you, too!' I thought, but said, "Oh, I'm sorry to hear that. When did you lose your job?"

"1998 -- and it's because of guys like you who buy foreign made!"

Now, math has never been my subject, but I didn't need a calculator to know that my purchase had absolutely no impact on *his* job in particular. I refrained from mentioning it, nor did I mention that the Prius was mostly assembled in Pennsylvania, from what I was told. Instead, and probably because my young son was there, I took the high road.

"Well, I'm sorry you lost your job, but I hope you can enjoy your Easter meal," I said, holding the door open for him and my family.

It wasn't the only time I had to defend her -- my Prius. Shortly after I purchased it, a coworker, known for his right leaning politics, eyed me with suspicion one day as I entered the building.

"You're not one of those left wing tree huggers, are you?" he asked.

Startled by the unusual morning greeting, I just looked at him, probably with a dumb look on my face. Warming to the attack, he shot a litany of questions at me, questions designed to "out" me as a liberal-socialistic-commie-pinko.

"Why'd you buy a Prius?"

"Do you believe in that whole global warming nonsense?

"What's wrong with American cars?"

"Who's on first?"

And so forth, causing my head to spin. I settled on answering just one of his questions.

"I bought that car because I drive 120 miles to work each day, it gets 50 miles to the gallon, and it is cheaper to drive," I said. Over the years I've found that, right or left, most people can relate to and even admire thriftiness. My coworker just nodded and walked away.

But this tale is titled, "Oh, Deer, part III," so you are naturally expecting a tale of deer or near-deer car collisions. I've already told you of the two I had with the old Chevy S-10. Now I'll tell you of the two collisions with the Prius.

***

There is a conspiracy, Good Reader.

There is a conspiracy in the animal kingdom, and I am going to reveal it now for the first time in print. (In total, this is the second time this conspiracy has been revealed. The first time was in the Geico car insurance commercial featuring the two hand-slapping, high-fiving squirrels. That commercial first ran on February 14, 2001, but I didn't make the connection until recently. It's true -- deer/car collisions are due to squirrel propaganda infiltrating the ranks of ruminant mammals, especially deer.

My third and final deer/car collision was as my family and I headed up north on Memorial weekend, 2008, just months after I bought the Prius. We were heading along I-75 north toward the Mackinac Bridge. It was very early -- still dark -- as we were trying to catch an early ferry to the island. Up ahead, on a long smooth straight-away, my headlights spotted a deer. It was a doe, and she was in the left lane, nibbling at something in the road. I slowed from 75 mph to about 50 mph and eased into the right lane.

Live and let live, that was my motto, and my intention was to glide right past Momma Deer without disturbing her roadside treat.

That's where the squirrels come in.

You see, I've learned with almost absolute certainty that they've been recruiting deer to join them in their sick game of dodge cars. Nobody's joining in on any reindeer games. Instead, the entire animal kingdom is getting in on the squirrels' game.

So as I eased past that doe on I-75, what do you think she does?

Does she stand there? No.

Does she run off the road AWAY from the oncoming car? No.

What she does is turn right toward my car, right INTO it, in fact.

The doe's body did a number on the entire driver's side, but my car also did a number on the deer. We pulled over and assessed the damage. My car was still going to make it to its destination, but that deer had, unfortunately, just met its destiny. I didn't think to look for squirrels at that time, but I'm sure they were lurking somewhere in the shadows, discussing the encounter like two nutty, play-by-play announcers.

"Well, Chuck, looks like our trainee has presented herself too early. That driver has spotted her and appears to be slowing," said the first squirrel.

"Chip, there's still time for a recovery. Look, that arrogant driver is only slowing down. She can still hit that car if she tries," said Chuck.

"Let's give her some encouragement!" said Chip.

"Come on, deer. This way. You can do it!"

<BAM>

And then Chuck and Chip do the Geico fist pounding thing. I'm sure it happened, though I didn't know to look for it then.

Being frugal, and since my car was still drivable, I decided to drive it like that until I had my second creature encounter. It was the fall of 2018, and I was taking Pennington Road east toward the big city. I was enjoying the back roads and spotted what looked like a bear cub (impossible) or a large raccoon on the side of the road -- the other side of the road. It appeared to be dining on something, and that should have been a clue. (Geico also has a commercial with raccoons eating trash. They are probably in cahoots with the squirrels.)

This time I did *not* slow down. Raccoons are reputed to be intelligent -- much more so than deer. And yet, as I passed on the *opposite* side of the road,

Ol' Rocky Raccoon bolted in front of my car. I didn't even have time to hit the brakes, and I saw it in my rear view mirror as I drove on.

The darned thing did a triple somersault, then flipped to all fours and ran off into the brush along the side of the road. Looking back, I'm sure he wasn't alone.

"Woo-hoo! That was a blast!" Rocky said as he slowed down less than ten feet from the road.

"Impressive," said Chuck. "You really are a tough guy."

"Tough?," Chip snorted, "I'll say! He's definitely tougher than that deer up north!"

***

It is 2026 as I write this intermission note, and I am happy to report that I have no more deer stories...

These Are The Days
(Giving Thanks for Thanksgiving)

Originally published November 24, 2021

In my 'new' office in Downtown Clinton, I'm still placing memorabilia, old photos and other objects, on shelves and on the walls. This Thanksgiving marks almost a year here, but I'm still not finished, and it doesn't take much these days for me to wax nostalgic.

Family photos tell their own stories -- Wedding Day to my wife, Deb, my four brothers and I clowning around, my son running hurdles or holding a soccer ball, my father's retirement (his second one) -- they tell tales both bitter and sweet. Bitterness is the taste of mortality each photo captures, the cold realization that those days will never be duplicated. Fortunately, the sweetness lasts longer; it lingers, and it can be recalled and retold -- replayed in the mind's eye and savored once again, often becoming sweeter with age.

Lately, and probably in light of Thanksgiving, my eye has been drawn to a game board I attached to the wall behind my office door. (See photo on opposite page.) It was crafted by my Uncle Ray, and it hung for decades in the basement laundry room of Raymond and Lillian Meyers in their Dearborn Heights home. It, along with a serving tray which had also once hung in their basement, have become tokens of the good old days of Thanksgiving as a kid.

Through most of the 60s and 70s, Uncle Ray and Aunt Lil (who were really my mother's aunt and uncle) hosted Thanksgiving dinner in their basement, and I will say (pun intended) that I relished that meal every year.

We would arrive early, about noon, but the house already smelled good, as Aunt Lil utilized two ovens to get the feast ready. She made almost everything from scratch. It was a miracle of synchronization, and she used Uncle Ray to man the basement oven, which held the turkey. We would watch as he opened the oven every 20 minutes or so, basting the huge bird with one of those long, yellow-bulbed basting utensils, spritzing the juice back over the top of the bird and then closing the oven door, but not before letting the tantalizing aroma escape.

In between oven duties, Uncle Ray stationed himself behind his basement bar, one of those remnants from the 50s and 60s with chrome bar stools, padded rails and wood grain paneling. Uncle Ray told jokes and served drinks -- fruity umbrella drinks loaded with maraschino cherries for the kids and hi-balls for the adults. Dad stayed in the basement with us and talked with Uncle Ray about football, occasionally watching as the Lions participated in their annual struggle against the Dallas Cowboys. We sipped our kiddy cocktails and marvelled at the decorations that hung behind the bar -- beer signs and bowling trophies. My favorite tokens were two bowling pins fashioned to look approximately like my aunt and uncle. (I would have kept them when we cleaned out their basement, but what was I going to do with them? Even a sentimental old packrat like me has his limits!)

When I was older, I'd stand around with the men at the bar and listen to Uncle Ray tell jokes. (He was a salesman of some sort, so he had a wonderfully engaging way of talking, with a warm, infectious smile that made you feel happy to be part of the conversation.)

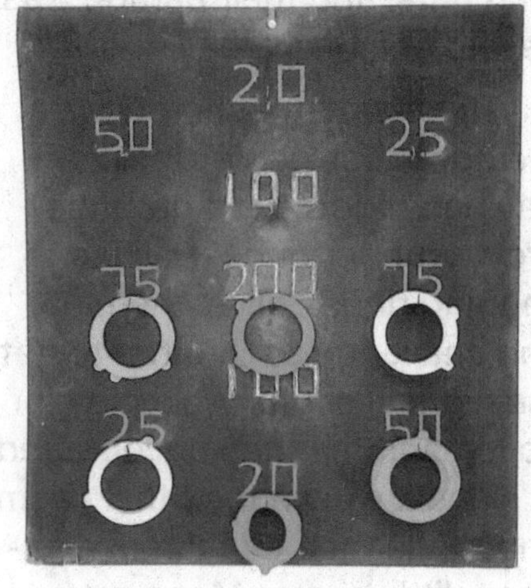

Memorabilia from Aunt Lil and Uncle Ray's basement bar.

When I was younger, my brothers and I would play games on the basement floor. The floor tile included a shuffleboard, and we'd play that for a while, then use the checkerboard patterned square tiles in the rest of the basement to play other, made-up games, like walking on only the white tiles. We were good at making up games back then, with none of the electronic distractions now available to kids and only one television per household, typically broadcasting shows the adults wanted to watch.

We tried playing outside, but their yard was much smaller than ours, and their garage was devoid of a basketball hoop.

The main attraction was the hoop toss game Uncle Ray had made. We'd grab the brown rubber rings (Ball jar canning rings), divvy them up, and challenge each other to get the highest score. We'd play for hours, and the men encouraged it, since it was in the other room and made their adult conversation a little easier. Mona was upstairs helping Aunt Lil, and eventually my grandparents would come over, too. Grandma Grace (Lil's older sister) would make a brief appearance downstairs to get her kisses from each of us, then she would ascend the stairs and take her place in the kitchen, as was customary in those days. Grandpa would join us in a quick game, tussle our hair, then join the men at the bar.

Eventually, dinner was served, and it was as good as any meal served since the first Thanksgiving Day -- turkey, real mashed potatoes with butter and sour cream whipped in, green bean casserole, both types of cranberry sauce, and Aunt Lil's stuffing, which featured raisins and little bits of turkey liver. (I had always despised liver, but her dressing was an unexpected treat.) Even her unique dessert -- lime Jello with pineapple and shredded carrots -- brings back fond memories.

This year, Thanksgiving for the Walters Family will be celebrated differently, in a restaurant instead of a home, but I hope it will be one to evoke sweet memories in the future.

Happy Thanksgiving to all of you.

Smiling Down From Heaven

Originally published December 23, 2021

Sunday was one of those landmark occasions.

Our only son, Nicholas, graduated from the University of Michigan as a computer engineer, and as parents, Debbie and I couldn't be prouder.

I must confess, however, that I am a glass-half-empty kind of guy, so my jubilation was briefly overshadowed by small, random clouds of guilt and regret that threatened to diminish the joy of the occasion.

During the long ceremony in Crisler Arena, my mind wandered back to when I was much younger, when I was about to graduate from college. It was the summer of 1984, and I was sitting at the kitchen table with Mona.

"Are you going to go to the graduation ceremony?" Mona

Debbie proudly poses with her college graduate, Nicholas Walters, after he received his diploma from the College of Engineering at the University of Michigan.

asked me.

"Naw, why bother?" I said, indifferent to the tenor of her voice.

She tried to sound nonchalant as she pressed the question. "Are you sure you wouldn't like to go? It's a big accomplishment!"

"Mona, it took me almost six years to graduate, and I paid for the whole thing. I don't need to pay for a cap and gown or any of that other nonsense," I said with finality. Young and selfish, I didn't even register the crestfallen look on her face at the time, though that look haunts me now.

It takes some of us years to realize what's important in life, and some of us never come to this conclusion: we don't (and shouldn't) always do things solely for our own benefit. Mona deserved to see her eldest son walk across the stage. It was a small ask, yet being that it was unspoken, I never heard it.

That is why I am so thankful today.

Deb and I did ask Nicholas if he was going to walk across the stage for graduation, and he said yes with very little hesitation. Maybe he really wanted to do it? He did work hard, after all. But I think he also did so for the benefit of his parents. He's much more thoughtful than his "old man" ever was, and for that, I'm grateful.

Mona must be smiling down on him.

***

It was a great moment, watching our son, who earned his engineering degree in just three and a half years, receive his diploma in a full auditorium. It was the first major ceremony near the end of the Covid-19 phase of separation and isolation. People were starting to gather again.

Debbie and I sat in our bleacher seats, hoping to hear the usual platitudes about how the young men and women who would receive diplomas had worked diligently thru a period of great strife -- the pandemic. We imagined the gushing praise for their fortitude and resilience.

Unfortunately, the moment came with political commercials...

As each speaker took the stage (and there were many -- almost a dozen), he or she, as if reading from the same script, worked the following four topics into their speech: Climate change, Black Lives Matter, immigrant rights for "Dreamers," and strong support for LGBTQ+ rights.

I don't pour bourbon on my corn flakes. I like bourbon, and I like corn flakes -- just not together.

I could have done without the politics.

I would have been equally offended if I heard every speaker opine on the "border in crisis," the ineffectiveness of masking up, stimulus money as reckless, inflationary spending, and the "Green Agenda" as a Trojan Horse for governmental control.

No place for it at a celebration. Shame on the U of M.

Spirit in the Sky

Originally published January 13, 2022

Thursday, January 6, 2022, 8:00 a.m. Pacific Standard Time -- I'm writing this as my son sleeps, here in Seattle, Washington. It is the day after getting out the weekly Local, and this week's edition was completed with Amanda Morris doing most of the editing and Sue and Chris Salcau doing all of the inserting, labeling and delivering. Though I'm confident they did well, I wasn't able to enjoy myself yesterday. You see, Good Reader, it was a long day of traveling for yours truly. The title this week relates to my long day of travel, specifically to the airline used.

Most who know me are aware of my generally frugal nature. Taking time off and traveling is extravagant for me, so I had to begin planning months ago, booking a hotel, plane, and rental car from the cheapest available sources. I was diligent in my search, and I am confident I got the cheapest rates. Of course, they say you get what you pay for...

My son, Nicholas, and I woke early and arrived at Detroit Metro Airport at about 5:30 a.m. yesterday. That wake-up time was not too much earlier than usual for me, but for Nick it was a feat, being accustomed to a solid 10 to 12 hours of rest. (Ah, I remember those days!)

In the airport, we figured out how to check our luggage and then queued for the preflight security inspection. Once at the table, we began to strip like Vegas show girls -- pockets emptied, belts off (from this point on I had to hold my pants up with one hand as I managed everything else), shoes off, open bags, open coat, say ahhhh, et cetera.

In front of us was a hairy man pleading with a female security guard.

“Really? Come on. It was a gift from my wife -- it's just a little itty-bitty knife,” he said, trying to look both incredulous and wounded as he begged. To my relief (and probably that of the passengers around us), the guard was resolute.

Once past the checkpoint, we waited until the flight

boarded. It was packed. Due to shortness of staff, other flights had been cancelled. The night before we had been offered hundreds of dollars to give up our seats. I considered it, but Nick reminded me of our goal -- to find a suitable apartment for him in Seattle, his new home. He had four appointments scheduled the next day.

Our airplane experience was long and grueling, partially because this discount airline had the smallest amount of leg room in any airplane I've ever been. We sat right over the starboard wing, and behind us was the emergency exit. Also behind us was Sagacious Sam and Adam the Acolyte, the first an older man who insisted on imparting his wisdom to the polite and tolerant younger stranger seated next to him -- *for the entire flight*. If I had a parachute, I may have used it to jump to earth in search of alternative transportation.

"I'm nervous about flying," said Adam the Acolyte.

"Odds are we'll be fine," said Sagacious Sam, "Only about a thousand deaths per year, in fact."

"Only a thousand?" Adam said.

"About 10,000 people die each year of the toxins in jet emissions," Sam continued, "and the worst airplane crash ever was actually on a runway in 1977 when two fully loaded airplanes collided."

As our plane began taxiing to the runway, I glanced at Nick, who looked a little green, and realized I was feeling a little anxious myself. I said a quick prayer and started a conversation with him, trying to drown out Sam's wisdom, which was non-stop, unlike our low-budget flight.

We were first heading to Vegas, baby! And after about four hours in the air, we landed and decided to fill our six hour layover with some gambling action. We caught a cab to Caesar's Palace, hoping to partake in a buffet for lunch. The buffet was closed, but we had a nice lunch anyway. With three hours left before we had to head back to the airport to catch our second flight, I thought I would teach my son about gambling in the city nicknamed 'Lost Wages.'

~~~

When I was young, my four brothers and I would gather at the kitchen table on rainy days to play board games or cards. Paul and I were older, and when we were about 10 or 11 years old, we'd coax our younger brothers to bring their
~~~

Nick chills for a few minutes (literally) at a Vegas slot machine during a layover on our way to Seattle for an apartment search.

birthday money to the table to play poker. (None of us had a lot of money -- just a few dollars, mostly in change -- but none of us had a bank account, either.)

We each snuck to our own respective hiding places and grabbed our cold hard cash to bring to the table.

Once there, we'd explain the rules to our younger brothers, who occasionally managed to get ahead of us, though they never ultimately won. Paul and I were juvenile card sharks, and our three younger brothers -- Mark, Joe, and David -- were baby sharks. (Do-do-do-do, do, do!) We cleaned them out quickly.

I could hear my mother and father in the next room...

"Ralph, what are the boys doing in there?"

"I don't know," he said, with practiced ease. "Just playing, I guess."

His focus on the ball game being broadcast on TV never wavered. Dad was a master -- able to maintain Zen-like concentration despite dogs barking, kids screaming, or his wife asking questions.

"Ralph," Mona said a little louder, "you'd better go in there and check."

So Dad came in and saw Paul and I with large piles of coins and our brothers with nothing. I'm sure we looked guilty when he asked what we were doing, but I'm certain we looked surprised by his response.

"Playing poker, huh?" He said as he came around the table, "Deal me in."

He made us give our little brothers their money back, but Paul and I did so willingly, especially when we saw him pull out a stack of dollars -- COLD HARD CASH!

Now we had a real sucker, or so we thought.

Paul and I won early and often, taking a good share of Dad's money before he decided to teach us about gambling.

"It's fun to win money like this, isn't it?" he said, dealing another hand. Paul and I looked across the table at each other and grinned. 'Yes, sir,' we thought, 'especially when we have a fish like you on the hook!'

"You guys have a lot of money in front of you," he said, nodding to our piles. We each had perhaps six or seven dollars, a fortune for us kids back in the early 70s.

"Why don't we raise the stakes, go double or nothing on the next hand?" He was smooth. Greed lit our eyes, and Paul and I felt invincible. We had been winning almost every hand. Certain of our luck, we readily agreed.

Now, Dad had been shuffling the cards an awful long time while Paul and I focused our minds on how we would spend our fortunes. I'm not saying Dad stacked the deck, but I know now, in my older age and with the perspective of a father myself, that he did have an agenda, and it was NOT to lose money to his kids.

The next hand of cards could have been better called a 'foot' as Paul and I drew nothing but losers. Dad managed an ace high flush, and, with great ceremony, swept both of our pots to himself.

Crestfallen, Paul and I just stared.

"How much money did you start with?" he asked, waiting for our answers.

"You lost it all in one hand" Dad said, matter-of-fact, and then paused for effect.

"Now you have nothing," he said, and Paul and I hung our heads. A few moments passed, allowing the lesson to sink in. Dad underscored the lesson with a final statement.

"Gambling is addictive. You should never gamble more than you are willing to lose," he said, and then he began counting out our money back to us.

"What are you doing, Dad? You won that!" I said.

"I know, but the lesson is more important than the money," he said.

I thought of this as I prepared to take my son into the gambling area of Caesar's Palace, hoping our experience would be as instructive as the one I remembered from my father -- and it was!

We decided to play a slot machine, selecting a Willy Wonka themed machine to swallow our money. We were going to be there for three more hours, so I put a whole $20 bill in each machine. We selected the Willy Wonka machines because we had recently rewatched the beloved movie starring Gene Wilder, and because it had a one penny wager button.

We sat side by side at the pair of like machines. Thinking this would last us until we needed to go back to the airport, I instructed Nick to push the penny button as I did the same.

The machines dazzled us with flashing lights, spinning dials, and a snippet of the immortal Wonka talking about Oompa Loompas. Then they stopped.

Despite the fanfare, we hadn't won, so Nick and I each pushed the penny button again.

Again, we didn't win, but we did hear a charming snippet of Wilder singing about 'pure imagination.'

We pushed the button again and again, but nothing happened.

"Dad, it's not working," Nick said as he slapped at the button. Mine had also stopped working, so we sat there a moment and stared at the flashing lights and the man in the orange top hat.

After a minute or two, we noticed the small print at the bottom of the screen, "Over 1,600 ways to win!"

"Dad, our first bet was over $16. The second bet took the rest," Nick said.

"But we pressed the penny-bet button," I said, a little angry now, shaking my fist like Veruca Salt's father, even though the ultimate goal -- to show my son that gambling eventually leads to a loss of money -- had been accomplished spectacularly!

We spent the rest of our three hours walking around The Strip, mostly looking at construction and sweating because we had to wear our winter coats and boots in this desert climate. By the time we got back to the airport, I was grateful to be boarding the tightly packed plane to our final destination -- Seattle, where we have slept since checking into our hotel, a little poorer in the pocket but richer for the experience nonetheless.

Sustainable Pizza & The Art House Nazi

Originally published January 20, 2022

Last week, I returned with my son from a trip to Seattle. We went to find an apartment for him as he begins his career in software engineering. We saw many apartments, most of them ranging from expensive to very expensive, the average being more than twice what one might pay in Michigan and perhaps three times what might be paid in Clinton.

The cost of apartments wasn't the only difference between my son's new homeland and our home here in Clinton.

On the positive side for Seattle, the roads there were in near perfect condition. We drove every day and came across only two small potholes. Compare that to our Michigan roads! The great condition of their roads is due to the milder climate, I'm told. It seldom snows there, so there's no freeze/thaw, freeze/thaw to buckle the pavement.

The roads there also differ from ours in their design. Because of our winters, we wouldn't dare design roads with the steep slopes found in Seattle. There, I felt like I was on the Mean Streak at Cedar Pointe, going up and down at near-impossible angles. Some of the overpasses soared so high that driving them felt surreal, like being on a life-sized Hot Wheels track.

Other differences were in the treatment of COVID and social distancing. Currently in Seattle, everyone wears a mask *everywhere*. The only time I saw anyone's mouth was in a restaurant, where signs reminded diners to put the mask back on when not ACTIVELY eating or drinking. (In the airport, an overhead announcer warned passengers that "keeping your mask down while holding a beverage is not acceptable.")

There were even Mask Police in Seattle.

On the third day of our trip, after Nick had selected an apartment in Bellevue, a suburb of Seattle, we decided to explore the town a little. We chose a trip to the Bellevue Art Museum, commonly referred to as BAM! (Exclamation mark included.)

Like almost every venue in that area, we were carded at the door -- yes, even an old codger like me! I kept my driver's license in my wallet, though, because their interest was actually in my COVID vaccination card.

Once we were found acceptable, we bought our tickets, discounted due to construction on the second floor. We were told to start at the top -- floor three -- and so we headed to the elevator.

I pushed the call button on the wall as Nick pointed out a sign next to the elevator.

'Please use the stairs if you are able,' the sign read. I gestured to the steps and began to walk in that direction as the elevator door opened. Out strutted a young man, probably mid-twenties, dressed in black with a black scarf wrapped around his neck and slung over his shoulder. He was carrying a black iPad, and his nose was so high in the air I could have given him a sinus exam if I'd had the inclination and a medical degree.

"C'mon, Nick," I said, now gesturing to the empty elevator.

"We're not going to use the stairs?"

I responded in the negative, and then, as the machine lifted us to our destination, gave my son a speech about hypocrisy, pointing out how that young man could certainly have used the stairs. Being a dutiful son, Nick just nodded.

We got to the third floor and looked at an exhibit of hanging pup tents with silhouetted figures inside. On the wall were details about homelessness in the Seattle area. While the exhibit was informative, it became more poignant when we saw the tent villages in downtown Seattle the next day. Much of the art was like that -- more politics than art, in my humble opinion -- though there was one artist whose work I admired.

Still, Nick and I probably didn't appreciate most of the "art." At one point, we came to two freshly painted walls and a twenty foot tall scaffold.

"They must be doing some work on this floor, too," Nick said.

"Unless that's also supposed to be a piece of art," I said in jest, laughing out loud.

Nick joined me, but then he found a placard on the opposite wall, one which had a twelve inch replica of the two-story scaffold next to it. The work was apparently titled 'Scaffolds: Big and Small,' or something like that.

Most of the placards spoke in polished prose about the artist's technique and intent. Most proclaimed their work as an embodiment of the struggle against 'the fascist U.S. government and the American industrial machine,' as well as climate change. Each of them also spoke in great detail about the "sustainability" of their art.

From that point, we voiced our regret about paying the admission fee, even though it had been discounted due to construction, but then I stumbled on one artist I liked (and a few more afterward, too). I asked Nick to pose for a photo that I could send to his mother. He stood in front of the piece, and, since there was *literally* no one else to be seen on the *entire* third floor, I told him to remove his mask for the photo. Three seconds later, his mask was back up and we moved on to the rest of the exhibit.

Two minutes later, as we moved into another room, the young man in black appeared in the opening elevator door and made a bee-line straight for us. I hadn't noticed his matching black jackboots before, but I marvelled at how appropriate they were as he came striding toward us with surprising intensity.

"Sir!" he shouted as he neared, "I must insist that masks be worn at all times!"

He pulled up at attention, back straight and iPad held up like a shield. I almost expected him to pull a sword with the other hand, or perhaps a lightsaber. At that moment, I was glad I had been wearing a mask -- he couldn't see my smirk.

I refrained from pointing out that our masks had been back up for a while or how short the maskless period had been. I also refrained from clicking my heels and throwing an arm forward, palm extended, and crying, "Jawohl, Kapitän." I just said, "Okay," and stared at him, watching to make sure he didn't draw that weapon.

Later, Nick and I figured that he had been using the iPad to watch patrons in the various parts of the museum. Perhaps he even had audio and couldn't wait to come chastise the unwashed heathens who had critiqued some of the displays. It was ironic, really.

We left BAM! and summarized what we had learned. We learned that the newest catchword is "sustainable," and the evidence became overwhelming as we continued our tour of the west. Sustainability was part of nearly every slogan and every sales pitch in Seattle.

The next day, as we queued for a boat tour, a young Asian man was telling his date where he planned to take them after the ride.

"Have you ever been to Joe's Pizzeria? They have great sustainable pizza," he said, smiling.

"What's sustainable pizza?" she asked, to which I silently said, 'Thank you, 'cause I have no idea either.'

Apparently, neither did the young man, but he gamely tried to respond.

"It means they grow everything right there at the store -- the peppers, the chicken, the dough," but his voice trailed off, probably because he realized how ridiculous (and how unappetizing) it sounded.

Nick and I had fun with the term from then on, even naming our team "Sustainably Local" when we took on an escape room near the end of our trip.

Alas, Good Reader, I must begin to wrap up this piece, as my discourse has become... er...
...unsustainable!

Who says this author isn't part of the artistic crowd?

***

Editor's Hindsight: A week or so after this article I received some cool comments from one of my staff photographers. He didn't find my amusement at what passed for art in Washington to be funny. I understood his perspective, of course; two of his daughters had chosen art as their career path.

I actually enjoy art -- real art that demonstrates real talent.

It was the middle school social studies projects -- floating tents with manikins and simple cardboard houses pasted to cardboard baseboards -- as well as the construction materials labeled as art that annoyed me; that, and the $24 admission fee per person (after the discount for the partial closure).

Call me old fashioned, but give me an oil painting or a piece of sculpture any day...

Goodbye, On-Site Tech Support

Originally published February 3, 2022

This week was a difficult one for me.

My wife, Debbie, and I said goodbye to our son -- our only child -- and sent him on his way across the country to begin his career. (For those of you who are thinking, 'Hey, I thought that happened weeks ago!' That was an exploratory trip to Seattle. Now he's gone -- for real.)

I really shouldn't be so gloomy. Nick has already called us, sometimes twice a day, and sometimes with video calls. Nonetheless, I really miss him.

Although, if I'm really being honest, I miss the on-site tech support the most.

These last two months, I've relied on Nick to help us navigate a new in-home wireless service, drop the satellite dish, change cell phone service and abandon our land line, not to mention the day-to-day angst of operating the remote controls. He managed to get us down from four controllers to two, but I still needed his help.

"Oh, Tech Support!" I'd yell from my recliner in the living room. "How do I ...?"

"His name is Nicholas," my wife would remind me, and then she'd proceed to snag him as he dutifully entered the room in answer to our call.

"Nick, how do I print this from my email?" Debbie would ask, and Nick kindly and patiently walked her through the steps. (He had set up the printer the week before.)

In just two short months, we got spoiled by his exemplary service. We came to relish our very own on-site tech guru. It sure beats trying to work with the guys in the cellular store, who promised me that my former cell service would "automatically be cancelled as soon as the number is switched over."

It was not. In fact, I still have to cancel my original plan. I've tried to reach the cell company's tech support team but haven't been able to get past the phone maze:

"Press one for this, press two for that..." No number is ever offered for a live person.

I did get a live person when I called to cancel my satellite service, which was a good thing because they had no online option to do so. I understood their reason for it after speaking with Clarissa from customer support.

"Can I have your account name and address?" Clarissa asked pleasantly. I gave it, stating that I was simply calling to cancel the service.

"Very well, Mr. Walters. I'll be glad to help you with that this evening," she said smoothly. "How are you doing there in Michigan?"

"Cold," I responded.

"I'm here in Galveston, Texas, and it's been unseasonably cold here, too. Do you have family there?"

I responded affirmatively, and she proceeded to make small talk, insisting that she was waiting on her computer to call up the account. (Had I had my personal Tech Support, I mean, Nicholas, with me, I would have checked her on that. Computers haven't taken that long since the Apple IIe.)

While waiting, I got to hear about Clarissa's four children and about how much she personally loved satellite television. After several minutes of this, I firmly reasserted that I simply wanted to cancel the service. I told her that we were now joining the millions who 'stream' their favorite programs.

"Ewww, you're streaming? Why would you want to do that," Clarissa hissed.

I hadn't heard that tone of voice since I was in middle school when my cousin Grace tried to set me up with a pretty blonde at the canteen. (Ewww, you want me to dance with him?)

Frustrated and tired, I again stated my wishes and was warned that I would have an early termination fee for less than two years of service. I told her that, fee or no fee, I wanted out. Our social palaver was over.

Now that Nick is gone, Debbie and I keep trying to pass the mantle of Tech Wizard to each other, and I think she's going to win that one. The other day, she figured out how to connect the sound bar to the TV, so naturally I thought I'd try out the title on her.

"Hey, Tech Support..."

Luckily, I managed to duck.

Can I Get An Amen?

Originally published February 10, 2022

Last week I had trouble sleeping.

It sometimes happens when I worry. I won't go into detail, but suffice to say that anxiety has led to some wakefulness in the wee hours.

I understand that I am not alone, and that some restlessness is even normal.

It happens more frequently as I've aged, and it bothers me because I always used to sleep like a rock.

Invariably, I turn to prayer when I have these moments, and soon I am at ease.

Sunday, my pastor read from the Gospel of Luke -- the story of how Jesus recruited his first two apostles, Andrew and Peter. Jesus asked them to take him out in their fishing boat, even though they had had an exhausting and unsuccessful night, catching very little. I was intrigued by this story as I sat there Sunday, even though I'd probably heard it dozens of times.

One of the first things to occur to me was how Jesus used boats and water and fishing to teach important lessons. In this case, when he caused their nets to be filled to bursting with fish, he showed them that they could count on him to provide.

Again in a boat some time later, Jesus stilled the water during a storm, reinforcing to his apostles that they should place their faith in him and the Father.

Some of you Good Readers out there may have stopped reading by now, thinking that I've gone off the deep end as some kind of religious zealot. I start this week's piece as I did to share what else was on my mind as I contemplated the Gospel Sunday, and I'm embarrassed to say it was not exactly reverent...

~~~

My father and my brother, Mark, were both avid fishermen. In fact, they took annual fishing vacations, often as far as Chapleau, Ontario, Canada. More often, the fishing trips were in-state, and on a couple occasions we chartered a boat
~~~

The Brothers:
The author (on the far left, grinning because he has once again made himself appear to be the tallest in the family), Mark (AKA Lips, Chico, and other less savory names), Ralph (Dad), Joe (AKA HoJoe and Joe Terro), Dave (AKA Dewey and Saucey), and Paul (AKA Froggy Philbuster and Juice).

with another avid fisherman, our Uncle Bill, who operated his charter boat out of Luna Pier at Lake Erie and out of Ludington at Lake Michigan.

Mark and my Dad were hankering for a fishing trip, so Mark called 'The Brothers' (as we were called by some), and we headed to Lake Erie for some Walleye fishing.

Uncle Bill introduced us to his first mate, and we cruised out to one of the "hot spots."

Nothing.

After 20 minutes there, we moved along to another part of the lake. Uncle Bill called for his mate to adjust the outriggers as we all sat and relaxed. I enjoyed the sun and the mist that came off the water as the hull sliced through the waves. Mark was getting irritated and started questioning the lures we had on the lines.

After another 45 minutes, Uncle Bill called other boats on his radio. To our chagrin (but not to our surprise), they all reported that they were not having luck either.

We continued to troll along, and the rest of the brothers decided to enjoy the contents of the cooler while Mark stewed over the lack of fish.

Having had a few cans of refreshment from the cooler myself, I started talking louder and making jokes. Mark thought we should all be miserable about the lack of fish, and he told us so.

"You guys need to be quiet. You're scaring the fish away," he said, "and save some of that beer for later."

"Relax, Mark. We'll catch fish eventually," I said, honestly not caring if we did or didn't, but it felt like the right thing to say.

"Yeah, right, we'd need a miracle," he muttered as he turned away to once again inspect the outriggers.

And that's when inspiration (combined with alcohol) prompted me to raise my hand and proclaim with televangelical zeal, "Can I get an AMEN!"

Two of my brothers (the ones who had joined me in raiding the cooler) gave me an "Amen," and I was emboldened.

"My brothers, I tell you in the name of Jesus, in the name of our Lord, that our nets will be filled," I shouted, hand still raised in testimony. "In the name of Jesus, when I touch this rod, God will cause fish to strike these lines until our boat is full!"

And then I brought my hand down. I missed the rod at first, my aim being a little off due to, ahem, circumstances, but then I tried again.

"In the name of Jesus, I command the fish in this lake to strike our lines!"

Now, for those Good Readers who have never been charter fishing, the fishing poles stay in holders along both sides of the boat until a fish strikes, and then the fisherman grabs the rod and goes to work. All afternoon the lines had been dead, but now they sprung to life.

Mark grabbed one line and handed it to Dad. Then a second one popped, then a third, and so on, until even the first mate and Captain Bill were holding a rod.

Twenty minutes later, we headed back to the pier with our limit.

Back ashore, my brothers and Captain Bill marveled at the "coincidence," but I knew better. After all, my mother's favorite Bible line had always been, "Ask and you shall receive."

And that's just what I had done.

So now, in the dark of night, I remind myself to put my worries in God's hands and ask for His help.

Can I get an Amen?

Life in the Fast Lane

Originally published February 22, 2022

Last week, I got in trouble with the police. Well, sort of...

You see, Good Reader, I got a text message from the Clinton Chief of Police Tony Cuevas. He sent me a clip from Facebook showing my wife, Debbie, in a conversation about the "speed trap" near the Shell gas station in the Village.

"Debbie is giving away all of our trade secrets," Tony texted with a laughing emoji.

Tony Cuevas is a good police officer, a very good police officer. I also consider him a friend, but I haven't always been friendly with police officers.

Now, don't get me wrong, I've managed to make it 60 years without acquiring a criminal record. Yet I haven't always had such a positive view of our men and women in blue...

When I was in my early twenties, I lived in Detroit, and I used to hang out at the corner party store called Hannon's. If you stuck around there long enough, you'd see just about everyone in the neighborhood. It gave me a chance to gather the local news the old-fashioned way.

A few of us would stand around at the counter and talk with whoever was working -- Arty, Tom, Lillian, or the owner -- Nabil, who went by Bill. If Bill was there, he'd let us buy a beer and hang around the counter, sipping our drink and smoking cigarettes. (Yes, smoking indoors -- it was a thing back then.) We'd have to hide the open beer cans if a non-regular customer came in, and we got pretty good at the cover-up.

Often, we were joined by Detroit's Finest. The Detroit Police had a height requirement until 1974. The minimum height was 5'8", but most officers were well over six feet tall, and the majority were male. I can still visualize our neighborhood's beat officers, though I no longer remember their names.

One summer day, the officers came in, and Bill offered them a cold one. They each grabbed a can of Schlitz and stood there with us (in uniform and on duty) sippin' on beers and talkin' 'bout the Tigers, a common activity in the old neighborhood.

One of the officers, whom I'll call Oscar, was mid-sip when his radio squawked.

"Car 57, we have a 10-23 in progress at 387 Piedmont. Do you copy?"

"Copy that," Officer Oscar said into his walkie talkie, which he then calmly replaced on his hip as he resumed drinking his beer and talking baseball. "Trammell and Whitaker are the best double play combo the game's ever seen!"

Big Gary, a sports nut and employee at the "book store" down the road (that never seemed to sell any actual books), took the bait and began to argue for Dave Concepcion and Joe Morgan of the Cincinnati Reds.

Bill and I looked at each other. We looked at the walkie-talkie. We looked at Officer Oscar, and we looked back at each other.

The great sports debate went on for minutes, with Bill and I exchanging looks that turned from questioning to concerned to panicked. Finally, Bill interrupted Officer Oscar.

"What's a 10-23?"

Officer Oscar looked irritated at being interrupted, but he apparently remembered who was the host, and so he answered.

"Domestic problem," and then he went back to the debate with Big Gary.

Apparently, his nonchalant answer had the same effect on Bill as it had on me. I visualized a woman, possibly a mother with children, being bullied or beaten by a drunken husband or boyfriend -- Burning Bed stuff. Bill must have had the same on his mind because now we both looked alarmed. Bill interrupted the sports talk again, this time with a note of anger in his voice.

"Aren't you going to go stop it?"

With eerie calm, Officer Oscar responded to Bill patiently, as if explaining to a preschool child.

"Nah, we let 'em get it all out of their system, and then we go pick up the pieces," he said, draining his beer. "We'll head out in about 30 minutes. Got another beer?"

Was there ever any wonder that the people of Detroit never really had warm, fuzzy feelings about their police force?

Good Cop, Bad Cop

In Memoriam

Tony Cuevas
Clinton Police Chief
2019 -- 2025

What makes them different? What is the difference between a "good cop" and a bad one?

Tony Cuevas was a good cop. Here's what made him different:

- Tony believed in law and order, and he believed in doing his job. (Others, well, you just read about the others, Good Reader.)
- Tony -- Chief Tony --- wrote tickets all day long, enforcing the speed limit in our sleepy town. (Other small town chiefs would spend the bulk of their days at a desk -- "why bother?")
- Tony Cuevas looked for ways to serve the community, regularly speaking to children in the township library, to senior citizens in church basements, to Rotarians over a home-cooked meal. (Others? Well, they may have made it for the meal...)
- Tony Cuevas created and ran a law enforcement club at Clinton High School because he wanted to share his love for his chosen field, wanted to pass the torch to the next generation. (Who else does something like that!)
- Tony Cuevas served his community by contributing regularly to The Clinton Local, first by reporting the monthly police statistics in a neatly typed, print-ready condition -- much appreciated by his editor -- and then also writing a monthly column called "Ask the Chief." (I don't think many communities newspapers can say they've received that level of involvement and cooperation.)

Tony was a good cop.

He was also a dear friend.

We shared stories from our careers over weekly coffee meetings whenever Tony could get away. (My "Coffee with Cuevas.") More importantly, we spoke of our love of family. Tony loved his wife, Rita, his children and his grandchildren -- Tony loved life.

He died suddenly on June 21, 2025, at his home.

Many miss him. I miss him.

~~You're~~ I'm So Vain

Originally published April 14, 2022

"Vanity, Thy Name is Woman" -- is often attributed to the great bard, William Shakespeare, who actually said "Frailty, thy name is woman" in the play, Hamlet.

It's probably no coincidence that vanity and frailty go hand in hand. My own vanity has indeed been a weakness.

Last week, I published a photo of myself and Clinton stylist Tishina Underwood in the paper to accompany an article about Salon 102 reopening in their new digs. The photo probably could have been best captioned as "Beauty and the Beast," and I don't really need to tell anyone who was "Beauty." Nonetheless, the mental image I hold of myself is a good three to five stars higher than reality, so when I get honest feedback, it sometimes rocks my world.

The Beauty: Tishina Underwood helped the author -- The Beast -- with a needed Covid trim.

After viewing the photo in the paper last week, a friend told me I looked like Mister Miyagi of Karate Kid fame. Now, I wouldn't mind if I was told I fought like Mister Miyagi, or that I had the mental discipline of a Kung Fu master, but the looks? My friend continued...

"Without your glasses, you look like Mister Miyagi, and with your glasses you look like Mister... what's the cartoon guy?"

I hesitated, dread creeping in, but an overwhelming sense of sardonic humor pushed me to offer... "Mister Magoo?"

"Yes! Yes! YES!"

The laughter was violent and disturbing, and in that moment I decided it was time for a change.

Too cheap to really consider plastic surgery, I looked to familiar territory -- my facial hair. I'd taken to growing a goatee this winter, which certainly lent itself to the Mister Miyagi look. It had to go!

Sunday, I drove to pick up some office supplies and added a beard and mustache trimmer to my pile of goods. I decided I would shave the offending mouth-mullet at the next available opportunity. On Monday, I dropped off packages of photos to the three school buildings, entrusting them to the coaches who taught there. As I was leaving Clinton Elementary School, I crossed paths with Lora Forgiel, the young middle school art teacher. It was a sunny and warm day, which matches Lora's personality well. I greeted her. Startled, she responded.

"Oh, my!" she said, "I didn't even recognize you!"

"It's been a long time," I said, thinking of the separation COVID has brought to us for the past couple years.

"No," she said, "I mean the beard. It looks really good on you!"

If Lora wasn't already my favorite teacher in Clinton before then, she certainly moved to the top of the list at that moment. (Flattery will get you pretty far with this old man!)

In a few minutes, our conversation concluded, though I can't recall what the rest of it was about. My mind repeatedly circled back to her flattery. But was it really flattery?

After all, she is an artist.

And artists definitely know beauty when they see it, right?

Or perhaps she admired my goatee because of the avant garde, artsy-fartsy vibe it exudes?

I guess that makes me either truly good looking or incredibly cool. I can live with either.

At home, I took a moment to look in the mirror, and reality crept back in with alarming speed. Miyagi or Magoo... I just look old! Maybe a little dye would do the trick?

But no, I recalled the time I tried that, about 10 years back..

I had purchased a package from the drugstore, one of those kits where you mix two creams into one paste and then spread it on your beard and mustache. The final mixture was a caramel color.

'How could that possibly darken my hair?' I thought.

I began to apply it and Debbie, my wife, came into the bathroom to tell me something. I finished applying the mixture and Debbie mentioned an issue with the kitchen sink. I followed her to the kitchen, looked it over, got my tools, fiddled a bit (in an effort to look like I was actually doing something), and continued to chit chat with her, forgetting about the mixture I had applied to my facial hair -- a mixture that warned DO NOT EXCEED 5 MINUTES.

Eventually, realization dawned on me, and I raced back to the bathroom. In the mirror, I was looking at Sir Graves Ghastly, my skin had achieved a pallor heretofore unseen due to my now inky black facial hair.

Frantically, I washed my facial hair a dozen times, finally resigning myself to live with my new mask of vanity until it faded, as everything, even beauty, always does.

I turned my one eye away from the mirror, preferring the vain perfection in my mind's eye, where my youthful countenance remains without blemish or wrinkle.

A mug only a mother could love...

The Dangers of Recycling and Online Surfing

Originally published May 19, 2022

Since I owned my first home in Redford in the late 1980s, I have been a conscientious recycler. I have also been an avid, and occasionally even apt, user of computer technology since that decade. Even with such a head start, I'm apparently fading -- rapidly -- to that lower level of functionality that we all end up at as we age.

We become our parents, as the commercial says.

Sunday is recycling night at my house, and so, after doing a few hours of yard work, I prepped the trash and recycling bins to be rolled to the road. Along the side of my garage I had leaned a large cardboard box to protect the surface against the weighty metal light fixtures I had stored there for scrapping. It looked tacky, especially after the work I had begun to beatify the flower beds, so I decided it was time to remove them. I packed the metal in my car (taking multiple trips with my little Prius) and finally cleared away the debris. Now came the time to cut the cardboard. I had just gotten a new razor knife and was enjoying the ease with which it cut. (Funny how a newer blade will make the job easier; I tend to use blades -- and everything else -- much longer than they were ever meant to be used.) I grabbed the box, set it up on top of the trash bin, and cut one side of it into six rectangular pieces, which fit neatly inside the bin. I then flipped it over to cut the other side and "Ouch!"

(Though if I'm honest, I said a lot more than that!)

A HORNET!

And it was on the tender inside of my left elbow, just above the joint. It was dangling there by its stinging tail, and I reacted...

<Slash>

I swatted at the little demon -- with my right hand -- yes, the one with the box cutter still firmly in its grasp.

Now the pain of the hornet's stinger paled by comparison to the new wound, though after a few minutes and a few paper towels, a little hydrogen peroxide and a dozen cotton balls, I was almost as good as new.

I was grateful for two things. The first is that I swiped at, instead of smacking, the insect. The second thing I was grateful for was that the hornet hadn't landed on my neck. (I could just hear my brother Paul standing over me at the funeral home, wondering aloud if I would win this year's Darwin Award.)

Friday the 13th had been the previous Friday, but I was starting to wonder if this was going to be a week for bad luck.

Debbie had a harrowing brush with an online scammer, one which caused her to head to the bank and change account passwords. She avoided serious damage, but then again, she's always been lucky.

Earlier that same week, Debbie asked me about our flight tickets for the Memorial weekend. I had booked the flight to visit our son early in March, but now, two full months later, I couldn't remember the details. (No surprise there!)

"I'll check my email to confirm our departure time," I said last week, but when I went to my email, I found nothing. Frantic, I checked all three email accounts I use -- nothing. Thinking that I had booked the flight at home on my cell phone, I checked it thoroughly. Again, nothing. Now I was beginning to panic. To my surprise, I remembered the airlines, Alaska Airlines, and tried to call.

"Expected wait times are currently between five and six hours," said the online recording, "and due to high volume, we cannot offer call-back service at this time."

It doesn't matter who you are; nobody (and I do mean nobody, despite my column a couple weeks ago) has that much time to wait on a phone call. I looked at the website and tried the "chat" option. The bar said my wait was only going to be an "estimated" 37 minutes. An hour later, I gave up on that estimate, sincerely hoping they did not use the same program to make other estimates, like the amount of fuel needed for a particular flight. I tried to chat again the next day, with similar results, though the estimated wait time was a provocative 17 minutes.

I thought some more and then remembered that I had used some of those online travel services in January when I took the first trip to Seattle with my son, Nick. Prior to that, the most recent flight I had booked was through a live travel agent, back when airport security was no tougher than hopping aboard a city bus.

When I had planned the January trip, I recorded every detail, sent copies to both Deb and Nick, and even "printed the internet," like those people from the television commercial who are "turning into their parents."

This time, I apparently thought of myself as an expert because I had done none of the above.

Monday, sliced arm still stinging, I went to my bank. The teller there found the payments to the airline and also noticed a payment to Expedia. I headed back to my office and -- surprise -- I found the confirmation on that site.

I'm still not able to print my tickets; that's restricted until 24 hours before the flight. I know that I could just load it onto my phone, but all the same, I think I'll print the tickets, too.

And then I'll recycle them.

That's Amore and Other Love Songs My Father Never Sang

Originally published June 16, 2022

A couple weeks ago, I promised I would write two stories this month in honor of the 25th wedding anniversary of my wife, Debbie, and yours truly. I tentatively titled the two articles "That's Amore" and "Dauntless Debbie and the Timeshare Triad."

"That's Amore" is the appropriate choice this week because it is also something of a Father's Day tale.

Mona (my mother) often referred to me as my father's favorite son. I refuted the notion that I was anyone's favorite, and I would point to my brother Mark, who was the best athlete in the family (and consequently got a lot of Dad's attention.) But I must admit that I always looked out for my father, especially when it concerned pleasing my mother.

"Ralph, will you stop watching the ball game long enough to mow the lawn today?" Mona would ask, seemingly oblivious to the fact that the Tigers were playing the Yankees in a Saturday afternoon double header.

Understandably, my father would start to grow angry at the thought of missing an inning or two, and usually I would spring up and offer to mow the lawn or handle whatever chore was at hand. (To be honest, it wasn't as noble as it might sound; I always preferred doing rather than watching -- I grew tired of watching sports on TV.)

Over the years, I would step up to help smooth the rough edges in my parents' relationship, and, consequently, I learned not to always go along with my father's thoughts on romance, occasionally guiding him in a different direction. (There was, of course, the time I went along with his decision to get Mona a frying pan for Valentine's Day. I was young then, but her reaction must have been impressive because, to this day, I don't even consider cookware as a gift for Debbie.)

When my parents' 50th Anniversary Party was being planned, Mona told me she would like all five of her sons to sing for her. She wanted us to sing as a group and as individuals. Raising five boys, she had heard countless people tell her we should form a singing group, becoming an Italian Jackson Five, or something like that. (Dad's friends always encouraged him to have four more -- so he could form a baseball team. To that, he would heartily agree, though not in front of Mona.)

My mother had been talking about the party for almost a year, and with a few months to go, I decided it was time to come up with a plan. I called my brothers and told them they had to each sing a song individually, and we got together to decide on a group song -- "That's Amore."

I knew this was going to be a highlight of Mona's life. She had been diagnosed with cancer a few years earlier, and after having a kidney removed, she had been on chemotherapy constantly. She was a fighter. She deserved the best, so I thought it would be special if I could enlist my father's help in selecting a song. I knew he wouldn't sing, but I figured I could sing on his behalf, kind of a Cyrano of Song, if you will.

"Dad, what song would you sing to Mom if you were up there?" I asked him one evening. He didn't even hesitate, bursting into a nasal rendition of Hoagy Carmichael's "Huggin and Chalkin."

"Ohhh, I got a gal who's mighty sweet,

Big blue eyes and tiny feet,

Her name is Rosabelle Magee,

And she tips the scales at three-oh-three..."

My mind filled with flashback images of that frying pan and what Mona might do with it if I actually sang that song for her anniversary.

I thanked my father and decided to step up to the plate on his behalf once again. I combed through hundreds of songs, looking up Billboard charts from their era and discarding them because I thought them silly. I moved on to my era and settled on Paul McCartney's "My Love." I had been a major fan of Sir Paul as a teen and figured I could tell the audience and my mother, by way of introduction, that I selected this song on behalf of my father, that it really expressed his feelings toward Mona.

I practiced that song over and over again in my car on the way to work and back -- two and a half hours a day -- for over a month. I must say, I sounded great, especially when I turned up the volume on the

The Brothers sing "That's Amore."

CD player. I was ready. Not only was I in good voice, but I felt I had selected the perfect song

My brother Paul, who always joked around, didn't plan anything but came in and picked out "Chantilly Lace" by The Big Bopper. Mark sang "The Way You Look Tonight" by Frank Sinatra. Joe sang Kenny Rogers' "Through the Years," and Dewey, the one with the real pipes, was to sing Josh Groban's "You're Still You."

But I was first, being the eldest.

I took the microphone and welcomed the crowd -- family and friends from five decades. Mona was beaming, and Dad looked proud. I regaled them with my introduction, swinging the mic smoothly from one hand to the other as I warmed them up with a joke or two. Then I got to the piece de resistance -- my song.

"Now I'd like to sing a special song that I think sums up how our father really feels about our mother. He may not always tell her he loves her, but the love between them is understood, like it says in this song..." and then I began.

It was going along fine, though the high notes seemed a little higher than they did in the car. Yet, I was gathering momentum, a musical juggernaut building to the crescendo that was the third and final verse, until...

Silence, except for me lamely continuing with the next verse -- unaccompanied.

I looked over at the DJ, a family friend, and he did a comically big shrug of his shoulders. Then I looked at my brothers, the four of them lined against the wall by the disc jockey. Three of them -- Mark, Paul, and Joe -- were pointing at the youngest, Dewey, who was just starting to realize that he had (mistakenly, he claims to this day) pulled the plug on me.

"You can start over," he said to me from stage left, and then to the DJ, quickly, "Just start it over, start it over!"

"I'm not starting over!" I nearly shouted. I honestly barely held it together, not seeing the humor everyone else saw in the moment until much, much later. But I managed to recover, which was good since I was the emcee. I even managed a gracious introduction for Dewey, though I had to force myself to stay away from the wall outlet.

We ended the singing spectacle with "That's Amore," which had been Mona's request.

All in all, it was a beautiful occasion.

I did get my revenge, however.

I had been videotaping the event, and I decided to produce a video of the occasion to pass out as Christmas gifts. All of us were at Mom and Dad's with our families, and we gathered around the DVD player. I watched Dewey out of the corner of my eye as we got to the show.

"You did a nice job as the host, Mike," Dewey said, possibly trying to soften the moment he knew was about to be replayed.

"Thanks," I said, smiling, "Here comes the song..."

"Wow," Dewey said after the first verse, "you really sounded good!"

"Sorry you pulled the plug on me? Huh?"

He stared at the screen a little longer. I not only sounded good, I sounded like Sir Paul McCartney himself.

I had synched my lips to McCartney's recording of the song almost perfectly. I say almost because it wasn't until a few seconds before the Great Unplugging that it became obvious ...

"You didn't!" he cried incredulously.

Yes, I did. Posterity be damned. I pulled a Milli Vanilli, and that's that.

Happy Father's Day to all of you!

Dauntless Debbie and The Timeshare Triad

Originally published June 23, 2022

There are moments when you just know that something is right.

Many of us, I'm sure, can recall that moment when we knew that certain he or she was the one we wanted to be with for the rest of our lives -- for richer or poorer. I believe I may have already shared that moment with you, Good Reader. Now I'd like to share another such moment, one that might come under the category of 'glad I did it.' It was the time my wife, Debbie, stared down a triad of evil timeshare salespeople in Las Vegas. I'll share the tale with you now, in honor of our 25th anniversary next week.

We were married on June 28, 1997, on a day that was every bit as hot as the ones we've been coping with lately. Deb nearly wilted on the altar in her full length dress, but she managed to hang in through the entire ceremony -- a full Catholic Mass at St. Christopher Church in Detroit, complete with family photos of every configuration afterward. Deb was a real trooper.

We paid for the wedding mostly ourselves, as both of us were a bit old for first timers. Additionally, our engagement was short -- a little over a year, not much time for saving. Consequently, we tried to do everything in a discounted fashion.

This naturally led to a few arguments. When I found out the four-tier wedding cake was almost $800, I lobbied for a sheet cake from The Warehouse Club (think Costco), and I lost.

We also had a 'wedding planner,' who helped Deb get what she considered a good deal on a dress and then helped tailor it. It did look beautiful, but her service could have stopped there. The 'wedding planner' was also supposed to make sure things ran smoothly at both the ceremony and reception, but she couldn't seem to get our photographer past the altar police (AKA a little old Polish woman) for up close photos as we said our vows. Every wedding ceremony photo was from the back of the church

-- almost 50 yards away! The wedding planner also apparently hadn't taken the time to make sure the disc jockey knew how to say any of the Italian names in my family.

There were a few other foibles on the day, but all in all it was storybook:

- The bride did not run away at the altar.
- Nor did said bride pass out in the heat.
- Nobody stood up to object during the ceremony.
- My Best Man, Paul, did not embarrass me during the toast. (Well, not really!)
- I didn't trip on Debbie's long dress during our first dance as Mister and Missus.

In the end, the open bar at the ceremony helped dissolve any anxiety or hostility left in the day. After a heavenly night, we celebrated Deb's birthday (which is June 29) with family and close friends, and then we packed to begin our honeymoon the following day.

We had spent everything on the wedding, nearly $12,000, a lot back then, but nothing like what many of our friends had spent. All in all, my new wife had the same frugal streak running through her veins as I had in mine. My mother, Mona, would have said it was due to our German heritage. (Dad was part German, part French, and half Irish. Debbie is also a mutt -- another thing we had in common.)

Unsure what we would receive in gifts, we didn't make any extravagant plans for our honeymoon after the first night. (You may remember, Good Reader, that we spent that night writhing in pain from food poisoning, a consequence of our excessively frugal nature.)

Deb and I were intent on spending two weeks for our honeymoon, so that left us 13 days. Our budget forced us to plan to spend all of those nights on a friend's floor in San Diego -- not romantic, but certainly economical, and it was warm and sunny.

Fortunately, an old friend of mine, John Manchell, gave us the use of his timeshare in Las Vegas as a wedding gift. It was a suite, with a lavish bedroom, a kitchen and a living room, and it was ours for five days and four nights.

"Could you just do me one favor?" John asked me after he bestowed the gift. How could I refuse?

I agreed on the spot, and then I told my fiance.

"Deb, we won't have to

sleep on my friend's floor for the whole two weeks!"

That was the equivalent of starting off with the good news, so then I naturally had to reveal the bad news.

"The only catch is that I had to agree to us sitting down for a 'brief' sales pitch so that John gets credit with the timeshare company," I said, almost exactly as John had told me, including, incredibly, the word "Brief."

Excited by this good news, Debbie made adjustments to our itinerary, delighted to find that flights to Las Vegas were considerably cheaper than those to San Diego. We would fly there first, drive to the fancy honeymoon hotel on the Pacific Ocean for one magical night, and then drive back to Vegas to enjoy the five day stay at the timeshare.

Being thrifty, we caught a red-eye flight from Detroit to Vegas, arriving around 6 a.m. We checked into the room, and I hit the bed, exhausted from the overnight flight.

Deb was invigorated by the new environment, so she went to the 'guest lounge' to check out the slot machines. I had barely begun to snore when she was looming over me in bed.

"Ooh, my beautiful new wife has come to wake me up," I said, mustering as much sexy swagger as I could, even though the words slurred out of my still sleepy mouth.

"No!" She said, lightly slapping my chest. "They want us to go down to their office."

'Well, that's not very romantic,' I thought, still groggy, and then stated the obvious, "Do they realize we just got in?"

Apparently they had, though as a sales technique, I have to say it isn't effective. I went down there feeling grumpy. It wasn't until later that I realized they favored the techniques used in hostage scenarios over those used by mere salesmen.

Truly dauntless, sixty-something year old Debbie mingles with the youngsters near stage front at a Faster Horses festival in Brooklyn, Michigan.

Deb and I talked resistance strategy on the way down in the elevator.

"You know that they are going to try to sell us a timeshare,"

I said, tensing my shoulders and setting my jaw in preparation.

"That's okay, we don't have to buy," Deb answered lightly, "And aren't we supposed to get tickets to a show or something?"

My new admiration for her began to blossom right there; she was like a convict facing the electric chair and asking, "What's for dessert?"

We reached the offices and checked in at a desk. We filled out a form, gave them our identification, and took a seat -- as if we had made an appointment. Deb asked about the tickets, inquiring if they had tickets for Siegfried & Roy, the famous magicians who also trained white lions and tigers.

"Oh, we have tickets for almost every show in town, all up and down the strip," the girl chirped.

"Well, can we get Siegfried & Roy tickets for our time here today?" Deb persisted.

"Oh, we'll have to see how your interview goes, but I'm sure I can find something for you!"

We didn't have to wait long as a steely-eyed woman in black pants and a dark suit coat came into the reception area. Her hair was short and looked to be dyed salt and pepper, making her look older. She turned her face with its sharp, narrow nose toward the bubbly receptionist, and told her, "Our guests will be meeting with Erica."

"Yes, Miz Turner!" Our bubbly secretary bounced up and led us past her boss, who appraised us like the witch in Hansel and Gretel. Erica was young, probably in her 20s, and seemed a little nervous.

'This should be easy,' I thought. 'I have students older than her. There's no way she's going to get us to buy a timeshare!'

Erica told us how much fun it would be to own a timeshare. She told us that all the cool couples had at least one. She showed us pictures of timeshares all over the world that we could use. And then she asked us if we would like to buy one.

"No, thank you," I said, politely but firmly. Erica looked sheepishly at Miz Turner, who scowled and glared across the room. She looked like an angry baseball coach, ready to walk to the mound to pull the pitcher, but who instead taps an arm to indicate that a relief pitcher should be brought in.

Across the room, a young man in his late 20s -- Patrick

-- came bounding toward us, tie loosened and shirt sleeves rolled casually to the elbows.

"Hey, how 'ya dooin'? D'Erica show you all the great places you could go?" Patrick said as he smoothly slid into Erica's seat and she headed back into the bullpen.

"What about our tickets?" Debbie asked as Erica walked away, promising to 'check on' our tickets.

Patrick went to work on me. He was casual and likeable, and I really didn't want to disappoint him. His pitch was smooth and seductive, and I was beginning to crack.

"Well, I guess it would be nice to go anywhere in the world..." I said, slipping into a trance.

"We're not getting a time-share," Deb said, breaking the spell. "We can't afford it."

Patrick pushed the book of pretty places in front of me (apparently hoping this version of a shiny object would keep me hypnotized) and turned his attention to Deb.

She was resolute, and she repeated her spell-breaking mantra."We're not getting a timeshare."

Patrick tried again with Deb, and then again, causing her to

Debbie and Michael Walters, 1997

forcefully say the phrase three times, and just like the Beetlejuice movie, it summoned a demon -- Miz Turner herself. (In fact, now that I think of it, her short spiky hair resembled that of Michael Keaton's in said movie.)

"I'll take over from here, Patrick," Turner said, placing a hand on his shoulder, black talons short but sharpened ominously at the tips. Patrick skulked back to the bullpen, where he and Erica both watched with looks of both admiration and fear, as if Zeus had descended from Mount Olympus to parlay with mere mortals.

Turner didn't even look at me, her years of experience and predatory instinct assured her that I would do as she bid -- if she could get past Debbie.

I looked at my wife, who had set her face like iron and stared back into the vacuum of Turner's eyes with conviction.

"We are not getting a timeshare," Deb said, unwavering.

It was a classic standoff, a case of the immovable object meeting the irresistible force. If it were a movie, I'd have queued "The Devil Went Down to Georgia" by the Charlie Daniels Band, or perhaps the theme music from "The Good, The Bad, and The Ugly."

Miz Turner tried and tried for almost another hour, but Debbie's resolve was unflagging. She occasionally altered her pitch, and sometimes her wording.

"This is an opportunity of a lifetime," Turner said.

"That's nice, but we're not buying a timeshare," Deb replied nonplussed. After a few more times, Debbie switched it up.

"You won't get an offer like this anywhere else. You'd be foolish not to take it," Turner said, now showing her frustration. She clearly was not used to losing.

"I hope not because we're not buying a timeshare," Deb said, and then started adding, "Where are our tickets to the show?"

After a few more times, Miz Turner curtly rose, turned on her heels, and marched to the reception desk.

"Give them their tickets!" she nearly spat at the once bubbly receptionist. "... from the second drawer."

After nearly two hours, we finally walked toward the exit, but first we picked up our hard earned tickets. My wife asked what show they were for, and the receptionist told us they were for a magic show.

"A really good one?" she said, trying to sound upbeat and cheerful. We went to that show, which was uptown in the old section of Vegas, and there were only 10 or 12 people in the whole place.

I enjoyed that show, but the one I remember best is the one my wife put on earlier that day. Her resolve to stick with our plan, to do what was best for our new family -- that was the real show.

That was the real magic show, and the magic has been there ever since.

Happy Anniversary, Debbie.

Country Road (Take Me Home)

Originally published June 30, 2022

I was wrong.

I always thought of the state of Ohio as flat, brown, and bleak, despite the fact that some of the liveliest characters I've ever met hail from there -- Clinton's Jim Rolland, my brother-in-law Jeff, and Buckeye Bub (Bob). I've considered all three friends even though all are stout-hearted Ohio State fans.

You see, Good Reader, I was raised a Wolverine fan. My brothers and I sang "Hail to the Victors" with my father every fall Saturday after every touchdown, and during the days of Bo Schembechler, that was a lot of singing!

It wasn't until I married my wife -- a Spartan -- that I had to set aside my Maize and Blue fervor. (We wouldn't have lasted 25 years if I hadn't.) Yes, it was difficult at first, but then I had to accept the fact that I never actually attended that school in Ann Arbor, so my zeal had no foundation. Now I root for both Michigan schools, but my disdain for the land down under (Ohio) had remained intact -- until last weekend.

Months ago, I asked my wife, Debbie, what she would like to do for our 25th anniversary. I expected her to request something in silver, as that is the traditional gift. Instead, she suggested we go to Hocking Hills in Ohio. I asked why, and she told me she had heard they had great hiking there.

I shuddered. 'Great, we're going into enemy territory to exercise?' I thought.

I searched the area on my phone and scheduled our getaway at an isolated cabin called 'Wildwood' in Ohio. I sent the information to Deb and let her do what she does best -- plan. My wife could make a living as a tour guide. Even in the days before we held computers in our hands, she would go to AAA and get something called a 'Trip-tik.' Every detail of every trip was planned in advance, which made things easy for me. (Just drive, Mike, drive.)

We headed out late last Friday morning, using our GPS

to tap in the address Deb had recorded from her research. We headed to Dundee, Ohio, home of the Wildwood Cabins. Partway through the trip, we realized the error and corrected to the Blue Rose Cabins, home of over a dozen cabins, including the individual cabin I booked, called 'Wildwood.' The error really didn't take us too far off track, but it did have an impact.

Our new cell phone service is spotty at times, and the cabin we rented had no service at all, so now we faced the weekend with no itinerary -- a first.

Our trip into Ohio started as I had expected -- barren flatlands with little scenery. We made it through Columbus, Ohio, and I felt a cold sweat on my brow. Looking into the rear view mirror, I realized I had worn my "Wolverines" tee shirt. I said a quiet prayer that our car wouldn't break down there.

Then we got into the rolling hills of southeastern Ohio, heading toward West Virginia, and the roads there were anything but flat. We turned onto the road that led to our cabin, and I was beginning to regret not doing more research before booking. The road was narrow -- so narrow that I doubted it would accommodate two vehicles (unless both were VW Beetles). The roads looked like a simple three inch layer of asphalt with no shoulder, and in places the road dropped into a ditch on either side (sometimes both sides). I drove slowly, and we approached the turn for our cabin when I felt compelled to stop.

"Ewww," escaped from my lips as I looked to my right and saw the messiest front yard I've ever seen. (And remember, Good Reader, that I worked in some very downtrodden neighborhoods in Detroit.)

The yard made that of television classic 'Sanford and Son' look like a pristine paradise.

'Uh-oh,' I thought, 'This romantic cabin in the woods idea might not have been such a great idea!'

"This isn't where we're staying, is it?" Deb asked, and I, of course, told her no, and then held my breath as we proceeded up the road.

After many twists and turns along a gravel road that just went up and up and up, we arrived at our cabin. It was neat and cute and certainly romantic. I exhaled.

We enjoyed a meal in town followed by some wine at the Hocking Hills Winery, which gave us a pair of wine glasses to celebrate the occasion. We went back to the cabin before it

'Honey, We're Here!'

This was the scene to greet our eyes as our GPS told us we were reaching our romantic destination -- yikes! Did I ruin our anniversary?

got dark and enjoyed the amenities there, and then we rested for our hike to see waterfalls in Hocking Hills. We had no internet service, so it was going to be an adventure. At dinner the night before, the hostess came over to our table with a slip of paper.

"If you're new here, you might like to see Old Man's Cave; it's handicap accessible," she said, and did she look at me at the end there? I think she did.

Nonetheless, we had thanked her for the advice and took her counsel that next day as we headed out. With no Triptik or plan, we defaulted to our only working technology, the car's GPS. We punched in 'Hocking Hills' and a long list came up. Deb selected one, and we went off on another adventure along narrow, winding roads.

Finally, we aimed toward the state park, where we realized that we were not alone. We drove around two packed parking lots before finding a third down the road which had a couple spots. The sign near the lot said we could get to Old Man's Cave from there, so we pulled in.

We were joined by a lady who said she had just hiked 12 miles and would like to join us on our way to the cave. We walked a while, mostly downhill, before we came upon a sign that marked the distance to the cave as another two miles.

"Two more miles from here?" I said, already hot and tired.

"I think it said point two," offered our companion, so we

forged ahead.

Clearly two miles later, we came to a one way sign on a path that led down to the cave. Determined not to walk any further before we actually enjoyed one of the sights, Deb and I went down the up stairs, "excuse me-ing" ourselves all the way down.

Thankfully, I hadn't packed another Wolverine shirt, or the annoyed stares we received may have turned ugly.

We got to the bottom and enjoyed the beauty of the area, and then I noticed a wedding at the far side of the area. I walked over and thought, 'How cool,' and then I thought, 'How did they all get down here in their fancy clothes?'

Deb and I finished up, walked up the up stairs and continued on the path, which conveniently turned into a broad parking area with a paved entrance into the cave, obviously the aforementioned handicap access.

The day was hot, and we were sweaty from our exertions, but we planned ahead for that -- we wore bathing suits underneath our clothing. I looked longingly at the pool that formed from the waterfall at this cave, but it wasn't more than a puddle.

Reluctantly, we headed back, mostly uphill this time, and finished this hike that was easily more than five miles. In the end, we survived. In fact, we took another hike of at least three miles. It made us feel younger, especially when we recalled hiking down terrain like this to get to a nude beach in California on our honeymoon, but that's a story that will remain untold -- at least for now...

***

The nude beach story is a real doozy, but I think I can leave some embarrassing stories untold... for now.

Permaflab
(or Let's Get Physical)

Originally published July 14, 2022

This week marks a birthday and an anniversary for me. Tuesday was my birthday, and I spent most of that day doing what I do every Tuesday -- assembling the Clinton Local.

Thursday, July 14, 2022, is an anniversary for me -- one year since I began exercising regularly.

A year ago, I started a program of diet and exercise. Though I've slipped off the diet and can't seem to get back on track, I'm exercising more often and more vigorously than I have in decades. This week on the exercise bike I found myself beating my 'ghost' by more than a minute. (That means I beat my previous record, which is recorded on the machine -- the marvels of technology!)

Before adopting my new exercise program, I must confess to fudging my numbers. Keeping track on a smartphone app, I'd give myself credit for everything:

- Walking? That must burn 100 calories per 1,000 steps.
- Gardening? That's easily worth 50 calories per half hour.
- Folding Laundry? Hey, that's a two-fer -- I get to count calories and get in good with the Missus.

I even read somewhere that if you chewed your food enough times that the act of mastication could outweigh the intake of calories. Imagine! Unlimited consumption!

Now that I'm into regular exercise -- five days a week for about an hour -- I can feel the muscles developing. The problem is that, since my diet has been less than successful, I am still unable to see those muscles. But I'm sure they're there, rippling under layers of what my cousin Tony calls "permaflab."

It can be disheartening, especially when I look into the mirror, but there is an upside. This summer, I am determined to redo the landscaping around the house -- upgrading and refreshing all the flower beds. Since my mind still thinks I'm in my thirties, I calculated that it would take two or three weekends at most. Now, I am hoping to finish before the first frost. I get out there and work, and not long after, I'm moving like the Tinman in The Wizard of Oz, complete with creaks and moans. But thanks to regular exercise, by the next day, I am usually right as rain.

These days, I often reflect on aging, and I recall the words of that great Clinton sage, Gary Couture: "It is better to be seen than viewed." (Gary was a funeral director.)

Thank you, Gary. I agree.

It is better to be seen -- permaflab and all.

***

Around August, 2022, I was committed to selling The Clinton Local to my lead salesman and friend, Sean McNatt. He needed it, and I needed out, to put it succinctly.

My stories tailed off -- the last couple being a collection of fragments really -- and then they stopped. The paper sold early in November, 2022, but I continued working as editor for a year to help with the transition. I told myself that I would begin collecting these memoirs into a book while I continued as Sean's editor, but then an opportunity to return to teaching appeared by Thanksgiving. I jumped at it.

Memoirs were forgotten as I balanced two jobs. When my mind returned to writing, I focused on publishing the works of others. Finally, the urge to tell my stories rekindled in the Summer of 2025, and I began work in earnest. (I even gave my son my handheld electronic toy -- an old Nintendo DS -- to avoid distraction. That may be the most embarrassing revelation shared in this volume, Good Reader.)

I have two more brief stories to share in this volume. I wrote them when I knew I had sold the paper; I wanted to get these two bits out before they left my head, as they focus on two of my all-time favorite people.

Beautiful Girls
(or Toes in the Sand)

Originally published August 4, 2022

Vacation time, and we're back up north again -- this time enjoying the convenience of a condominium complete with heated pool, but our vacations haven't always been so comfortable and luxurious.

For most of the 25 years Debbie and I have been together, we've gone camping, and for most of those years, we were at rustic campsites. Rustic camping (no water and no electricity) is fine if you're taking your son out with the Cubs Scouts for an overnight trip to work on a fire starting or knot-tying badge, but for a two week vacation?

Let's just say I look back on it now and wonder how we did it.

~~~

Since Nicholas, our son, was a year old (Summer, 2001), we have headed to the west side of our great state. In those early years, we went to Orchard Beach State Park in Manistee. The park is set atop a sand dune and has a spectacular view of Lake Michigan, especially at sunset. The only drawback was the beach (now gone due to erosion), which was down a flight of stairs -- 65 steps each way!

Since we had a young child, we brought nearly everything you could imagine down to the beach so that we could spend nearly the entire day there -- a large cooler filled with ice, food and drinks, folding chairs, beach blanket, a small tent in which young Nicholas could take his naps (often with Dad!), puzzle books, putters and golf balls, Hot Wheels, and the usual bucket of plastic sand-shaping instruments.

All of that stuff was heavy and required many trips. Fortunately for me, Debbie did most of the hauling. After helping carry a few items on our first trip down the steps, I eagerly dove into the job of helping our son craft Putt-Putt courses in the sand.

"Aren't you going to help bring the rest of the stuff down, Mike?" Debbie would ask, though eventually she knew better. For my part, I extolled
~~~

her stamina and strength, loudly if necessary.

"Babe, you've got to be the most physically fit woman on the beach! Look at how strong your Momma is, Nick!"

Nobody's fool, Debbie rolled her eyes and assigned me to lunch duty, which meant one more trip up the stairs for the day, but that still kept the ratio of trips below 3 to 1.

We enjoyed that beach for many years, crafting golf holes and race tracks in the sand, collecting Petosky stones and other pretty pebbles (which I used one year to make a statuette for my mother), and even swimming, on occasion. Once, when Nick was five, the two of us had an adventure, taking our inflatable kayak along the shore to the beach in town, about two miles south. (I heard about it from Debbie, too!)

"What possessed you to take our son so far in a kayak on Lake Michigan?" Debbie said to me as I pulled to shore. (She had run the whole distance along the beach to catch up with us.)

"He wanted to go for a ride to this beach," I said, as if it made perfect sense.

"Our three-year-old wanted to go, so you went?" Deb said, and, thankfully, that was the end of the conversation.

Sunny days on the beach -- that's the prime memory of those days, until one week in 2008. The week had been unusually gloomy -- rain and cooler weather -- not suitable for spending the entire day with toes in the sand. After the second day of this weather, we decided to take a ride up the coast. It was late morning when we left, grey skies sending us away from the beach for the first time in all the years we'd been heading to Lake Michigan for vacations.

We took US-31 to M-22 and cruised the upper west coast of Michigan through Onekama, Pierport, Arcadia, and Elberta. As we continued north and rode through Frankfort, the sun poked through the gloom. We stopped at a roadside turnout and discussed the possibility of stopping somewhere nearby to enjoy the day. I suggested we continue north a little longer, so we hopped back into our silver Dodge Caravan. When we got to Empire, we saw a sign directing us toward the public beach.

The beach in Empire, Michigan is actually a two-fer. On the west side of the public parking is Lake Michigan, with its silky, sugar-sand and big waves. On the east side is South Bar Lake, considerably warmer and with fewer waves and some shade trees. As the day had heated up nicely by this time, we opted for the latter and grabbed our blanket and cooler. Nick saw some kids jumping off a dock into the shallow lake, and he managed to talk his athletic mother into joining him. I opted to spread our blanket and prep our site (which in my mind included sampling the contents of our cooler).

I looked to my left at a couple sitting on a blanket under a tree. Wishing I had their spot, I stared a little, but then realized that my gaze had locked on them for a different reason.

"Anthony?" I said, first to myself and then again out loud.

I began to walk toward the man on the blanket with confidence as my early recognition was confirmed -- it was my cousin, Anthony, who lived nearly 20 miles away near Interlochen. He was sitting on a blanket with a friend, a woman named Kirsten. Ironically, Nick had already struck up a friendship with her sons and was running and jumping off the dock with them.

We spent the rest of the afternoon there with them, having a great time, and then continued it at his house, where we slept overnight. The next day we returned to our soggy campsite and packed our vehicle, then we returned to Tony's house and finished our vacation there.

My cousin, Anthony, was like an older brother.

From that point on, we decided to move our vacations further north. Since then, we've enjoyed almost exclusively sunny days, but not on the very first night in our new vacationland. That is another tale, one which I'll save for another time.

For now, it's time to hit the beach!

***

The next year, we booked our vacation at a campground near our cousin, and the story of how we got there would begin with the classic, "It was a dark and stormy night..."

My Grandfather's Chair

Originally published August 11, 2022

Up North again this week, and we were invited to my Godmother's house for a family get-together. My Godmother, who is also my Aunt Alberta, moved up here several years ago from her home in Detroit to be closer to two of her four children. I'm sure if she could, she would have the entire family together living in a single compound. It's that important to her.

After a sumptuous meal, I sat with Aunt Albert, a few of my cousins, and their grown children. We talked about good times in the past, lamenting the traditions lost (and silently, those dearly departed people who helped make those traditions). Contrary to what you may be thinking, it never sunk to doom and gloom. Many stories were light, like my recollection of my first pet -- a goldfish that lasted less than a day.

My father and mother decided that we should each have a pet of our own, so Dad took the five of us young boys to Korvette's Department Store on Joy Road in Detroit so that we could each pick out a goldfish. Dad bought a bowl, a little gravel, and a deep sea diver with a treasure chest to decorate the bowl. I can remember how we each excitedly told the unlucky teenager who waited on us which exact fish we wanted of the hundreds schooling in the tank, our eyes tracking his little net with barely contained elation.

"I want the one with the white speck on its tail... No, not that one! The other one!"

He had to do that five times, but I think I had been the most demanding. I knew what my fish looked like, and when I had to put it in the bowl with my brothers' goldfish, I followed it carefully, pointing out to them which fish was mine. I think we stared at those fish for hours that afternoon and into the evening.

The next morning, we ran to see our new pets in their bowl, which rested on a stand in the kitchen next to our wall mounted telephone. My excitement drained quickly as I observed that my fish was floating belly up at the top of the bowl. I had made such a big deal about what my fish looked like, there was no way to deny it, so switching with my younger, more naive brothers had been made impossible.

Dad took mercy on me, or perhaps it was Mona. Either way, I got to select a new fish later that week, and this time I chose one that looked a lot tougher. It was a black goldfish (if that's not an oxymoron!), and it was bigger than the other fish -- appropriate, since I was the eldest.

My new fish was a bully, picking on my little brothers' fish and eventually killing all four of them by the next morning. My brothers were distraught, but Dad could see a pattern emerging, so to avoid making endless trips to Korvette's, he decided to go big, and we got our first full aquarium set up -- a 10 gallon model. He let us pick out more than just one fish, and it worked -- we didn't become nearly as attached to any individual fish.

Except me, of course, because my black goldfish had survived, and it took to the new aquarium like, well, like a fish to water. In fact, it thrived and grew to about three inches long in a short time. Dad bought a 20 gallon aquarium, and old 'Black Beauty' grew to about six inches long.

She hadn't stopped her bullying ways, either, and more and more swordfish, mollies, guppies and neon tetras ended up dead. When the big silver angel fish went belly up, it was decision time. Dad saw another pattern developing, and he suggested we find a more suitable home for my fish.

My cousin Anthony, who sat across the table from me last week as we traded stories, had a big aquarium -- 100 gallons, I think -- with a few oscars, which are sturdy fish. Anthony adopted Black Beauty, and she grew to be bigger than the oscars, her tail fanning out behind her unlike any goldfish I had seen up to that point. I marvelled at her glory every time I visited.

We lived close to family back

in those days. Everyone in our family -- grandparents, cousins, aunts and uncles -- lived within a five mile radius near the Detroit/Dearborn border. Its not like that anymore, as we are spread to the four winds, it seems.

Our maternal grandparents lived less than half a mile away -- a short walk. Grandma Grace, who lived to be 102, would walk over every day to help Mona with housework. (She never learned to drive.) Grandpa Ale (We called him Grandpa Grace for a while until my mother corrected us) picked up Grandma with his tan station wagon after he got off work. We always looked forward to his arrival.

When Paul and I were maybe four and five years old, respectively, Grandpa played Hide-and Go-Seek with us. He'd tell us to count off to ten, and then we'd try to find him. He always hid in the same spot -- sitting in an old purple crushed-velvet, wood-framed chair at the top of the stairs in our dorm-style bedroom.

Paul and I crept toward him with caution, giggling nervously. He wasn't playing Hide and Seek after all. He was playing "Iron Claw."

"Is he asleep, really asleep?" Paul would ask.

"I don't know," I offered with just a hint of doubt, which was dispelled as Grandpa gave a loud snoring snort.

Paul laughed.

"Should we wake him up?"

Realizing I had a guinea pig, I suggested, "Why don't you touch him and find out?"

Paul reached out his hand and touched Grandpa's left forearm, and, with cat-like speed, Grandpa's eyes opened and his left hand shot out and firmly grabbed Paul's arm.

We were hysterical with laughter (after the inaugural round of this game) and Paul tried to pull away, shouting, "Let go. Let go!"

"What do you say?" Grandpa said, not relinquishing his grip. "What are the magic words?"

Paul had forgotten, so I prompted him in a whisper, "Say Iron Claw!"

"Iron Claw!" Paul shouted, but Grandpa's grip remained firm.

In his excitement, Paul had forgotten the complete phrase, but a moment later he recovered and released the full magical power: "Iron Claw, please release!"

Grandpa's left hand sprung open, and Paul was able to

retract his arm. Both of us were still laughing the entire time, but I stopped as Grandpa's right hand shot out to grab my forearm.

"Iron Claw, please release!" I shouted, too smart to be caught for as long as my brother.

Or so I thought...

The solid grip remained. I was trapped. Now Paul's laughter seemed a little more hardy than mine. I tried the magical phrase again.

"Iron Claw, Please Release!"

Nothing.

Now Grandpa seemed to be falling back into sleep, but his grip on my forearm remained firm. Paul stood by me, and he tried the magic words on my behalf. Still nothing. We repeated the magical phrase several more times, each time with a different inflection. I think we even threw in an 'abracadabra' and a 'presto' for good measure.

Nothing.

"I guess you'll have to just stand here until Grandpa wakes up," Paul said, and he didn't seem at all phased by that prospect. Mona had called us to dinner, and I knew my faithful brother would abandon me at any moment. I tried one last time.

"Iron Claw..."

Grandpa's left eye, the one nearest to us, opened and he whispered, "That's not the Iron Claw. That's the Steel Claw!"

"Steel Claw, Please Release!"

Grandpa's right hand snapped open, and before we could get away, he took each hand and tousled our hair, then pulled us close for a bear hug. We all went downstairs for dinner with the family. Afterward, my cousins came over for cake and ice cream. (It must have been someone's birthday. It was a tradition.)

Last week, at my Godmother's table, after we had exchanged many stories and lamented bygone traditions, my head was filled with memories. Later, while driving home, I realized that this was at least the third year in a row that we had gathered at her table while on our summer vacation, each time sharing old memories and making new ones.

"Wow," I thought, "My Godmother is a crafty one!"

She had established a new tradition right under our noses!

POSTLUDE

So, that's it, Good Reader...

Well, not really.

If you enjoyed these stories, you may enjoy the companion volume to this tome, Memoirs of an Average Man: Seven Years Below the Masthead:

- It is the story of yearning for and then buying the newspaper from the cagey Maryann Habrick -- nobody's fool.
- It is the story of an intrepid, yet hapless, school teacher who attempts to transform into a businessman.
- It is the story of an editorialist who tried and failed (miserably and repeatedly) to stay in the middle of the road concerning the Coronavirus and Donald Trump.
- It is the story of an average man's dreams abandoned before they could be dashed upon the rocks.
- It is a story of...

Well, just read the story if you want to know what it's about! It will be available by Fall, 2026 on Amazon.

Until the next release, if you'd like to hear another story about one of my wonderful vehicles, email me at ***LocalMediaNowLLC@gmail.com***, and I'll send you the story of my 1980 Volkswagon Rabbit diesel engine and place you on an email list to get updates on future books.

Thank you for reading along with me.

Michael J. Walters
June 12, 2026

ABOUT THE AUTHOR

Michael Joseph Walters was born July 12, 1961 at Providence Hospital in Detroit, Michigan. That facility was closed and demolished decades ago. He attended St. Christopher Catholic School and Benedictine High School, both in Detroit and both closed. He grew up in a small home on Detroit's west side with both parents, four brothers, and a dog. That house still stands.

The author received a BS in Education (majoring in English) in 1984 from Wayne State University in Detroit. He taught at his high school alma mater for one year before beginning a 31-year teaching career in Detroit Public Schools. He earned a Masters in Education Administration in 1996, married Debbie Mosher in 1997, moved to Clinton, Michigan in 1998, and bought the Clinton Local newspaper one year before he retired from teaching in Detroit in 2016.

Mike planned to own and grow the newspaper for 10 years, and then retire again, but Michigan law changed in 2022, allowing retired teachers to re-enter the field while retaining their pension.

Mike sold the newspaper to his salesperson and friend, Sean, and then joined the teaching staff at Madison High School in Adrian, Michigan, where he enjoys a shorter commute and a near idyllic atmosphere for education.

Mike hopes to follow this book with three others, God willing...

March 7, 2026

www.ingramcontent.com/pod-product-compliance
Lightning Source LLC
LaVergne TN
LVHW040216110826
845146LV00005B/1314

* 9 7 9 8 9 9 4 6 9 7 7 1 9 *